The Tene

QUILLEM MCBREEN

HEROIC

Heroic Books

First published in Great Britain in 2021 by Heroic Books.

Paperback ISBN: 9781914342004
Ebook ISBN: 9781914342097
Audiobook ISBN: 9781914342189

Printed and bound in Great Britain by Clays Ltd, Elcograf S.p.A.

www.heroicbooks.com

This book is printed on paper from responsible sources.

To you, in truth.

PROLOGUE

The chime of a bell hung in the air, clear and crisp and tinny. It had taken Sentenza a long time to find this place—*too long*, he thought bitterly. He had already counted two summers, and here was the second early winter whipping at him. The ragged hillside tracks he'd been wandering for weeks gave nothing away, and less and less stood out the further he progressed across the wind-blasted wilds. Snow already covered the ground at this altitude, and it would not be many moons before it blanketed the lowlands as well. Nearly three cycles he'd been searching—he just hoped the man he sought would still be here. Would still be *alive*, he corrected himself.

Wits alone had helped him pick up the trail again, just when he'd almost lost hope. Now he had the name of a possible location: a remote spot, more than a day's ride from anywhere and deeper and higher into the wilderness than he might have wanted—and yet, a sense of anticipation kept him spurring his lumbering horse on even as his frozen body protested. Not many ventured this high into the hills, and even fewer were mad enough to settle here.

'Old Ballir keeps mostly to himself,' the trader had told him. 'Ain't really no one goes up there much, and Ballir only comes down once in a blue dawning to sell some hides and get the odd thing. Don't seem to need much in way of supplies, though. No one but him and his two boys up there, besides those women of his, o' course.'

Sentenza wondered how anyone managed to keep going in such a place, miles from anywhere and without the support of neighbours. No one in their right mind would try to grow crops up here; surely Ballir would need grain for animals and food and drink for him and his, no matter how resourceful he was. Setenza asked himself again whether Ballir was in fact as mad as he suspected or whether he just didn't want to be found. It was this burning question that had brought him to this isolated part of the Mata Mountains, where the rocks seemed to grow straight out of the ground, tall and sharp and jagged like great teeth. These, next to the grey and swaddling sky, made every step feel like a descent into the mouth of some terrible beast.

Pushing the thought from his mind, Sentenza squinted on through the snow. There was nothing to see; outlaws and heretics were the only people stupid enough to journey so high in the ranges— fools on a fool's errand, of course. The Church of the Righteous Truth would follow criminals even to these lengths, all in the name of the One True Goddess.

The path eventually levelled and the clouds seemed to rise, revealing a wide landscape divided by stone walls and copses of felled trees. Then, at last, the outline of a large building in the distance: a farmhouse. The sense of satisfaction spread warmth to Sentenza's frozen bones. *Who in their right mind would set up to farm a mountainside?* In truth, he didn't much care. He was here to do a job; once it was done, he'd return home and forget this inhospitable place.

He spurred his mount to a trot, the sound of hooves resonating against ice and stone and snow. He caught a tune on the wind once again: the erratic rattle of wind chimes. They were closer now, chattering like noisy birds, perhaps meant to ward off ancient spirits or the ghosts of the long since dead. Sentenza knew better: it wasn't the spirits you needed to worry about.

He passed beneath a canopy of trees, hunching against the sudden snowdrift falling from the branches. The note underfoot changed, and Sentenza hurried to wipe the snow from his face. He blinked into the new light.

The ground was no longer frozen. Instead, he was greeted by a carpet of green: luscious young shoots of grass and the splash of colourful wildflowers reaching as far as the mist-shrouded feet of the mountains beyond. With a start, Sentenza realised it had been cattle bells he'd heard calling on the breeze. Indeed, there they were: a few cows picking among the pastures and at least twenty sheep besides.

It was unnatural.

Sentenza's horse became skittish, and he bent to give her a soothing pat on the neck. The snow-covered peaks lingered above the sun-bathed farmland, jarring and incongruous. *What kind of magic has Ballir got himself involved in?* Sentenza could usually smell a user half a day's ride away, and knew that his target was certainly not a Wielder and probably not a Cognator either. Ballir was a dry old hack, and it was fair to say that Sentenza did not remember him as a particularly shrewd or clever man. Although, *best to give the man his due*, he thought. He'd certainly been a stubborn son of a bitch to find.

The path opened out upon a small courtyard, terracotta sand almost glowing in the mountain sun. A mule was hitched to a water wheel and began to bray as Sentenza approached. Two boys stopped dead in their tracks, nervous eyes following the intruder. Sentenza reined his horse in and climbed from the saddle. One of the boys dropped the bundle he was carrying and ran, bare feet pounding a double-quick rhythm toward the main house. It wasn't a big house, but good enough: a simple kind of place that Sentenza wouldn't mind settling down in himself one day. Still, that wouldn't be for a long time yet, not if he had anything to do with it.

Wooden steps drummed out a warning and the remaining boy jumped into the waiting arms of a woman, eyeing him cautiously. Sentenza tethered the horse, climbed the steps, and walked past the woman. Broom in one hand and boy in the other, hate shone in her face. He could almost taste it: an ice-cold loathing frosting over in this unseasonal oasis. It was certainly dramatic. He met her stare with one of his own, hard and uncaring. She was not his concern; not the one he was here for.

The house was sparse, with little by way of decoration. Tools of the trade hung on the walls alongside an upright time piece. Sentenza stopped to marvel at the contraption. He'd seen only two in his lifetime—one in the Capital and the other in the Misty City. This reminded him of the latter. A priest's instrument, full of a magic he could neither sense nor understand, though his mentor—the same man that had once owned this device—had taught him to read them. He peered outside, bobbing his head slightly to assess the position of the sun, fingering the delicate clock hands until they read two-eighteen. 'Quite a nice old thing,' he said, not looking at the woman who trailed behind him, 'when it's set right.'

He turned and strode deeper into the house. Instinct always drew him to the backs of buildings. The business end. Pantry, kitchen, liquor—they were always hidden from prying eyes.

He tried the door at the far end of the hallway, opening it onto a stone-floored kitchen and dining area. Pots sat on a wood-burning cooker, the smell of meat and grease and sweet pine filling the air.

In front, at a large wooden table, sat a fat man in his late-middle cycles, noisily eating from a bowl of bread and beans. He looked up when Sentenza swung the door closed and, at once, stopped. He put down the spoon and seemed to rearrange himself, sitting up a little straighter in the wooden chair. Looking away from Sentenza, the man towelled away a morsel of his stew, gave a satisfied belch, and took a slurped gulp from a tankard of what looked like rough ale.

'What are you doing here?' he said at last, placing the tankard back down with unexpected care. 'You don't even knock?' The fat man's voice was lazy; words tripped against each other and dripped from his mouth like spittle.

'You've done a good job of avoiding me, Ballir,' Sentenza answered, slowly crossing the room. He kept his manner light and easy—nothing too ugly too early. He took a seat opposite his reluctant host.

'It's not always wise for a man to let himself be found,' Ballir answered, eyeing him warily. 'I'll ask again. Why are you here?'

'You should know why I'm here. You know what I do.'

Ballir's eyes twitched.

A slight movement over Sentenza's shoulder. He swivelled in his chair to find one of the boys standing in the doorway. Sentenza placed him at fourteen, maybe fifteen cycles at best. Still, old enough to be a problem.

'Alear, go help your mother,' Ballir commanded. 'I have an old friend here for a chat, and we don't want bothering.'

The boy left without a word, cold eyes never leaving the *old friend*.

'Cute family,' Sentenza said with a smile. He helped himself to a hunk of bread. 'I didn't think you'd have had time. How long has it been? Five, maybe six cycles? I'll tell you what, though: you've done well for yourself here. Landed on your feet, so to speak. Must take a lot of work, just you and the wife and those boys. No one else here to help you, hey? Takes a lot of planning, something like this.' He reached forward, taking the tankard and helping himself to a long mouthful. It was strong and gritty, but surprisingly cold.

'Now look here, Sentenza...'

So, he does remember me—and best that he does.

'You can tell Sakani that I never planned anything,' Ballir said.

Sentenza smiled. 'You took off pretty quick. Sakani doesn't like people walking out on him in the middle of a job, especially when that someone has a whole pack of *things* belonging to him and the Church.' He let the words hang in the air.

Ballir sat silent for a moment, just looking at Sentenza. Assessing the situation. Beads of sweat glistened on his wide forehead. Then, to Sentenza's surprise, the man laughed. A short little guffaw that threw the other man off. 'Listen,' he said, relaxing back into his chair. 'If that's all this is, I can pay the money back.' He made to stand. 'Let me shout the boy. He can go get—'

'Sit down, Ballir,' Sentenza said sharply. 'Sakani doesn't pay me to act as bailiff. You should know that.'

'But, Sentenza,' Ballir implored, spreading wide his stubby hands in a submissive gesture.

'But nobody. I've got a job to do, just like everybody else.' Sentenza took off his hat, laying it down onto the table in front of him. His eyes met Ballir's. There was less fear there than he'd expected, but maybe that was for the best. Less messy that way. Less pleading.

'We go back a long way,' Ballir said, a slight whine to his voice. 'Just let me sort things out here.'

But Sentenza didn't respond. He took another drink.

6

'Things aren't what they seem.' Ballir gestured to their surroundings, urging him to take it all in. 'The money isn't why I left. Truth, I hardly even need money here. Look at this place. I have everything I could ever want. It should be the middle of winter, and yet look outside. Go ahead'—he pointed to the window—'you must have seen on the way in. Cattle in the field, corn in the sheds.' He was talking quickly now, fat chins quivering. 'I still have most of that cash. It's yours, all of it. I don't need it.'

Sentenza raised a single eyebrow. It was an interesting offer. Ballir was still gazing at him, and he was unsure if this was an act of defiance or submission.

Finally, Sentenza sighed. 'In truth, I don't think it was the money that bothered him, do you? You betrayed his trust, Ballir. You got greedy. You took something that he actually cared for.' He looked about, letting his shoulders relax as he gestured about the room with his tankard. 'Look at all this. Do you think it can all be that simple? You know why I'm here. You've got one chance to tell me what I want to know. Where is she?'

The man's watery grey orbs flickered; not much, but enough to give a warning.

A soft click came from behind and Sentenza kicked down hard, throwing himself and the chair he was sitting in to his right. A clunking twang and a hiss, and something zipped and puckered the air to his left. Instinctively, he rolled onto his side and reached out, first with his hand and then beyond—or, at least, that's what he tried to do. He'd performed the act countless times before. Why had nothing happened?

There should be something there, he screamed to himself, a force or power that lay just beyond his hand, waiting for him to tap into as he had done all his life. His heart skipped, empty fingers fumbling uselessly in the air. There was no time. He forced the

7

panic down and rolled, his hand whipping down to one of the short blades he carried at his belt. *I'll have to do this the old-fashioned way.*

He pulled the dirk free, drawing onto his knee. The arm arced and swung upwards, snapping taut with sudden force. He released his grip, sending the blade swimming neatly across the kitchen. A wet thud signalled his success.

Sentenza rose to his full height and strode forward to where Ballir's eldest son lay bleeding on the floor, blade sunk in his chest. The young man's slippery hands fingered the hilt clumsily. Breath came hard in short, desperate gasps. Then, all at once, he was done. The body dropped, hazelnut eyes losing their pain and anger, drifting into the lifeless void.

Sentenza stopped to retrieve both the knife and the crossbow, surprised that such an antique could still function. *Almost as big as the boy is... or was,* he corrected himself. An anger flared in him. *He could have killed me with that thing.* Turning back, he saw that the boy's quarrel had flown right past his now-vacant chair. Wood lay split and splintered where the bolt had hammered through the table and pierced the boy's father as if he were a hunted boar. Blood seeped from the deep wound in Ballir's stomach and his hands flexed against the table, his teeth grinding.

Sentenza straightened, fixing the man with a glare.

Ballir braced, knuckles white with effort. He coughed, blood spattering down his chin.

Sentenza dropped the crossbow and moved slowly back to the table. He placed a hand on the edge, resting his weight there. Ballir's eyes bulged, the barbed head of the bolt sinking further into the man's ruptured flesh. A dull shout rumbled through him in broken stages.

'That's no way to treat an old friend,' Sentenza's voice was cold and hard. 'You *will* tell me if you have any more of those skulking around the place, won't you?'

'S-Sentenza,' Ballir spluttered.

'Too late.' Sentenza took an old rag from the table and used it to wipe the boy's blood from his knife. 'We've talked long enough.'

'Wait,' Ballir gasped. 'The healer.' His hand moved down to the puncture as he spoke, as if he needed confirmation of the wound.

Sentenza dropped the rag, gaze fixing the blubbering mess before him. As always, he took care to focus on the job, not the man or the words he was trying to push out. It was better that way—or, at least, easier. If you listened to the words, you sometimes started seeing the man for who he was.

As far as Sentenza was concerned, he had a task to complete. Sure, he could leave Ballir to slowly bleed out, but that could take days, and there was always an outside chance that something would go wrong. The wife, the other kid, a passing stranger, or someone else he had failed to notice; any of them could fetch help before the end. Besides, Sentenza bore Ballir no personal malice. This was just a job, after all.

The blade shone in the morning sun, clean and crisp, like the healthy mountain air. He placed the knife at the man's clammy neck, skin already growing pallid. 'The healer, Sentenza,' Ballir repeated, eyes redder and wetter than they had been before. Tears flowed, streaking his dirty cheeks.

Sentenza paused. What could this fat farmer know about healing? Healing was a gift bestowed upon the Church, and they certainly would not waste it on a cretin like Ballir. Yet something tugged at him—in all the confusion, he had almost forgotten about what had just happened. He was what the world termed a Wielder and, for as long as he could remember, his power had always just *been there*: a fundamental constant, like the sun rising in the morning and the moon bringing in the night. He couldn't see, smell, or taste the power, yet when he needed it and reached out for it, it was there. Until now.

Could Ballir have found himself a local healer? Could he have somehow changed the way the magic worked around here? That would take some serious power. The thought piqued his interest.

'What about a healer?' He eased the blade's pressure on the man's throat slightly, bringing his free hand to rest on the shaft of the quarrel still jutting from Ballir's fleshy stomach.

Ballir grimaced. 'A travelling healer,' he coughed, bloody spittle forming around his lips. His words were strained, but the tiny glimmer of hope gave him voice. 'That's what he said he was. I was hiding, trying to keep quiet... Things weren't going well—the girl, the animals, the cold.' He coughed again, eyes rolling about his skull. 'We couldn't survive here... She was ill, dying anyway—sweating sickness, maybe, I don't know. Nothing we did was working. He said he could help... could save the girl and change everything, for a fee. I had no choice. I don't know how he did it, but it got better almost overnight. We've been... happy, Sentenza, with more than we could ever need. It's like a permanent summer.' The man's head sagged, and he began sucking in desperate gasps of air.

Blasphemy. Only the Church could sanction the use of healing. It was one of the central Tenets. Pain and sickness were given by the Goddess to punish sins. As for this other magic—well, Sentenza had never heard of anything like it before. Even listening to Ballir's words might cast him as a heretic.

No, he realised. Ballir was just buying time. A man would say anything to save his own skin, and that was doubly true when he had a bolt in the belly. A nice try, but pointless. 'And you think this would interest me?' Sentenza asked, believing the tale less and less the more he considered it.

'What? No,' Ballir croaked. 'You could find him. You could find out what he used and take it.'

'Do you have an address for this "travelling healer"?' Sentenza said, voice thick with sarcasm.

'The payment. You could use it to track him down, like you did me. Take the money I have here from Sakani.'

Sentenza couldn't deny that. He sighed. 'You have my attention, Ballir, but I thought you used the money to pay this healer?'

Ballir spluttered a guttural laugh that seemed to cause him far more pain than anything else. 'I didn't pay him in money, but good, good—I knew you were a man of sense. Now fetch some help.'

'Tell me first,' Sentenza growled, pressing down on the feathered end of the quarrel. Ballir tensed, his lips rippling against the pain—or was it something else? Something deeper and more emotional. There was guilt there, Sentenza realised, shimmering beneath the surface. 'You know what I did. Don't make me say it. I can't. Ask the woman... She has hated me every day since. Just get help.'

'And the money?'

'Under the fire grate,' Ballir breathed. 'Now, for the love of... Please!'

'You wouldn't make it anyway,' Sentenza replied, and dragged the blade free and clear. There was only soft resistance, like slicing pork for the pot.

Ballir gasped—a mixture of gurgling and the hissing of air.

Sentenza stood, not looking back, and plucked the rag from the table. Wiping his knife, he turned back towards the door.

I trust unto you these words, inviolable truths passed down by the Goddess herself, whose name remains so sacred and sacrosanct that none may utter it. 'I give to you my Church,' said the Goddess. Given to all so that we may find truth. For there is no evil that she cannot help us overcome if we only bend to her will; no disease or illness we cannot cure if we but submit to her Church of the Righteous Truth, for only through her Church can we ease our pain and suffering.

-From the Tenets of Truth

CHAPTER ONE
SOLATTA

The Southern Estates

The tent had grown hot and humid, packed tight with people.

Solatta struggled between two more faceless men, trying to cross the great crowd. If she weren't so nervous, she might be more irked—it was silly to be nervous. This wasn't her night after all. She wouldn't exactly be doing much, she was just there to help. The bitter thought annoyed her.

The blue hour of dusk seemed somehow shorter here, and the light was fading dramatically. She hastily lit several more of the special candles that Tervan liked to bring out on such nights. These had a nice smell to them, but were a lot more expensive than the day-to-day ones. 'They help to set the scene, my dear girl,' Tervan would announce in his most theatrical voice whenever she asked him about them. She secretly liked it when he did this, and so she had taken to asking the question whenever they set up. Other candles had been placed around the tent earlier that afternoon, some standing upright in long, slender holders, while others hung from chains slung from the tent poles. Solatta placed two of the newly lit brayberry candles into holders before pushing on, narrowly avoiding a swung elbow.

In the middle of the tent, a rough circle had been left clear by the gathering hopefuls. They nudged one another eagerly as they waited and murmured, but not one encroached beyond the line of straw. A man stood proud within that circle—slender and dressed too finely to be a local. His shoes were of smooth and polished leather, and his trousers were dark blue, made from a lush and soft fabric that, Solatta supposed, must feel sumptuous to the touch. His shirt was pristine and white, showing no marks or sweat stains, and over the top was a deep green waistcoat. He was resplendent in his frippery.

This was the very definition of a gentleman, Solatta thought. She moved closer, positioning the candles to provide more light for what was yet to come. She looked up at the still-silent man, absorbing the feeling of the crowd. It was as though he were drinking them in and assessing them. She wondered how she might feel if it were her up there instead—excited, perhaps, and powerful. For now, though, her stomach was a ball of tension. Still, it was nothing new: she always felt like this on performance nights. What if something went wrong? What if she froze in her tasks or someone got hurt?

Tervan's hand had drifted down to the pocket of his waistcoat, his fingers fondling something inside. Solatta knew it to be the smooth black stone he carried with him like a token. It was his good luck charm, he'd told her once. He caught her eye, almost as if he had sensed her gazing at him, and gave her a wink. The evening was about to begin. Wait—was she going to be sick?

Tervan raised his hand high into the air, commanding attention. Slowly, he began turning on the spot, looking out into the assembled faces as he did so, meeting their expectant eyes. The crowd grew quiet and still. He stopped and raised his other hand, demanding complete silence. Eyes followed his every move, moths fixated on a flame.

'Ladies and gentlemen,' he began, his voice strong and resonant, 'welcome, and thank you for coming.' He paused, but didn't allow the silence to settle. 'You, the lucky few! My tent is not big enough for all who would benefit from my words tonight, but this cannot be helped.'

Solatta gazed about her. Although she had seen the performance many times before, she still found the spectacle no less entrancing. Not just Tervan and his show, which in truth was miracle enough, but also the way this one man could take a group of strangers and pull their strings as if they were old puppets, keeping them hanging on his every word. She took in their faces: sun-beaten and weather-worn, lined perhaps beyond their time. Mouths held agape, uncertain what they were in for—but Solatta knew. She was almost jealous of them; she wished she could again see Tervan's show for the first time, watching with the eyes of a child, fresh and innocent to the world. These people had seen a lifetime of hardships, and she was glad that, for once, they would be witness to something bright and spectacular. A magical escape.

'You may not realise it, ladies and gentlemen, but I come to you as a brother,' Tervan called out, his voice beginning to take up a rhythm. 'I may be a stranger to this town, but I come to you as a brother in Truth, and I know that you want the Truth. I know that you deserve the Truth.'

Solatta kept her vigil, silently watching how the crowd reacted. Some locals were already nodding, and she almost breathed a sigh of relief.

'I look around here today and I see people that are desperate for the Truth.'

One of the women in the crowd whooped in acknowledgement.

'That's right, my friend,' Tervan affirmed, picking up on the woman's exclamation. More of the crowd were nodding along now and, as ever, Solatta was astonished at how quickly they responded.

'That, my brothers and sisters, is the sound of someone searching for Truth. The sound of someone who has heard enough lies.'

More calls of assent were now coming from the crowd—some *Yeah*-ed and others just *Mmm-mmm*-ed their responses. It was clear that these people were desperate for a release. Solatta could feel the tension building, and she wondered what kind of lives they led to be so wound up so easily. Were they so starved of entertainment? They had been timid on arrival, she remembered, as though anxious at being caught. Did they live in constant fear? If so, of what? Their masters? Each other? Perhaps even the Church? Tervan told her that they should never trust the priests, and yet here he was preaching the Truth.

'Now, I may not be a man of the Church—I have not taken those vows nor dressed in those robes—but I am a man that walks in the Truth, and I am a man that deserves—no, *demands* the Truth!' His voice followed an entrancing cadence, rising and falling; one moment a gentle sea lapping at the shore, the next a fierce wind striking up. 'Among you, I know that there are those who have found it hard to listen to the Truth.'

A few gasped at the thought of such blasphemy, but none recoiled as Solatta had expected.

'It's okay. The Church of the Righteous Truth cannot condemn you here, in this tent—in this sanctuary. I may not be a man of the Church, but I am a man, and this tent is *my* church, a church of man—a child of Al Ma'Ath, the mother of us all.'

There were now more people making some kind of noise than not, abandoning whatever fears they might have had of being associated with these incredible (and almost certainly sacrilegious) statements. Tervan excelled at this, she knew—presenting himself as absolver had long been among his talents. Solatta could feel the energy in the room; the heat and humidity made it feel more like a bath house than a tent, and sweat gleamed on her brow, hot and sticky. Tervan, however, still looked relatively cool. She would never understand how he managed that particular trick. Readying herself, she wiped her clammy hands against the grey fabric of her skirts.

* * *

They had arrived at the outskirts of Doarson six days ago, heavy with dust and the weariness of yet another long journey across open country. The region was so large that it could still take another six or so days to reach the Citadel itself. Here, they were far from the bustle of the large towns. They struck a simple camp, with only their vardo-style caravan and a small fire to warm themselves.

'These are busy people with more on their minds than the two of us,' Tervan reasoned, eyes glinting in the low firelight. 'Simple people do not notice other simple people quite as much as they do outsiders. We need to be as invisible as we can. Then, when we ourselves go unseen, we will find what otherwise goes unnoticed

17

and ignored.'

Each small village and settlement looked much the same as the next. Workers in the fields paid no mind to two more drudge-faced hacks, and the days melted into one another like lard in a skillet. Not that they were working in the traditional sense; no, their task was to take quiet notice of the people. Get a feel for them, single out those individuals who didn't look so good. Tervan was a Kellawayan, after all, a member of the ancient nomadic race that wandered the known world, passing on their beliefs and heritage. Even after the Great Wars of the Expansion they had retained their ancestral right to roam; it was a tradition so deeply ingrained in their culture that it had endured every fresh obstacle of the modern era. An indentured workforce, only just on the right side of slavery in Solatta's opinion. Most people around here were born, raised, lived—if you could call it that—and died within a day's travel, unless their service was sold on and shipped off to some other House-Lord. Mostly, though, they were simply left to tend the land. Generation after generation... no schooling, not much else either. It brought Solatta to tears just to think about it. Even the House-Lords might only visit for three or four months during each cycle.

But then it wasn't the nobility that interested Solatta and Tervan. As far as they were concerned, those types could look after themselves. They were only here for the lowly: those men, women, and even children who toiled day in, day out, month after month, scraping together an existence while the nobility grew fat off their labour.

'These simple people have little to exist on and even less to dream for,' Tervan had told her when she was still a child, 'and there are few things in this world that are as sad and as offensive to the Goddess as having nothing to live for. So, we give them hope and belief.' He gave her a smile and ruffled her hair playfully.

'Hope and belief?' she queried.

'That's right. Hope that there is something bigger and better in this world, and the belief that someone actually cares about them and their lot. And, in that way, we do something to spread the ideals of the Goddess. We put a little of her Truth into the world.'

It always struck her as strange, this conflict within her guardian. Often, he seemed at odds with the Church and its teachings, even going so far as to say some of the most terrible things—things that might get them into trouble if they were overheard and reported. While most normal people would go to their local church day after day to pray and give their offerings, she couldn't remember the last time they had been near one, never mind inside. Then, at other times, he talked of wanting nothing more than to spread the Truth of the Goddess throughout the land, of all the miracles that she performed and how she made the world and brought light and hope. *That's just Tervan*, she supposed, *a bundle of confusion, and the source of all irritation.*

On their third day in the Southern Estates, they stopped for refreshments in a local alehouse popular among the villagers of Sia. Not that it could be called much of a 'house'—to Solatta it looked more like a wooden shack beside a dirt road. Upturned crates stood in for tables and buckets acted as stools. Judging by the smell, the buckets were fresh from the privy house. It was here that she had seen him.

She noticed his hands first. Well, not so much his hands, but his fingers. Fat like a chicken's legs, the nails thin and glass-like. The man himself had a tired and weathered face, with sallow-looking eyes that looked empty and lost. As Solatta watched, he began coughing with such fury that she was sure he was about to dislodge a lung. Tervan considered him for a while, his eyes drinking in every aspect of him. Finally, he nodded and they left, paying for their drinks and the man's, though he appeared not to have touched it.

That evening, they moved their caravan closer to the alehouse and, on the following day, went about the area, spreading news of a famous Kellawayan who was soon to arrive.

＊

Solatta smiled to see so many now gathered in the tent. Strangers mostly, but many faces she recognised from their short time in the little village of Raon, one of Lacustria's southern estates. Easily two-score now stood excitedly, scandalised by what they saw. There were men and women of all ages, though Solatta was sure many were here just to find out exactly what a Kellawayan was. *Never mind*, she thought. *They will see soon enough.*

She realised she was fidgeting with her skirts again, her idle hands tugging and pulling at the freshly laundered garments. She still wasn't used to them—around town, she'd worn only grime-stained rags and, while she had no doubt that Tervan was right that no one would recognise them, the new clothes felt stiff. Her mind began to wander and, once again, she caught her hands reaching for her skirts.

She closed her eyes and inhaled deeply, picking out the different aromas of the tent. She was good at this game, and it was one of her favourite lessons: recognising the many herbs and tonics they used. Days-old sweat and soil predominated, both intriguing and off-putting at the same time, like mouldy potatoes baked in cumin. She wrinkled her nose at the idea.

Tervan's melodic voice swam back into her ears. She smiled as he allowed the crowd's excitement to grow, lifting them up with his words and carrying them along on their own emotions before dropping them back into quiet contemplation. The crowd looked on eagerly, willing him to continue his sermon, and yet he remained speechless, holding his tongue so long that the audience became restless and the atmosphere uncomfortable. At last, he moved into the crowd, stalking through the throng like a cat creeping up on a mouse. The people moved back instinctively as he came towards them, carving a path that closed behind once he had passed through. A slow, deliberate passage.

'I can see that some of you are suffering,' he called out. As he walked, he peered into their faces, studying the eyes of those nearest to him. He approached one woman straight on, singling her out. The cat had found his mouse.

The tent grew quiet, all eyes turning to focus on the pair. Tervan searched the woman with his eyes, staring as though through her, *into* her. The air seemed to thicken, a great silence about to break, and Solatta realised that she too was holding her breath. Tervan placed one hand on the woman's forehead.

'This woman,' he said in loud and clear voice, the sound rumbling through the silenced crowd. This particular mouse was certainly a comely woman, Solatta thought, rolling her eyes—dark hair and somehow even darker eyes that now flicked nervously between the people around her. 'This woman. Oh, this woman has known sin and untruths,' Tervan continued, shaking his head.

Some people nearby gasped and edged away. Others nodded in agreement. One woman who Solatta could not see even voiced a loud and knowing confirmation.

'We are all children in the light of the Truth, my daughter. Do you accept the light of the Truth into your heart?' Tervan waited for a response, but the woman seemed too stunned to know what to say. 'I ask you: does the light of the Truth reside in your everlasting soul?'

Slowly, the woman began to nod, and Tervan's hand moved along with it. He raised his free hand high into the air above him, his fingers balled into a fist.

'Let the Truth of light and life focus on me and flow into your heart!' He opened out his upstretched hand. A blue wisp of flame sprang from it and leapt into the air before burning out. The woman screamed, as did several others—the gasp of air, a collective intake of breath, Solatta included. Quickly, Tervan leaned forwards, his mouth close to the woman's. Solatta could see that his lips moved, yet she could not make out what, if anything, he was saying. Without word or notice, the girl collapsed to the ground.

This was her cue. Solatta turned to the table, crouching down to find the small leather-bound box she'd placed there earlier. Quickly, she opened it, revealing a range of tubules and phials of coloured liquids, and, fingering through them, she selected one. None of the potions held either label or description but, even at a distance, she could recognise them by smell alone. Spirit of Hartshorn: made by slowly boiling hoof filings in urine. It was a wonderfully rousing tonic. She had painstakingly learned to make each of the potions in the box—following patient instruction from Tervan, of course. She crossed to the woman, un-stoppering the phial and passing the acrid-smelling spirit under her nose while lifting her head slightly. It smelled of cycles-old horse swill and was enough to sting the eyes, even at an arm's distance. The woman took in a sharp and violent gasp of breath, as if someone had landed a punch to her midriff. A mix of coughs and tears welcomed her back to reality.

Unperturbed, Tervan moved on through the crowd, seemingly ignorant of Solatta and her nose-stung friend. He stopped here and there, pausing beside someone or another, leaning close to them and whispering something in their ears. Each time, the effect was the same. Even without the theatrical burning palm, the person would drop to the floor, only to then be revived by Solatta and her stinking spirit. The onlookers gasped and shrieked with delight at each new person that she brought coughing and spluttering back to consciousness.

To them, the whole show was a marvel—'A parody of death and rebirth,' as Tervan had once phrased it.

Three of the people he had felled—two women and an older man, though there had been more besides—had taken more than a few nervous wafts of Hartshorn before their watery eyes had looked up thankfully at Solatta. Even with the pungent potion, it was hard to miss the fact that the old man had freshly soiled himself, and she was suddenly grateful for the masking odour of horse pee.

Finally, after almost a complete lap of the tent, Tervan paused in front of the man that Solatta had pointed out in the alehouse.

It had been a wager whether news of the travellers would make it to the man, and an even bigger gamble on whether he'd turn up. It was not unheard of for a person not to attend the tent on the first night; it simply meant that the pair would carry on spreading the word throughout the following day before setting up the tent again each night until he or she arrived.

Tervan looked at the man in front of him, unblinking and transfixed. Eyes boring deep: assessing him, studying his character. 'You are in pain, my friend,' he said at last. His words were softer now, more comforting than before.

For the first time, Solatta noticed how painfully thin the man appeared, with skin that looked to be stretched too tightly over his bones. He slumped forward, and a young, dark-haired girl, possibly his daughter, helped him up. He lifted his head to look at Tervan, but the action seemed to pull at his throat and chest, bringing on a coughing fit. Dark red gobbets in savagely contrast with his pale flesh. Some of the people nearest to the man edged away, eyeing the mucus fearfully. Solatta could hardly blame them; there were sharp notes of foulness that clung to the man. Greasy and feculent, a miasma of fetid lardy-cakes.

'What is his name?' Tervan asked the girl.

'It is Coln, sir,' she replied in an uncertain voice, lost to the crowd.

'Is your faith in the Truth strong, Coln?' Tervan asked. It was no use, though; the frail man's breathing was too ragged for him to respond, and Solatta wondered whether he'd even heard the words.

'Oh yes, sir,' the girl interjected. 'It is strong, sir—stronger than most, I'd dare say.'

'Very well.' Tervan stooped, slipping one arm around the waist of Coln to take the bulk of the man's weight. 'Help me walk him to the table, child,' he said to the girl. 'Solatta, please clear the table and fetch a bowl with some fresh water.'

Solatta was already moving, having anticipated his request. Bending back down to her potions box, she replaced the Hartshorn and removed a heavy glass bowl, filling it with water from a pitcher nearby. The bowl was good and deep, decorated with intricate patterns and engravings that hardly seemed to align— indeed, in certain lights they seemed at odds with one another. A competition of engravers and artists must have worked on the thing, each adding their own distinctive markings. One area had tiny animals etched into the glass: cattle and other grazers, birds and flying things, fearsome beasts that stalked and hunted. Another featured plants and flowers, while yet another showed heavy clouds and a sea ravaged by storms. Here there were body parts: hands and eyes, arms and legs. Solatta had never thought of the bowl as particularly pretty, and yet, somehow, she liked it. It felt like her own, even though it had been in Tervan's family for generations. No, she thought. That wasn't how he put it. It had been with *him* for generations. He was forever mixing things up and saying them wrong.

She carried the bowl and a clean cloth to the table, placing them neatly, and moved some candles to give them more room. Tervan and the girl positioned Coln in front of the table, his back to it, and helped him up, lifting his legs so that he could lay him down.

The man hardly seemed to notice. His eyes displayed neither alarm nor anxiety, although, in truth, they did not display very much at all. Alone or perhaps free at last, they stared off somewhere far ahead. *He looks to be in a worse state than most of the others*, she thought, the knot of anxiety beginning to strengthen in her stomach once more.

The man began to cough again, his head jerking to the side, where the young girl was on hand to catch a fresh mass of bloody sputum with an old, stained rag. Solatta positioned herself at the end of the table and waited quietly for further direction. Tervan, having helped his patient onto the table, now moved to its side.

The smell of wet dog and tobacco made Solatta turn. There, wide-eyed behind her, stood an eager-faced boy dwarfed by the leering crowd.

'Some of you may know this man named Coln,' said Tervan as he turned up his sleeves. He stressed the man's name for all to hear, but at the same time seemed to speak directly to Coln himself. 'He lives with you in your community. A man who has given his life and his health to work the land in order to grow another's wealth. You may know him as a goodly man, or as a man of poor character—I do not know.'

Some people in the crowd, including Coln's daughter, seemed aghast at the suggestion, and shook their heads at the idea. One woman called out, 'No, sir!'

'What I see,' Tervan continued, shutting out the noise of protest, 'is a man in need of help. A man who, on this day, needs to find Truth in his world.'

His forearms now bare, he turned to Solatta, winked, and dipped his hands into the bowl, rinsing them before allowing her to quickly towel them dry. She smiled back at him, proud.

The girl—not Coln's daughter after all, Solatta thought, for they were too alike in age—stood nervously to one side. Solatta studied her: she and Coln had the same high cheekbones and dark hair, only Coln's was thin and matted with sweat. His sister, then? It mattered not—she couldn't stop Tervan now if she tried. Still, better to be safe than sorry. Solatta took her arm and pulled her near. 'What is your name?' she whispered.

'Shohanon, miss,' the girl whispered back, evidently afraid, unable to pull her eyes from the scene. 'Please, what is going to happen to my brother?'

'Shhh,' Solatta answered, smug at having guessed correctly. 'Everything will be okay. You just need to trust in Tervan—he knows what he's doing.'

Shohanon slowly nodded her understanding, though her body was trembling.

Tervan unbuttoned Coln's once-white shirt. It was not that the shirt was dirty, Solatta realised, but rather that it was old and worn to the point of exhaustion, like the clothes of so many others here. Now, it looked greyish-brown, the colour of untreated wool. Coln's exposed chest showed far too many ribs, furrows and ridges that hardly moved under the man's laboured breathing. The people in the tent inched forward for a better view, only to shrink back at the ugly reminder of the harshness of their lives.

'This man is diseased,' said Tervan, his voice rising again, cutting short the murmurs.

Fearful of the word, the front row of people stepped back, treading on those behind. Angry mutters passed among neighbours.

'A disease is like a poisonous rumour spreading through a village, eating away at the community,' Tervan continued, louder still. 'It relies on darkness and mistruth to carry it from one place to another, growing in strength all the time. Feeding.' He held out his hands to the crowd, palms outstretched, before lowering them to hover over the man, one above his chest and the other over his navel. At once, Coln drew a sharp intake of breath, as if someone had slipped ice down his back.

'Trust in the Truth!' Tervan said, more for the benefit of the eager crowd than the man on the table. 'Accept the Truth into your heart. We are all born of lies and untruths, and it is only in the blessed light of Truth that we can find redemption.'

Again, calls of assent and confirmation came from the baying crowd. Solatta could feel their heat, could almost taste the anticipation.

Tervan slowly pressed his left hand against Coln's chest, conjuring a paroxysm of coughing. With his right hand, Tervan reached under the palm of his left, searching for something, digging into skin. There was a loud pop, and the crowd shrieked—nervous. Even Solatta jumped, worried that something had gone wrong. A trickle of crimson began to spill from Tervan's hand. Solatta felt Shohanon go limp against her. *So much blood.*

Tervan pulled his darkly stained fist free. Something red and meaty came with it. Screams and cries. Shouts of disbelief. Setting aside the bloodied mass, Tervan moved his hand again to the man's chest. A second pop. More blood, and another fleshy mess pulled in his eager grip. The crowd teetered on some unacknowledged brink—they could easily be lost. Solatta knew that they had to work hard and fast. Shohanon was distraught, grabbing at Coln's hand. His chest was thick with blood, but his body seemed peaceful. And then, sudden and desperate, a breath—a gulp like a freshly landed fish. Coln coughed, a blessed noise, the first cry of a baby. Tervan held his bloody hand aloft, gristle knots glistening.

'Solatta, could you clean Coln off please?' he said, stepping back from his workspace, looking suddenly tired, though his eyes retained their mad gleam.

Solatta moved quickly, panic rising. The water felt warm on her hands, almost hot. She mopped at Coln's chest, sloughing away the scarlet stain, scattering the meaty debris. *What if it's gone wrong?* A fear she'd never managed to shake. Three wipes, dunk, wring. Four wipes, dunk. Finally, the viscera was washed away and the chest almost clean. Where Solatta half-feared a gaping wound, innards exposed, there was nothing, just a pink-washed glaze. There should be holes torn into the flesh, the crowd knew it—they had seen Tervan tear into the man's chest and pull out the disease in one bloodied fist. She could hear their muttering, even now—their disbelief and wonder. She knew exactly what they were feeling; she'd felt it herself. She supposed she still did, only muted. It was not the spectacle that moved her now; it was the results. The days to come.

'Faith in the Truth. Faith in our ability to overcome the lies and torments of our lives,' Tervan intoned in a clear and solemn voice.

The crowd hushed.

This is the Miracle of Truth, Solatta thought, looking at Coln. She felt proud at the part she'd played, however small. She looked to her guardian, his waxy skin now pale and drained. She wanted to go to him and wipe the bloody residue from his hands, to care for him the way he cared for others. The way he cared for her. But she knew not to. He would take himself off to be alone, like always. She felt a pang of sorrow mixed with something else—something like annoyance.

'Pray for Coln to be received of the Truth, that his heart and body will be cleansed of lies,' he continued, his voice faltering. 'Pray, too, for your own salvation in the Truth, and for the love of the Goddess to become known to you for all time.' Wearily, he looked to Shohanon. 'Coln should remain here overnight. You may keep your vigil if you wish, but let him rest.'

With a final smile to Solatta, Tervan walked from the tent. The crowd cowered as he passed through them. Fearful or reverent, she never could tell. They had just watched him perform possibly the greatest blasphemy possible, though she knew they would tell no one. How could they? If they did, they admitted their part. They were complicit sinners.

The buzz of voices started up as soon as the tent flap fell. No one seemed to know exactly what had happened. 'Is Coln even still alive?' Solatta heard one woman ask another. None dared to get close to his prone body, but many watched his sister, how she went to him, terrified and tearful, but not, it seemed, in mourning. There was solace in her action. It seemed to confirm their worst fears: not that he was dead, but that he was still alive. Saved—even cured. As though the Goddess herself had come down and taken away his ailment. But only the Church had that power.

Solatta had no answers, not that anyone asked her. They kept their distance, eyeing her strangely. She was used to it by now, but that didn't quell her annoyance at Tervan—how like him to walk away and leave her to pick up the pieces. *Are all men this lazy?* This was life with Tervan, she supposed—his was the show, the pomp and the pageantry; hers was the real work. She was the one who roused them, cleaned them, tended to them, cared for them, and she was the one who was left with them afterwards. She threw the rag into the bowl and began to angrily blow out candles. She muffled a cry when hot wax splashed onto her fingers. She felt tears forming. *Fine for him to help people he doesn't even know, but where is he when I need him?*

She knew the words were unfair as soon as they formed. He *had* always been there for her, for as long as she could remember. In fact, he was all that she *could* remember. He was her teacher and her guardian. He helped her when she hurt herself and tended to her when she was sick. He provided food for her and together they travelled the world in their little caravan. Yes, he made her mad at times, but he also made her smile and laugh. He was the father that she often wished she had known, and more than anything he was a kind and caring man. He was her friend.

She busied herself with her bottles, clinking them back into the leather box alongside the bowl—*her* bowl. The tent had emptied, and only stragglers dallied, all hushed voices and furtive glances. She heard a new voice, weak and scratchy. A mouse, perhaps.

'Where am I?'

'Shh.'

She turned to see Shohanon bent over her brother, stroking his thin hair.

'You're going to be okay.' There were tears in her voice.

Solatta had lost count of how many times she had witnessed such scenes. Still, each time she saw the reactions of family members and loved ones, it brought it all back to her—the sheer tenderness of it all. The honesty and Truth in what she and Tervan were doing. They were *helping* people. They did more to help the people than she had ever seen a priest do. She had no idea how they did it, or even whether they should be doing it. The Church said no, she knew that—according to them, only the Goddess's love can heal and only her Church can administer to the sick. 'That's only so they can charge for the service,' Tervan would say. The priests called it a sin to heal, that the Goddess sends pain to punish those who have turned away from her, but Solatta couldn't believe that. How could the Goddess hate her people so much? It made no sense to her.

She walked uncertainly towards the pair and, as though sensing her, Shohanon turned to look at her. Immediately she broke down: great sobs of relief, all snot and gulps of air.

'I can't...' she began. 'I don't know what happened or what to say. You've done so much. I can see it's him. It's my Coln. He's back. I can never... thank you. Thank you both for what you have done.' She threw herself around Solatta, sobbing into her shoulder.

These were the moments, she knew—the times when she finally understood that what they were doing was right, and that she had her own part to play. It wasn't just Tervan. It was another gift he had given her. He had brought her into the show, added her to the spectacle. *He doesn't walk out to let me pick up the pieces,* she realised. *He does it to give me these moments. The recognition and the glory.*

'I give to you my blessed Truth,' the Goddess said. Those who believe in her and the sacred veracity of her words alone will be saved. Cast out false idols and un-Truthful representations, for they pervert and twist her blessed Truth. Trust in her Church and dwell not in the dark and evil places of old, which should forever remain buried.

—From the Tenets of Truth

CHAPTER TWO
AL-DREBAN

Baile Saor

Sweat stung the young priest's eyes, and he stopped to take a drink. It had been a foolish thing to trek to the summit of the Knap during the heat of the morning. Still, he supposed, it had been his feet that brought him here, not his head. That had been too full of questions to worry about where he was going, too busy with daydreams to care. He couldn't help imagining the glory that awaited him when he presented his findings to the Church. For now, though, all he had were suspicions and ever more questions. Now that he had finally crested the summit of the butte, however, he wondered whether it had been worth the effort.

The Knap was little more than a hill with a tor and impressive views over the Lacustrian Plains, but it had taken him almost the full morning to climb. Now, nothing but rocks and gale-battered trees greeted him. He felt deflated—despite the sun, the wind slapped at his face like a rebuke. This was meant to be a holy place. Not one in Truth, but from the age before the Church: a time when the realm of Alytheia was split into factions and people believed all kinds of superstitious nonsense. Those days were gone now, thank the Goddess. It was almost unsettling to think that heathen mystics might have practiced their mumbo-jumbo here. Automatically, he began to raise his fingers to his head against such wickedness, but he stopped himself, remembering with a start that he was supposed to be travelling in secret. It wouldn't matter up here, of course— there was no one around to see him—but still. Alone he might be, but he didn't *feel* alone. This place felt odd and uncomfortable, as if someone was watching...

A gnarly old tree shook an arm at him, rattling in the breeze. He shuddered, though he wasn't entirely sure it was due purely to the wind. He reminded himself that he was a man of reason, soon to be ordained proper into the Church of the Righteous Truth. He was not interested in fireside tales and ghost stories. He was here to find truth.

People had gone missing. More to the point, priests had gone missing—two of them, in little over two cycles. He had been sent to find them, or else discover what had happened to them. His search had led him here, the market town of Baile Saor. Too big to be a town, too small to be city. It answered to the administrative centre of Doarson—or, rather, it should have. Only, no one had been to pay the taxes in over two cycles. It was a coincidence that made Al-Dreban suspicious, though that wasn't the only thing.

The town was busy, prosperous even, full of people coming

and going without a care in the world. He had lost count of the number of people who'd greeted him with a smile and a nod. Not once had he been stopped and asked for his documents, and he'd not seen anyone else detained either. It was as if the city's people answered to no one. Where were the patrols? Where were the authorities? Someone, somewhere should have asked to see his travel chit. He'd gone to enough trouble to have one forged, for Truth's sake! Everyone needed a chit, except maybe the king, but even then, Al-Dreban couldn't be sure. He had never been exactly clear on how the law applied to royalty. He assumed that the Church held authority—but then, he was biased.

For hours he'd wandered the streets of the town. He had a great time. The market was full of stalls selling all kinds of goods, the traders all vying for custom. He'd been given so many tastes and titbits that he felt full, and yet he hadn't had to part with a coin. Spiced hams and cheeses, mutton cooked in gravy, and an off-cut of pheasant that had been stuffed with other little birds. The grease had dripped down his fingers and he'd sucked away on them long after he'd finished crunching on the little bones. And that was just the food—all kinds of goods were on offer. Weavings and cloths that were rich enough for any High-Lord or High-Lady. There was no mistaking it: this was a rich town, a town that should be paying much more in taxes than it was. He had seen the records during the briefing from the Golya of his order, probably the most eminent priest in the entire region. Above the Premiero of the Citadel, even. It still made him tremble: here he was, little more than eighteen cycles in age, not even fully ordained, and yet he'd been called to see the Golya. It was enough to make a mother proud. At least, most mothers, Al-Dreban thought with a smirk. His hadn't once bothered to check up on him after handing him over to the Church. She hadn't even looked back, they told him, after leaving him on the step. *I wonder, did she even think of me on her death bed?*

Al-Dreban shook his head. Now was not the time. From here, he could just about make out the gleaming roof of his lodgings—the Golden Hart, an out-of-the-way inn on the road out to the Knap. The proprietor was a friendly sort. Eager to please. He'd almost seemed affronted when Al-Dreban had offered his travel chit and identification (though, not wanting to be fingered as a priest, he'd ensured the papers dropped the honorific 'Al'). They recorded him simply as Dreban, a Kikkuli—like all good lies, it had an element of truth. His father before him had been a Kikkuli, and well respected at that. Al-Dreban couldn't remember much about him. He'd died when Al-Dreban was still a boy, back when they'd still held a position on the estate.

It had been the innkeeper's wife who'd taken his details in the end. A stout-sided woman who was the perfect foil to her husband. Her name was Kareti. A fittingly plain name, Al-Dreban thought. She was a dour woman of little humour, or at least none that she cared to show him. He'd heard the place referred to as the Old Moose about town, though he doubted anyone dared use that name in front of her. The woman made him feel uncomfortable for some reason—it was something in her eyes. They were small and piercing, like those of a shrew or stoat. They'd look more at home on her husband, the weasel-faced Tefarnin.

'Travelling through are we?' the innkeeper had asked him. 'Not had many of them in a while. The travelling-through kind, I mean. Not really something you see much of, is it? No one travels through anywhere, do they? Market town, you see. Folk tend to travel to it, or they travel from it. Not heard of anyone travelling through it before. What you travelling for anyway, young lad like you?'

It was a serious question, Al-Dreban noted. There was no

hint of challenge.

'Work?' Tefarnin continued apace, giving Al-Dreban little time to think, never mind respond. 'A Kikkuli is it? Well isn't that great. Can't think we've had a horse trainer stay at the Hart before. How d'you get into that then? No, don't tell me,' he said immediately, 'it's the father, isn't it? Always the father with proper trades. You ever meet a smithy, then as near to the truth is his father was a smithy too. Stands to reason. No High-Lord can afford to let them go, see. When Dad dies, who's the smithy then?'

For once, the man actually waited for an answer. It was all so close to the truth that it left Al-Dreban flustered.

'Well it's the son, isn't it. Like you,' said Tefarnin, with such an expansive smile that it seemed he'd just solved an ancient riddle. 'Used to work with horses, you know? Wouldn't have minded training 'em myself. Bloody big things, mind. Were then, still are now. Off to see an uncle then?' He stole a glance at the documents that still lay on the counter. 'They must have got a goodly amount of coin for your services, I bet. Either that or you greased a palm or two to get your hands on a travel chit all the way down to Doclea.'

Again, the comment was intended innocently enough, but it struck far too close for comfort. While the man was oblivious, the po-faced Kareti snatched the documents from view and thrust them back to Al-Dreban. He was certain that she had read more into his fluster than she admitted, but she kept her counsel and shot a baleful look at her husband. Al-Dreban was the happier for it.

His rooms were at least more comfortable than the conversation, though he slept poorly. His head was filled with indistinct, half-invented memories of his father, his wrinkled face warped and translucent like a rainbow. Each time Al-Dreban thought he was getting closer, the damned figure would disappear into mist. Even the legacy of his name had been lost, given away on the day his son had been given to the Church: the day that Dre'Bhan Ul-Mutti, Kikkuli—Drea, son of Bhan, Master of Horses—had become the son of no one, child of the Church. The day he had taken up his name in Truth: Al-Dreban.

Tefarnin invited him to break his fast in the morning and, to his delight, he found Kareti to be a fabulous cook. Her small, dark eyes were as sharp as an owl's, and many a time Al-Dreban felt them boring into him when his head was turned. Still, it seemed as though she had not gained her tongue during the night. It mattered not, for her husband kept the conversation flowing even more than he did the food and small beer, though Al-Dreban only had a head for the talking. He forewent the ale after the first cup, fearing that he might become befuddled before his task here was even begun.

'Where did you say you were from?' Tefarnin asked between mouthfuls of pork and bean stew.

'Sestria,' he replied. A town he had memorised but never visited.

'In the north, is it?' Tefarnin asked, 'sounds like it's northern. Had an uncle who was northern once—not so far north as to be distasteful, mind. He still knew right from wrong and left from right an' all that. Did have some bloody funny ways about him, though. They all do up there. Did you know that the women used to chop off a finger for every child they lost? Childbirth, finger gone... flux, finger gone... drowned at sea, finger gone.' He demonstrated on a hand, folding a finger down with each death he counted. 'No wonder some people don't let the children out of their sight. Too bloody worried about how they'll pick their noses otherwise.' He bellowed at his own wit, but was soon quietened by Kareti's withering glare. He leant in conspiratorially. 'Then again,' he attempted to whisper, but was somehow louder than before,

38

'at least they'd have fewer to bloody wag at you, eh?' he said, and guffawed all the more.

Al-Dreban couldn't help but like the man, because of rather than in spite of his unguarded tongue. He was sure the man had received a well-placed kick to the shin from his wife for that latest transgression, and when he described a House-Lord's daughter as buxom, Kareti took away his ale and left the room. The act had conveniently masked over Al-Dreban's question as to whom their House-Lord was, and he wondered if it wasn't deliberate.

'If you don't mind,' he asked, hoping to return to safer and less controversial ground, 'I'd like to pray and give thanks to the Goddess before I set out for the day. Do you have a shrine I might attend for a short while?'

He waited for a response, though it might have taken all day. It was the first time he had found his host lost for words. The man just looked at his bowl, frozen in time.

'An altar, then,' he offered, more to break the awkwardness than anything else.

'No shrine, no altar,' was the flat response.

It was all he could do to stop himself from making the ritual blessing. A house with no way to pay homage to the Goddess? It was close to seditious.

'I'm sorry,' he found himself saying, as though he'd mentioned someone recently deceased. 'Maybe there is a church I might attend? In the town maybe?'

'Church is gone,' said Tefarnin coldly. All humour had fled him; he seemed now just like his wife. 'There was a fire. There hasn't been the time to rebuild.'

'I see.' He was almost relieved. 'But surely your priest has reported this to us? The Citadel must be making plans as we speak. A town without a church is hardly a town at all.' It was out before he realised what he was saying. Had it been a trap? No, it can't have been; Tefarnin had not even flinched at the admission. A slip of the tongue, that was all. 'Us' instead of 'them', a simple error anyone could make. Gloss over and press on. 'And this being such a fine and growing town, I'm sure the priests will be arranging to rebuild a bigger church for the burgeoning community and families.'

Now the man looked up. Had it been overkill?

'I think it's time for you to leave, Mister Dreban.'

'What? But I'm not finished—I mean, I only arrived yesterday,' he stammered.

'My wife and I have things to be about, and I'm sure you have things that you want to achieve before the day has raced away from us. Evening meal is served an hour after sundown, but you'll have to let us know before you leave if you are planning on eating.'

'Of course.' He might have cried with relief. The innkeeper stood and began collecting the table things. Al-Dreban rose with him, spilling some of his uneaten stew in his haste to help.

Tefarnin snatched the outheld bowl and glared up at him. 'I don't know what it is you think you're doing here, mister. But it ain't right to go sticking your nose in where it doesn't belong. This town has given up a lot—more than most would like to admit. We don't appreciate the likes of you reminding us of the things we've lost. Hard times make for hard decisions. It ain't an excuse, I admit, but we judge ourselves far harder than any outsider could, so I'd thank you to keep to your own business.'

With that, he turned and stormed out. Al-Dreban was shaken. His words had been a clumsy attempt to cover his own indiscretions, not intended to stir the memories of his host's haunted past. He hurried to his rooms to collect some things, but was accosted along the way by Kareti. She appeared from nowhere, like an apparition.

'I've been watching you and I see,' she warned ominously.

'See what? I assure you, I have done nothing.'

'Nothing is it? Well I see you and I see that you are not nothing. You are far more than you admit to being, young man. Far more than you might even know yourself. But you might find us more than we seem, too. These are a goodly people, just that some of those are led by foolish men who wouldn't know the Truth if it bit them like a snake. But then most men wouldn't. Not even you.'

Her words cut and she pressed them home, jabbing at him with a finger as if she was poking a fire.

'Oh, don't kid yourself on that,' she started anew, cutting short any protest. 'You're nothing but false and full of lies. Like a child's plaything, all dressed up and painted like a puppet. Well if you go sticking your beak where it shouldn't be sticked, then you're going to get your strings cut—and that's for sure. My advice to you, mister whoever-you-say-you-are, is to get while the getting's good.' And with a final jab, she was gone, leaving Al-Dreban with a throbbing pain in his temples.

By the time he left for the day, his head was low and his spirits grew lower. Foot followed foot and before he knew where he was, he was already winding up the Knap.

Now, peering out at the land stretched below, the wind called to him, whistling between the stone mounds, some as tall as a man. The old stumped tree shook its withered arms. It seemed to want him there as little as the old moose and her husband had. And to think, he had taken to the man.

He kicked at the earth, a thick cloud of soot brushing up underfoot. His nostrils filled with the scent of charred wood and dirt. He crouched on his haunches, touching the black soil. *A fire*, he realised, casting about. The whole place had been ablaze, and recently too. Or at least a large section. It must have been visible for miles around. *Who in Truth would be setting a bonfire up here, and for what purpose?* It was just another question for his already lengthy list, and he'd be lucky to answer half of them if the whole town clammed up like Tefarnin and Kareti had. He stood, looking down upon the town. It seemed suddenly as hidden and full of secrets as the mighty Marandum Forest, its people as unreachable as the peaks of the Mata Mountains. He sighed—it was not just the morning's conversations that needled him. There was something else too, something that he knew rooted it all. Some other mystery hidden behind the false smiles and niceties. How could a town not have a church? Where did they pray? Evidently not in their homes. *If it were my town*, he thought, *I'd be breaking my bones to build it myself.* Who would want to bring a child into a place that has no basis in faith and Truth?

And there it was: the thing he had missed. The answer to the question he hadn't even asked. Where were the children? He'd not seen a single one.

It was time to go back into town.

The descent into Baile Saor was much quicker than the trek up, but each step felt like a climb into the abyss. By the time he was back in the town, the sun had almost completed its own laboured journey across the sky, and Al-Dreban cursed the idiocy of not taking his hat. His face was caked in grime and dust, but he didn't stop to wash. He felt very much the bit between his teeth. There were layers to every story, he knew. This one would be no different. The missing priests, the unpaid taxes, the empty pleasantries— and, most of all, the children.

He strode through the bright streets, passing tradesmen hawking wares, crowds of laughing townsfolk, relaxed workmen wandering between sites. They sickened him, all of them—such profanity! He needed to find the mayor or, if they could not be found, then some other authority. If they refused to answer his questions, well, he would have no option but to send for the Suers of Truth. The thought made him shudder, and this time he did touch his fingers to his forehead: *Might I always know Truth.*

The Suers would get to the bottom of things, though they would not be discrete, let alone delicate. That was not in their nature. Cruel and wicked he had heard them called, but only by those who might hide the Truth and defy the Goddess's word. The Suers were a tool of the Truth, nothing more. He had never seen them in their work and prayed he never would. The stories were enough.

The light was beginning to fade. He sped his weary legs, stumbling a little on the cobbled ground. He must have appeared a madman. The people gave him a wide berth, smiling oddly or frowning as he passed. No matter. There: the town hall—a great stone building, wide facade resplendent in the late light. Now he would get his answers. Only, it was closed. Shuttered even. But surely, Al-Dreban thought, surely there had to be someone. He walked around it fully, searching for a minister, a staff member, even a maid. Nothing. He made another circle of the building, people stopping in the street to watch him. He felt like some deranged animal.

Halfway round again, he saw an open window. What if he were to climb in? What answers might he find? He scoured the street, looking for something that might help him in. It was then that he spotted it: small and unloved, an insignificant bit of rock, with neither paint nor embellishment, half-hidden under weed and moss at the corner of a snaking alleyway. A small stone shrine. The sight took him aback. It was the last thing he had expected to find, and it ripped the wind from his sails. The first image of the Goddess he had seen since entering this Truth-forsaken place, and it told him everything he needed to know. He hurried for the thing and crouched low among the bracken, desperately trying to scratch some life and dignity back into the stone. It was a futile effort. His head fell forward, chin hovering above his chest. Tears began to glimmer in his eyes. He tried to utter a prayer—something to purify, to renew. It was no good. The words would not come. *The heathens!* By the Goddess, they deserved the Suers. He made to stand, but saw something at the foot of the shrine. 'What new heresy is this?' he uttered.

He picked it up, turning it over in his hands. Hessian cloth, roughly sewn, stuffed, and fashioned as some idol. Crudely stitched features gave it a fearsome-looking face. Its nasty little mouth twisted open, as though it were shouting some blasphemy. It was a wicked thing, Al-Dreban was sure—a tool used in dark practices to conjure the false earth magic of old. It was not of the light and certainly not of the Truth. He had a mind to toss it back to the ground and stomp it into the dirt. 'No,' he heard himself saying. 'I'll keep it. It will be more evidence of the evil that is happening here. They damn themselves with their own actions.'

'Good day to you.' A man's voice from behind.

Al-Dreban turned to see a stately looking man, well-dressed and well-fed. His highly polished boots felt too close in his crouched position. He stood, his anger ready to boil over, but saw the man was not alone. Two much more powerful looking men flanked him, faces set.

'Good day, sir,' the portly man repeated. He had an air to him, as though he was used to being listened to. 'Allow me to introduce myself. I am First Citizen and mayor of Baile Saor. Mayor Prefeito.' He smoothed his moustache with an air of self-importance.

Al-Dreban was unsure of how to react. His blood boiled at the arrogance the man showed, even in the vicinity of this abomination. The mayor watched him in silence, waiting on his response no doubt, as though they were set to play out some farce of formalities. *How dare he*? Al-Dreban reached for his pocket, intending to present his documents. It would be sweet to watch the man's look of superiority slip, to see him drop to his knees and beg for forgiveness in the face of the Church that he and his town had betrayed and insulted. His fingers had closed around the papers when he remembered: they were false. He was nothing more than a horse trainer on his way to take up work with his uncle. *Passing through*. Worse still, the papers were forged. The mayor waited.

'I... I am...'

He swallowed. His predicament had cooled his anger, though not his indignation. He wanted to say more, but only stumbled forwards, one hand still clutching the hessian poppet, the other reaching forward to steady himself. The mayor reached out and grasped the hand as though to shake it, enveloping it within his hot and sticky palms.

'Oh, don't worry, young man,' said the mayor calmly. 'We imagine that we know exactly who you are.'

Panic began to spread within Al-Dreban and he tried to pull free. One of the two men stepped forward, a slender leather cosh in his fist. It described a swift and smooth arc before his eyes. Al-Dreban dimly registered a searing pain in his head that quickly spread out across his body. He felt his legs begin to sway and pondered their movement until, steadily, an all-engulfing darkness washed over him.

* * *

Night had fallen, as had the temperature. Al-Dreban's head throbbed, and he wondered how serious his injury was. He

45

tasted the iron-salt of blood in his mouth and he had the sluggish recollection of an impact, though it flittered somewhere at the edge of his memory, much like the lights that glimmered at the edge of his vision. He was outside—were they stars? It felt like they were, so twinkling and elusive. They were growing, he realised, larger and brighter. He thought to move. Something nagged at him to get up and run, though he couldn't remember why. He tried to stand, only to find he already was. The wind clawed at him, and he shuddered. Something waved an angry fist and he flinched. Something strong and solid held him. Slowly, the world came back into focus.

He was back on the Knap. There was the same acrid smell of burning in his nostrils and the same angry old tree rattling its branches in the wind. There were new things too: the two men that held him fast, for instance. Neither said anything, not even when he struggled and lurched against them. It wasn't long before he stopped resisting altogether. After all, where could he run? He was miles from anywhere, without his horse, and no doubt he had been divested of his things, including his travel chit.

The lights continued towards him, growing like the knot in his stomach. They swam slowly from the darkness. Before long they resolved into individual torches, each one carried by a face Al-Dreban half-recognised—townspeople? Men and women he had seen these last days, had even spoken to. At their foremost was the mayor.

'What's going on?'

He got no answer. Just the faces, resolute and cold. The mayor halted several paces from him, meeting his gaze. Torchlight flashed across his face, sending shadows skittering over his features. His dark watery orbs burned orange, hiding something behind.

Then, apparently satisfied, the mayor turned away. He held

his empty hands aloft in front of the crowd and called for their attention. Silence followed—expectant, not reverent. He was equal among them, not exalted. Al-Dreban looked beyond him to the faces. Haunted and troubled. They looked drained but resigned, as though they had been here before. He felt a dark foreboding grow within him.

'What is this?' he called. He searched out the faces of people he recognised, silently imploring them to answer.

'Good citizens,' the mayor called to them. 'We meet here again too soon. I am as disappointed and anxious as you are. I thought we ended this, as did we all. We have tried to move on, to get on with our lives. We have shown ourselves to be a happy town, welcoming both merchants and strangers. Gods know we have tried. We have all taken these people in—into our town, into our lives, and even into our homes. Offered comfort, succour, and even, in some cases, our hearts to these people.' He paused, allowing his words to filter through. 'But when those people come to us to trick and to lie and to bear false testimony, with nothing but malice and wickedness in their hearts, then what are we to do? We have no option but to strike out, to cut the head from the snake.'

Al-Dreban swallowed back the fear rising in his throat. He squirmed against the grip of the men holding him, but his efforts served only to focus them, and they tightened their grip. It agitated the crowd, who began to murmur.

Now the mayor turned, looking at Al-Dreban almost with pity—or was it shame? 'This very day,' he continued, 'this very afternoon, in fact, I found this scavenger. This weaselling meddler, ferreting in our town. This worshipper of false prophets, watching and spying on us at the bedrock of our community, which we hold so dear and have given so much to build.'

The crowd focused on Al-Dreban, their faces angry, distorted in the low shadows.

'I just stopped to say a prayer at the shrine!' he shouted, voice cracking.

Sharp words ran through the crowd like bushfire, intensifying as they went.

'You hear it from his own mouth!' the mayor cried. 'Like so many of the idolaters who came before him, spreading their lies and filth, his intent was clear: to bring us back under their yoke. To enslave us once again and make a mockery of what we paid so highly for. He planned to take away what was promised to us, just like the rest.'

The mayor stopped and stared into Al-Dreban's face for a long moment. Al-Dreban wondered dimly what exactly the man was looking for. He felt that whatever was going to happen next hinged upon this moment.

'In his pocket, he carried this,' the mayor added, his voice so thick with regret that Al-Dreban almost felt sorry that he had to deliver such bad news. The mayor reached into the pocket and took out a cloth bag. Reaching in, he pulled out the hessian poppet with an exaggerated flourish. The crowd gasped, recoiling, as though the man had presented them with a live viper. Voices were raised in chivvying heckles.

'Witchery!' one woman's voice exclaimed from within the crowd.

'The Other's magic!' decried another.

The mayor held out his hand again, and an unsteady quiet followed. 'Yes, my friends,' he said sadly, 'a witch's cursing doll. Why would a man who claims to pray at the altar of the Church of Truth carry such a wretched thing—that is, unless he is full of lies and deceit?'

'I found it!' Al-Dreban cried, trying to pull himself forward, 'there, on the floor, by the shrine!'

But they seemed not to hear, or else did not want to.

'Burn the witch!' came a cry from the crowd, a man's voice this time.

Al-Dreban froze. Such words were inflammatory, likely to catch hold and spread like wildfire.

'No, my friend.' The mayor's voice cut through the baying masses, much to Al-Dreban's relief. 'No, we are not like the petty-minded men of the false church—men who hide behind misspoken words of false piety while stealing and plotting in the shadows. Neither are we like the power-mongers in their towers—thieves and hoarders all, schemers and connivers—who would buy our blood with lies.'

'He can't just walk away! He has seen too much.' It was a man's voice, but none that Al-Dreban recognised. His tongue was dry as ash in his mouth, and his limbs grew heavier by the second. Was this the magic of their false gods?

'No. No we cannot.' The mayor turned to look at Al-Dreban, and again he seemed to consider him, a ponderous complexion causing his moustache to tug in towards his nose, consuming his otherwise blandly flaccid face. A face that, for the moment, Al-Dreban could kiss. *Yes, yes,* he wanted to scream, but couldn't. *Listen to him.*

Still, he was not stupid—he knew he had seen too much. Even without the words, without the profane bile that had been spouted, he knew. The poppet, the untended shrine, the lack of proper checks and legislators in the town: all these things were enough to doom these people. With his added testimony, the Suers would be ruthless. And even after that, for a heresy such as this, there would be watchers. Promulgators of Truth. For cycles to come, the lives of these people would be heavily monitored and regulated.

Neighbours would be called upon to denounce their neighbours, their own relatives even. A misplaced word, a skipped prayer—all could earn a visit from the Suers of Truth. No, he was too dangerous to these people. His best hope was that it would be quick, whatever they did.

The now-familiar scent of burnt soil sprang to mind and a cold shiver passed through him. He prayed to the Goddess that he would not become the crowning centrepiece of some hideous bonfire.

The mayor nodded, his contemplation complete. He turned back to address the crowd, arms out to them. *Is he placating them or agreeing to their terms?* Al-Dreban could not be sure and, for the moment, he did not want to know. Was he... preaching? The thought sickened him more than the thought of his impending death.

'We will return him to the ground then,' the mayor said with an air of finality. 'As was the way before—the way of our ancestors.'

The words rang in Al-Dreban's head. It had all the finality of a proclamation, and he felt the tension lift from the crowd as if they had been removed of a great burden. *Returned to the ground,* he thought. *Surely, they cannot think to bury me?* He tried again to struggle against his warders, earning grunts from one and an elbow in the back from the other. He sagged, his body collapsing so suddenly that the men almost dropped him.

'Bring him,' the mayor commanded. He made his laboured way to a seemingly free-standing stone. It was taller than a man, wider even than the mayor. Al-Dreban followed in the arms of his captors.

From here, Al-Draban could see the stone was smooth and irregular in its regularity; not rough and cracked, as might be expected of stone, but perhaps hewn from some large quarry, carefully sculpted, and brought deliberately to this place. Al-Dreban kicked feebly, sending clouds of dust into the night air, but the men ignored him. Other hands clasped him, dragging him on, and his legs gave way. With a gesture from the mayor, several more men appeared at the stone, putting their backs to it and hefting it aside.

Al-Dreban's throat seemed to seal entirely, the surface rough and sticky. Where the stone had once stood yawned a black concavity, a tunnel sloping gently deep into the earth. It was roughly the size of a man.

At another signal, Al-Dreban was pushed forward. He fell to his knees, his hands clawing at the hot earth. If only he could get some purchase, he could stay here—he could kick and scream and drag at the floor until they all left him alone. He wouldn't say anything, not now. The men that had held him lifted him from the floor as if he were only a doll or, he thought suddenly, a hessian idol...

'No!' he shouted, faintly surprised by the desperation in his own voice. 'You cannot do this—I am a member of the true faith! A man of the Church and one of the Goddess's representatives on this world! You will bow to my authority.'

The mayor shook his head as though in disbelief, looking deeply worried and concerned. He still held the poppet and looked to it now. 'As I said, an idolater. A liar and a charlatan, sent here to spread lies and deceit.'

'That's not true,' Al-Dreban managed, but he knew his argument was false. He *had* been sent to the town under false pretences. He *had* lied about his business and his intention to spy on these people and report back his findings, all in the name of Truth.

He gazed up to see the mayor's face ripple with something like despair, his small eyes blazing. 'Your Church has done nothing for this town,' the mayor growled, the sound incongruous and strange, 'except to rob it of its resources, its pride, and its legacy. Where was your Church when our families were forced into serfdom? Where was your Truth when our ancestors were forced to renounce their own faith? Where was your Goddess when our wives wept for the children that were taken from us?' He spat, tossed the poppet to the ground, and spun on his heel.

Al-Dreban lurched forward, struggling to his knees. He would follow—he would run. But a booted foot planted itself between his shoulder blades and pushed him down into the dirt. Something jabbed him in his side and he winced, the world swimming before him. The end was coming.

And then she was there: a familiar face. A dream? She had a fierce, almost maternal concern in her eyes. Black and stoat-like. Kareti. Even she had come to taunt and maim him. No doubt her husband was here too. In fact, it had probably been they who had reported him to the mayor. She bent down beside him, picking up the poppet. He lifted his eyes to her, unsure what to expect.

'I warned you,' she said softly. 'I told you not to go poking about here. They don't welcome your Church. It isn't what was promised.' She glanced past him and her eyes took on a faraway look. 'She told me it would be different.'

She snapped back to him, took the poppet, and held it up to her face. 'It almost looks like her, you know, from an angle.'

He had no idea what she was talking about. He didn't care. She was mad—they were all mad. He'd have spat at her if his mouth weren't as dry as the soil.

She whispered something to the poppet, words so quiet and delicate that Al-Dreban couldn't hope to hear—but then, he'd heard enough of their lies for one lifetime. She looked back to him. 'I did warn you,' she repeated, and her voice was tender. She stood, shook her head, and tossed the poppet at his feet.

A canvas bag joined the poppet while another man drove a flaming torch into the ground. Al-Dreban staggered back onto his haunches, shuffling further down into the tunnel to avoid the flames. He struck something and tumbled back, spitting earth. When he peered up, he found his vision of the world sliding away. A terrible rumbling met his ears: the sound of stone grinding against stone. It trumpeted his fate, but Al-Dreban heard only the thumping of his traitor heart. The entrance diminished, a window to the world outside—the real world—eclipsing before him.

But Al-Dreban was no longer there. He was a child again, staring from the window of their family home, watching the faded path. Then it was gone.

Torchlight danced on the craggy surface of the stone. A whimsical jig, all light and warmth. Mocking him—both what he had been and what he had become. In part, Al-Dreban agreed.

'I am the source of all power divine,' the Goddess said. In her might and majesty, she created all things both on this world and beyond it. No magic can exist that does not emanate from her and the Truth of her Church. Evil and sinful is all magic not used for Truthful purposes, and for the benefit of the Church and its holy congregation.

—From the Tenets of Truth

CHAPTER THREE
TEFARNIN AND THE COLONEL

The Barracks of Barkathet

Tefarnin felt as if he'd woken from a restless sleep. It was not his usual routine—normally he'd slowly shake off the night, wipe sleep from his eyes, and cuddle into his wife before gulping down a fix of strong coffee. This was more instantaneous, as if someone had interrupted a comforting dream by dowsing him with cold water. Worse, he was sat fully dressed and upright in a wooden chair in a room that he did not fully recognise. Blank, whitewashed walls opposed him, inset with two simple windows that allowed the room its illumination. Bright daylight poured in. It was not morning.

Something was very wrong.

The sound of men's laughter rang aloud, and he knew that if

he got up and looked through the window he'd be able to see who was there. Yet, for some reason, he felt compelled to stay exactly where he was. Not moving, not speaking. Waiting. The laughter was split by the sound of a thick, ragged cough, and the hefting-up of phlegm that was, a moment later, spat to the ground.

A door swung open to reveal the outline of what at first appeared to be an enormous container. It was a few seconds before Terfarnin's eyes adjusted enough to discern... a barrel? No, a man—a huge one, eclipsing the sun and sending the room briefly into shadow. He might have been from a circus of some sorts. His dress was flamboyant, audacious even. A dark blue kurta, pulled tight around the waist with a scarlet cummerbund, embossed with golden trims. Entwined into this was a sabretache housing a long-sheathed sword that shone with colour as it toyed with the light. Stepping into the room, the man took a simple look at Tefarnin, rubbing thick white gloves on his dark and thickly bearded face in evident contemplation. A much thinner and sleeker looking man, moving with an easy and flowing manner, glided into the room behind the barrel-man. The two looked around, assessing their surroundings before coming to rest some way in front of where Tefarnin sat. The barrel remained standing while the thin man sat on the table in the room's corner, his feet resting on the chair in front of him. Terfarnin wondered whether any chair could manage the weight of the barrel.

Another shadow appeared at the door and a third man entered, much better-proportioned than the first two. His simple clothes betrayed a well-muscled physique that expressed an eagerness to fill and even break through the white blouson and black dress trousers covering it. His dark, piercing eyes roamed the room briefly before settling on Tefarnin. He felt as if he knew the man, or at least the eyes, and that he would know them anywhere, even had he only glanced them fleetingly and from a distance. They penetrated rather than looked, cutting to the quick, as if the owner could know what you were thinking on a whim. There was a coldness to them that not even this bright, sunny day could warm.

Somewhere deep within his mind, Tefarnin scrabbled for a name. It came to him as a distant thing, half forgotten. The colonel. Tefarnin shuddered. He wasn't certain he had actually met the man before, but he was certainly familiar. A knot of dread welled in the pit of his stomach.

'What is he doing here?' the colonel asked, his voice flat and uninterested.

'My lord—' Tefarnin began in a small and stammering voice. Before he had chance to continue, however, a swift backhand from the barrel connected with the side of his head. It was so unexpected that it knocked him half from his stool and into the table next to him, sucking the wind from his body and leaving his face stinging. Beyond this, there was no acknowledgement that he had even spoken.

'He arrived almost an hour ago,' the thin man said. 'One of the kitchen maids spotted him and sent word to me directly.'

The thin man's voice was reedy and nasal. *Like a magpie*, Tefarnin thought as he righted himself and rubbed at his face.

The colonel seemed to consider this for a moment.

'It's his conditioning,' the thin man continued.

Turning, the colonel stared at Tefarnin. An intense chill spread throughout his body, passing as quickly as it had come.

'Do we know him?' the colonel asked.

'I don't recall his face, but then we have so many like him dotted around the region. I have whispered to so many that I can't remember half of them,' the thin man answered.

The barrel remained silent.

'Well then, Susurro,' the colonel said, 'let's see what he has to say.'

The thin man—Susurro, Tefarnin figured—nodded and moved closer. He stooped until his face was so close that Tefarnin could feel warm, moist breath upon his cheek. Susurro brought his hand up and cupped it around both his mouth and Tefarnin's ear with such speed and suddenness that the innkeeper flinched. When nothing else happened, however, he relaxed, only to realise that Susurro was talking—well, not talking exactly, but his lips were moving rapidly. Tefarnin strained to listen, but it was like trying to hear the flapping of a moth's wings. *But there*, Tefarnin thought. *Was that my name? It can't be—he doesn't know it.*

As he strained to listen, Tefarnin began to feel more and more distant, as if he was being stretched somehow, his head away towards the farthest horizon and looking lazily back. He could see himself, but only as a tiny pinprick. The world became very dark, and this time he definitely heard his own name being spoken, softly at first—a new voice, not Susurro's, and yet he felt he did—or perhaps only should—recognise it. He had heard it before, he was sure. His wife? No, not his wife. *Anneach, my girl? Is that you?* If he were anything more than a grain of dust, he might have wept. But no, it wasn't her. The voice was male.

The murmured words seemed to release a great pressure that had been building within Tefarnin. It described a great many things, retold a great story: a stranger had come to visit and stayed at an inn. Somehow, it was *his* inn. The Hart. How could this unseen person know these things? The goings-on within his home; conversations that had been shared. He knew, had he been a man, that he would feel uneasy about it all, that he might resist. But how could he? He was nothing but dust. What cares did dust have? An argument over breakfast. The worries expressed by his wife. The tears she'd shed and the fear they shared. Secret things that were precious to him. Things they couldn't be certain of. Lies and duplicity. This boy, a visitor, no horse trainer. A deceiver. Heated words between a man and his wife. Harsh words, belittling words. All fed by fear. And, at last, a dark congregation called.

The voice left out nothing. Tefarnin speaking with the mayor, something he hadn't done since—well, since Anneach. His wife's pleas and, behind them, the quashed yearning that he could somehow make it all better, bring her back.

For a moment, his mind was tugged away. He felt, inexplicably, the sudden bitterness and resentment of human life. He—and he was, he thought, a 'he' again—resented the Church, the mayor and, most disgracefully of all, his wife. His eyes were filling up, and he thought that he might cry. But for the words, he may well have. Susorro's voice, however, his whisper—it feathered his ear gently, pulling him back from the harsh memory until, once again, he felt calm and soothed. The unseen man was nearing his end. The story was coming full loop.

'And then,' Tefarnin said, his voice distant and almost disembodied, as if they were no longer his own and were instead being projected into him from somewhere far away, 'I felt a pull, and remembered the calling of the words—the words that tie and the words that bind—so I came here, where I knew you would be.'

'Where will they take this Dreban?' the softer voice of Susorro asked, so close to his ear that he hardly needed to even whisper.

'To the sacred place. To the sprouting of the tree and the Womb of the World.'

'It was all nonsense,' the colonel said, staring out of the window. 'Maybe you've gone too far this time, Susurro.'

Susurro shook his head. 'I don't think so, boss. You can tell it by the eyes. They'd be glazed and dead to look at, but this one's still got life in him.'

The colonel considered this, eyes fixed on a bird outside taking a dust bath. There was little breeze and the air in the room had grown stale. Truth was, he hated these still summer days. Give him the icy sting of winter any day.

'Sir?'

The colonel sighed. 'Well? What is he talking about then, Captain? You're the Cognator. Cognate, or whatever it is you people do.' He was being unfair and he knew it, but he didn't want to be cooped up in the stifling heat any longer than necessary.

Susurro looked aggrieved. 'Do you remember the stories about old Pliney in these parts?'

'A little,' the colonel replied lazily. 'Crazy old hermit, lived in the hills, dug his house in the ground. Didn't he get eaten by snakes?'

'Kind of, boss. It was during the Emendation, after the Great War of the Expansion. There was a great purging. The Church dispatched the Suers of the Evulgation around the land to help make sure that those who had recently converted to the Truth remained committed and didn't fall back into their old ways.'

'Good old rock and tree worship,' the colonel said, a grim smile bending the edges of his lips.

'Well, yes. It sounds ridiculous to our ears, but we live in enlightened times. Before the Church took people out of the dark, people paid homage to what they saw and what they knew. Who could blame a farmer whose crops rely on the sun and the rains for praying to them?'

'Rocks and trees,' he repeated.

'Quite. Trees are symbols of growth and strength. They stand watch over an area, much like Braga here.' He nodded to the big man. 'Stones can represent the earth or strength and security. Truth is, people would worship snakes as fertility symbols because they look like a cock. I didn't say it had to make sense. The point is, the war was over and the king and the Church had won. All the old principalities where they practised the old ways were finally subdued and brought into line. Job done—only, of course, it wasn't. It's all well and good forcing the princes and the great houses to submit to the Truth, but what about the people? The peasant? Who stops shit-for-breath here'—he gestured to the innkeeper—'from carrying on with his old beliefs? Who prevents him from sacrificing his neighbour to some fire god because his house burnt down? Or selling his children to a witch so she doesn't turn his ale sour?'

The filthy innkeeper lurched suddenly forwards, retching onto the floor around his feet. Susurro edged away from the man and glanced down at him, his nose wrinkled.

'Beliefs are long standing,' he finished sourly. 'They sit deep within the roots of a community, like a nasturtium.'

'Nasturtiums?' the colonel asked dryly.

'Exactly. If you need to get rid of one, you can't just pull up the odd flower. It roots so firmly that it just keeps growing back, cycle after cycle, generation after generation. These things have been passed on for aeons. You can't get rid of it without digging it all up, each and every remnant of root, or by burning the ground completely. Even then, it might grow back.'

'If we can't root out the weeds then let them burn, my

old friend.'

'Exactly, boss. That's what the Church thought. But then they realised that, rather than try to tear out the weed, you can turn it to something you want. Like nasturtiums. What was a weed is now a plant.'

'A plant, Susurro? It's hot enough to bake a turd in here and you're talking to me about plants?'

'But that, in effect, is what the Church did, sir. It took the disparate beliefs of the heathens and remoulded them, forced the old folk to change how they thought about them. They spent decades, centuries even, reshaping the old religious sites. Got an old temple? Thanks, we'll have that and tell everyone it's an altar to the Goddess. Pray to the sun spirit after the harvest? Okay, we'll hold a bigger celebration to the Goddess and call it Wepet. You see? We used the old ways to make the people believe that they'd worshipped the Goddess all along, only they didn't know it. And over time, people forget.'

'Susurro, unless you're about to use your Cognator skills to implant your point directly into my head, I suggest you hurry it up. There's only so long I take the smell of our guest here.'

Susurro gave a flurry of nods. 'You're right, you're right. Pliney really *was* a crazy old hermit. He spent most of his adult life scraping out a miserable existence in the hills, digging tunnels until he became lame, with no one to talk to but the snakes. But he was also something of a shaman or mystic of sorts, an old man dedicated to the old gods—Mu-Alman and the like. Really though such men were nothing more than members of a cult that worshipped snakes. They were thought to both watch over the dead and give fertility. Either way, it was a heresy that the Church could not stand.'

The colonel stared, his face flat, and Susurro gave a nervous grin. 'Anyway, the Suers were dispatched in all their righteous fury, but this little old man, supposedly so frail now that he needed a stick to walk, refused to recant. Instead, he struck out at the six Suers like a coiled cobra. Three of the six died where they stood, and the three others forced the heathen back to his cave. The old man hissed a curse at the Suers, thrust his cane deep into the ground, and blocked himself in. The Suers waited for him to come back out, but overnight, the stick had somehow taken root—by morning, it was a full tree. The three Suers returned to the Misty City, but the story spread. Hundreds, even thousands flocked to the site. Of course, the Church hated this, but realised they couldn't stop the story now it was out. So, instead, they changed it. Now it was the Suers who had been defiant in the face of adversity. They became three, not six, and old Pliney became an evil sorcerer who'd divined his power from the entrails of village children. He called forth an army of snakes but, somehow, the Suers managed to stand true in the light of the Goddess. They vanquished the old man and banished the snakes, sealing them and Pliney's body in his own tunnels. Afterwards, they prayed to the Goddess for her cleansing Truth. *They* planted the old man's cane into the ground, and it was the Goddess who breathed life into it. And, just like that, the narrative was changed. Now, the story is key in the promulgation of the faith. It reinforces the notion that magic is evil and dangerous when not in the Church's control, and people from that region fear snakes to this day.'

'No, Captain. People are scared of snakes because they are creepy and slimy and they can bite and kill you,' the colonel said, kneading his forehead. 'Why are we still talking about this? Please tell me before I slit the idiot's throat and drown you in his blood.'

Susurro gave an ingratiating chuckle. 'The tree is nearby, sir. In Baile Saor. It's where the idiot comes from.'

The colonel turned from the window, more interested now.

'And "the Womb of the World" is what locals call the old tunnel network up on the hill there. It used to be a pilgrimage site, but no one bothers with it anymore.'

'None but our guest here and his equally insipid priest friend,' the colonel offered.

Susurro stood, stretching his limbs and rolling his shoulders as though testing them. His joints audibly cracked into place. 'Should I inform the adherents, or shall we go directly to the Citadel?'

'With this?' asked the colonel with an air of distaste. 'And tell them what? If you think for one minute I am letting you bore the teats off anyone of import with your crack-pot stories then you don't know me half as well as you should by now. No.' He stood, repositioning his hat. 'Wait until we have spoken with this Dreban directly. Then we'll notify the Premiero. I want to know why they've sent this pup spying in the first place. We'll take a hand of men at first light.'

'A hand? Won't they know anyway? If we send that many men then they will demand an adherent be attached.'

'That's why we won't send anyone, we'll take them. We might not be ordained adherents, old friend, but we're both anointed in the faith. It might not stand for much with some these days, but we can still just about pull rank over the lower orders they send here to be forgotten about.' He kept his tone dismissive, but knew it barely masked the resentment he felt. He had been barely more than a boy himself when he'd begun running *errands* on behalf of the Church. They had offered him untold riches, a life of ease, but these promises had never materialised. Now, here he was at the edge of the world. Only the frozen north was more remote, but at least there it was cooler.

The colonel straightened and made to leave. Casting one more look back across the room, he remembered suddenly the innkeeper, grime-caked and lost.

'I don't think he's of any more use to us.'

Susurro nodded. 'What should I do with him? Do we risk sending him back to the town?' His hand slunk towards the blade hanging at his belt.

'No. Whatever else he is, the boy must be someone's puppet. If we send this oaf back, he's sure to raise someone's suspicions. We don't want the strings cut before they've been pulled, now do we? Didn't he mention a daughter? Maybe she is part of this project the king is consumed with. Let's send him there and maybe he can find her. I've ever been a sucker for happy endings.' He smiled. 'Braga, you're with me.'

The massive man had stood eerily silent throughout. He finally roused, moving to the colonel's side, and the colonel felt as if a shadow had engulfed him. He welcomed the cool.

'I shall leave you to it, Captain.' And with that, the colonel turned on his heel and marched out into the blazing sun. Despite detesting the heat, he had only little time for the strange effects of Cognator mind magic, and he cared not to linger. A Wielder himself, he had little experience of Susurro's grotesque methods, and he wished to keep it that way. He had his own secrets to keep.

The barracks square was busy. Soldiers rushed in formation from one place to another, kicking up dust from the baked earth. He was comforted by the steady music of their march and drill, and fell into step as he crossed the great parade ground. He felt the presence of his pioneer sergeant fall in over his shoulder. It was hard not to; it seemed that the big man's step was a tad keener than usual, but then the colonel knew that he had never liked Susurro's mind magic either. Unlike most, he had seen it in action—and to devastating effect. It was not a thing upon which a man was likely to dwell.

'Well, Braga, my aphasic friend, it looks like the barracks are yours while we are away.'

As usual, Braga gave no reply, not even a murmur or a cough of acknowledgement. He merely waited for his commanding officer to give him a nod, then continued on his way towards the troop rooms. The colonel smiled warmly to himself. *If only more people were as easy to get along with as Braga.*

'Colonel!' A voice sounded in the near distance, distracting him from his distraction. 'Colonel,' the call came again. A sharp and over eager voice, slightly nasal. Annoying.

He turned at the sound. Long experience had taught him that to ignore the man was futile. A man some cycles short of his middle age approached, his short steps placed gingerly to avoid dirtying his expensive clothes. He was a short man, though the colonel preferred to think of him as a little one. A man of his standing should hold himself taller, but the younger son of House-Lord Aargau, Dritsek, was just too stiff in his efforts. It gave him an air of flustered superiority that attracted the kind of mockery no amount of money or influence could guard against.

Dritsek had been a go-between for his father and the court for some four cycles; it was a position the colonel felt was as pointless as Dritsek himself. The army and its barracks, however, were held in thrall to the noble lord who bankrolled the operation, and so the colonel accepted this minor intrusion as the price of holding a force just shy of two thousand men.

'Ah, Dritsek,' he said absently as the man came to a stop next to him. 'How might I assist you?' He oozed false courtesy—a dangerous game.

'Military Intermediary Officer Aargau, if you please, Colonel.

I do you the honour of using your title around the men; I would appreciate it if you were to repay me the courtesy.'

It was an honorary title at best, something his father had invented to appease the boy and keep him away from court.

The colonel took a drawn-out and deliberate look around the deserted courtyard, finishing his slow visual scan of the area before finally meeting the eyes of the other man, who seemed to visibly shiver in response. 'As I said, what do you want? I'm busy.'

'There have been reports of seditious activity in some of the southern estates,' Dritsek responded, attempting to regain some dignity but only managing an air of standoff pomposity.

'Good, I will send a hand of my men with Braga. It's been far too quiet around here of late, and the men could do with some exercise.' The colonel allowed his sentence to trail away, distracted by the growing smile forming on Dritsek's usually resentful face. It was unsettling.

'I think not, Colonel.' Dritsek's manner became more confident despite his awkwardness. 'You see, this situation is said to involve the spreading of a particular philosophy at odds with those accepted as authority. That's right, Colonel: heresy. So, you will attend to this personally.' He reached into the breast pocket of his jacket and withdrew some parchment, unravelling it ostentatiously. 'I think you will find the details to be to your satisfaction.' He began reading the letter aloud, taking his time as his eyes flicked back and forth across the page. 'Dear Colonel Sentenza... to personally spearhead the immediate deployment... no greater numbers than a finger of men... delicate situation requiring a delegate to represent the council of Doarson and the Church of the Righteous Truth... so on and so forth.'

Sentenza was no longer looking at Dritsek when he snatched the letter and scanned through its contents for himself. He could *hear* the exaggerated grin on the other man's face and, while internally he felt like shoving the parchment back down his throat, he knew it would be an error.

'Signed, with his seal, by appointment to the Citadel and to the realm, for and on behalf of the City-Lord... now, who was that again? I forget, and yet it is so very familiar. Oh yes, that's it. How silly of me. House-Lord Aargau.'

'From the ruins I brought you light and life.' Those were the words of the Goddess. Out of the darkness of lies and distrust she gave us Truth, for she alone is creator of the world and all that exists. There is no god but her; no power other than hers. She is the beginning of all beginnings and the end of all ends. Trust in her and in her Church alone, for theirs is the only Truth.

—**From the Tenets of Truth**

CHAPTER FOUR
SOLATTA

The Southern Estates

Solatta woke to a clear and crisp morning. The smell of jasmine was rich in the air and the happy chirrup of morning birds lilted in the low breeze.

Quietly, she rose from her pallet, stretching the sleep from her bones. Her fingers lightly brushed against the clerestories of the caravan. It was a vardo, wooden and compact, full of trinkets and knick-knacks and colourfully painted on the outside, though the interior always felt dark, despite her best efforts to brighten it up. She stroked the lace trim she had recently added to the window and smiled. She felt warm and cosy; comfortable even. It was home—the only one she remembered. She yawned, and a rasping snore answered her from behind the curtain covering the top bunk. She stifled a giggle and crept her way around her own bunk. The wooden steps creaked as she stepped out into the day.

It was good to feel the grass between her toes. She always liked to walk barefoot; it made her feel free. She had vague memories of walking like that in the snow, but it had been so long since she'd seen any that she barely remembered what snow was like. Her young cycles were lost to her. Like dreams, the memories danced beyond her remembering. Shadows at the edge of the clearing. Ghosts in the woods.

She washed her face using icy water from a pail. It was crisp and fresh, like the morning itself. Smoke lifted lazily from the flue. It would be a while before Tervan awoke. He always slept in after a show, meaning she'd have time to look in on Shohanon and her brother before breakfast. When she arrived at the tent, however, she found it empty. The table stood forlorn, bowls and cups still standing there, food half-eaten and seemingly abandoned. The air was hot and sticky, the scent of trampled grass mingling with smoke, sweat, and mud. She should have known.

'There are always more people to help, my girl. Remember, we do the Mother's work,' Tervan would say if he could see her. But, for once, she wanted to feel it herself. She wanted to see the face of a sibling, the tears of happiness in their eyes. She wondered if she even *had* any siblings. That was all her childhood amounted to: whispers and unanswered questions. Gaps where the images of her loving parents should live. A little hole in her heart.

'Daughter.' It was a woman's voice, soft and lovely like a bird singing in the sunlight. Solatta turned towards it. 'I'm sorry,' the woman said again. 'I don't mean to presume, but you feel like a daughter to us is what I mean.' She was short, big dark eyes set deep within a friendly, weather-scorched face. Her hair curled tight, framing a broad, bright smile.

Solatta didn't know what to say. It was an odd comment.

'To us all,' the woman tried to explain, sensing her confusion, 'you and your father feel like family. You've done so much to help already. I've known Coln since he was a boy, his sister too. What you've both done for him... I know he would have died before the turn of the cycle, we all did. We were just waiting on the day. But to see him up on his feet like he was this morning? It ain't nothing but a miracle. Now, in truth, I don't know how, and I know the priests would say it's wrong'—she touched her fingers to her forehead, then kissed them—'but it can't be right for a young man to waste away like that. And not just him, but his sister too. She don't ever leave his side outside of work, and she'd about die with him if he went.' She looked at Solatta, her eyes big and watery. Tears or old age? Solatta couldn't tell. She felt as if the woman was waiting for her to say something, but she didn't know what.

'We don't have much,' the woman said awkwardly, 'but I wanted you to have something for your efforts. I dare say we all do.'

A boy appeared, as though he'd been hiding in the woman's skirts. Her son? He looked anxious, as though Solatta might be a witch. *They probably think I am*, she realised. His mother pushed him forward and he almost tripped over his own feet. He regained himself and came on uncertainly. In his hands he held something wrapped in linen. He made it halfway to her then looked back to his mother. He had gone far enough for his liking, and dropped the parcel to the ground before racing back to the safety of her skirts.

They were not the only visitors. The woman was quickly replaced by another. This time, Solatta recognised the face from

71

the night before, but nonetheless the same awkward conversation repeated itself and another package was left. Then another—a man this time—and another. Like courtiers visiting gifts upon a princess, the locals piled in, each leaving gifts and offering embarrassed hugs. It was soon too much, and Solatta made her excuses and fled back to the vardo. The pile would continue to grow, she knew—it always did. She could still see the slow procession of villagers from her spot by the window. The poor always gave, and the poorest the most. It was they, she supposed, who truly knew the value of life and the cost of sickness. When everyone else had forgotten, they remembered the kindness of strangers.

She prepared some tea absently as she watched. A cleansing tonic. The smell of citrus enveloped her as the herbs and bitters infused in the pot. A hand on her shoulder made her jump.

'Good morning, little one,' Tervan greeted, softly kissing her on the head and settling onto a stool.

'Morning? Some of us have been about our chores already,' she chided playfully.

'Well, early risers get all the fun I guess.' He smiled back at her.

'And lazy bones will be lucky to get breakfast!'

The sun was young in the sky and its warmth was yet to touch the clearing. A thin layer of dew clung to the ground and their breath fogged as they joked with each other. Solatta grinned as she used a hem to lift the steaming pot from the fire, gesturing with the spout to her guardian. He responded with two tin mugs and she filled them with the sweetly perfumed tea.

'Did you sleep well?' she asked, returning the pot to the fire.

'I did,' he said, smiling in return. 'You know that I always sleep well after we perform.'

She noted his use of the word *perform*. 'I don't think it is simply a performance,' she said, taking a small sip from her mug. It was hot, almost burning—just as she liked it.

He frowned. He was forever telling her off for drinking tea too hot.

'Well,' he paused, raising his own mug to his nose. He sniffed at its contents and winced slightly. 'When you get to be as old as I am, my dear, you'll understand that everything is a performance of some sort or another.'

'How old are you exactly?'

'I'm old enough to be your father's father's father.'

She knew it was a joke, but the words burned hotter than the drink. She bit back a reply. She didn't know her father, let alone her father's father's father—how could she know how old that was meant to be?

She turned from him so he might not see her disappointment. 'Don't tease,' she said, though the mirth had evaporated from her tone.

'Who said anything about teasing?' He must have heard the change in her voice. He kept his own light, trying to cajole himself back into her good books.

'You can't be *that* old.' She searched for a kerchief, fearful that she might cry. It was silly of her, she knew. But how many times had she asked about her family only to receive a diverting response?

'I'm sorry,' he said. He'd crossed to her and now placed a hand upon her shoulder. The touch was instantly comforting. 'That was insensitive of me. I mean to say that I am old, that is all. Older than most people you will have known, even if you cannot remember them. I am tired after last night, and my mind has not quite caught up with me—nor my manners.'

She felt abashed. He had not meant to hurt her feelings. He never did. But it was difficult not knowing who you were or where you came from. She clung to her mug as though it were a comforter, hugging it close.

'How old was my father?' Her voice waivered, close to breaking. 'I mean, last month was Res Satti—the start of my seventeenth cycle, right?' Month of the elephant—an animal famous for never forgetting. The irony was not lost on her.

'I remember the day I first met you,' he said, turning her to face him. His eyes searched hers, and she could see her own pain reflected in his, and was the sadder for it.

'Your mother was heartbroken to see you leave. But your parents had their own troubles and knew they had no choice. Theirs was a very different path and they couldn't take you with them. If they had, well, who knows what would have happened, but certainly not everyone would have survived. Your mother knew you would grow to be a strong and beautiful woman. She held you to her for so long that I thought we'd be too late. Eventually, your father took you and passed you on to me. We expected you to cry, but you didn't. You gave a funny little smile and took hold of my hand. Only then did your mother cry, but they seemed like warm and happy tears. She knew I would take care of you and that you would be safe and happy. I'd not long met your father, but your mother I had known for some time before that. Distantly at times, but I always kept an eye or an ear out for her.'

Solatta struggled hard to remain in control, not wanting her tears to disturb the story. It was the most he had told her, though she still had no answers. She was so confused; angry and happy all at once, lost in the images his words conjured.

'Fittingly, it was Choton Satti,' he continued, 'the month of sanctuary, at the beginning of the cycle Arah Nisanu. I shaved your head in the light of the sanctuary fire.'

'You shaved my head?' she laughed a mix of tears and snot and pawed at her eyes. She touched her braid as though to check it was still there.

The story had warmed her like the rays of the rising sun. She smiled uncertainly. Was he trying to distract her?

'Of course. That's the point of a sanctuary fire,' he said with a glint in his eye.

'To shave someone's hair?' She laughed, in earnest this time.

'No, to purify. You cut away the old life and all its links. Pain, suffering, anguish, sorrow—all of it. You're cleansed in the light of the Goddess. The hair grows back, just like you grew, free from what went before. New.'

'Well, I think I like my hair as it is these days.' Her eyes settled on the campfire. 'Just to be certain, let's not go near a sanctuary fire any time soon.'

He smiled and ruffled her hair, and she scowled at him. 'Don't worry,' he said, 'they aren't just any old fires. Their spark can only be taken from a sanctuary stone.'

She raised her eyebrows. It sounded very much like one of his stories.

'You don't believe me?' he said, acting wounded.

She said nothing.

'You'd know if you saw one. They're big—huge, in fact. As big as a man, or bigger even.' He held out his hands, stretching them out as far as he could. 'Shiny and smooth to touch. At night, they look like great big bears, rearing up on their hind legs. Once, they numbered in their thousands. Standing proud at the edges of the forests and woods, like gleaming gateways. They used to be sacred—had some connection to the old magic, they say. They were a community of sorts. Each one linked to the next, like a web of magic running through the ground.' His eyes grew distant, as though he were struggling to recall something.

'Really?' she asked quietly, trying not to sound as doubtful as she felt, though not wanting the storytelling mood to leave him. 'What happened to them, then? How come I've never seen one?'

'Oh, some king or another had them all knocked down.'

'What?' This time she simply could not disguise the doubt and disappointment in her voice. 'You can't just finish it like that. *Once upon a time, there was a whole load of huge magical stones all over the place, but someone knocked them all down and that's why I've never seen one.*' She looked at him questioningly. 'Now you're definitely teasing me.'

He held his hands out to her, warding off her accusations. He smirked. 'Okay, okay, so I may have embellished a little bit. But truly, some of the stones are there, just forgotten. Many were stolen. I don't think there are many left now, though there used to be one not far from here.'

'Can we visit it?' She was suddenly interested.

He thought for a moment, rubbing at the fresh growth of stubble sprouting on his tanned chin. 'I don't see why not,' he concluded. 'It would be good to see one again. That's the thing about the past, you see—even though no one remembers or believes in it, it still shapes things around us.'

'In what way?'

'If you don't know the history of a place, then you don't know the place at all. The stone of an old market town, for example. Before that, it was a sanctuary town, a place full of old magic, but no one remembers. Now it's just a market.'

Like me, she thought. *Just a girl that doesn't remember her past.* The thought was bitter. 'Then let's go and see it,' she said sharply.

Too sharply, she realised.

Now, her guardian seemed unsure. 'I don't know,' he said. 'Now I think on it, these types of towns attract the wrong types. Officials and Churchmen. We're better off travelling south.'

'Of course,' she snapped. 'Why would we want to find anything with a past?'

He felt the words like a slap—she could see it in his face. He tried a smile, though it did not quite fit his face. 'Yes,' he said quietly. 'I suppose we could go to visit. I had a friend there once. Perhaps...' His words trailed off and he walked back to the fire, staring into the flames as though looking for something there.

Solatta cursed herself inwardly. She felt as though she had poured water all over his attempts to win her round. Still, she thought, it was his evasion that had brought them here. She felt frustrated all anew.

'It was all such a long time ago,' she heard him say, the words like the mutterings of an old, lonely person: absent, thin, and easily lost.

'What about my hair?' she called to him, trying to end on a more pleasant note.

'Mmm. Your hair?' He didn't look at her.

'Yes, you're not going to cut it all off at the sanctuary stone, are you? You won't use it to start a fire there? You must need a stone to set a sanctuary fire.' Clumsy, she knew, but it was all she could manage.

He stood and headed to the doorway. His hand closed on the doorknob..

'How did you cut my hair?' she said quickly, voice rising, betraying her anxiety. 'If the stones were all stolen a long time ago, where did you find the one you used for the fire?'

For a moment, he did not answer. His hand dropped to a

pocket, fingering what was inside. He regained himself, his words falsely bright. 'You got me!' he said. 'I was tricked by an old hag. She told me the story of the sanctuary stones. That's how I know about them. She sold me a sacred fire and I gave her half of my food for good measure. Silly old fool. Never trust an old hag, I say.'

And with that, he was gone.

'So we're moving on then?' she called after him, unsure why she felt so bad. *All I want is the truth.* Yet whose? The simple truth was that Tervan was her family. She knew that every time she asked about her past, she came across as ungrateful, as if her guardian hadn't been good enough and so she dreamed of another life with the family that had abandoned her. All he'd done was provide and comfort. She gulped back the lump in her throat.

Their breakfast was a simple and quiet affair, just enough to get them going. The conversation was as sparse as the meal. Cold cuts and cool words. Though, as the sun rose and the day warmed, so too did their spirits. Just as well, Solatta thought. It would be difficult to take down the tent if they were not speaking.

They found the tent strewn with parcels. It took them almost as long to gather them together as it did to collapse the tent. The selflessness of the poor people warmed Solatta's heart, and she knew Tervan felt the same. It was hard not to be touched, after all, and they were happy to share the moment together. Once they had finished, their smiles for each other felt as genuine as they did humble.

By late afternoon, the village was behind them. It was their custom to leave early on the day following a performance and to drive as far as they could before the sun dwindled into twilight.

'You never know who comes to watch us,' Tervan had once told her. 'The Church is constantly looking for people like us. The hidden ones.'

'What do you mean?' she'd asked. 'I've never met anyone like us.'

'There are some. Maybe not exactly like us. What we do is the Goddess's work. We spread the real Truth. I don't think there is anyone left who can do what we do, but here and there you will hear of someone who has the gift. The old crone that everyone thinks is mad. The young woman who has a head for tonics.' He looked at her with a knowing wink. 'You won't find them at the Misty City, but they're watching. The priests are always looking for people they don't approve of, listening to the gossipers and the tittle-tattlers for hints and clues.'

At the time, she'd thought it just another of the tales he told to keep her mind from wandering on their travels. Now, though, she realised he believed it.

Only once he felt they were far enough away from whichever village they'd left behind would he stop, and they'd set up camp for the night. The next few days were always the same: long treks punctuated only by the occasional break. They kept away from the busy roads, choosing dirt paths and woodland where they could, skirting the estates of House-Lords as they criss-crossed back across the plains. They took turns to drive their little horse, Cobb.

When he was not driving, Tervan took stock of the gifts the villagers had left. Solatta, on the other hand, worked at her lessons. Numbers and letters were expected, though she didn't like them and often found it difficult to apply herself. Only their application to her potions made it worth the effort. After all, while it was easy enough to memorise the simplest tonics and teas, the more demanding ones were best recorded by hand. Still, it was a tedious task. 'Words and numbers are not my cup of tea,' she announced to the caravan. 'Tea, on the other hand, now that *is* my cup of...' She felt the caravan come to a stop and hastily packed her phials and writing things into her box, where they fit snugly next to her bowl.

Their meal that night was a stew of beans and vegetables prepared by Tervan while Solatta brushed and tended to Cobb. The night sky was clear and, as the sun set, stars winked into life in the distant heavens. Solatta poured Tervan and herself steaming mugs of tea—valerian root and passion flower. It smelled both sweet and earthy, like violets after rain. She hoped it would soothe her aches and pains, though, in truth, what she really needed was the time to relax and wash away the heavy days of travel. Nestled next to Tervan, she peered into the campfire.

'Would you tell me a story please?' she asked.

'Well, what story would you like?' He leaned back against the stump of a tree and she murmured in annoyance, repositioning herself in the crook of his arm. All frostiness had been left behind on the road and now it was just the two of them—or three, she supposed, glancing at the still-grazing Cobb. A better life than most, she realised. They might not have much, but they had all that they needed. They had each other. And she would protect that, as he protected her.

'A new story, I think,' she decided. 'One I've not heard before.' She slid down and lay her head against his knee. The tea was hot and a little sour, just as she liked it. She had little time for people who could not take their tea without honeying it first.

'Well, let's see now,' he pondered, his hand gently stroking her braid. 'Okay, I think I have one. Long ago—long before you were born—before even *I* was born...'

Solatta smiled.

'There was darkness and there was cold. All the people in the world lived together in one place, but it was so dark that they could not see. In fact, the only thing they could make out was a great solitary eye that glared down at them from the sky above. Everyone knew that the eye belonged to an enormous and terrible beast, so they cowered away in terrible isolation, fearful that they might attract its attention and draw down its ire.'

Her smile began to waver. This was not how relaxingstories started.

'The beast had lots of names: Vayron, Qilish, Niceni, and many, many more besides. It lived only in darkness and had only ever been alone. It never slept, and it was wrapped so tightly around the place the people lived that it could not move or speak. For centuries upon centuries, it lay silent, watching the people. It saw them move and sleep and speak, and it grew very, very jealous. So much so that if it heard anyone speak, it came crashing down and ate them with its huge mouth, crushing them to bits with teeth that were bigger than trees and sharper than swords.'

A chill spread down her back. It sounded monstrous.

'One day, a baby was born. But instead of being joyous, her mother and father were afraid that the baby would cry and the beast would hear. Then, they thought, he'd come down and eat her. So they hid their daughter, and because the baby was so small, the beast didn't even see her. Although she was quiet for almost three weeks, eventually she became hungry, and the little baby started to cry and scream for her milk. Well, the beast heard the cries of the baby, and it followed the sound until it found her. It ate her, gnashing her up with its great teeth and swallowing her down. The father tried to stop the beast, but how can a man fight a beast so big? It ate him up too.'

Solatta stared at Tervan, eyes wide.

'The distraught mother cried silent tears,' he carried on, not giving her the chance to stop him, 'so as not to attract the beast's attention again. She cried for cycles and cycles—huge salty tears that ran down her face and onto the ground. She cried so much that the ground couldn't absorb any more of her tears, and soon rivers began to run from where she sat. Then, one day, she found that she had cried silently for so long that she could no longer hold back her wails of anguish. She had held them back and stored them up inside her for so long that, when they were finally released, they ripped from her like a thousand storms.'

Tervan's voice rose suddenly, and Solatta jumped. 'Thunder shook the world! The mother's anger enveloped her and lightning streaked from the clouds. The flashes illuminated the sky, and for the first time the people saw that the world was completely flat. They saw too how barren and bare the ground around them was, because the beast had kept the world in darkness, stopping anything from growing. The mother became even angrier with the beast and screamed out to it, and it responded with all its usual jealously and hatred. It swept down to devour her, but the little woman used her anger and fought back against the monster with her lightning and her storms.'

Solatta realised she'd been holding her breath. 'Then what happened?' she managed.

Tervan smiled down at her, though his features were hidden in shadow. 'The beast carried the woman up into the darkness of the sky, and all the people watched in awe and horror. For many days and nights, the two battled in the skies, and with each bolt of lightning that the woman sent out, she punched a small hole into the blackness of the beast's body. Light streamed through the holes until the black sky was littered with a thousands upon thousands of lights. Still, after months of fighting, it looked as if the beast would triumph. It took hold of the woman in two of its clawed fists, trapping her arms to her body so that she could not fight back and bringing her up to its huge mouth... but the mother was not finished. As the beast was about to devour her, she thrust out her tongue, which became a mighty sword, and she hacked the beast straight through the jaw, separating the top of its head from the rest of its body. The lower jaw and the body of the giant beast fell back down to the ground and, wherever they landed, the huge bones created hills and mountains across the landscape of the world. The mother too fell back down to the world. She looked up to where the single eye of the beast still peered down upon them. Without the rest of its body, it could no longer swoop down to attack the people. All it could do was watch. The sky was no longer solid black—now half of the sky was flooded with beautiful warmth and light, and not only from the pricks of light in the beast's skin, but from the great cut the mother's sword had made. At last, the people could move around freely and see the world for what it was. The people were still afraid, however; they had been ruled over by the beast for so long and could still see its horrible eye watching them. They complained to the mother, asking her to rid them of the eye, too.'

'Yes!' Solatta announced suddenly, leaning forward. 'Yes, she should kill it once and for all!'

Tervan tutted softly, shaking his head. 'What she knew that you don't, little one, was that she could not totally blame the beast, because it was only doing what it had been born to do. It was the only truth the beast had known.'

Solatta frowned and slumped back, her eyes upon the swimming stars above.

'Still,' Tervan went on, 'to satisfy the people, she made the world move so that for part of the time, the beast would be hidden away from them. During that period, they would have warmth and light as they worked and played, but then she would let the beast look down upon them when the people slept, so long as he promised to watch over the world while it rested in darkness.

'For many cycles, the world turned from darkness into light, and the great white eye watched while the people slept. When the people were awake, however, they still complained to the mother, saying that they were hungry and that the world was too hard and dusty for them to sleep on. So she used her sword to chop off her right arm, and that severed arm grew into the mother's sister. But the wound hurt the mother and the pain made her cry. The sister gathered up all the tears from the mother and scattered them about the dusty land. Then, for many, many cycles, the sister travelled across the world and scattered the tears onto the bare ground. Everywhere they touched, flowers sprung, and trees, and grass, and the many strange and wonderful animals that live on the land and in the waters. The people marvelled at the new world that the mother had given them, and they worked the land, farmed the animals, and fished the seas, and at last they were happy.'

Tervan paused for a long moment, and Solatta wondered whether he thought she'd fallen asleep. 'Is that the end?' she said at last.

Tervan gave a sad smile. 'If only it was, dear heart! After many happy centuries, the people came and complained to the mother again. This time, they said there were too many people to live together, that there wasn't enough room or food for everyone. So, again, the mother used her tongue-sword and chopped off her left arm, which grew into another sister. Once more, the wound hurt her and made her cry for many cycles. The other sister collected these tears and set about travelling the land, scattering the mother's tears just as the first sister had. This time, instead of the tears growing into flowers, tress, grasses, and animals, they developed into illnesses and diseases, crime and corruption, wars and famine.'

Solatta's eyes began to fill with tears of her own now. After a moment, she felt Tervan's long fingers pass gently over her braid.

'After that, the people didn't complain to the mother anymore. They were too busy—not only working the land, fishing, and hunting, but trying to deal with the consequences of their earlier discontent. Now, the people had illnesses to contend with, and failed crops, leaving them to go hungry once more. The people began to know death and suffering at their own hands. They too became jealous of those who had more than them. Inevitably, they began to fight and squabble with one another. Families joined together to become tribes, and tribes formed together to become nations. Tribe fought against tribe and nation fought against nation. The mother saw all of this and was saddened. Her sisters went to comfort her, but it was no use—they could not stop the mother's tears, and soon all three flew from the world to escape their pain. Some of her final tears, however, had soaked into the soil, and they imbued the ground itself with a strong magic. Other tears formed into droplets and rolled away, where they sat for many centuries until some grew into people. These were the mother's special tribe, who she created to travel throughout the world and remind the people of her and her story—to tell everyone how the mother loved them and that they were all brothers and sisters. This tribe was the mother's priesthood among the people.'

'The Church of the Righteous Truth?' Solatta asked eagerly.

Tervan snorted. 'Mother no, child! These were the original Kellawayans. But the people soon forgot how to listen. They were eaten up by their jealousy and hatred, and no longer listened to the words of the mother. Instead, they heard only what they wanted to hear, and some of them used these interpretations of the mother's sacred words to steal power from others, setting up their own church in the process. *That* is what we now know as the Church of the Righteous Truth.'

Solatta was shocked. Tervan was unorthodox, sure, but she had seldom heard him be so blatantly, well, *heretical*. She had seen the signs in the towns, the Tenets written large for the people to see; she had heard the Promulgators as they wandered the streets, expounding the Truth. She had sensed too the dangers of going against their teachings, though few spoke of it. Suers. Those who sought the Truth. These were not the whispers a girl wanted to hear. She looked around, suddenly frightened, but saw only Cobb, trees, and the stretching grassland beyond.

'The false church grew over time. It assumed positions of importance throughout the world until there was almost nothing that it didn't control. They all but destroyed the true memory of the mother, stamping out anyone who spoke for her or against them. Many fights were fought and even wars waged to ensure that the Church's version was the only one remembered. Some people try to hold on to the memory, but it has been so long and it's so dangerous.' He paused, and his voice caught in this throat. 'It's important not to forget the past.'

When he looked at her, his eyes were full of sorrow and apology. 'I'm sorry, Solatta. I truly am. Sometimes I wish it were my head that had been shaved; my past that was cleansed.'

She looked up at him and he leant forward, kissing her on the forehead. 'I think,' he said, rising. 'That it is time for an old fool to go to bed.'

They bid each other goodnight and she soon followed him into the caravan. She had grown cold, though the night air had not. She wrapped herself in an extra blanket, shutting herself off from the world outside.

Sleep came fitfully for Solatta, and was beset by dark dreams of a world living in fear of a dark insidious force, always watching from a distance too great to fathom.

Place Truth at the centre of all things; love of family, love of an ordered and balanced life, and, most of all, love of the Goddess. For all of these to flourish, there must be Truth. Without Truth, we are less than the shadow of deceit that stalks the night, forever destined to die in darkness.

—From the Tenets of Truth

CHAPTER FIVE
AL-DREBAN

Baile Saor

Al-Dreban could feel the cold deep in his bones. He pressed himself against the great stone barrier yet again, straining with all he could muster, but it was no use. His shock at being entombed had finally abated, thank the Goddess—all that remained now were disbelief and a growing sense of furious panic. He shouted again, but the rock took little notice. So far, he'd managed only to tire himself out and gravel his already dust-choked throat.

He slumped onto the floor, faced with a helplessness that he had not felt since he was a child. *They mean to leave me here.* The tears come unbidden. It was something he had not given into since his mother... no, he would not think of it.

'Stop it,' he forced himself to say. He refused to be consumed by self-pity. 'Stop it. Stop it. Stop it. Stop it. Stop it. Stop it,' each time with more force and volume until he realised that he was shouting again. He attempted to gather himself, wiping the moisture from his cheeks. He had to think clearly—like a man, not a child.

He snatched up the torch. For one horrible moment, its light spluttered, but then burned all the brighter. The snap of the flames echoed in the darkness like a distant laugh, mocking his misplaced resolve.

Throughout the ordeal, he had been focused on the outside world, too consumed with getting out to even consider what lay deeper in the hole. Now, after the faces and the shouts were little but memories, he needed to assess his situation and adapt to this bleak new truth. Well-formed earthworks loomed in the torchlight. Beyond them, smooth, well-compacted clay and hard-hewn stone combined with rough brickwork to form a long and intimidating tunnel. He had no choice, he knew. The mayor and his cronies couldn't free him even if they'd wanted to. Their actions had damned them long before they had damned him.

He sat, peering into the inky dark, his breathing and the lick of the flame the only sounds. The air smelled earthy and sulphurous. He needed to move, lest he expire right here. He clambered up, realising for the first time just how raw his hands were from pounding against the rolled stone. And then he saw it.

'That Goddess-damned poppet! If only I'd just left it where I found it.'

It stared up at him through black and uneven eyes. He stamped on it. Perhaps he'd be able to grind it into the earth. 'No,' he said aloud, surprising himself. 'I'll keep it. Carry it with me like a token. Once I am out, I will present it with glee to the Golya. Then they'll know.' He picked it up, turning it over. 'Then you'll know!' he shouted at it. 'I am a priest!'

He thrust it into a pocket, furious once more. He snatched up the bag that had been thrown in with him. Inside were bread, some cheese, and two canteens. He sniffed at them. Water and some kind of vinegary wine. 'So they hope for me to linger rather than die too quickly.' For once, they were in accord.

The tunnel was twisting and sloped constantly downward. Al-Dreban had the feeling he was being delivered into the belly of the world. Though it eventually levelled, it did not straighten, and he had no way of keeping track of the twists and turns he had made thus far. Rocks in the darkness conspired to trip him, while low-hanging beams and buttresses struck out at his head as he tried to keep his feet. The tunnel seemed alive and determined to thwart his progress, but he was resolute. With each step forward, the air grew thicker, the heat terrible.

Hours passed, or so it felt. He had no way to tell. His legs were heavy and, when a stone took him unawares once again, he decided it was time for a rest.

The canteen was heavy in his hands and the wine sweet. Too sweet, he thought bitterly, and the tunnel too dark. No, not dark. His eyes were closed. He wanted more wine. Wine to sooth his throat. But his mouth sucked only at the ground onto which he'd slumped. The taste of soil and dust made him recoil but, by then, he was already asleep.

It was late in the cycle, just a few days into Touro Satti, month of the bull. People had only just shaken off the excesses of Wepet, the annual feast to mark the passing of the longest day. Ul-Mutti had been chasing butterflies in the long-grass meadow. They leapt at his approach, dancing on the air as they somehow defied even the slightest of breezes. So delicate, like a promise. How unfair it was that such a small thing could fly and he could not.

The meadow attracted hundreds of butterflies of all shapes and colours, flitting from grass to grass and flower to flower. Sometimes, he would stand still for a long time with his arms outstretched, waiting for one to alight upon him. He watched as they folded and unfolded their delicate wings, patterns alternating from bright to dull. He would let them sit there and stretch out their wings in the sun, staying still for as long as he could, and then watch them skip back into the air as his arms tired and began to tremble.

His favourite had almost see-through wings and was half the size of his hand. Only when they caught in the sun could you see their silver linings. Sometimes, they looked just like shadows, but if they quickly opened their wings out and the sun caught them just right, they became a pair of staring eyes. Spirits of the field, he'd taken to calling them.

It was mid-morning, and the day was already too hot for chores. The sun was slow and angry at this time of the cycle. The last two weeks had been especially sun-drenched. The flowers were dying early, which meant fewer butterflies.

Ul-Mutti's father had sent him to the fields almost two hours ago. He was to check the hay meadows for signs of flashfires, since the weather had been so dry. Really, his father was still suffering from too much sweetgrass wine during the festivities, and was using the threat of fires as an excuse to be left alone in the stables.

It was only a few weeks until the grass would be harvested, dried, and stored to feed the horses during the barren months after Samu Satti, month of the monkey. It wasn't even Ul-Mutti's job to check the fields; that duty should have fallen to Basl and Tarthyn, Cosl-Ewdryth's twin boys, but they would be out sounding with the priests and all the other children.

It meant he had the day to himself, without interruption—

until, that is, they finally reached the fields. It was the last day before the workers would descend with their scythes and his butterflies would vanish for another cycle.

He allowed himself to wander as his thoughts meandered, his hands outstretched and brushing the tips of the long grasses. Insects leapt into the air at his approach, but it was a stranger sound that caught his ear: it barked and grunted in the stillness of the day. An animal in distress? It was almost rhythmical, low and gruff. Snuffling? He tuned his ears to the sound, blotting out the buzz of the bees and the chirping of other insects, searching out the direction. Louder now. There, towards the boundary of the estate. He hadn't dared come so close to it before.

Something moved in the shadow of the tree. His heart pounded. *A boar? A bear? A night-crawler? No, it can't be. It's daytime, idiot.* He ducked low in the grass, creeping closer. The noise was loud now— he was almost on top of it. Soft and wet sounds, like kissing. Hard breaths and a muffled groan. At once: a figure. Mousy blonde hair flowing over hunched shoulders. The girl was crouched low in the grass, lifting herself up and down slowly. It looked for all the world like she was riding. She made such noises as he had never heard before—harsh and excited, all breaths and pants. She was looking down, reaching her hand out. Straining, he could see that there was someone else. A man. He did not look very comfortable. The man's hand reached up and caressed her—wait, she was naked! Without knowing it, Ul-Mutti uttered a gasp. The woman's head snapped up, her eyes wide and alert. Too late, he ducked. For one horrible moment, their eyes had met.

Ul-Mutti turned and scrambled away, panic coursing through him. He crouched low, insects buzzing around him, and tried to forget what he had seen. He knew she would not recognise his face, but anyone would recognise hers: House-Lord Nylu's only daughter, the

Yia, Del-rey!

The Yia's scream echoed behind him, a horrible sound that sent birds skittering. Ul-Mutti cursed and broke into a full-blown run, chancing a look behind him as he cleared a scruffy copse. The man. Naked and furious, scrabbling with his trousers. He fell. It gave Ul-Mutti a chance and he sprinted on, but soon enough the man was on his feet, lumbering after him.

Ul-Mutti tripped, almost stumbled. He slammed into a sapling, tangling with its low branches. They grabbed at him, tearing at his clothes, but he couldn't hear the rip above the thumping of his heart. A glance backwards. The man—or boy, really—had seen him, wild eyes shining among the grasses. A field hand? Was it Basl? No, Basl had only a cycle on Ul-Mutti. There was an older brother though—Vetl. Ul-Mutti had no intention of waiting to confirm his suspicions. He ran on, the tree line of the woods looming ahead. He was almost safe.

It was just after dark by the time Ul-Mutti arrived back at the family house. It was a larger-than-average home on account of his father's title—they even had stairs, and he did not share his sleeping quarters. Yet it was so close to the neighbours and the walls so thin that it sometimes seemed like they shared their living space. Already, Ma-MaMul was opening her door to see who was approaching so late. He was certain that she was a bat; her ears picked up everything.

Their door was already open. There, in the doorway, stood his father, his silhouette dark and immovable. Ul-Mutti knew he was in trouble before he even opened his mouth. What had he expected? Hours late, clothes dirty and torn, covered in bruises and cuts—he looked more a lostling from the forest than the son of a horse master.

'Where have you been, Drea?' Bhan'Va Yax-Kikkulisan looked

94

his son up and down. His voice was barely a whisper, which Ul-Mutti knew to be an ominous sign.

'I am sorry, Father,' the boy replied. 'I was playing and lost track of time.'

'Playing, Drea?' his father repeated. He stepped aside, allowing his son to enter the house. He did so tentatively, knowing that his father was angry—it was the only time he ever used his formal name.

The small room was still laid out for supper: three empty bowls sat on a table, and the warming smell of stew clung to the air. Evidently, his parents had waited for him to return before eating. Ul-Mutti hung his head, but his father's rough, strong hand gripped him beneath the chin.

'Look at you. *Playing?* Lying, more like!' his father bellowed. 'Where did you go playing that your clothes have become so torn and dirty?'

Ul-Mutti searched for something to say.

'Look at me, son.'

The day was fresh, the memory etched deep. It would be for a long time, he knew.

Ul-Mutti grimaced in pain, his father's grip tearing at a split lip.

'Tell me, what you have been doing?' He dropped his son's chin and grabbed him by the shoulders.

Ul-Mutti cried out.

'What is this?' his father asked, spinning him roughly around and dragging the back of his shirt up, revealing a network of cuts and bruises. 'You have been fighting. These look like strap marks.' His father spun him back, looking deep into his eyes, waiting for a response. 'I am Kikkuli to the estate. Do you understand? You are the son of the horse master, not the thug brat of some stable hand. What if there is a complaint?'

His father waited, but there was no answer. He raised his arms in the air, a prayer to the Goddess. 'Give me strength to find some small Truth in this child.' He was red in the face.

And there was truth, but it wasn't one that Ul-Mutti could tell.

'Do you know how worried your mother has been?' his father asked. He seemed flat, as though his usual happy demeanour had been drawn steadily from him.

The beating he'd received in the woods had been hard and brutal. Vetl's blows had seemed all the more furious for his fear of what Ul-Mutti might say. If it became known about the estate that he was tupping with the Yia then his life would not be worth the living. Stealing the virtue of the House-Lord's daughter... Ul-Mutti shuddered at the thought. The girl was said to be tipped for the Seers' Tower. She would never outlive the shame, but she would outlive the boy, that was certain. Vetl had stressed this: if there was any risk to him, then it would be the worse for Ul-Mutti. Vetl's father would be sure of it. He drove the message home with fist and foot and belt. 'And this is just a taste,' he warned. 'My pa'll do worse to you and yours if you so much as squeak a word.'

Ul-Mutti did not know what to say. How could he describe what he had seen? How could he explain that scene to his father? What would his father say when he told him that he had crouched there in the grass, spying? He chose to say nothing. If he could not tell the truth then he wouldn't tell at all. At least his family would be safe.

'So,' said his father. He closed his eyes, as though offering a silent prayer, a final hope. 'All I ask is for the truth, boy. But you cannot even give me that.' He glanced back at his son, but Ul-Mutti could not hold his gaze.

He felt lost and empty. The utter disappointment in his father's eyes would haunt him for cycles yet to come. It left a knot in his stomach that hurt more than the beating.

'If you cannot tell me the truth, maybe you will the priests. You will take yourself to the chapel in the morning, Drea. For now, fetch my riding crop. Evidently, you need to be taught that it is wrong to fight.'

Later, after his father's lesson had finished, Ul-Mutti lay abed, eyes raw from tears. It seemed that no one could have cried so much in one day. He curled into a tight ball, trying to shut out the world, trying to forget what he had seen. He felt small and very much alone. He drew a final dry, wretched sob and lay back, sucking in breaths. Then, amid the chirping crickets, he heard an old and familiar melody rising lightly through the otherwise still house. It was a lullaby, one he thought he had forgotten. He called out to his mother, but she did not respond. *It must be her, though.* She was the only other one home. His father had left, unable to even look at his liar son.

Ul-Mutti gathered himself, rising from his bed, though his body screamed a protest. The sound grew louder: a woman's voice, thin and weak. Was it his mother? He could barely remember the song. He followed the sound, half-forgotten words drawing him up the stairs. His legs ached. All of him ached. A curtain separated his parents' room from the house, and her from him. He watched his hand reach out and draw it back, unbidden. Disembodied, almost. He ought to tell it not to.

The room was dark and bleak. A solitary candle battled in vain to spread its light, but even it struggled against the swaddling shadow. His mother sat on the bed, her back to him. Dressed in black, she melted into the gloom. A wind called through the open window, but instead of shuttering it, she stared into the night.

'Mother,' he called again. She did not stir from her vigil. The singing grew louder. He pushed into the room, struggling against the curtain like it were a barrier—or was that the dark?

'Mother,' he said, louder this time, almost shouting. His voice sounded old, he realised, and desperate. Her hand sat loose in her lap. He reached for it, taking it in his. Thankfully, she responded. Her fingers closed. They felt thin and frail. His were dirty from the fields and woods, but hers were clean and soft like old leather, wrinkled and bleached by the sun. He worried he would get dirt on her and tried to pull free, but she held him fast.

'Mother?' he said.

Still, she did not turn. The singing had grown loud—too loud. He pushed between her and the window, squinting to see her face.

It was not there.

She was blank. No eyes, or nose, or lips. Not even a mouth. Nothing. A blurred, grey, vacant space, crushing in its emptiness. Grey wisps of hair fell like strangler vines, framing the void. All the while, the song grew louder and louder until Ul-Mutti felt his ears might burst.

When Al-Dreban woke, he found he was screaming. He cast about as though expecting to find the faceless thing still there with him, but he was alone again. Beside him lay the bag and the torch and the poppet, and echoing more and more distantly were the ghosts of his own screams.

It took a moment for him to remember where he was, or even who he was. *I was so young*, he thought. *Just a boy. But I am a man now, and a man of the Church. That was many cycles ago. Those people are gone now.*

A lifetime ago, it felt.

We believe in the one True Goddess, for she alone gave us life, light, and the holy Truth. Before her there was nothing, and after her there shall be nothing once again. There are no gods above her, nor demons below her.

—From the Tenets of Truth

CHAPTER SIX
SENTENZA AND BRAGA

The road from the Southern Estates

The hour was late. Dogs barked warning songs from somewhere outside, and Sentenza winced. The barracks was sweltering, but he felt the heat only as pressure mounting in his head. He pinched the bridge of his nose as though he could somehow massage the ache away.

'Susurro, you're not helping.'

His captain stopped pacing. 'But you can't just go, Colonel.' Sentenza felt that he had said the same thing a hundred times already. 'If you do what he says then he's won.'

'You seem to forget our position here, Captain.' The last of the sun had faded over an hour ago, but he had ordered candles not to be lit. He hoped the dark might ease his head.

'No, sir. It's him who forgets. You're the colonel. You are in command here, not him. What is he? Intermediary officer? I've never heard such pish.' He was pacing again.

Sentenza could hear his tread. 'And who do you think we answer to?'

'The Church and the king.'

'No, Captain. The king holds no standing army except his own guard and the barracks in the Capital. The Church hasn't held an army for centuries. They exercise their political and cultural power to control us, just like they do with everything. No, the army answers to the City-Lord and his appointed council. More specifically, the barracks are responsible to whomever the City-Lord appoints as colonelcy to the army. That just happens to be House-Lord Aargau.'

It can't have been the first time he had explained this—not even the first time that afternoon, never mind the cycles they had been here. Was Susurro being deliberately obtuse? Admittedly, Sentenza had been enraged by the temerity of Dritsek too; it had crossed his mind to ignore him out of hand, but something in the letter had piqued his interest. What would Dritsek's lord-father see as important enough to order *him* to attend to it? The old rogue was in rough health; there were questions as to how long he would last, but he had always been a wily old dog. Much more so than his pompous son.

'He's a cockwomble, sir.' Susurro nodded firmly, more to himself than Sentenza. He'd evidently reached some hard-sought conclusion.

'No,' he said, although he agreed in principle. 'I think he's right.'

Susurro stopped pacing. 'What? But what about the priest? Surely you want to know what the Church has been doing behind our back?' The captain sounded almost hurt.

'I'm sure it will come to light at some point. Besides, Braga can deal with a priest in over his head. I'm more interested to know what the council classes as seditious.'

'Do you think treason?' Susurro sounded suddenly excited.

Sentenza shook his head. 'I doubt it. That would require a much bigger response. It would need to be seen. Plus an emissary would have to be sent for. No, this is something more subtle.'

Sentenza thought for a moment. It would not be the first time that he'd been used for somebody else's dirty work. He had been tutored by Golya Sakhani, after all, and not only in the ways of Truth. He had done a great many things over the cycles that the Church might not see as fitting, all in the name of the Golya—not that he would ever actually put his name to it. Sentenza was under no pretence that if he were ever called to answer for these *tasks*, a visit from the Suers would follow soon after. And yet he'd been powerless in the old priest's presence. Sakhani had that effect on a person—he simply couldn't be refused. It had crossed Sentenza's mind on more than one occasion that his former teacher might be a Cognator. But now was not the time. He pushed down the bitterness that was beginning to swell and turned back to his nagging captain.

'But a finger, sir. Four men. It's little more than a fire team. A colonel should lead a fist at least. It's a deliberate slight!'

Sentenza took a clay jar and cups from a stand. The sound of the stopper was almost as satisfying as the deep, sweet smell of brandy that filled his nose. He stood, handing a cup to Susurro.

'Hopefully this will shut you up for a while.' He poured two more cups. 'What say you, Braga?' he said, handing the big man the drink. It seemed small in his hand.

The pioneer sergeant cocked an eyebrow, his lips curling into a smile.

'As ever, you have taken the words from my mouth, old friend.' He clinked his cup with Braga's and took a deep draught. The taste was delightful, the liquid warm and full of body. It filled his head. 'There you have it then,' he said to Susurro, turning on his heel. 'Braga agrees. Besides, four men are more easily overlooked. It will give us a chance to speak with the locals down there. The council aren't the only people with connections. I still have some old friends that we might call on without the Church breathing down our necks.'

'Won't you have an adherent with you?'

'Now you are being deliberately stupid. There won't be an adherent because you're coming with me. If it were just me, then there'd be a remote chance they could insist on sending a representative. With the pair of us, they wouldn't dare challenge.'

More importantly, he thought, *it will give me a chance to do some snooping of my own*. Where there was talk of healers, it set his thumbs itching like an old pickpocket. Even if there was the slightest chance of a link to Old Ballir, he had to check it out.

'Has it come to this?' asked Susurro. 'When even the colonel can't be trusted to govern his own men?'

Sentenza laughed. 'Would you trust me if you didn't know me?'

'It's because I know you that I don't,' Susurro said, shaking his head wryly. 'I remember when we first met. Artless boys! No family, no home, no hope. Just ripe for the plucking.'

'Perfect for the Misty City to snatch us and swallow us up,' agreed Sentenza. 'There are days when I feel grateful that Sakhani got his claws into us when he did. Could you imagine if we'd been allowed to go through the testing?'

'We'd either be running the place or dead.'

'Or wishing we were,' added Sentenza. 'I sometimes wonder.'

For a second, he looked almost wistful. 'Would we be sat somewhere, shrouded in mist up some dark tower, pulling the strings? Having Sakhani jump to our tune for once?'

'I doubt it. Spiders don't get tangled in their own webs.'

'Very true,' agreed Sentenza. He smiled to his old friend and raised his cup. Even Braga seemed to be enjoying the conversation— and that was saying something.

Dew still clung to the ground as Braga readied his horse and men the next morning. Altogether, they were a hand of forty mounted infantry, and would likely make Baile Saor in a little less than three days, all being well. Then the simple task of finding the priest who wasn't a priest and escorting him back to the Citadel. Simple orders: exactly how he liked it. In Braga's opinion, people used far too many words. He was a man of few, though his thoughts meandered like the mighty Waipera River—it had long been a failing of his.

'Remind this town where their loyalties lie,' Sentenza had told him. 'Rattle your sabres, so to speak. Frighten the shit out of them, and out of this damned priest while you're at it. Just find him and make sure he is unharmed. If you need to crack a few heads then do so, but try not to kill too many. We don't want to make an unnecessary scene. Tensions are running far too high as it is.'

The obvious question to Braga—one that he did not voice— was where indeed *did* their loyalties lie? They were Doarsi—they should have been loyal to their House-Lord and, in turn, the City-Lord. Market towns tended to be different, though. They developed ideas above their station. It happened when people got that sense of freedom, Braga knew. They saw people with travel chits coming and going all the time. It got people thinking—and not thinking of the straight variety.

Yes, they were dangerous places, market towns. Tongues

became freer, and that was the most dangerous freedom of all. People were bound to the lord that they served and that was the simple truth of it. Once they started thinking they were free to move and speak, there was no telling what else they might do. *Like kidnap a priest*, he thought.

For himself, Braga had always known his place. A soldier. *Always have been and always will be.* Still, things might have been different; the future, Braga knew, was always changing based on the most menial, minor things. *Had I known my father, I might have been something else. Maybe he was a forester or a stonemason, or even a tailor.* He held his large hands out to inspect them, and laughed. As if he could have been a tailor! No, more likely his father had been a blacksmith. *Yes. I should have liked to have been a smith.*

'Sergeant.' The voice of Sergeant Joyne interrupted his thoughts. 'Are we taking the river road? Wouldn't it be quicker to take the old road through the interior? Although, it will give us additional time to drill the men. I don't know about you, but it feels like a while since anything interesting happened around here.'

Strange. The kid never calls me Sergeant, Braga thought. Few did—his official rank was much higher, but he retained the title as a kind of homage to his adopted father.

Still, he was right—Braga had allowed their route to hug the river. It was far too hot to trek through the interior, and they would only lose a half day by sticking by the water. Surely the priest would wait. Besides, by taking the less travelled road, they were more likely to root out bandits along the way. Outlaws and brigands plagued the nearby towns, Braga had heard, gangs of runaways and escapees from the estates. Some ran to escape injustice—the beatings and the rapes—while others ran for love. It didn't matter to Braga. The liberty was not theirs to take. Their reasons were for nought in the eyes of the Church and the king.

Sergeant Joyne was trying not to stare, still waiting for an answer that, in truth, would probably not come. Pioneer Sergeant Braga was known for many things: his size, his outlandish uniform, his prowess, his name, and his silence. Words he left to the likes of the colonel. Now there was a strong and confident speaker! When he spoke, people stopped to listen. Sure, partly because of his rank and position, but sometimes just because of the way he said things and the looks he gave: a glint in his eye that warned of a hidden danger, for example. When the colonel spoke, you knew you were being spoken to.

Captain Susurro, on the other hand, was a different dish of lizards altogether. His words were quick and oily, like he was greasing you up to be fried. You always knew you didn't want to listen, but that was just it: you had no choice. When he got real quiet and you could hardly hear what he was saying, that was when you knew he'd got you. Braga had seen it: people altered somehow, either by what he'd said or the way he'd said it. He had no idea how or why, and he was certain that he didn't want to find out.

Still, both men had been raised in the Misty City. That had to mess with a person's head. Braga had little time for such methods—words and magics both. Give him a weapon in his hands any day. Thankfully, given his stature and his reputation, he'd found he needed neither words nor magical abilities to get orders across to his men. He could afford to be economical. He'd seen how powerful words could be; he wasn't about to waste them.

As Braga followed his meandering thoughts, ignoring the foot-tapping Joyne, another man reined his horse in alongside them. He was severe and stern-looking, the kind of man who had to look very hard indeed to find pleasure. Taut and angular, he reminded

Braga of a pit viper. Braga peered at him, his face giving nothing away. He knew who—or rather what—this man was: his uniform singled him out. While Braga's own colourful uniform was full of life and character, the newcomer's drab blacks marked him as an adherent: the attached representative of the Church.

Al-Eldar had been a late inclusion to the hand. It should have been Al-Razovel, but there had been an accident: the old fool had missed a step and fallen down the stairs to his quarters. A shame. Braga had a soft spot for him. They'd joined the barracks at roughly the same time and he always had a calming influence on the men. Al-Eldar, on the other hand, left tense and bickering soldiers in his wake. He had a way of gnawing at the nerves with his constant talk of Truth and quoting of the Tenets. It was tiresome but necessary, Braga supposed. How else would the men know that they marched in the light of Truth—and how else would the Church keep track of where exactly the men marched?

'Pioneer Sergeant,' the adherent said tersely, nodded a greeting. 'Sergeant Joyne.' Braga noticed how he fought back a sneer. *There is trouble brewing here*, he thought. 'I hoped that we might have time for a briefing.'

Braga considered him. The man was too sure of himself; he'd arrived only days before, and was already acting like chief chicken in the coop. *Next he'll be ordering me to brief him.*

As he saw it, there was nothing much to talk about. He had already given the men their instructions, which, as ever, had been simple and to the point: 'Ride to Baile Saor. Rescue this capercaillie from the hermit's place and take him back. No deaths, just split heads.' It was that simple. He had little time for Sergeant Joyne's small talk, and even less for Al-Eldar's pious peacocking. He gave a non-committal grunt and spurred his horse into a trot. He'd spend the rest of the day at the front of the column.

It was nearing nightfall on the second night when Braga dropped back to re-join the hand. The sky was torn with jagged stripes of red and orange clouds as if on fire. The chirping of insects and low moans of animals drawn to the Waipera River filled the air. Braga had the definite feeling of unrest. Had he been a superstitious man, he might have knuckled his brow or spat over his shoulder— or, if he were a religious man, he might have invited the knowledge of Truth by touching his fingers to his forehead. But Braga was neither of these things. He was just a soldier. Still, when the scream of the go-away bird split the air, even he considered it an ill omen.

Sergeant Joyne gave orders to stop for the night and set up camp, and the men seemed grateful for the distraction. The cooling breeze rolled from the river, and yet still the heat lingered. Thankfully, they had made good time and the crest of the Knap could be seen in the distance. In the morning, they would break camp and follow the river as far as the old river fort, Golem Grad. It was an eerie old place, with little to offer besides snake pits and rubble. The only battles it fought these days were against time and decay, and no one won against those foes.

Braga ate with his two officers but took no part in their bickering. After, he walked among the men. It was here that he felt at home, basking in the shouted jokes and laughs of his rank-and-file. They were family to him: the one he'd never had and the only one he would ever now need. His mind drifted to Sirle. He hoped that, despite everything, she was still waiting for him. His face flushed beneath his thick beard and he felt his mood sour. The damn thing was supposed to shield him from the world, but now it just made him feel hot. No wonder he was the only man in the barracks permitted to grow one. A historic privilege of his rank, as was the gintarcz, the length of cloth wrapped about the head. Ancient tribes in the far north wore similar items for religious purposes, or at least they had before the War of the Expansion. They were still worn by some for modesty, but there was little of that among his men. Their spirits were high and the camp had the feeling of a field drill rather than that of an actual operation. Braga couldn't blame his men—he felt it too. It was difficult *not* to feel relaxed. A full hand of men to babysit a single priest? It was like using an axe to snap a twig. He smiled at the image. Another symbol of his rank: a huge battle axe, a gift from Targus.

He left the men to their stories and their jokes and their songs, full of the warmth of their affection. It was a disappointment to return to his officers. The air felt as dark as the night, a contrast to his walk among the troops. He sat between the two, offering a barrier.

'The position of the army is to enforce the will of the Church, wouldn't you agree, Pioneer Sergeant?' said Al-Eldar. His voice was tight and nasal, clipped and proper. A true southerner. To Braga, it sounded forced and uncomfortable. He was trying too hard to engage. Braga guessed that the pair had been arguing or at least disagreeing, probably since the moment he had left them.

'The Church supports the king and the army is there to keep the king's peace,' countered Joyne. It had the feel of a well-worn discussion. 'The Church has a poor record where the army is concerned. That's why the law forbids priests from holding any rank; you just can't be trusted with power.' He sounded pleased with himself—a point scored. 'It's not the only thing you can't be trusted with. Otherwise we wouldn't even be here, would we? I can't imagine the Church being tasked with the rescue of a soldier that had gotten himself lost pretending to be something he wasn't now, can you?' Joyne was lost in mocking scorn, his eyes alight.

Al-Eldar's eyes narrowed and he drew himself up. Braga could almost imagine his tongue tasting the air like a snake's. There was something about the adherent that he didn't like, but he couldn't quite say what. It was as though he had hidden layers. Maybe it was just that he didn't know the man. He was a man of Truth, after all.

For a moment, the adherent's eyes flickered to Braga. Surprise registered fleetingly, replaced by something else. Braga gave a slight frown. Was it irritation he saw or admonition? He would need to deal with that.

'Both king and army only exist thanks to the Church, and you would do well to remember that.' The adherent's heckles were up. 'If it weren't for priests, no one would walk in the Truth. You'd still be separate little tribes fighting your petty battles. It was the Church of the Righteous Truth that forged one mighty kingdom from the flames. As for our task here, it is clear. Priests do *not* simply go missing. Why else would a hand be mobilised? The town must have been complicit.'

The fire crackled, though all else seemed to have grown quiet. Even the dusk chorus of birds faltered. Braga chewed on the adherent's words. What an odd conclusion to arrive at. The correct one, yes—to a degree, at least. But he was not to know that. He'd replaced Al-Razovel at the last moment and hadn't even been party to the briefing, not that it had gone into much detail. Could this be one man's overzealous assumption, or did he know more of the truth than he should?

'You people see conspiracy everywhere, even when there is none,' said Joyne testily.

'*You people?*' the Adherent's voice was ice. 'I hope that you are not referring to the Goddess's representatives on this world in such a demeaning fashion, *Sergeant* Joyne.' He spoke the title like an insult, drawing the word out and turning it into a threat.

'What?' Joyne seemed uncertain. He knew, as did the rest

of the hand, that it was part of an adherent's role to report back on the mission. That included the men—*and* the officers. 'I—I meant nothing by it, Adherent, it was a harmless jibe. A throwaway comment.' He had turned pale, Braga noticed.

The adherent's lips curled into a satisfied half-smile. 'I should think so. As you know, *Sergeant*, my role here as adherent is not only to act as a spiritual link between the men and the Church, but also to provide a much more physical and detailed report on the practices and attitudes of the men within this hand, *including its officers.*' The explanation was not needed. The viper had struck.

'Enough,' said Braga. His voice came out hard and final, surprising even himself with its forcefulness. His two officers looked at him and then quickly away, like children being scolded. *How do these people get to become part of the Church? Petty-minded individuals whose farts have more body than their shit.* He was of a mind to say something further, to well and truly put an end to the matter, but decided against it. There was something in the words of the adherent that he did not like; an implied threat not just to Joyne, but to his own authority. He would need to watch his Church attachment.

As if on cue, the call of the go-away bird rang loud and clear in the near distance. The night air might have cooled but the atmosphere was still thick, and not just between his two officers, Braga realised. The smell of heavy smoke clung to the night, woody and acrid. Too much to be from the camp: there were a bare handful of fires lit, and even they were little more than embers. He cast about for the source, and there it was: a light in the distance, raised somehow, licking into the sky. He wasn't overly familiar with the town, but he knew that Baile Saor sat in the shadow of a hill— the innkeeper had told them of it. He'd also spoken of bonfires up there, and the townsfolk congregating.

Sergeant Joyne had the scent of it now. He looked eastwards, following Braga's gaze.

'I'll get the men saddled,' he said, springing up, overeager.

'No,' barked Braga. 'Quiet. Just us.'

The three men readied quickly. They were barely an hour from the town and, as mounted infantry, they travelled light and fast. They found Baile Saor deserted. Only an old drunk greeted them, and most of the lamps stood extinguished. Braga had a feeling of something scurrying in the dark recesses and alleyways. Shadows seemed to follow them, or at least he felt they did. It was a far cry from the Citadel, that was for sure; there you would find municipal lighting in the main squares, torches burning brightly in wall sconces, all provided by the great houses. Here, a man would be lucky to find a candle in a window.

The fire announced itself proudly, blazing atop the hill. The Knap, the innkeeper had called it—nothing more than a mound of earth between the town and the river. A single road led them from the town to the Knap, and they ascended slowly, single-file. They aimed to surprise, not to be surprised. Closer to the summit, they stopped and dismounted. Braga led his men away from the path, where they tethered the horses to a low scrub. Then, the beasts' low whinnying the only sound, they crested the hill, keeping low and moving quickly. The dull roar of the flames and the booming voice of a lone speaker—a man—echoed from above.

An expansive plateau met them. It looked as if a giant had torn the top from a mountain. Huge boulders and rocky crops peppered the surface, and not all looked natural. The bonfire had been heaped near the centre of the plateau, where it burned fiercely, casting the massed congregation in hues of orange and red.

The three men dipped in and out of darting shadows as the flames licked higher and higher. Braga fancied he could feel hot breath on his face. Beyond, silhouetted figures danced in the firelight. Not imaginings—actual people. Hundreds. A horde, basking in the fierce heat. Spumes of smoke gushed out, engulfing at least a third of them before receding. Two men fed the beast with greenwood while a third raked them into position.

'What in all fuck is going on?' Joyne whispered.

'Shush,' the big man hissed, though he knew they couldn't be heard. The crowd were transfixed, bent into poses of adulation: arms stretched skyward, rhythmically fanning the flames, almost as if praying to it. Voices mixed with the roar of the blaze, low and musical. Chanting perhaps; he could not make out the words. Maybe there were none. It all felt terribly, obscenely old. Braga pictured bees swarming around a dripping hive.

A heavy-set man stepped from the crowd. He went confidently, head held proud, nodding to those he recognised. Evidently a man of position, Braga thought, despite his drab roughspun tunic. The man stopped and stared into the fire. It was unclear what he gleaned from the flames but, after a long moment, he turned back to the crowd, seemingly invigorated, and raised his hands—a mirror of their own salutes. The congregation fell quiet. Even the bonfire seemed to lower its voice. The man held them there in silence, allowing the tension to build.

'Friends,' he said at length. His voice was strong and welcoming, like an older brother's. It cut across the plateau as though amplified by some unknown force. 'The longest day has been and passed. Some of you have worked hard in the fields. Some of you have toiled tirelessly in your shops and the rest have worked and played longer and harder in your taverns and inns.'

The crowd murmured a half chuckle, seemingly appreciative

of the levity. Braga understood: they knew the seriousness of their situation. Even by being here, gathered together in such a way, they were exposed. If but a whiff of this were to be received by the authorities, it would sentence them all. A visit from the Suers would be the least of their concerns.

'We have seen loved ones leave us,' continued the man. 'Called back to the earth by the Other and returned to the Three. Pity them not, for they go on in the glory that lies in wait for us all. Pity instead those that are left behind, beset on all sides by the harshness of this world. We hide ourselves away from a vain and inglorious church that does nothing to honour the True Goddess; it exists only to twist the Truth and hide it away from the rest of the world.'

Shouts and calls rose from the baying crowd, each man and woman exultant in their approval, their voices together as one. Braga could see their faces in the orange and red light, eyes wide and shining. There it was: convicted by words, as are most. Braga shook his head softly.

He felt movement. Al-Eldar pressing forward, all elbows in his haste to be upon the heretics. The man was incandescent, ablaze with righteous fury.

'Wait,' Braga growled. It was a deep and gravelly command. It carried his full authority, and needed to. The adherent frowned, eyes narrow slits that shone a reptilian yellow, but stilled. For now, at least.

'What fate has befallen our children?' the ringleader cried.

'They took my son!' one anguished voice cried.

'They took all of our children,' he said, voice even. 'Our sons and our daughters. For fifteen long cycles this has been the only truth that we have known. Fifteen cycles since the promulgators of lies stole our joy away. Taken to a better place, we were told—a place where they could be taught and educated. A place where they

113

could learn the Truth. Where they could be looked after properly and offered better futures. In honour of this great act, they gave us freedom...'

A man in the crowd howled like a wounded dog at this, interrupting the speaker's oratory. He waited again for quiet.

'A freedom we accepted, though with heavy hearts. A price worth paying. Who would not want a better life for their children? We were not the monsters that day, though we bear our own share of the shame. We became a free market town with no ties to the land and the City-Lords, gained a future we thought we could never have offered our young. We paid the price. And paid, and paid again in full. Each morning when we rise, each evening when we lie down to sleep, and every waking moment in between. And yet still they came. Still they tried to take from us, despite what we had been promised. Despite what we had given up. They brought their lies with them, hiding them as they hide their true nature. Snakes in the grass. But we have ways to deal with snakes, friends.'

Fierce voices shouted back their approval, faces contorted in pain and fury.

'Just as we deal with our loss every single day. Ours is a community joined in sorrow. I know that some of you have tried to move on, to start again and bring new life to the town once more. Other faces, just as familiar to me, stalk the nightmares of others, too haunted with grief to try anew. Who among us knows not that false hope when a distant traveller grows closer, their features so familiar? But of course, these strangers are never our boys, our girls. And so we gather here again, as we always do, to call upon the Three. To ask their forgiveness. That they may pity we blinded fools and answer our prayers—now, at this turning of the season, more than ever. It is time to clear away the old growth and cut away the spent crops. We ready ourselves for the long, dark nights, and prepare for the bleakness that reflects our own hearts. May we too prepare ourselves for the darkness, in the hope that the coming cycle will bring new growth and happier times for us all.'

The man lapsed into silence, mournful eyes searching out faces in the crowd. Braga didn't doubt his pain—he could see it in his lined face, his hunched posture. No one spoke. Even the fire was swallowed in the silence. It was the man himself who broke the spell. It had to be, it seemed. He walked to a nearby tree, addled in its posture, aged and embittered. Leaves flicked dull green and fiery orange. He picked up a machete from where it lay on the earthen ground and, reaching up, took hold of a branch and hacked it free. Tucking the weapon into a rope belt, he returned to the fire, seemingly the centre of his world. He held the branch aloft, saluting first the fire and then the crowd. 'First,' he intoned, 'we offer this up to Al Ma'Ath, goddess of balance and justice. May she see this sacrifice in her honour—a symbol of the strength and purity of the mighty ash, rooted deep in the ground yet reaching up to the heavens. Protector of innocence and Truth.' And with that, he tossed the branch into the fire. It was swallowed greedily.

He took something from the pocket of his robe and placed it on the ground by his feet. Then, untying the rope around his waist and pulling his robe up and over his head, he bared himself to the night.

None flinched at his nakedness. They were used to it, Braga realised.

'Second, we offer this to Hothorisis, goddess of birth and rebirth. May she see this sacrifice in her honour, a symbol of our birth, that we may be as a new-born child in her eyes. May these rough fibres scratch away old sins so we can be born again from the ashes of her holy fire.' He tossed the robe into the inferno. It spluttered and flared in happy receipt.

He bent, lifting the item he had placed on the floor and holding it out to the crowd, demanding they see it fully. It was a doll—a child's plaything, though badly done.

'This, third and final, we offer up to the Other, goddess of death and the end of things. May she see this sacrifice in her honour, a symbol of ourselves, that she may know us in her final loving embrace.' He cast it to the flames. Braga stared—it seemed to release something in the people watching. They began to sway, almost as one. A soft and mournful song rose from the crowd as the man once more took up the machete and walked into the crowd, handing it to a woman. She took it from him without question. Cutting her own branch from the tree, she carried it reverently to the fire, removed her clothes, and added them both to the blaze. This done, the woman passed the blade on to another member of the crowd, who also played their part. As did another, and another, and another. It took an age, each person following the same procedure until they all stood naked, swaying to the sound of their words. Braga thought he understood. In this, at least, they truly *were* free.

Slowly at first, hesitantly, hands reached from one to another. Tender touches and sensual strokes. Woman to man, man to woman, woman to woman, man to man—it mattered not. There were no bounds, no constraints here. Neighbour explored neighbour with increasing abandon.

It was enough. Braga signalled to his officers and edged away from the scene. They would gain little else by staying. In the distance, the tune changed. It became loud and raucous before losing shape altogether. It no longer held words—was no longer really even a tune. Braga felt a shiver go down his spine. It was the sound of a town that had turned its face from the Truth—or, rather, that had found a Truth of its own. Braga thought it sounded wonderful.

The Goddess is the fruit and food of life. Her love and light are ample nourishment would we but open our hearts to her and her Church. As She gives her love freely to us, so too should we give our love freely to one another. Where there is need, the Truthful will give without prompt or question.

—*From the Tenets of Truth*

CHAPTER SEVEN
AL-DREBAN

Baile Saor

Al-Dreban stirred suddenly, blinking ash and filth from the swimming gloom of his sight. It was dark—it was always Goddess-damned dark. How long had he even been down here? Hours? Days? Surely not weeks... but then, he had no way to tell, not even the usual rhythms of sleep. The air had grown so hot and stifling that he had repeatedly fallen in and out of intense dream-thick sleep in the cloying darkness.

His torch had long since expired. Half-realised figures came and went, and he bore them no mind. His eyes adjusting, surely, or perhaps just the desperate imaginings of a fading mind. The thought brought him odd comfort, and he laughed despite everything. *I will make a new home here*, he thought, *in the very bowels of the world*.

Sleep had become a predator, stealing up on him and sinking its fangs in deep. He swung wildly from energised and determined to overwhelmingly tired. Time was a liar. What might have been a blink became sleep. How many times had he fallen from his feet to nestle among the stone? He wasn't sure. Were it not for his cruel dreams, he might sleep forever.

But no. Instead it seemed he was doomed to revisit periods of his life best left forgotten. Memories long-buried were dragged to the surface, images of his parents (or at least as much of them as he could recall) distorted and stretched in his mind's careless eye. Trivialities were born again as epicentres of apparently great significance, while recent events were hidden behind smoke and fog, all except for one: Kareti. Somehow, her face lingered, crisp and clear. She quickly became a recurring theme, and Al-Dreban began to wonder whether he hadn't become a reborn teenager pining after his first crush. Another laugh, the sound high and manic.

First, the day of their meeting and the truth she had tried to pass onto him. Her intense eyes, the way she stared into him with a keenness he had not at once noticed. Those eyes had seemed to pity him later, in those moments before he'd been buried. *Not buried*, he chided himself. *Entombed, or something. Not buried. Buried is what happens to the dead! I'm not dead. I am not dead!*

Or, he thought suddenly, maybe he was. What if he had already expired? Somewhere, deep beneath the ground, his emaciated body might already be festering, withered and dried like a fungus—or, worse still, a feast for worms. Was this really all there was afterwards? He touched his fingers to his forehead and offered a brief prayer to the Goddess, though he doubted even She could hear him from down here.

Shame hit him with cold, sharp clarity. How could he even think such a thing? A heinous blasphemy. He was a man of the Church; he lived his life by the Tenets. The glory of the Goddess awaited him after death. He was bound to walk in the light of Truth, not dwell in the depths of despair. *I am just tired*, he thought. *The mind plays tricks on a person when they are too tired.* In fact, now that he thought about it, he did feel a little sleepy. He would feel much more himself if he were to rest a little. Not long—just a short nap, then he would feel fit to continue. He realised he was already sitting down. His eyelids were heavy. He wondered if she would be there again, waiting for him. He tried not to think of her. But, as he drifted off, it was her voice that he heard, whispering softly in the darkness.

The little house was one of gloom and neglect. Tattered rags hung from the windows, as though they too wished to leave. A miasma clung to the air. Everyone sensed it. Even the nosey Ma-MaMul left them to their own devices, as though she feared to catch whatever it was that ailed them. Ul-Mutti knew what it was. He had felt it since the loss of his father.

Two cycles had passed, though each one had felt a lifetime in itself. There was little work for him on the estate except general labour. He was no Kikkuli—he had neither the age nor the training. His head had always been too full of meadows and insects. If only he'd focused on the there and then, maybe the here and now wouldn't be so difficult. He might have a trade and fond memories of time spent with his father. Instead, he had darkness and despair, and a mother lost in grief. He could hear her now, upstairs. Singing her lifeless songs, each one the same as the last. Each a dirge, no matter the lyrics or the tune. She removed all life from them. She removed all life from everything.

'Did she really?' asked the voice in his head. It was her

again—Kareti.

'Will you just leave?' he called to her.

'Are you talking to me or your mother?' she asked.

'Cute. Very cute. But don't forget it's me that wants to leave, not her. She is happy to stay here and die. She's already a ghost.' He rounded on himself suddenly. 'Why am I even talking to you?!' She was not his friend, he reminded himself. Goddess, she wasn't even real. Maybe she was a manifestation of his stress, he thought, quietly impressed by his own logic. His body's way of dealing with the situation in which he found himself. Yes, that was it.

'Then it's myself I cannot trust,' he said aloud.

'That's the first word of truth that's come out of your mouth,' came Kareti's sardonic response.

Distantly, he heard a woman's sobbing, as miserable as it was pitiful. It both stung and pricked his senses. Unable to provide a solution to her woe and angry that she allowed it to absorb her, he slammed the house's crumbling front door, hoping to shut in the noise.

The sobbing stopped. 'Hello?' came his mother's voice. 'Who is it? Ul-Mutti, is that you? Are you there?'

He strode on, blocking out her tremulous whine. *Silly old crone.*

'She wouldn't even recognise me anyway,' he reasoned. 'And good that she doesn't. Ul-Mutti is a child's name. Only she calls me that. I am the oldest male of the family now; I deserve a man's name. My name is Drea, as my father called me.' He realised he was shouting, hands balled into fists.

'Did that make you feel better?' asked Kareti. Her words were barbs, deliberate in the way that they clawed at him.

'Yes. At the time it did,' Al-Dreban answered indignantly. 'It made me feel like *I* was in charge of my life for once—as though my destiny was not tied to that pathetic woman, who was too busy wasting away into nothing to notice anything around her.'

Kareti was quiet for a moment, letting his words hang in the air. 'And this was the last time you saw your mother?' she said at last.

'No,' he said, the edge from his voice tellingly absent now, replaced by an unexpected longing. Al-Dreban felt something prickling inside of him. It was difficult to recall these images and feelings; he had not thought of her in many cycles, possibly since he'd joined the Church. To his shock, his voice wavered and he found himself on the edge of tears. 'I saw her again some cycles after this. She was thin—almost nothing left of her. Just bones with too little flesh to cover them. Skin stretched too tight, like the wings of a bat.'

'It was hard for you to see her like that?'

'No,' he said more confidently, regaining himself a little. The flatness of his own voice surprised him. 'No, of course not. I was already invested in the Church as a novice by this time, I think for more than a cycle. The beginning of my training, before I was eventually sent to the Misty City. I'd wanted to be sent sooner, but they insisted on "a period of reflection" before leaving my old life behind.'

'You remained on the estate?'

'No, though not far. Less than a day's walk. It helps students to acclimatise without the fear of having truly left.'

'So it makes it easier for them to tear you from your loving family,' she said.

Al-Dreban snorted. 'False. Being housed near to our childhood homes, yet outside of them, allows us to see our old lives with new eyes and new objectivity. To see things that we hadn't previously and recognise the mistakes and opportunities that we were previously too blind to see.'

'Those sound like someone else's words.'

'What do you know?' he hissed, flushing hotly. 'The Church gave me purpose. It took me in when I had nothing—gave me food and shelter. Without it I would be nothing, or worse than nothing. I would be just like—'

'Her?' Kareti said softly. 'Just like the woman who gave birth to you, raised you, and loved you? You still had a home then, and someone who cared for you. There was still food, even after your father died. The estate gave an allowance to the widow of their esteemed horse master, but you turned your back on that and on her.' Her tone was accusatory now.

'She was nothing more than a wraith!' Al-Dreban shouted. 'She didn't see anything or anyone. She was so absorbed within herself that she didn't even notice when I left.'

'Is that so?' she asked and, as she did, the dream changed.

Ahead, an open window. The sun shone across fields and a light breeze blew, loosely tugging on a battered and greyed curtain. It snapped half-heartedly into view, limp and tattered. It clung desperately to the frame; suffocating. The world too felt tired and washed out, as if bleached of life. Loneliness and desolation crept across the dream; it touched Al-Dreban and he felt all colour draining from him. A haunting melody engulfed him, incessant and wordless, fluttering around at the edges of his hearing. Then a harder sound below: a shutter or a gate closing. A feeling of hope flared and, for a moment, he thought that he saw a suggestion of colour flicker across his vision like the first blooms of spring. He turned from the window. He knew this room far too well.

'Va? Ul-Mutti, is that you?' a thin whispering voice croaked, cracking into nothing. It did not so much ask the question as plead with the emptiness. But the emptiness remained. 'Anyone?' the weak voice tried again.

The bang of the door was the only answer.

Al-Dreban turned away. He hoped the shame would consume him and burn him from this wretched world. And then the tears, each one leaching at his vitality, turning his world grey and cold. 'Stop it. What is this? Whose dream is this?' he pleaded.

'These aren't dreams, Al-Dreban,' came Kareti's cold voice. 'These are memories. The Three bear witness to all and remember all. Hothorisis, who is there at the birth of all things. Al Ma'Ath, who lives with us throughout our lives. The Other, who embraces us at the end.'

'What? What nonsense is this?' Al-Dreban felt his guilt give way to something new, something hot and angry. 'You are a witch! You are nothing more than a heretic—an abomination against the one True Goddess!'

'How can this be magic, Al-Dreban? Magic is guarded jealously by your priests, and only the Church can control its use. It says so in your precious Tenets. Only the Church has been invested by Her Holiness the Goddess with the power of magic!' Her voice had grown theatrical and mockingly self-important. 'In which case, how can I be both witch and heretic? Magic can only be invested by the Church. Why would a heretic be entrusted with its power? Either way, we all know that women can't use it. You don't even test us.'

'This is just a dream then. It cannot be anything more.'

'That's for you to decide,' she replied softly.

Quietly and slowly, the dream changed again, though the foreboding veil still clung, stifling everything it touched. He was outside now; it was possibly late afternoon. The sun hung low and miserly in the sky, refusing to give up its warmth. It cast elongated shadows that seemed to gather in the near distance. Al-Dreban was

125

aware of motion: slow and difficult steps along a dust-covered path. He could feel a tightness around him, as if a constrictor held him in its coils. They seemed to tighten with each breath. A building loomed, cold and ill-boding. He thought he recognised it... yes, the church seminary where he took his vows. It was bigger and darker than he remembered. The walls were not so tall as this, and he could not recall them being so black and unwelcoming. A familiar, bat-like hand reached into view. It struggled to knock against a wooden door, though even as it did a young man dressed in grey robes opened it. Had he been expecting the call?

'Hello sister,' he said, voice gushing with a buttery, sugary smoothness, both empty and devoid of feeling.

'My son, Ul-Mutti?' the woman said. Her voice was barely a whisper; so racked with effort that the breeze might have stolen it before it could be heard.

The young man helped her inside, taking her to a well-lit vestibule. A fire burned in the hearth, though the room held no warmth. The young priest helped her to a chair before leaving her alone in the room.

Al-Dreban was aware of time passing. It stretched before him and his mother like an ocean, treacherous and unnavigable. She looked weary and older than he could bear, and yet there was a brightness about her; a spark in her eye that he had not seen in a long time. Despite her cycles of solitude and neglect, she seemed alive. With a terrible plunging of his stomach, Al-Dreban realised why. Hope—she had hope, for the first time in what might have been months or even cycles. The air was filled with the sound of singing. The same awful tune he remembered her singing by the window, only now its rhythm had changed. The melody was exciting, no longer haunting. It was full of promise and possibility.

A door creaked open. Another man entered, older than the

last, dressed in the full robes of a priest. Black, like the shadows that followed him.

'How can we help you, my child?' His manner was calm, warm even. He seemed eager to help, though his expansive smile never touched his eyes.

'My son,' she repeated. 'Ul-Mutti.'

'Yes?' the priest replied.

Al-Dreban felt a fresh gust of hope flood the dream. Light filled the room, dancing on the walls like scores of butterflies. He tried not to breathe. If he stayed as still as possible, perhaps the feeling would stay with him forever.

But in his heart he knew his mother had not heard the question in the priest's response. She had thought it recognition; hope had blinded her to the truth.

'I am afraid to say that we have no one by that name here,' the priest said steadily, his smile broadening.

'Yes you do!' Al-Dreban called into the dream. 'I am here! I mean, there. I am there!'

'But he came here—my son,' his mother's voice croaked, somehow even weaker than before. Each word seemed a hundred lashes across her back.

'I am sorry, my daughter,' the priest said. 'Your child is not here. Though rest assured we are all children of the Goddess. Find solace in that.'

'Please,' Al-Dreban begged. 'Please, I am here. Please find me. Please bring me to her.' Even as he spoke the words, he could feel the final vestiges of colour escaping from the dream, and an all-engulfing greyness swept from the fringes. A bitter cold wrapped around him, and he feared that he might never be warm again. 'Ask for *me*, mother. Ask for Drea. They will find me.' It was no use. Her light was already fading.

'Come, child,' the priest said, taking the woman's arm and helping her from the chair, 'let me show you out.' He walked her back the way she had come, back to the large wooden door she had arrived at. He smiled at her and then touched the forefinger and index-finger of his right hand first to his forehead, then to his lips, and finally to his chest, intoning, 'Truth be in your thoughts, in your words, and in your heart, my child. Now, go in Truth.' He smiled down at her.

The woman's hand raised automatically, shakily mirroring the priest's actions; actions she had been taught as a child and which she remembered teaching her own child in turn. She stopped after touching the fingers to her lips, wet now from the tears that were tracing down her face. The priest stepped back beyond the door, closing it on the frail old woman and leaving her alone once more.

The woman stood for a moment, staring blankly at the door. Gradually, as if borne on a gentle breeze, the distant melody began to swell. Al-Dreban tried to ignore it, but it grew louder and darker, full of doubt and fear. The hour had grown late. The sun, smouldering beyond the horizon, spoke of the coming dark. With no other choice, the old woman turned and started back along the crumbling path.

Al-Dreban found that he was weeping. The sound of his sobs mingled with the hollow footfalls of the woman and the ever-present lament stretching tuneless across the vacant plains. Mercifully, Kareti remained silent.

He watched her through half-closed eyes as she staggered on. Finally, with terrible inevitability, the woman's tired and lumbering gait became too much for her weak frame, and her body seemed to crumble beneath her. Slumped there in the dust, one leg folded awkwardly beneath her and the other stretched out behind, she seemed to contemplate getting up... but it had been such a long day.

She had walked so far, only to be disappointed. She was tired. So tired. Maybe, if she could just lay there for a short while...

She lowered her chest to the ground and rested her cheek on the path. Her breathing was so light against the dirt that it hardly disturbed the dust. Steadily, the evening grew colder and darker. Shadows closed in around her, eager and hungry. Al-Dreban saw her dreams and her thoughts—how, in those final moments, she remembered a time—so faint now, like a seed caught on the breeze—when she had been happy. A long time ago, when she'd had her husband and son. Her family. Her *va* and her *mutti*. She closed her eyes, allowing her breathing to become more and more shallow and her thoughts to drift like dead leaves away.

Al-Dreban opened his eyes. It was dark, but it no longer mattered. He tucked his knees up tight into his chest and held his wretched face in his hands, his back up against the cold rockface. He cried hard, in great racking sobs, like a little boy looking to his mother for comfort. 'They said she had been wandering the streets,' he said between tears, gasps absorbed by the emptiness, 'they said she had gone mad. That she hadn't even known herself at the end, never mind her family. They said...' He fell into silence, his emotions overcoming him. Shame. Anger. Guilt. Pity. All engulfed him, dragging him down into the pit. Time passed, he supposed, but not enough of it; not enough to entomb him. He wanted only for the darkness and the tunnel to swallow him whole, for his bones to become dust and crumble into nothing. *Let this whole thrice-damned world come to ashes.* For a long time, the only sound in the tunnels was the echo of Al-Dreban's tears. No matter how much he wept, there seemed to be more tears ready to fall. Finally he lurched forward, spitting dust and tears and mucus into the dry dirt, and howled into the black. He wanted there to *be* something. Why had no one screamed at him and asked him why he didn't do more?

Why hadn't he helped her when he'd had the chance? Why had he let her down so horrendously?

From the darkness came a familiar voice. 'They lied,' said Kareti.

Only this time, she was no longer confined to his dreams.

The Goddess gave life to the world, creating first people to populate the land. She then brought forth all of the things that swim in the waters, that fly in the sky, and all the things that walk and crawl upon her bounteous lands. Only the Goddess has the power to bring forth life, and only the Goddess determines when it is to be taken away.

—**From the Tenets of Truth**

CHAPTER EIGHT

SENTENZA

The road from the Southern Estates

The air burned.

The sun had long since passed the zenith, but it was still hot enough to cook rocks. That was just how it was in the interior: the heat seemed to keep on rising. Sentenza wiped at his brow with the back of a gloved hand. Dust rose in choking little clouds, kicked up by the horses. It tasted bitter and, despite the heat, he wished he'd brought a scarf. A myriad of flies and other biting insects buzzed around the heads of the four men, hungry for blood. No doubt this was precisely what Dritsek had hoped for; unable to do any actual harm, he'd instead planned to let the insects do his dirty work. *A true bureaucrat.*

Susurro coughed as he drew alongside. The man practically simmered in the noon heat, and his ratty and sullen face was glazed with sweat. Sentenza took his canteen and passed it over to his captain. A rich red wine he'd picked up from the estates, full of berries and summer fruits. At least that brought the shadow of a smile.

'Thanks,' said Susurro, wiping his parched lips, 'at least the journey wasn't totally wasted.' He handed the canteen back and the colonel took a pleasingly long draught. It was a happy thing to do, and brought back memories of simpler, more carefree days. There were times when he longed for those days. A horse, the open road, a skin of wine, and a head full of dreams: what more could a young man want? It was a far cry from the petty squabbles of the barracks and the even pettier posturing of the High-Lords.

'You think it was a waste of time?' he asked.

'Of course it was. Dritsek sent us to chase ghosts and fairies, and that's exactly what we did.'

Sentenza smiled. 'Ghosts and fairies,' he repeated.

'What? You think it was anything more? We're sent to "uncover sedition" and all we find are scratchily written leaflets about some farmyard healing? Hardly necessitates the involvement of the army, does it? The local sheriff should have just rounded up a couple of old crones and had a witch trial. They could have used the posters as kindling for the bonfire.' Susurro gave a crooked grin.

Sentenza rolled his eyes. His friend had always had a morbid sense of humour. 'Those poor old dears,' he said. 'Say, wasn't your very own mother handy with herbs?'

Susurro shot him a glance, though there was the hint of a smile in his eyes. 'If it wasn't a fool's errand, then what was it?'

'Maybe you're right,' Sentenza said, reining his horse to a stop. Susurro feigned surprise. 'But you're also wrong. This was no goodwife sewing herbs and curses into dolls. They'd do exactly as you say—a witch hunt, handled locally. Does no good to have so many eyes on a few women. You heard the rumours: the boy that should have died. There was a man involved in this. A healer, and not of the Church. Why else would they send for soldiers and why else would the Citadel demand the colonel? It's all too subtle to be a deliberate slight—Dritsek's not that clever. No, the more I think of it, the more I think we really could be chasing ghosts.' He cast his mind back many cycles. One of the Golya's little tasks: an overlong search in the mountains, only to find whispers and echoes. It had been a healer then too—a strong one. And a girl. He'd been too late then too. 'Ghosts and fairies,' he repeated. 'Could it possibly be...?'

How close to the truth you might be, old friend, he thought. He could almost imagine the ghost of Ballir laughing at him right now, chins wobbling and splattered with blood.

'Who? The Aargaus?'

'No matter, Captain. But once again, you're right. I think when we get back, we need to do a little prying of our own. It's possible that I may have underestimated Aargau.'

'Dritsek? You actually think he's worth more than cattle piss?'

'Not the little lordling. The father. House-Lord Aargau. Maybe there is more to the man than the story of his illness suggests.'

'He could do with a healer himself from what I hear,' Susurro said. 'Though if you believe what you hear, half the bloody council is waiting on the Other's embrace.'

The colonel looked to him with mock reproof, touching his fingers to his forehead and lips. 'Truth, Captain. And you, anointed in the Church. How many cycles did you spend training in the

Misty City?'

Susurro grinned. 'Only one less than you, Colonel. Which is how you know exactly what my mother was capable of.'

They dismounted and picketed the horses. Susurro dispatched the two remaining men of the finger as instructed and began gathering wood to set a small fire. When Sentenza asked whether it wasn't hot enough already, he said it was to keep midges at bay, though Sentenza knew that his friend feared worse night-shrouded biting things than midges. *Superstitious old goat*, he thought, turning to stroke his horse's smooth snout. The late sun burned a brilliant orange as it began to set, lighting the sky in fiery tiger stripes. His horse's coat shone like burnished gold as he brushed it down.

'I hadn't even heard of House Aargau before Dritsek,' said Susurro, appearing next to his own horse. The two men quickly fell into the comfortable familiarity of tending to their horses. It was as pleasant an evening as they could have hoped for given the heat.

'There isn't much to know,' replied Sentenza, almost absently. 'They're an old enough house, but they fell out of fashion. Caught on the wrong side of some dispute centuries ago. Since then, they've been trying to get back into the Church's favour. Marrying into the right houses, grandiose acts supporting this and that City-Lord, even bankrolling the local military.'

Susurro snorted. 'Truth knows how they manage that. Look at Dritsek. He hardly has a head for the army.'

'None of the family do. They're miners. Or, at least, that's where their coin comes from. The Goddess must have smiled on them, for their lands were found to sit on seams of metal ore and black coal. Recently the Church has been clambering over themselves to trade the stuff.'

'Convenient coincidence.' Susurro did not sound convinced.

'Certainly is,' the colonel said, more to himself than to his captain. House Aargau certainly had ambition, but their House-Lord had been absent from council for over a cycle because of his health. As, in fact, had City-Lord Phaedra. Another coincidence? Sentenza had little belief in them. But why send them out here? True enough, it had been a leaf-counting exercise, but some of the ghosts and fairies they'd been told about by that handful of superstitious and filth-encrusted peasants might just be real. There was too much to consider; too many answers when he didn't yet know the questions. Still, one thing burned in his mind, as it often did when he thought of healers: that day, long ago, when his Wielding had failed him. To shut down a Wielder like that would require tremendous power—something he'd never experienced before or since. If a man could take that power and harness it, possess it even, they'd be unstoppable. What any magic user might not give for that. He eyed his old friend with a newfound suspicion. True, Susurro's was a different type of magic to his own, but wouldn't anyone betray their closest friends for power like that? He decided to keep his own counsel on the matter. 'Dritsek can move in his own little circles and play his petty games,' he said, taking care to keep his voice casual, 'but we'll figure out what he's up to once we're back, eh? Then we can cut him a slice of his own arse and feed it to him.'

The two men smiled: Susurro to his colonel and Sentenza to himself.

The animals snickered and whinnied, pulling at their tethers. Sentenza fetched a handful of cobnuts from his saddlebags and stroked gently at the muzzle of his horse, his mind drifting. He felt a distant excitement stirring. It would be good to visit even some slight revenge upon Dritsek. The lordling was an upstart and little more, but he certainly couldn't be allowed to flex his muscles. Once he returned, Sentenza would submit a report to say that they'd found nothing of concern: no seditious rebellion, no herbalist crones, and certainly no mysterious healers. Then he would firmly plant his own spies at the centre of House Aargau. A servant in the young lord's quarters, perhaps, an elderly adherent to pray for the House-Lord, or even an attractive attendant to Lady Aargau. She was said to be something of a beauty, though distant from her lord husband these past cycles. Maybe her head might be turned elsewhere?

At once, Sentenza's gelding yanked at the reins, snorting. It threw its head, wide eyes darting over the grasslands beyond.

'Easy, boy,' he said, stroking the beast's ear, 'what's the matter with you, eh?' He looked about. All seemed still. Susurro was a few strides away, busy adding crushed apple to a pail of water. *I don't know why he always does that. I've never seen a horse deliberately die of thirst.*

Something was upsetting them—even the captain had noticed it now. Sentenza walked his horse to Susurro. 'Here,' he said, handing over the reins.

'What is it?'

'I'm not sure. There's something not right.' The two men scanned the area back along the road. There was no sign of anyone following. Indeed, there had been little sign of anyone for their entire journey, except for peasants working the fields. The roads were always empty these days. Even traders and merchants were being increasingly forced to use the king's canals.

'Where are the others?' asked Sentenza.

'Over there.' Susurro nodded in the direction of the scrub. Beyond stood lazy fields of corn. Tall and wiry now, heaps had been left to dry in the late-season sun and used to feed livestock. It presented a perfect cover—but for what?

'I'm going to see how they're doing. Stay alert.'

Somehow, he knew something was wrong, even though all seemed still. He strode quickly to the other men of the finger, sergeants Annahr and Zubana. Neither seemed concerned, though they had their backs to him. They appeared busy, their attention on their tasks—collecting wood, Sentenza supposed, or foraging.

He chided himself for having not been more thorough and attentive. The two weren't busy at all—they were slumped. Sentenza cursed and spun on his heel. Their journey had been too uneventful, and they'd lapsed into a false sense of security. A life of drills and training kicked in. His senses sharpened, muscles tightened. There was no time to worry about what they hadn't done—only what now needed to be done. Wolves did not dwell on the past.

'*Captain!*' he roared to Susurro, his hand already on the sword that hung at his waist. Instinctively, he felt for the presence of Wielder magic, ready to bend it to his will. It was always a comfort to him, like a blanket or a lover—always there to be held.

Feeling exposed on the path, he dropped down to one knee and drew his sword. The ground either side of him was bare and unprotected; even with his power, he was a sitting duck. For a moment, he wondered if it would be best to retreat to the horses, but then he thought he heard a noise coming from one of his two officers, and his mind was made up. He had no way of knowing who or what was waiting up ahead, but his ability to Wield was stronger than that of anyone he had ever met. He heard Susurro making progress behind, and soon his captain drew up next to him, his sword held ready.

'What is it? What do you see?' Susurro asked, dropping down to one knee alongside him, eyes scanning the horizon.

'Up ahead, Annahr and Zubana both down,' Sentenza answered.

'Shit. Numbers? Did you see anything?'

'No, just more of that damned maize. They must be using it as cover. Shall we find out for ourselves, old friend?' He shot Susurro a tight smile. It felt natural—it was, in truth, an age-old ritual the men had shared for most of their lives. Somehow, it felt right.

Susurro nodded, and wordlessly the pair started forward in a stooped run.

They made it to the edge of the scrub patch and dropped down. Just ahead lay the two slumped bodies. From this distance, it was clear they were dead. A brace of black-fletched arrows protruded from each corpse like the antennae of some insect. One lay crumpled in a heap, bent face down over some bushes, while the other stared up at the brilliant sky, lifeless eyes that now burned orange like something from a nightmare. The same black fletching nestled beneath his jawbone.

'They probably got him first,' Sentenza said, indicating the man lying on his back. 'The first arrow to the chest took him by surprise, and the second was on its way before the first had even struck. Caught him as he was falling backwards. The other guy had probably turned to run when they got him.' He had no idea why he said it—just words to keep his mind from freezing. An old soldier's trick. He knew it made no difference how and in what order; it was the who and the where that mattered now.

'What do you think?' Susurro asked. 'Bandits?'

It was possible. Escaped estate workers living off the land—they could be found all over the kingdom, stealing from travellers and merchants. They even raided the odd estate from time to time. But to attack soldiers? They would have to be incredibly desperate or incredibly stupid.

'I don't think so,' Sentenza said. He pondered for a short

while, his eyes constantly searching for the slightest movement. Each swaying stalk caused his hand to grip ever tighter upon the hilt of his sword. He almost hoped there was someone still there. He crawled to the nearest corpse, tugging at an arrow. It moved little and noisily. 'Pretty well made,' he observed, 'and all the same. Bandits steal and scavenge. They don't make neat, consistent arrows.' It didn't change things. Just made their foes more interesting.

A noise from the cornfield forced their attention. Susurro dropped prone behind one of the bodies. Sentenza reached out reflexively, holding on to the feeling of power just beyond his physical self. Ready.

To the left, a clattering of jackdaws rose noisily into the sky. Dark screams and black wings, feathers cutting at the air. Susurro sighed in relief, but Sentenza stiffened. A hissing noise cut towards them and Sentenza surged forward, pushing out with all his weight. A heavy block of air formed instantly, a thick plume of dark-grey smoke, and the space he Wielded became dense. The arrow—black, he thought, like the others—careened off harmlessly into the scrub. He threw himself down just as a second arrow flew narrowly overhead. Two heavy thuds as metal bit flesh to his right. He spun to Susurro, expecting to see a third corpse, but the captain was unscathed. The two arrows had found their home in the back of Zubana.

More sounds crashed in on them, these lacking the subtlety of arrows. Bodies moving through maize, tearing stalks free. Stems snapped and men yelled war cries as Sentenza rose, sword held ready. These were not the screams of the desperate. They were direct challenges, specific threats—the shouts of men who had shouted such things before. Sentenza counted at least six, plus a single archer at the edge of the field. This one worried him the most. Even he couldn't hold those arrows forever.

Sentenza swept to his left, putting distance between himself and Susurro. It would make the hand-to-hand fight harder, but it would split the archer's aim. He couldn't hit them both at once.

He flexed the fingers of his sword hand, loosening his grip to allow for more fluid control of his strikes. He planned to rush the bowman, hoping that Susurro might distract him for long enough to buy him an approach. The captain was already finding his feet, short sword drawn, steel flashing like fire in the evening light.

The onrushing men had halved the hundred or so paces to the field, faces alight and eyes set on the colonel. He wished he'd buckled on his great sword or, even better, that they had Braga and that huge axe of his with them. Still, there was no time to dwell on what might have been. The bowman was already nocking another arrow. His arm stretched and his eye sighted. The strum of release and an arc of feathered iron raced towards Sentenza. *Why do they always go straight for me?*

The first man came in low, sword sweeping upward. Sentenza caught it on his short sword and kicked out, buying a moment's breathing space. His shoulder ached. There was a blur of faces and bodies as others joined the melee, flashes of steel licking out. The arrow screamed. He pushed out with his Wielding in response, air thickening and coalescing around him. There was a cracking sound as the wooden shaft splintered, relief flooding him. Too soon, the sound of another arrow being loosed struck his ear.

A blade came from above, framing its wielder's twisted face, angry and intent. Sentenza parried then barged the soldier with his shoulder. He spat in the man's eyes and flashed his own fangs. Fighting wasn't pretty. The man drew back, cursing and wiping at his face, then lunged, his sword arcing downwards in a two-handed attack. The blow would have gone a long way to splitting

Sentenza down the middle, but it was clumsy and rash—no trouble for the colonel to step into the man's reach. He deflected the strike and used his attacker's own momentum to pivot him at the hip. The man's back was forced up and out—right into the flight of the archer's arrow. Sentenza felt the impact. The body shrunk into him like a child searching for succour. His last exhalation, wet and noisy on Sentenza's neck, faded to nothing.

There was no time to breathe. A second man charged, a third not far behind. The dark fletching of another arrow flashed far too close for his liking. *For Truth's sake,* he thought. *I've got to stop him.*

The first new attacker—a thin, wiry man with hard eyes—lunged sharply, blade arm searching for Sentenza's chest. The colonel leaned back, tripped, and fell. His attacker straightened and raised his sword. Gasping from the exertion, Sentenza struck out with the Wielding. A solid block of force crashed into the man's leg, crunching bone, and the soldier fell in a rage of screams.

The other man stabbed down at the prone colonel. Sentenza rolled, narrowly avoiding the blade before licking out with his own short sword. Steel cut deep into a black-clad leg. The figure dropped and Sentenza's blade found him again—his throat this time. There were no screams, just a low gurgling.

Sentenza regained his feet. Immediately he threw out his Wielding: a dense block and the menacing thud of yet another arrow. It was taking more and more effort.

A third and fourth man joined the fray. A blade jabbed towards his face. He dodged back, bringing up his sword to block. Steel bit steel. The dark-eyed man grinned, then threw his head forward viciously. Sentenza felt pain searing through his nose and eyes. For a moment, he felt blinded. The air swam with shadows. He thrust out with his Wielding, a simple and instinctive push. The man staggered.

The next man—a bearded giant with wild eyes—chopped at his head with a wicked-looking blade, part machete, part saw. Sentenza blocked, his sword catching in the nicks. The other man pulled back, trying to tug the colonel's blade from his grip, but Sentenza pushed his weight behind his sword and sank it deep into the man's chest. Spittle frothed red. More screams joined the tumult.

Another flash of metal: the third man swinging. Sentenza kicked out, catching the man's knee and sending him sprawling. He spun away, reaching out to catch the oncoming arrow as if between unseen fingers. The man, growling, threw himself forward, blade hacking low. The colonel stabbed his sword down, blocking the slice at his legs, then dragged downwards with his Wielding, twisting as he did so. The arrow, caught still in the air, hammered suddenly into the man's eye. He dropped without a sound.

Sentenza spun, ready for the next combatant, but found none. Susurro was still fighting, but he knew his captain had his own particular skills. Already the effects were clear: one of his assailants was screaming and stumbling, sword forgotten, clawing at his face and torso as though beating down flames or fending off bees. The others circled Susurro, probing and prodding with their swords. Sentenza might have rushed to help had the air not sung out a warning. He ducked in time to see the arrow whip over his head. *Truth, that archer's getting tedious.* He turned, sword held ready, and charged the distant bowman. Susurro would have to fend for himself for a while.

The archer rushed to nock his next arrow. The man's aim was true enough, but the draw was shallow and weak. Sentenza pushed his Wielding forward as he ran. It took more energy and was harder to maintain, but he didn't need it to block the arrow, only to deflect.

It worked: the arrow went wide.

The archer panicked. Throwing down his bow, he turned on his heels and fled into the cornfield. Sentenza followed, dry reedy stalks slapping and beating at his face, the air thick with birds, the thrill of the coming kill—and then the trail stopped.

The archer had gone. Sentenza stopped, spinning in place. Flies buzzed at his sweating face. His breaths came hard and fast.

One second became five, may have become hours for all Sentenza knew. Then, at once, a flash of movement—and strong arms crashed around him. One held fast around his shoulder while the other clawed around his neck. A short blade sliced towards him. He twisted, pulling the arm forwards and away. The grip released and the man slipped. He spun to face the colonel, adopting the posture of a street fighter: a wolf ready to maul. He stabbed forward, feinting, marking his ground.

Sentenza smiled. He had played this game before. The archer prodded forwards once more, but Sentenza met him with his sword. At the same time, he thrust with his Wielding. It smacked clean into the face of the archer. The crunch of air split the man's cheek and he swung, eyes wide with something like surprise. The air churned. Another sickening crack cut deep into his jaw. Lips split to the teeth, already red from blood. Two more in quick succession, and the man's face began to pulp. He ran at Sentenza—too little, too late. The archer met the tip of the colonel's blade with his chest and was still before he even slumped.

The soil sucked the blood greedily, and Sentenza felt the full weight of his fatigue crash against him. 'Damn archers,' he said.

A haunting scream cut the air. No birds this time; it was a man in distress. Sentenza hurried towards the sound, his apprehension building. It had not been Susurro—had it? He burst from the cornfield to find the captain grappling with one of the attackers. They were locked in a close embrace, Susurro's mouth next to the man's ear, his lips working quickly as he spoke his dark narrative. The man's face was a fixed mask of horror: eyes wide and manic, mouth contorted into an endless scream. He was already lost, Sentenza knew. Just as well too, as Susurro's sword lay several paces away among a patch of grass.

Sentenza had seen the likes before. Where Wielding was forceful and aggressive by nature, Cognating was more subtle, or at least appeared that way. Its effects were anything but. It was frightening to see the impact a few choice words could have. A Cognator with enough skill could imbed something into a man's mind without them even knowing, but it took time—something that Susurro didn't have. Sentenza could tell. Instead of deftly and delicately weaving a narrative into the attacker's mind, Susurro had hammered it home. It was the loosest form of control, often involving the first thing that came to mind, but it was still effective. A person could only fight one battle at a time, after all.

Almost gently, Susurro pushed the attacker away and allowed him to fall to his knees, useless: a sobbing, twitching wreck. It was pitiful. Wan-faced, Susurro plucked his sword up and, with a short scrape of the blade, put the man out of his misery.

One man was still screaming, now crouched alone some distance away, and the final attacker—white-faced and wild-eyed but determined, it seemed, to fight until the end, rounded on Susurro. The air was strangely still. Even the flies seemed to have stopped buzzing. For a moment, Sentenza felt as if the whole world had stopped to watch. The man kicked up a cloud of dust and lunged with a single grunt of effort. His attack was wild and Susurro sidestepped, parrying easily, the clang of metal sharp and resonant. The man staggered, off-balance, and Sentenza felt himself relax. A simple backward slice of the captain's blade and it would be over. The man's foot tripped on the corpse of his comrade and he dropped to one knee, taking him under the sweep of Susurro's blade. Steel hissed through air. It was a terrible sound—an empty waft of traitorous air.

Sentenza's stomach lurched.

The kneeling man's eyes bulged as he thrust upwards.

Susurro's face didn't immediately register what had happened. He peered down curiously at the hilt jutting from his gut, the swelling bed of red bubbling from his tunic. Sentenza took a single lame step, but the world had slowed. Realisation crept across the captain's face, slow and terrible. This could not have happened. He had been on top, in control—there'd been no way, no way...

With crooked slowness, Susurro's head swivelled to find Sentenza. The captain's cold blue eyes burned into his, and Sentenza felt his whole body shudder. Why hadn't he helped? Why had he not rushed straight in there and saved the idiot?

Susurro stumbled, his legs losing strength. The sword tore deeper. The captain's eyes flickered, the light there dimming. They should have been windows onto a life well lived. Now they were nothing but lies.

The world came rushing back—quicker, louder, more intense than before. The heat, the noise, the truth: it was all too much. Sentenza wondered for what felt like a long time whether this was something he could endure; whether it might be the thing that would finally overwhelm him. But it would not. He knew that. That was his truth in the moment of it all: that *he* was the colonel. That that was all he'd ever been.

He crossed to the body and, with one fluid motion, stabbed down once. The captain's killer never made a sound.

Sentenza felt cold despite the heat. The captain was dead.

He let his sword fall from his hand and fell into a crouch beside his friend. With a numb hand, he reached out and closed Susurro's eyes. It was the least he could do. He had known the man for most of his life; they had almost grown up together, ever since they'd met in the Misty City. He had been his oldest friend.

Still, Sentenza would not mourn him. He had never mourned anyone or anything, and he was too old to start now. He felt a streak of cold flood through him and, with it, clarity. He would not waste time crying over the dead. Instead, he would discover who was behind this. He would take revenge on the person responsible.

Already, the flies had found Susurro. Sentenza stood, collecting as he did so his sword from the earth, and, with a final glance at his friend, walked away. From a dry copse of ragged trees, the last of the assailants staggered towards him, still scratching and clawing at his now-raw face. The colonel dispatched him with a single swipe. He felt nothing. No pity, no remorse. Was it just his training? Could he really be that disconnected? He was uncertain, but it was what he needed: to be focused, not emotional. He was a soldier, after all. The colonel.

He checked the dead man. He was young and pale, but there were no identifying marks—no uniform, no house markers. For all intents and purposes, the men had been only a ragtime bunch of bandits. Only, they weren't. They'd been too well prepared, too clean and fed. Sentenza was confident they'd received training somewhere, for all the good it had done them.

He returned to the horses, pausing only to retrieve an arrow. He stroked at the fletching idly. It was a thing of beauty—well balanced and exquisitely made. Five black notches marked into the shaft. A signature of sorts? It was a starting point, at least; his route to the truth.

He would avenge his friend's death. He would kill whoever

had tried to have him murdered out here. But before any of that, he and Dritsek needed to have a frank and pointed talk.

Place your trust in the Goddess for she is your Truth and your Church, your light and your salvation. Put your faith not in false prophets and enter no false church. For in these places you will find only darkness and damnation.

—From the Tenets of Truth

CHAPTER NINE
BRAGA

Baile Soar

It was an unholy thing. Intoning the Three, denouncing the faith... even Braga had to admit it was shocking. For Adherent Al-Eldar, it was a thing of utter obscenity and he remained indignant with righteous rage. *Frothing for blood*, Braga thought ruefully. To discover one such miscreant would be difficult enough, but a town full of them? And so wholly given over to perversion.

As soon as they had re-joined the hand, the adherent demanded the men be mobilised. He wanted each and every man and woman involved to be dragged through the streets and hanged. 'Naked as they were!' he cried. 'Let the Goddess view them for what they are! *Sinners* and *fornicators*.' He spat each word with more venom than the last. Braga worried the man might explode if he didn't calm down.

Yes, the townspeople would have to answer for their crimes. That was the way of things. A person couldn't blaspheme out in the open like that and expect to get away with it. Still, it wasn't Braga's job, nor the job of his men. They weren't Suers; they were soldiers, and they already had a job to get done. He still had no idea where this priest was, and his recovery and return to Doarson was the hand's only goal. Al-Eldar could go whinging to the Church *after* they had completed their mission.

The big man shivered despite the heat. He certainly would not like to be in the the mayors shoes when the Suers got hold of him— but, then, he would never have been stupid enough to cavort naked at some form of heathen fire ritual in the first place.

Word had spread quickly through the hand, and the men were agitated. The adherent had certainly done a good job stoking their fires. Braga marched among them, ordering restraint. When the adherent confronted him, demanding action, Braga met his insistent ranting with stone. Only after the adherent finally quietened did Braga repeat his orders. Perhaps the adherent would prefer to wait in quiet contemplation of the faith, he suggested, while he and Joyne travelled back into town to confront the mayor face to face.

Al-Eldar's dark eyes burned with an odd intensity and, for a fleeting moment, Braga didn't trust him. There was more menace in this man than he cared for. Perhaps it'd be better to have the priest somewhere he could keep an eye on him. Only, the man would be too quarrelsome to take with them in his current state; and besides, by leaving him behind, he'd be out of harm's way— and, more importantly, at a suitable distance from the heretics.

Braga and Sergeant Joyne broke camp around dawn and travelled the short distance to the quiet town. A light mist still clung to the morning, swirling about them as they rode through deserted streets toward the centre, the clopping of their horses' hooves like slow applause. It was easy to locate the mayor's residence. Clean and well-built, with good straight lines and whitewashed walls, the house towered over the surrounding homes. Braga wondered idly how the man had come into his position. Had he been a merchant, or was his leadership the product of bullying and positioning? Either way, his house certainly seemed out of place at the intersection of worn and lived-in streets.

The two soldiers tethered their mounts to a fence towards the front of the house, which appeared empty. It mattered not; locked doors were not a problem for a man of Braga's size. It took but a slight shove from one of his burly shoulders to break the front door's flimsy lock. The interior was surprisingly sparse, with none of the official trappings that might have been expected. It appeared that the mayor was not one for trinkets and knick-knacks. Joyne moved on ahead, scouting upstairs before confirming that there indeed appeared to be no one at home. Nodding silently, Braga sat down at a large stained-wood table. Sergeant Joyne made himself even more comfortable, finding some coffee, and was busy fixing a fire in the grate for a kettle when they heard the door moving on its battered hinges.

Braga could barely equate the man who had led the previous night's ceremony with the man who had just walked through the door. He seemed smaller somehow, more like your typical snooty bureaucrat. Thankfully, he was now both alone and robed. He looked up warily at the two men and, whilst not completely taken aback by the two strangers in his house—they had tied their horses out front, after all—he did seem surprised to see soldiers, especially one as large as Braga.

Within the time it took the mayor to regain his composure, Joyne had crossed the room and grabbed hold of him by his shoulders, manoeuvring him onto a stool. The man looked as though he might protest but, at the sight of Braga, the words died on his lips. The pioneer sergeant raised a stout, bear-like hand, demanding both silence and attention.

'Before you speak,' Braga said, his voice seeming to rumble through the room, 'I am not interested in your perversions.' He paused to allow this information to sink in.

A look of relief touched the corner of the mayor's eyes, but was quickly replaced with one of suspicion. 'My name is Prefeito, I am the mayor of this town and carry a writ of freedom for it—'

Braga cut the mayor's protestations short once again with a simple motion of his hand. *I may not have the ability to control minds like Susurro, but I must carry some weight*, he thought, and fought back a smile. Relaxing into his chair, he began anew. 'I want the pre—'

'Priest? What priest? We haven't had a prie—' the mayor began, prompting Sergeant Joyne to step around the chair and rain down two fast blows to the man's body, forcing the air from his lungs and leaving him spluttering for breath.

Joyne waited for the mayor to cough a few times and then grabbed a handful of his dark hair and yanked his head back. He brought his head close to the man's face so that he could look into his watery, bloodshot eyes.

'This can go one of two ways for you,' Joyne said in a calm and dangerous voice. 'You answer our questions when we ask them, and we all go away happy. Or, I force answers out of you and *we* go away happy while you scratch around in your own shit, trying to find your teeth.' He waited to see some recognition in the mayor's eyes: a flicker of fear to establish that he understood the situation. 'Right, then I'll ask you again,' he said. 'Like the man said, where's the fucking priest?'

Only the pioneer sergeant himself seemed to have noticed that he had not asked about a priest. He had, in fact, been about to say 'pretender'. It appeared, however, that the Mayor Prefeito was fully aware that Dreban was a Churchman. That made his crimes much more serious. As if kidnap, heathen fire ceremonies, orgies, and denouncing the faith weren't enough? And what was all of this nonsense about being a free town? The Suers were going to have a field day. He tried not to think about what his adherent might do.

'But I don't know anything about a priest. What priest? We haven't had one here in months. The Church has stopped sending them.' But the mayor's words trailed off at the sight of Joyne flexing his arms. Braga understood; Joyne had the look of a man who enjoyed casual violence. 'We haven't sent for a priest,' he said at last, voice barely above a whisper.

'Why would you not send for a priest?' the sergeant asked.

A stupid question, Braga thought. The man had seen how the town liked to spend its evenings. The last thing they would want was the Church breathing down their necks. The outrage that had followed the two priests disappearing had been bad enough; it even reached the barracks. There were rumours that a black-robed body had been found not far from here, floating face down in the river, but the Church had hushed it up.

'We don't need priests—I've already told you. This town is a free town. We are bound to neither the Church nor the king.'

This earned the man another punch from the sergeant, and Braga could not exactly blame him for it. The mayor was talking nonsense—no towns were free.

'There hasn't been a free town since before the last war,' said Joyne, stretching his fingers.

The mayor's lip had split. A solitary bead of blood traced its way down his chin. He looked confused and lost, and Braga might have felt sorry for them if he weren't being so idiotic.

'Where is he?' asked Braga, his voice rough and ragged. It seemed to carry more threat than Joyne's fists.

'We found the boy. He was difficult to miss.' The mayor seemed to visibly deflate as he spoke, as though by speaking he was giving up on a great many things. A future full of dreams and potential, perhaps, now suddenly seen for what it was. 'He'd been skulking around the place for a couple of days. We knew that they would go back on the deal—priests, emissaries, they're all the same. None of their words ever hold the truth. Just another lie dressed up in a silly outfit and delivered with a fancy seal.'

Braga was uncertain what the man was talking about, but he didn't want to risk interrupting the confession.

'The boy was just another instrument: a torture sent to mock us. Every time we thought we'd turned another corner, put things behind us, there they were with their spies. It's too much. People can only take so much, give so much, before they break. Well, we damn well broke.' The mayor's voice broke too, and Braga found that he *did* feel sorry for the man, despite everything. He could understand the pressures heaped upon the people at the bottom. He'd seen enough of them: the rules and the demands. It never got easier, even in the army. Guiltily, he thought of Sirle, the woman he'd left behind, wondered whether she was still waiting for him. Would he have waited for her were their situations reversed?

He pushed the thought from his mind. That was just the way of things. Who was he to change it? A soldier, nothing more. He had a role to fill, just like the mayor did.

'Where is he?' asked Braga once more, his voice harder, a new danger to his words.

The mayor looked worried. 'We took him to the Knap,' he answered. 'You've been up there. You've seen we don't exactly hold with the Tenets.'

Braga recalled the ritual at the bonfire. So the mayor had known they were watching.

'I swear if you roasted that poor bastard on the fire, I'm going to put my foot through your fat piggy face,' the sergeant growled, grabbing at the mayor's collar.

Mayor Prefeito looked appalled. 'What? No! We didn't burn him. We made him do the same thing that they made us do.'

The two soldiers frowned. What was the man talking about?

'We try to live without the shackles of the Church and the burden of our shame. They forced us to do that. They forced us to face our own fears. Have you ever done that?' For a moment, the man's lost look was replaced with a flash of anger. 'Ever been made to look deep within yourself and start again? Each and every one of us chose how we live today. Yes, we turned away from the Church and the Tenets, but we embraced the Truth. *Our* Truth. That's a choice that boy will now have to make for himself. He'll search himself and see if he can live with what he finds.' The mayor's scowl faded, and he sat back—slumped, almost. Braga figured he'd been waiting a long time to say those words.

'And what if he doesn't?' asked Joyne.

Mayor Prefeito raised his eyes to the pair. 'I don't know, in truth. We all made the right decision. I suppose that, if he doesn't, he'll either go mad or die.'

Braga rose, shaking his head. *This whole damn town must be mad.* They had to find the priest—only, what had they done with him? Braga recalled the strange words the innkeeper had said to Susurro. Something to do with an ash tree and a womb. He'd seen an ash on the Knap last night, and the mayor had himself admitted that that was where they'd taken him. What about the huge standing stones? What were they *for*?

'I won't ask again,' said Braga. This time, it was he that stood and flexed his fists. 'Where is he?'

'We put him in the ground,' replied the mayor, shrinking back into himself.

'You bastards buried him?' Joyne struck the man about the head sharply. 'I knew it. You killed him!'

Why does no one settle their differences with a proper fight and then just let things be? Braga thought as they part-dragged, part-marched the mayor back up the Knap. They could have just beaten the priest bloody and sent him on his way. But no, instead they had to bury him, all for—what was it?—the chance of 'rebirth'. The captain had said it was all about snakes and old magic from some time before the Church. But Braga knew better—it was all the same really, just with one god or goddess or mystical mountain beast swapped for another. The Church believed in the Goddess and the town believed in—well, he wasn't exactly sure, but the important thing was that it was all about control. The Church had control and the people wanted to take that back. The Church sent a priest to spy on the people, so the people twisted that back around on the Church. Only, the Church was much more powerful than the town.

A boulder almost the size of the pioneer sergeant marked the entrance. It took surprisingly little effort to manoeuvre the stone out of the way. Braga hoped this fact didn't indicate how often it was used. What was clear was there was no sign of the priest inside. Inky darkness and distant echoes were all that greeted them.

'That's it?' asked Sergeant Joyne. Braga could understand the man's frustration. 'How far does it go?'

As if in answer, a musty wind moaned through the tunnel, its breath cold on Braga's face. He almost thought it... it *hissed*. Joyne had heard it too, he knew. He caught the man touching his fingers to his ear and forehead as if warding off the wicked sound. The pair of them, he thought suddenly, superstitious fools! Only, one has the backing of the Church.

'That's it,' answered the mayor, breaking the spell. 'Follow it through to the end and you should find him.'

He must think me as much a fool as that damned priest.

'Lead the way,' said Braga, shoving the mayor ahead of him and into the mouth of the tunnel. The man stumbled in a few steps, but seemed oddly calm. Braga turned to leave parting instructions with his sergeant before following Mayor Prefeito in. He only hoped that the tunnel had not already become the priest's tomb.

From the Goddess comes light and life. In the beginning, she created the world and all the things on it, all of the trees and plants and animals. Do any of these want for warmth or food or water? Let the Goddess forever be the light that shines in your heart, the food that fills your soul, and the water that sustains your very life.

—**From the Tenets of Truth**

CHAPTER TEN

AL-DREBAN

Baile Saor

The silence was a comfort. It was the only time that she, Kareti, left him to his own devices. It had come on in stages. At first, the dreams. Her narrative laid atop images from his past. Now, though, it was more frightening. At least in dreams there was an air of the fantastic. Anything could happen in a dream. But when a voice invaded the waking world? Al-Dreban wondered once again whether he'd gone completely mad. Her voice was a near-constant companion—his only one in this darkness—but he much preferred his prior loneliness. At least then he'd known what was in his head and what was real. He'd known who he was.

At first, he'd thought her words mocking, as if they belonged to some deeply hidden part of himself that despised what he had become. It was not a side he recognised. He had always known himself, how he had to get away from that estate to truly blossom. He had known what he wanted and where he wanted to be. Now, he didn't have a clue. Kareti's voice had caused him to turn and spin so many times to see who might be there that he no longer knew which way he had come in and which way he intended to go. He was convinced that the woman had somehow stolen into the tunnels to torment him. At first, he had tried chasing down her voice, only to find himself further lost.

'Who are you?' he'd screamed.

There came no response—just the sounds of crawling insects, the constant drip of water in the distance, the rushing of his heart.

'You know who I am,' came the eventual response. 'You sat at my table. You ate with me and my husband.'

'But that can't be true,' he reasoned, almost pleaded. 'You can't be here if you're... not here.' His voice cracked, throat sore from the dryness of the air. A terrible fear settled upon him as he considered the slow fragmentation of his mind.

'You should first ask where *here* is and why *you* are here at all, Drea, son of Bhan,' said Kareti, her disconnected voice seeming to surround him.

Her use of his boyhood name disconcerted him. It belonged to a past he'd handed over to the Church. Dreban was an adult name—the name they had given him. Though now, he even had a title, an honorific. *Al-Dreban*. That was the name of a man who meant something; who would do things. A name in Truth. He felt his chest swell with pride, but the feeling passed quickly. An icy draught blew and his mind flicked back to the image of his mother, cold and alone, desperate to see her son one last time.

'This used to be a place of faith and magic,' said Kareti.

Where he might have expected scorn, her voice was warm and understanding. Not for the first time, he found it unsettlingly comforting to have her words with him. *Goddess help me.*

'Oh I know,' she said, as if in response. 'The Church tells you that only it can use magic. That it is a gift of the Goddess herself and only someone anointed in the faith can harness it without causing harm and damage. But it wasn't always this way. Magic could be anywhere and used by anyone.' She sounded wistful.

'And look where that got us,' Al-Dreban answered. 'A land full of warlords and false prophets. A hundred princes trying to enslave the people on one hand and a thousand so-called priests trying to steal their souls on the other.' His words were bitter, but it served her right for intruding on his self-pity. 'If it weren't for the Church of the Righteous Truth, there would be no kingdom. People would still be fighting their petty wars and magic would be used falsely to dominate us all. Only the Truth brought us all together. It brought the cities under control and it brought control back to magic.'

'The Church has about as much control over magic as you have over me.'

'We'll see about that,' he said. He clasped his hands over his ears. It was a childish gesture, but he knew that she was a figment of his imagination. All he had to do was to focus on shutting her out. He forced himself on through the dark, stumbling ahead. He almost tripped but managed to catch himself. He could almost imagine his fingers reaching out. Another trick of the mind, he supposed. Still, it seemed to be working: Kareti had fallen silent.

Despite himself, he couldn't help but turn her words over in his head. The Church did use magic, he had to admit, but only to protect and defend the people and the Truth. It was dangerous to use it for anything else—worse, it was sinful. It said as much in the Tenets. Absently, he wished he had the ability. *If I were a Wielder I could have bashed my way out of here by now. In fact, they'd never have got me in here to begin with.* His testing, however, had turned up nothing. He'd taken a two-week journey to the Misty City for an interview with one of the Golyas that had lasted minutes. He hadn't even been given the chance to speak. Even now, the memory caused him to flush with embarrassment.

'Aww, poor little man. Weren't allowed to play with the big boys, eh, Drea?' Kareti's voice was sudden and mocking. It caused him to stumble again.

'What do you know of it?' he bit back.

'Everything. Just like every other woman who feels the pull of magic but doesn't even get close to the Misty City.' Her words were cold.

'Don't be ridiculous. Women can't use magic. It says so in the Tenets.'

'Does it? Where exactly?' She was indignant.

He racked his brain, trying to think, but couldn't. There was nothing. No passage, no statement. No absolutism that categorically denied the use of magic by women.

'Everyone knows it, that's how I know. If they could then the Church would test them and there would be women Wielders and Cognators everywhere.' He hoped his uncertainty hadn't come through.

'Of course,' she answered. 'I guess you're right. I mean, the Church never misleads or lies to people, does it? Especially not young priests who have just started their journeys.'

'What is that supposed to mean?'

'Think about it, Drea. When did you make your journey?'

He thought about it for a moment, trying to piece together the events.

Kareti laughed. 'I'll remind you, shall I? The day after your mother arrived at the door to the seminary. The day after your own mother died.'

The words struck Al-Dreban like a hammer to the gut.

'No,' he murmured, 'it can't have been.'

'Al-Eff took you on that journey to distract you, Drea. You know it. You said yourself that you saw her from a window.'

'No, I didn't. I wasn't sure it was her. It was dark. It could have been anyone.' He felt tears forming unbidden and forced them down. He did not want to let her make him cry again. He'd cried his tears long ago. He wouldn't give in to her, not like...

'Not like she did,' Kareti said.

His anger flared. 'Stop it,' he snapped. It kept his shame and guilt at bay. 'You're making things up to confuse me; using my own sketchy memories against me. Get out of my head.'

'Your old tutor, Al-Eff. It was he who broke the news of her death, wasn't it? Just before you arrived at the Misty City.'

'What does that matter?'

'Think, Drea. How could he have known? You travelled together. Did you receive a messenger on the way?'

He fought against her words, dug desperately into the images that twisted and turned in his head. There had been no message. There had been no one. Just Al-Eff and their driver. When they had stopped to board the ferry and cross into the city, the old priest had taken him aside.

'You need to be brave,' he'd said. He took Dreban's hand and pointed to the looming towers, shrouded in mist. Hundreds of pointed spires reaching into the grey sky.

'I will be,' Dreban answered. 'I am ready to have my Truth tested.'

'I know you are, my child. But that is not what I mean. You have to be brave for another reason. I have news from home.

163

Though it may not be happy news, it is Truth. And we must always trust and accept the Truth, mustn't we, Dreban?'

'Of course. I will always walk in the Truth.'

'Are you sure?' asked the priest. 'I wouldn't want it to interfere with your testing. I know how much magic can mean to a young man.'

'It won't. I promise. I am ready.'

'It is your mother. I'm afraid she is dead,' the old priest said bluntly.

It took a moment for the words to sink in.

'How does this make you feel, child?' Al-Eff asked.

In truth, Dreban wasn't sure. His mother had been absent for many cycles, lost in a dream world. His throat felt suddenly dry. A gust of wind must have swept his face, for he felt his eyes begin to fill. He coughed the tears down, refusing to let himself be overcome. He had no time for tears; he had shed enough over that woman already. No, he was a priest now, and was here for a reason. He would not become lost in her lies again.

'Are you sad or afraid, Al-Dreban?' Al-Eff asked pointedly. It was the first time anyone had given him the honorific. A man's name, at last. Dreban felt pride tear at his guilt, his sorrow. Finally, he had been accepted. For the first time in his life, he truly belonged.

'No,' he replied, a little too eagerly. 'No, Superior Al-Eff. My mother died a long time ago. The Church is my only mother now.'

In the dark of the endless caves, the memory tore at Al-Dreban. So it was true. His old mentor had known about his mother's death all along. He had used the knowledge like a tool, stringing his young apprentice along like a puppet. No, Al-Dreban told himself. Al-Eff had protected him, that was all. He had used the excitement of the testing to help Al-Dreban deal with the shock and the pain of his loss. He found he was crying. The tears burned his eyes like smoke from a fire. Before he knew what he was doing, he had broken into great sobs, shame and anger roiling within him. He felt small and stupid, and terribly, unutterably alone. He realised then that he had always been alone, ever since the day he'd left the estate; the day he'd betrayed his father and turned his back on his mother.

'I am sorry for your loss,' Kareti said softly.

'Sorry?' he sniped back. 'Sorry for invading my head? Sorry for tearing at my heart? Sorry for digging up memories that should have remained cold and dead? Sorry for having me buried in this, this tomb?!' He stormed off, further into the squalid black. The tunnel turned and twisted round and back on itself but still he went, wiping at his tears, before tripping and slumping against a cold stone wall. His fingers seemed too long and thin.

'Wait,' he called in surprise. 'My fingers. I can see my fingers.' A clear blue light hesitantly spread its tendrils into this section of the tunnel, and Al-Dreban could see a bend in the gleaming stone ahead.

'We're here,' Kareti said. She sounded resigned. 'Now we'll see.'

'See what?' he barked.

Whether she responded or not, he couldn't say—he'd stopped listening. He was at last *somewhere*. If there was light then there was some way out to the surface. An escape. *His* escape.

He rushed towards the light, each step bringing more detail. Beyond the bend, the tunnel opened out onto a vast chamber with columns of ancient rock strung from floor to ceiling. Tunnel after tunnel fed off from this central pavilion—how many, he couldn't tell. A dozen or more people might be stuck in them, just like he had been. At another time, he might have felt angry, but not now; he was too full of hope. He stumbled into the cave, his feet catching in his haste, and a cloud of bats erupted from the shadows, tearing through the air in a frenzy of screeches.

Al-Dreban watched them go, weaving between the columns of crepuscular light that shone into the cave from above. They seemed sent by the Goddess. A small pool stood at the centre of the cave, collecting the heaped light within it, blue and soothing.

He rushed to it, grabbing at his empty water skin. He could taste the grit and soil in his mouth, his throat dry and cracked. He longed to plunge into the pool and drink it all so that he might never be thirsty again.

But something stopped him. He lingered above the pool, peering at his reflection. He looked old and worn. His fingers stretched on for too long, their lengths thin and brittle. Bat-like skin pulled between them. He pulled away from the pool as though burned, a memory stabbing at him.

'What's the matter, Drea?' It was her again. Even now, when he was about to be free, she couldn't help but torment him.

'I know what you're doing,' he said. He looked about him as though she might finally have joined him from one of the other tunnels. Of course, there was no one.

'What am I doing exactly?'

'You're in my head. Planting thoughts and images into my mind. Making me think of things that I don't want to. It won't work. Not now, not here.' He struck his hand out. It shone in the light, as though made of crystal. 'Here,' he said, with increased confidence. 'I walk in the light of Truth. You can't hurt me.'

'Very good, Drea. You're finally starting to make sense.'

'What?' He snatched his hand back, suddenly uncertain.

'This whole journey has been about Truth. Not just your passage through this tunnel, but every step you have ever taken. Every heartbeat, every breath. They have all been taken in the light of Truth, Drea. Each person has to come to terms with their own

166

Truth. It can't be found in the seminary or hidden in the books they make you read. The Truth can only be found within. It is something that we take with us.'

Al-Dreban shook his head, harder and faster, as if he could expel the tiny woman who apparently lived inside him. But it was no use.

'We have to recognise ourselves before we can find it. Here, in this place, you can reflect upon your life. Confront the things in your past that have made you who you are. Ask yourself if the choices you have made have been the right ones. Then, when you have truly looked at yourself, see if you can still open your heart to your Goddess. You can choose to continue down the path you have started down, the one other men chose for you; or you can choose your own life, your own Truth. This is within your power.'

The cave grew still, so much so that he thought the pool a mirror. He looked at himself. A man grown now, a man of the Church. 'Is that it?' he asked. 'You dragged me down here for days, weeks even, for this?' He plunged his hand into the waters, filling his canteen. 'It's cold.'

'It's dangerous,' she countered.

He pulled his hand back out and his image shattered into fluid fragments, a thousand versions of his own face staring back at him. They were him and not him all at once. Some were old, others young; a lifetime of faces and emotions. Slowly, the ripples faded, his fragments swallowed by one monolithic reflection. He looked terrified.

'This water holds an old type of magic, one that your Church certainly wouldn't allow. It will give you life if you drink from it, but I don't know how you will be changed. No one I know has ever tasted of it.'

'This is nonsense,' he spat. 'I've made my choice, now how

do I leave?'

The surface puckered with tiny little droplets, each sprinting away from him like skimming stones across the surface. He followed them with his eyes. Beyond stretched two smaller tunnels hewn into the stone. Somehow, it was clear that these led away from this place, not deeper into it. They seemed to absorb the light that eked into them. Al-Dreban felt cold creep over him once more.

'There, Drea. They are the exit.'

'What do you mean?' He was growing tired of her twisted responses.

'That is where you make your choice. One exit leads you back to the person you were before you entered. The other, well, that leads to a new you. The Truth you had then versus the Truth you have now.'

He could bear it no longer. Slinging the water skin over his shoulder, he crossed to the paired mouths. All was still as he stood before them, eyeing each in turn. They appeared the same—both were little larger than he, and both were blacker than night. He could see nothing beyond them. There was no way of telling where they led. He stepped towards the one to the right. Immediately, he knew it was the one he wanted. It was easier: larger, somehow more comfortable. If he took this one, he felt, he would be out in no time. He stepped forwards, hands held out to either side. He realised they were trembling.

'Are you sad or afraid, Al-Dreban?' Kareti asked, though it was no longer her. Not even her voice. Not even female.

He turned back to the cave, expecting to see her—or him, whoever he was. There was no one. Even the light seemed to have dimmed. The silence was a shroud trying to smother him.

Suddenly, that exit didn't seem so appealing. The air smelled dense and putrid, the darkness more threatening. He felt it clawing at him, dragging him towards it. Instinctively, he backed away and inspected the second tunnel. Yes, it was smaller, the ground more uneven, but it was his exit. His Truth. He stepped inside.

The mouth seemed to fade into nothing behind him, and Al-Dreban found himself in darkness. He pushed on, crawling when he had to, undeterred by the pressing stone. The ground grazed his knees and knuckles but, somehow, he knew it was right.

At once, light and sound exploded. Trees, birds, insects, the low wind. None noticed him, didn't care about the dishevelled, crying, laughing thing that had emerged among them. His eyes watered even now, even beneath the yellowing moon, but he didn't care. He breathed in, taking in all the glorious smells. The air, the grass, the plants, the life. It was so good to be out, to be free. He rolled onto his back and soaked in the night. Millions of stars blinked back at him, all framing the great moon's indifferent gaze. Dreban beamed back. The relief flowed through him, threatening to swallow him up. Finally, he stopped laughing and pushed himself up, first onto his knees and then onto weary, uncertain legs. He would cry if he weren't so dry. He took the water skin and drank deep. The water was icy cold and joyously fresh. It dribbled down his chin. He poured it over his head, happy to wash away the remnants of the tunnel, and, for a moment, all was good and right with the world. He closed his eyes, taking it all in. He felt like laughing and crying all at once. Singing for joy.

Then, at once, silence. Dreban opened his eyes. The animals had scattered, and muted wings burst suddenly from the underbrush, diving above him. An owl hooted its impossible question. For a fleeting second, it sounded like her. 'Who,' she asked. 'Who are you?'

Sudden pain tore up from somewhere deep within him, as if something thin was prying the flesh from his bones. He cried out and lurched forward, icy cold seething within him. The water—she'd said it was dangerous. Bolts of fire and ice ran through his body, striking at every nerve, turning first to steam and then to fire. Lights danced bloody chaos in his swimming vision and vomit bubbled and receded, cloying in his throat.

He staggered, crashing through the clearing, through the trees, through the night. Birds flew from his path. Animals took flight at his terror. Only the owl remained, calling to him, mocking him with her inescapable voice. Dreban no longer cared. His shouts ripped through the air and, all at once, so did he. He hadn't seen the cliff, didn't even see it as he tumbled over. He wasn't truly aware that he was falling; all he knew was that he was suffering. All the night knew his scream—and then a splash before the quiet. The silence was a blessing.

When the rain falls and waters your crops, do you bemoan it and demand the rain withdraw? When the Goddess sends the sun to rise and warm the world, do you decry it and pray for its light to fade? No, you do not. So if, in her eternal wisdom, the Goddess creates pain and illness and suffering in the false and unTruthful, why would you question her?

—From the Tenets of Truth

CHAPTER ELEVEN
SOLATTA

The road to Baile Saor

Solatta awoke to the sound of screaming.

It was awful—an animal? A bird? It had to be something terrible. A night-stalker wailing at the door, searching for a way in? A one-eyed beast waiting to gnaw her bones? The idea penetrated her head, filling her with dread. Rolling over on her pallet, her sleep-fuddled head started to clear. There was nothing trying to get her. She was in the vardo, alone. She screwed her eyes shut, trying to concentrate. *The kettle, that's all.* Tervan must have set it to boil, and there it was, whistling merrily.

171

She dragged herself up and welcomed the morning. It was already bright by the time she stepped outside, though still she felt foggy. She brought the kettle, adding hot water to cold in a bowl. She mixed in a little rose oil and breathed in. Warm and flowery; the scent of lazy summer mornings. She washed her face and hands, pleased with the fragrant aroma, feeling for all the world like a sophisticated lady rather than a travelling tea-maker. At least it would stop her smelling of horses for a while. Still, it wasn't not like there was anyone to impress. Tervan would never notice, and wouldn't say anything even if he did. She sighed.

'What more do you need?' she asked herself. 'What more could a girl on the verge of womanhood possibly want?' Her voice was sarcastic. It might even have been an impression of Tervan—she wasn't sure. It had been a timid effort, as though even thinking it amounted to an act of disloyalty. She sighed again.

'Attend to your lessons, Solatta. Practice your numbers, Solatta. Learn your letters, Solatta.' Now that she was in full flow, she was definitely mimicking him. 'Well, what if I don't?' she harrumphed. 'What if I don't want to learn? Maybe I want to run away with bandits, living off the land and my wits. We'd hunt by day and sing and dance by night under the light of the moon.' She twirled around the campsite, humming a tuneless melody under her breath.

When she tired, she finished washing and made a potent mug of tea using five-flavour berries. *All a girl needs to put fire in her belly.* She took a stool by the fire and spotted a note on the floor. 'Just like that man,' she said to herself, picking it up. 'Won't wake me to say he's leaving like a normal person. No, he has to write a letter, just to force me into practising my reading. Well, I'll show him. I'm not going to read it. Whatever it says, he can tell me himself when he gets back.' She relaxed with her tea, savouring the complex mix of flavours. Her fingers drummed against her leg. She eyed the note suspiciously.

It was no use. She put down the mug and opened the note.

Dear Sol, it began in his fluid, slanted script. *You were snoring loudly when I woke, and so I thought that I would let you sleep.*

'I do not snore!'

I have gone into the town across the river to sell some of the items. Her finger followed the words across the lines, chasing them to the finish. *This will not take long, and I shall bring back some food for later. There is cheese and bread for your breakfast.* He signed off with a simple, *T.*

See, it said further down. *That wasn't so hard now, was it?*

'For Truth's sake,' she cried, screwing up the note. 'Stubborn as a mule! Wasting good paper just to prove a point. I should tether that man up to pull the vardo. You can come and ride with me instead, Cobb,' she called to the horse.

It was a beautiful day, and the birds kept her company through the morning. They skittered about the clearing, darting in to tidy away any crumbs they might have left lying about. All the while, they filled the air with their pretty little songs and chirrups. What a nice way to be woken, she thought. Better than a screaming kettle any day.

She made light work of her chores, aping the birds as she darted here and there, all tiptoes and spins. She was a lady at a ball. She laughed to herself. *You've never even met a lady, never mind been to a ball.* That brought her back down to earth. Dirty hands pawed at her work-worn dress, adding fresh marks to the fabric. She felt her cheeks redden.

Suddenly self-conscious, she fled back to the vardo and changed into a fresh tunic, stuffing her grubby dress into a basket.

The day was still young; she had plenty of time to wash them in the river. She knew exactly the place: a slow-moving section of water downriver from the fort, peaceful and private. She might even have time to bathe herself.

Sure enough, the water was crystal clear and cool, and felt soothing in the growing heat of the day. Just what she needed after so much scrubbing and cleaning. Looking to the bank behind her, she felt good about her day's work. A little time to relax and clean away the afternoon would do no harm. A little self-indulgent, but why not? There was no one around to stop her. A family of black moorhens paddled away from her across the water, disappearing into some nearby rushes. She smiled at her companions, following them until her eyes caught something else in the water, bobbing gently nearby. It moved slowly, passing behind a collection of larger stones. She rose, her buoyant mood gone, and waded closer, almost fearful. For a moment, it almost looked as though it could be a...

Solatta screamed. The grey ghost of a heron shrieked into the air. Other birds took to the wing, suddenly desperate to be away. Two booted feet jutted out from behind the rocks, bobbing in the eddies. Ice bit into Solatta's spine. She covered her mouth, bit down into her fingers. She didn't want to look—but then, she couldn't just stand there. What if it were Tervan? Each step felt like a lifetime. She checked herself, not wanting to go further. She was almost at the rocks. One more step and she would see clearly over them. How could she move? How could she face a sight that would surely haunt her nightmares forever? She steeled herself. *What would Tervan do?* He wouldn't think twice. He would wade into that water and drag whoever it was out. *But he can't drag himself out.*

Solatta swallowed the lump in her throat. *That's why you have to do it. You have to be brave—for Tervan.*

She forced herself forward, one terrible step at a time. Each one threatened to bring her world in about her.

The man was face down, his body sprawled across the rocks, which anchored him in place. She reached out to him, hands trembling. She held her breath. Closed her eyes. 'Dear Goddess,' she choked. 'Don't let it be him.'

She pulled the man onto his back. Matted black hair covered his face. She breathed. A long, loud, and blissful breath. Joyous, even—part laugh. Tervan's hair was short. It wasn't him.

She bit her lip, suddenly guilty. She'd rejoiced while this man lay dead or dying, she knew not which. *What do I do? What do I do?* Her whole body shook. *Focus, Solatta. This is what you do. You help people who need it. You make people better.*

But it wasn't true—that's what Tervan did. She was just another pair of eyes.

'Exactly,' she exclaimed aloud. 'You watch. You've seen him do this. You know what to do.'

She dragged at the man, stumbling and slipping over the rocks, until his body lay sprawled across the riverbank. She knelt by him, her hands shaking as she considered what came next. She dropped her head to his chest, listening for breath. It was there. Shallow and fragile, but there. It was enough.

'What happens when people fall into water?' she asked herself. 'They drown, silly girl. He hasn't though, so what else happens?' The talking helped; it eased her fears. It was just another lesson, she told herself, a test of memory. She was good at those.

That farm girl several winters ago—Tervan had dragged her from a river. No, a pond. She'd gone straight through the ice. They'd gotten her out quick enough, but the cold had set in fast. 'You have to keep him warm,' Solatta breathed. 'But he's soaked.'

She looked around. The clothes that she'd washed were drying in the sun, pegged out across the branches of a nearby alder. She tore them down and ran back to the man's body, her practised fingers worked at his clothing. Methodically, she divested him of the wet garments. She felt no shame, no embarrassment—there was no time for such things. In that moment he was no longer a man, only someone to be saved. She swaddled him in the dry clothes as if he was a baby. That done, she ran.

Back at the camp, she stoked the embers of the fire, bringing glowing coals from the vardo's stove and breathing life back into them. She heaped kindling upon the fledgling flames, then filled the kettle, leaving it there to heat. She harnessed a wooden pallet to Cobb and drove him back to the river. The man was still there, still clinging on. She rolled, dragged, and screamed him into position. By the time he was in place, her clothes were more worn and dirty than ever. It mattered not. Cobb carried them both back to the vardo, back to the fire.

'What now?' That was all she remembered Tervan doing. He'd kept the girl warm. The kettle whistled, making her jump. 'Tea,' she said. 'I'll make a tonic.' She grabbed her box of potions, riffling through it. Hurriedly, she mixed dried leaves into her crystal bowl. The familiar actions were a comfort. At last, she felt confident. Nettle leaves and seeds, goldenseal, ginseng, arnica... she mixed them all with fresh honey. In went the hot water. The aroma was immediately warming and Solatta took a deep breath, her muscles relaxing. She poured a cup and took it to the man. Already he looked less pale. She brushed the hair from his face. Not a man, she realised—a boy. Only a little older than she. Nineteen, twenty cycles, maybe. Pale skin, at least for the region. Still, she'd seen paler. His skin was soft as sand and cold to the touch. At once, he lurched. Coughed. His breaths came louder now. It must be a good sign. Solatta brought the cup to his lips and they parted at her touch, allowing the tonic in. He spluttered, but managed to swallow. Solatta sighed with relief.

'That should do you plenty of good,' she said. She sat back and stroked his sand-matted head. 'How, by the grace of the Goddess, did you get yourself in such a state? Never mind. You just rest a while. There're few that can't benefit from my tonics.' She relaxed onto her haunches, the tension draining from her in long, trembling waves, and she almost felt like crying. She found herself taking a long draught of the tonic she had made. Her crystal bowl seemed to shimmer and sparkle. A ray of light struck it and split into a thousand shards of colour that played across the surface. A storm of rainbows, both violent and beautiful.

The man's eyes flashed open. Solatta jumped, sending the cup tumbling. She covered her ears when he screamed, the sound pained and awful.

Something was very wrong.

Just as the Goddess breathed life into your soul, our mothers bring us crying into the world, gasping for our first breaths, perfect in our own selves. So too at the end, we are to remain perfect in our own selves. Let no blade tear at our skin, let no animal eat of our body, and let no fire burn our flesh away.

—**From the Tenets of Truth**

CHAPTER TWELVE
BRAGA

Baile Saor

The dark grew and brooded, as did Braga. It seemed to press in on him, watching him, considering him. Over the many hours he had spent following the mayor through the guts of the world, he'd felt *lessened* somehow—a shadow of himself, or of the mayor. The tunnel snaked back and forth, consuming itself and tying a person in knots. It felt treacherous and wrong, like it actively wanted you to take a wrong turn. Had it not been for Mayor Prefeito, Braga would have. Through short-cuts and niches, the big man stuck to the mayor like a limpet. He was not some green-faced recruit; no way was he going to be shaken off. A man could be lost in here for days, weeks even. Men *had* been lost in here, he knew. He could smell it. Were lost in here still, he hoped. If the priest was already lying cold and broken somewhere, whether insane or dead, Braga would have nothing to return with. Still, where there was life there was hope. *And where there is hope there is life?* He hoped so.

The mayor led them to the terminal point of the tunnels. Around the chamber, dozens of dark mouths fed off Goddess knew where—deeper into the dark, the damp. A spectral light filled the place, ghostly shadows Braga couldn't explain haunting the extremities. Bats chattered in the eaves, passing their black commentary on the pair.

'An ill omen,' the mayor said.

Superstitious bastard, Braga thought. Still, even he could start to believe such fairy tales in this place. Shafts of light poured in from cracks in the distant rock, striking the oddly blue water. Them seemed magnified somehow, almost opaque.

They searched the cavern. Braga knelt by the pool and reached in as far as he could, dredging for the priest. The mayor would not go near it, instead choosing to rub at his filth-streaked face as though washing it of some evil. Another ill omen, no doubt. Braga seethed. He pulled his hands out of the pool, quietly savouring the damp, tingling cool.

'Well?' he demanded.

The mayor shrugged. He seemed too afraid or shocked to speak after seeing Braga disturb the waters.

There were easily more than fifty tunnels branching off from the chamber, perhaps closer to a hundred. They could spend months, the pair of them, searching each one alone. It was no use. He would either throw the idiot into the pool and leave him here to rot with his omens, or drag him back to town and wait for the rest of the hand to join them. By first light, he could have parties of men tracing the lengths of this labyrinth.

They paused only to eat and drink before snaking their way back to the entrance. Even Braga had to admit that the silence was oppressive. The tunnels felt as if they were closing in—although, for the massive Braga, they may as well have been.

The first rays of the morning greeted them as them emerged. Happy little songbirds skittered away on the breeze. The cankered old ash was the only witness to their rebirth into the world. Joyne had left his post. Braga was furious; he would never have guessed it from the man. He would be sure to put him on a charge before the day was even warm.

A lazy morning mist was meandering through the sleeping town when they returned, the dawn light granting it an ethereal glow. Braga thought again of the inscrutable pool and its dark home. Everything about the town seemed still, even the air. A shroud of silence settled in the streets. If it weren't for the scent of fire emanating from the shuttered houses, Braga would have thought it deserted. The smell grew, bitter and acrid. It stung at his nose and eyes. Something was wrong.

Mayor Prefeito had sensed it too. 'Where is everyone? It's too quiet.'

'It's early,' said Braga.

'It's a market town—everything happens early in the day. The streets should be bustling.'

Braga knew the man was right. Had known it all along. He recognised the smell—he just hoped he was wrong. Even before they reached the centre of town, however, it was clear he was not.

Houses stood ransacked. Shutters had been ripped from their hinges, doors torn free. The scattered debris of life lay strewn about the streets. Here an upturned goods cart; there a broken barrel. Here a dress, torn and discarded, its wearer nowhere to be seen.

Not a soul they could question. Homes stood broken and bared to the world. Others barely stood at all.

They passed a stand of stables. The smell of burnt meat was overpowering.

'What by the Mother has happened here?' the mayor murmured. Had he been of the Church, he might have touched his fingers to his forehead. Had Braga been a more religious man, he might have done so himself. But there was no ritual to ward off whatever this was. Nothing so simple could protect against death.

They made slow progress towards the town centre. Neither spoke—there was nothing to say. It was the mayor that broke the silence: he half screamed, half wailed. He buckled at the knees and dropped to the floor. Ahead stood the remains of the town hall. It had been a prim building, Braga remembered, its white paint and straight lines snubbing the other, less well-dressed buildings around it. It now lay charred: a battered mass of burnt and smouldering rubble. Within, curled among the shattered stones and blackened husks of beams, lay what looked like hundreds of blackened bodies. They were bent and coiled, fire-tortured into ashen sculptures. Smoke still rose from the bodies like still-chained ghosts yet to be released.

The smell was too much to bear and the mayor retched, vomiting nothing but bile and water. He fell to the ground, a terrible vacuous croak tearing its way from his throat, his tears welling and then coming all at once, tracing thick streams down his ash- and dirt-streaked face.

Braga's hand gripped at his sword. He longed for its comfort, its promise of control. Useless. If there was someone here to fight, to punish, he might have at least felt some sense of purpose. But what good was a soldier here? What solace could he offer the mayor? Worst of all, how could he begin to make sense of this? He cursed himself for ordering the hand to stay encamped. Had they been here, they could have fought. They could have saved the townspeople. He looked away from the mayor, shame settling around his shoulders like a damp, cold blanket.

Then, to his right, movement: a dark shape among the mist and smoke. A dog, perhaps. Something alive at least. He followed it without really knowing why. Maybe he wanted to rescue it, or maybe he wanted it to rescue him. Maybe he just wanted to be away from the mayor and the nagging sense that, one way or another, he was to blame.

The dog led him to the town square. This had once been a place of festivals and festivities, of trade and life. Now, it was a grim forest of death. Dozens—no, hundreds of heavy wooden stakes had been erected among the cobbles, each hoisting a contorted body. Inexplicably, Braga thought of the barracks, of soldiers arranged in the parade ground ready for inspection.

Men, women, soldiers. *His* soldiers. Their faces frozen in silent screams that would never end, that would haunt him forever. Some perched atop their murder trees while others had slumped, allowing the sharpened spike to split clear through. Carrion birds had already claimed some, their black forms pecking frenziedly, tearing entrails from split stomachs.

The smell was foul—the sickly sweet odour of blood mixing with the heavy stench of piss, shit, and vomit. Braga had been a soldier for many cycles, had seen—had *done*—terrible things. But nothing like this. This was a charnel scene torn from the history books, an atrocity from the early religious wars, a dark age long past. How—why—had they regressed so far? Braga stumbled on unsteady legs and turned away from the carnage, no longer able to see it.

Automatically, he returned to the mayor. He felt the strange, foreign urge to join the man, to slump down with him and never stand again. Those staked souls had been his men. He should have been there for them; *with* them. Maybe he could have made a difference, maybe not. It didn't matter. At least he would have tried. Instead, he'd abandoned them to their grisly fates. What kind of leader was he? His mission was a profound failure, his hand slaughtered. But when the mayor looked at him, Braga felt something stir. The man was utterly lost. Only pain remained—pain and confusion and impotence. Braga had seen it before, even in the eyes of those he'd once known, even cared for. He swallowed, something hot and terrible and powerful swelling inside him, and Braga remembered who he was. He had a duty. He was a soldier—a pioneer sergeant—and he had work to do.

He offered a hand to Mayor Prefeito. It was not healthy to sit and wallow. A man could get lost that way. The mayor looked at him expectantly, his blank face blazing suddenly as the early sun struck it. Slowly, he reached out and grasped Braga's hand. The man stood.

'Why?' he whispered.

Braga had no answer. Had nothing to offer except his arms, his legs, and his strength. He knew he would need all of these before the day was through. Both of them would.

If the town hall had cut to the core of the mayor, the sea of spikes threatened to cleave him in two. The charred remains had been one thing—unrecognisable bodies that barely resembled people—but to see the faces of people in all their gruesome agony? It was something that no one should ever see. That no one would ever forget.

Still, they couldn't leave them. And so the two men set about their grizzly task. They worked all through the day and night, stopping only to refresh themselves. They hardly ate—the smell was too strong for anything but bread. And always the feasting birds. The buzz of flies.

Tirelessly they moved. Carrying, fetching, arranging. Sweat and toil and blessed distraction. Come nightfall, they were ready. More than one hundred spikes, each one packed tight with kindling and faggots of wood. Braga was impressed by the mayor's stoicism. Truthfully, he was impressed with his own too. Through each new spike and new body, each fresh punch of recognition, each pang of guilt, they went on like machines, fetching and loading and setting. From each of his men, Braga collected a coin, the name of each etched into its surface. These were the only physical memories his soldiers had left, but they would live long in Braga's. If not each face, then each name.

As night fell, the two men walked between pyres, touching torches to the heaped wood. Braga handled the townspeople, while the mayor lit soldiers. It felt right that way—or easier, at least. He felt that he was respecting the town, while the mayor was respecting the hand, each man appreciating the other's loss. Neither of them spoke as the flames fed and grew, sending cascades of sparks glittering into the night sky. What words could they say? What words could possibly assuage the staggering loss assembled before them?

The mayor held his hands to his chest, one pressed upon the other. Braga placed his own hand over his heart. His white gloves were stained red, he realised—his entire damn uniform. Blood and soot and dust. He hoped the dead did not take it for disrespect.

He recited the names as the pyres blazed. Not all were accounted for; a small number were missing, absent among the dead. Joyne, for one—the sergeant he'd been ready to reprimand for leaving his post. His guilt flared afresh. Al-Eldar was missing too. Braga hoped he had escaped, that he had been selfish enough to run. In his heart, though, he knew better. Al-Eldar was a man of the Church. A shepherd until the end. Braga imagined him ushering his flock to the town hall, claiming sanctuary. Who would burn a priest? Who would commit such crimes as these?

Both men were exhausted, physically and mentally, but neither wanted to seek shelter in this place of death.

'There is nothing for me here anymore,' the mayor had said. It was natural that he rode with Braga. No one would want to be alone after this.

At the camp, they found no answers. Only more death: the three missing soldiers, their throats cut.

They piled stones on the bodies and gathered what supplies they could.

'What now? Where do we go?' The mayor seemed lost. Braga understood—everything that had once made him who he was had been taken away.

He could offer only one answer: 'The barracks.' The only thing he had left.

They reached the river as the sun broke, spreading warmth over a world they hardly recognised. It would be a long time before they would feel anything but cold. The sounds of life were all around, mocking their sombre silence. The old fort loomed in the distance: the Isle of Snakes. It had stood for centuries, protecting the region. Now, it had finally failed. A cry rang in the air. Birds took flight. It sounded bestial.

'Just birds,' said the mayor absently. Braga wondered who he was reassuring. They rode on, the town and its horrors behind them. A familiar call echoed in the distance: a bird whose warning Braga wished he'd followed. '*Go away. Go away.*'

A figure waited ahead upon the old crossing point, on foot and alone. Braga stiffened. He could sense the unease of the man riding next to him.

'Who is it?' the mayor hissed.

'Good day, gentlemen,' hailed the stranger as they approached. He was tall and wan, with thick dark hair framing an amused face. He perched on a thick case, looking up before bending back down to fix his boot. Then he stood, offering his hand.

Mayor Prefeito recoiled. Even Braga's hand slid to his sword.

'Who is it?!' the mayor repeated. Then, to the man, 'Who are you? Who are you with?'

The man withdrew his hand, now uncertain himself. 'Is there a problem?'

The question was a trigger. The mayor charged suddenly, kicking out at the man from his mount. His horse twisted and bucked, throwing its rider, and the mayor tumbled forward onto the stranger, a mass of flailing arms. The two spilled to the ground, the man's case breaking open and shedding all manner of wares—household items, metalware and trinkets, even children's toys. All seemed to offend the mayor, each a mark of guilt.

Braga climbed from his horse. The mayor rained blows upon the man, shouting and sobbing, and Braga took several quick steps forward, seized him by the shoulders, and dragged him off. This nonsense would get them nowhere. The mayor spun, face a mask of rage, and for a taut moment Braga thought he was going to attack him. Then the man broke down. He flopped forward, crying like a babe into the barrel chest of the pioneer sergeant.

Braga had little time for this. He sat the mayor down then turned to the stranger, who had scrambled up, face red, and backed away, eyes darting between the weeping mayor and the gigantic man studying him. He was a wiry man, clean and well-dressed.

Ordinary in all respects, Braga thought, except for the fact he was alone on the outskirts of a town that had recently been wiped out and carrying exactly the types of thing they had seen scattered about the bloodied streets. What part could this man have played? Was it a coincidence? Braga did not believe in them. It seemed a stretch that this one man could have massacred a whole town, to say nothing of his own hand of trained soldiers. Still, there was something strange about this man. Was he a distraction? Were other men silently stalking them? Slowly encircling them, ready to pounce? There could be bandits in the area—desperate men ready to do desperate things. He did not look desperate though. He looked thoroughly cared for.

'Papers,' said Braga. He waited, but the man made a mummer's farce of searching about himself for them. Finally, he shrugged and explained that he didn't have them with him. Another convenience? A Kellawayan out of Southlea trying to sell goods at the market. Without his papers. He'd left them at his camp across the river, apparently. He could take them—if they wanted, that is. Not half a day's walk.

Braga sniffed. It had the smell of something, but he almost believed the man. What would the colonel do? He knew what Captain Susurro would do. He'd lay hands on the man and pour words into his ear. He'd know the truth of it soon enough. The colonel though? He'd play the man at his own game. He'd keep him at arm's length, waiting for the right moment.

'Show us,' he said at last.

'What?' called the mayor. 'You can't honestly believe him! Did you not see what they did? They could do the same to us if we just walk—'

Braga quietened him with a stern look. He ordered the stranger to ride with the mayor—always slightly ahead, always in view. Braga rode behind, a hand on his pommel. They rode through the morning and into the afternoon. They rode across the river and over grasslands and back to the river's bend. They found no camp, though they found no one else either. He was certainly hiding something from them, but Braga was lost if he knew what it was. The more the day dragged on, the more settled the man appeared to become.

The sun passed its zenith and the pioneer sergeant finally called an end to the charade. They were returning to the barracks—all three of them. The stranger protested, but Braga would not be dissuaded.

Slow and sombre they rode. Braga was glad of it.

Weep not for the dead, for they have returned home to the Goddess, who, just as a mother might welcome a child back to her bosom, does welcome her children back to everlasting Truth.

—From the Tenets of Truth

CHAPTER THIRTEEN
SOLATTA

Baile Soar

How could she have been so wrong? No one had ever reacted in that way to her tonics before. The man had gone from freezing to burning up in the space of a few mouthfuls. Panic grew and Solatta's stomach churned. She was sure that she'd used the right herbs; she'd used them plenty of times before. *If only Tervan was here. He'd know what to do.*

She tried her best to comfort the man, but he roiled against her touch. She padded the pallet with spare clothes, trying to make him more comfortable at least. His own clothes were still soaked, and she hung them near the fire to dry. He moaned again, making her cringe. What if he died? She rummaged through his things, hoping to find some clue that could explain his terrible reaction.

Maybe he'd already eaten some poison berries. Water dropwort grew by rivers—had there been any nearby? She didn't think so. She withdrew her hand and stared: just a child's doll and a water-spoiled travel chit.

'D-r-e-b-a-n,' she read slowly, sounding out the unfamiliar word. 'Dre-BAN. DreBan. Dreban. That's his name?' She looked at him quizzically. 'What kind of stupid name is that? It sounds like something a frog would say.' He twisted on his pallet and she swivelled quickly away, placing the torn and sodden chit next to the fire to dry, hoping it was not beyond repair. Her joke felt clumsy now, empty and childish. She fingered the doll absently. *Oh Tervan, you stubborn man. Where are you? Trust you to go and leave me now of all times.* Worry twisted at her insides, gnawing at her nerves. She paced about the camp. The man had not improved; if anything, he seemed worse.

Stuffing the doll into a pocket, she made her mind up. Solatta packed away the camp. Pots, cups, crockery—everything was returned to the caravan. With a great deal of heaving and pulling, she managed to drag Dreban up the steps. He groaned a protest at her rough treatment, but it was the best she could do. She closed and secured the door before sinking down onto the step. It had been difficult and tiring work.

If Tervan won't come here, I'll just go to him.

She hitched Cobb into his hames and connected them to the vardo. Before too long, they were moving. It felt good to be doing something.

They crossed the river near to the old fort, not far from where Solatta had first found the man. It was the quickest route, and she hoped that it would be the same one Tervan had travelled. With luck, they would meet him on his return. A single dirt road led to the town and, as she joined it, her heart began to race. A thick curtain of smoke was blowing across the road, leaving a bitter taste in her mouth. 'What is happening today, Cobb?' she coughed. 'The whole world has gone topsy-turvy.' She tried to keep her voice light, but in truth she was terrified. What if Tervan had been caught up in a fire?

When she reached the town, she found it silent. There was no one around—no children running to and fro, no bustling or chatting or cursing. There was only smoke; smoke and a deep, lingering stench. It was so strong that it burned Solatta's nostrils, and she wrapped an old bit of cloth around her face. It offered little relief. Despite herself, she drove the horse on towards the source of the smoke. All the people must be there, helping to fight back the flames.

At the centre of town, she stopped the vardo. Trembling, she climbed from her position, her legs threatening to give way at every step. A great numbness washed over her. Ahead stretched a great forest of smouldering stumps. The burnt remnants of people— hundreds of them. Solatta stared, feeling nothing but the distant throbbing of her heart. A great evil had come here.

So many people. It must have been the whole town. Men, women, she couldn't tell. Children? Goddess, she hoped not. At once, feeling came rushing back and she staggered, retching into the ash and dirt. Tears flooded her eyes. How could someone do this? She would scream aloud, but she feared she might never stop.

After what felt like an age, awareness dribbled back. Fear began to spread, eating at her. What if the people who did this were still here? Maybe they were watching her, waiting to grab her and add her to the pile. Then the real terror struck.

Tervan.

She forced herself to her feet. He had to be here somewhere.

She raced around the empty streets, trying house after house, but he was nowhere to be seen. Finally, she came back to the grim field of death. She peered up at the nearest corpse—nothing but a charred lump of dead flesh—and turned away. No, not here. If he were here, she didn't want to see him.

But what if he wasn't there? What if he had never been to this sorry town in the first place? Hope flooded into her heart. He'd be alive and back at the camp, helping her with Dreban. But as quickly as it had come, her fledgling hope was torn away from her. The truth was that Tervan would never have left her like this. For the first time in her life, she felt dreadfully alone. This time, she did vomit.

A thought came to her, an unbidden and unfamiliar voice: 'There's nothing for you here, little one,' it warned. 'You shouldn't linger.' It was right. She shouldn't linger. It wasn't just her anymore; she had Cobb and Dreban to take care of.

She returned to the vardo. Cobb was skittish—Sollata knew he could tell something was wrong. She soothed him, calming him as she turned them around. The sooner they could be away, the better. She never wanted to think about that place again. She drove Cobb hard, keeping the smoke and the town behind them. A little after twilight, she brought them to a stop on an empty road. She fought hard to still her trembling hands before finally allowing herself to lay her head down and weep. She wept for the hollow feeling inside and for the suffering of the people in the town. Mostly, though, she wept for the loss of her guardian and mentor and friend. She wept for Tervan.

Place your trust in the Church and its priests. They alone are the instruments of the Goddess, ordained to give light and leadership to the many so that they may come to know the blessed Truth and bask in the holy light of the Goddess.

—**From the Tenets of Truth**

CHAPTER FOURTEEN
DRITSEK AARGAU AND PREMIERO IRMAO

The Citadel

Two men walked through a lavish and fragrant garden. Gravel crunched satisfyingly underfoot and the air was warm and balmy. Dritsek Aargau waited at a respectful distance as his host stopped to take in the scent of a bloom. It was deep red, reminding him of blood. The colour almost matched the high priest's cap. Dritsek tried not to notice as the older man sniffed at his pale, wiry fingers. There was something distasteful about it, almost sexual. Predatory.

'I am afraid, Dritsek Aargau, the news will not be to your liking. My sources advise me that no word has come from your delegation to the Southern Estates for some days now.' The Premiero's voice was cold and distant, though oddly soothing. Practised and honed.

'Your Eminence,' said Dritsek, trying his best to steer the conversation. 'I have already sent out a party to take stock of them. I expect them any time now.'

'Please, Dritsek,' the priest said. 'We are old acquaintances and quite alone here. You may dispense with the title for now.'

'Of course, Irmao,' Dritsek said, bowing his head out of habit. It was difficult not to show some form of deference even though the two men were almost of an age, though the Premiero affected an air of a man almost twice his cycles. Maybe it was his training in the Misty City, or maybe it was just a way to project his power, he could not be certain.

'Tell me, what will this party find? Have all arrangements been made?' The Premiero stopped once more, this time waiting to hear what the other said.

'It will be as required, Irmao.'

The priest turned to face Dritsek for the first time, his strong dark eyes fixing on his companion. 'It had better. You can afford no errors at this late stage. Positions have been set and all the counters are in place. If you fail now, you will never have another chance. I hope you realise what we place at risk here.' His voice had grown dark and malevolent. It left Lord Aargau with no question of what was at risk—or, rather, *who* was at risk. The threat angered Dritsek and, for a brief moment, he was piqued. *I would do well to swallow that pride here*, he thought. In such circles, emotions could be dangerous. Better to be an insulted fool than an imprisoned one. Or worse.

'We cannot fail in this,' said Dritsek. 'The colonel and his cronies are out of the way. The machine has already been set into motion. Once the news of his removal gets out'—he glanced around as though they might somehow be overheard—'then there will be no other option available. Don't you see? We've already won.' His excitement grew with his confidence. He reached out, intending to take the priest's hand, but found only his arm. Irmao's body stiffened at the touch. Dark, disparaging eyes followed the movement.

'You forget yourself, second son of House Aargau,' said Irmao, snatching his arm away. There was an icy edge of danger to Irmao's voice. It unnerved Dritsek. He bowed his head in supplication.

'I apologise, Premiero, forgive me. I only meant to say—'

'Enough. I've already heard what you have to say. Be careful that your overconfidence will not be your undoing. There is still further to go and much more to be done than you seem to credit, and you cannot even give me confirmation of the smallest part. May I remind you that City-Lord Phaedra still sits in the Palace Tower. I assure you, he will not sit idly by and allow someone else to call himself City-Lord in Doarson while he lives, no matter how frail and weak he might appear. Meanwhile, you have not even completed the simplest step.' The Premiero turned his back on his guest, returning his attention to his beloved flowers.

Dritsek understood. The audience was over. He forced himself into a stiff bow—it would not do to be caught disrespecting the Citadel's second most-powerful man. *The fool can have his flowers and his expansive estates. Just as long as he delivers on his promises.*

It took an age to leave the gardens behind. Yet another affectation. 'All the other House-Lords build towers, but no,' Dritsek mumbled as he walked, 'he has to have sprawling estates. Here, in the Citadel! There will be some big changes one day,' He had to admit, however, they were the most beautiful gardens in the entire region.

A man awaited him beyond the limestone baldachin. Its many gables and pinnacles seemed to loom over him, making a mockery of the city's skyline. Yet another not-so-subtle symbol of power.

'Big changes,' Dritsek mumbled once more.

'My Lord?' the footman asked.

'What now?' Dritsek spat. The man lowered his eyes in deference. *As well he should.* Immediately, he felt better; bigger, almost. At least this man knew his station. He would not dare to dress him down or dismiss him as the Premiero had.

Uncertain of himself, the footman said nothing. He was new.

'For Truth's sake, man, you were sent here for some reason, so deliver it. Deliver it, or must I have it beaten from you?'

'A message, my lord. From Barkathet. I was despatched to inform you directly.'

'Well? What is it?'

'The party has returned and awaits your pleasure, sir.'

Dritsek felt elated. It was the news he had been waiting for. News upon which a great many things depended. And they certainly would be great. All they needed was this small catalyst— the tiniest of sparks that would ignite all of his plans and set the region alight. 'Excellent. At least some good might yet come from the day. Have my carriage brought immediately. I will attend the barracks directly.'

The footman turned quickly on his heels, disappearing through an iron gate. Moments later, he returned and ushered Dritsek into a waiting carriage. The young lord settled back and watched the towers of the Citadel recede into the distance. It would take him the rest of the morning to reach Barkathet—hours of rough and uneven track that would jolt and jar. For once, though, he felt he might actually enjoy the journey. It would be the first of many between the city and the barracks. Only, very soon they would be *his* barracks.

Premiero Irmao watched from a small niche as his guest's carriage drew away. He worried that he had been too stern with the younger man; he had treated him like a boy, but in truth Irmao was only a few cylces senior. Aargau was a hot-head but, with the right hands on the reins, he would be a valuable asset. One that he fully intended to use.

Climbing from his perch, he found himself wiping—or perhaps wringing—his hands. A familiar knot had started to develop in his stomach. He forced himself to clasp his hands behind his back. It was best to project an air of comfortable self-dominance, even when there was no one to see him.

His walk through the gardens was slow and deliberate. Pleasant, certainly, but Irmao knew he was only delaying the inevitable. All too soon, the staged and perfectly manicured terraced gardens slipped past him and he found himself surrounded by tangled scrubland. The plants here were choked out by weeds, and brambles and nettles swelled in great rolling bales. Even the insects seemed fiercer; gone were the happy little bees and butterflies, replaced by wasps and hornets and all manner of biting things. Their very sounds made his skin crawl. It was an area of the gardens that he cared not to visit, and it showed. Still, the Premiero picked his way on, passing across the difficult terrain with an ease of foot that would have eluded most. It might not have been his favourite area of the gardens, but it was one with which he was very familiar. Intimate, even.

An old and decrepit bench waited for him under an even older and mostly dead yew tree. Pausing to compose himself, he sat down with a heavy and resigned sigh. 'Here we are again, old friend,' he said, though his words hardly carried. It mattered not. He didn't even know to whom he spoke, but even in this place it was difficult to let his guard down. An ill wind swept through the handful of branches left on the tree. A smell of decay clung to the breeze. Above, a ragged-looking raven pecked hungrily at a clutch of the vivid red berries that somehow managed to grow on the gnarled yew. Its caw sounded disturbingly like laughter.

The Premiero grimaced as he picked one of the berries, crushing it between his fingers. The sap was sticky against his skin and a sickly sweet odour wrinkled his nose. What had he expected? It was ever the same: always verging on putrid.

There was a flat, smooth stone next to the bench. He touched his sticky fingers to its surface, marvelling at how warm it felt. Almost immediately, the sensation changed. A tingling started in his hand and quickly travelled up his arm and through his entire body. It felt as if his nerves had been set suddenly alight. Each crackled and sizzled and Irmao hung for a taut moment, suspended somewhere between agony and ecstasy. It was not something he enjoyed.

An icy cold descended upon the gloomy garden. Everything but the stone seemed caught in its frosty grip. Irmao found his hand held fast in position, as though fused to the stone. Despite himself, he gasped.

'You are there, my child?' A voice hung in the air, having arisen from some indeterminate place, rustling through branches and rumbling up from the ground all at once. It was an old voice. It rasped and crackled like dried leaves. Still, after all this time, he'd not grown accustomed to the sound.

'I am, my lord, as ever to receive your guidance and wisdom,' the Premiero responded. He bowed his head, touching two fingers to his forehead—an unnecessary sign of subservience.

'Then allow the Glorious Goddess into your heart and speak the truth. Has it begun?'

'It has, my lord,' Irmao responded. He hoped the voice had not noticed the words catch in his throat.

'Excellent. Your endeavours in preparing and coordinating this incident will not go unrewarded, my child,' the voice fizzed gleefully.

'Forgive me, my lord. I ask no reward. To merely serve and further promulgate the greater glory of the Goddess is reward enough for my simple soul.'

'Indeed, you are ever the servant, child.'

Irmao flushed. Had he imagined it, or had the voice emphasised the diminutive? Either way, his spine stiffened and he felt his jaw clench. He was thankful that the link between the two men only transmitted their voices and not an image, like the devices he had seen used elsewhere. 'And what of the king, my lord?' he ventured.

'Do not concern yourself with such matters,' the voice snapped in response, earlier traces of conviviality now lost. 'The king has his own council of advisors, among which we are well placed. Even then, we need only control the flow of information in order to contain the response. You are to ensure that no messengers leave the Citadel with news intended for the king's ears. Station guards on the surrounding roads and have them double the patrols. Detain anybody travelling under forged documents, even if they are produced by our own clerics. Use your man in House Aargau to hold them so as not to arouse suspicion. Do not fail in this, First Child of Doarson.'

'You are as wise as you are Truthful, my lord,' Irmao replied—but the tingling sensation in his hand had already vanished. His audience was over. He was once more alone in the gloomy section of the gardens. He removed his hand, wiping it on his robes. It still felt slightly tacky. He grimaced—whether in response to the dirt on his hands or the recent conversation, it was hard to tell.

Ironic, Premiero Irmao thought, *that lying to the Great Pillar of the Universal Church, Vice Regent and Protector of the Holy Truth, comes so easily.*

Irmao smiled as he emerged back into the brightness of the day, released at last from the dark confines of the old gardens. He felt his hand twitch and he moved once again to wipe away the sap on his robes, but he checked himself in time, instead clasping it firmly behind his back. He felt the warmth of the sun against his skin once again and puffed out his chest a little as he strolled back among the glorious blooms and scents of the flowering terraces. The plan *had* to work. There was little scope for failure. He had staked too much on it to fail; they all had. Yet he had gone further than most, indulging Aargau too much and acquiescing to his foolish whims. He just hoped that the idiot did not overstretch himself, though in truth it was Irmao who had crossed the line. He personally had ordered not one but *two* unspeakable acts, all in the name of Truth. He just hoped that somehow the Goddess would forgive him.

Remain plain and obvious in the eyes of the Goddess. Scheme and plan not, for she is ever-present. Those that plot and obfuscate her holy Truth will forever be blinded from her grace and eternal favour.

—From the Tenets of Truth

CHAPTER FIFTEEN
DRITSEK AARGAU

The barracks of Barkathet

The barracks of Barkathet buzzed in the heat. A hive ready to swarm.

Dritsek's carriage pushed through the main gatehouse. Just short of twenty-five hundred men made their home in Barkathet, but there was space to easily accommodate more than double that number if there was cause to raise the indentured militia. Dritsek felt himself swell. It would all soon be his. With the colonel disposed of, it would be a simple matter for him to assume control. His carriage drew past the neat little buildings that framed the central parade ground, and he paid little attention to the various drills and exercises taking place. A small ball of tension hardened in his stomach. *This is how it will all start to fall in to place,* he thought. *How the second son will reach beyond the constraints of his family and rip what is duly his from under their noses.*

The carriage stopped, snapping him back from his daydreaming. The footman stood ready with the door already open. Dritsek paid him no mind as he descended and stalked off toward the clerk's office. A plain looking man sat waiting within, simply dressed. Everything about him was unremarkable and forgettable. The perfect spy.

'Well?' Dritsek demanded.

'Sir?' The man appeared hesitant, and his face held a moment's reluctance that Dritsek understood as insubordination. The young lord felt his eye twitch, but decided to let it pass. He would not mar this day with anger. A crowd of men stood in lines outside. Dritsek closed the door on them, forcing himself to remain calm.

'Report, then.'

'I returned this afternoon, sir,' the clerk answered. 'Sending straight for you as instructed. I travelled south as far as the river and then made my way towards the Southern Estates. I found the bodies on the road almost two days short of the Southern Estates, near to House-Lord Wolden's lands.'

'Bodies, you say? How many? Did you count them? Could you identify them?'

'Nine, sir, and yes, I was able to identify some. Captain Susurro, for one...' The man trailed off, giving weight to the name he had just delivered. He seemed momentarily unsure of the information he was providing, but whether it was because he had reason to disbelieve his own words or because he feared his employer's reaction, Dritsek could not tell. 'And Sergeants Annahr and Zubana,' the man finished.

'What? That's all? Who else?' Dritsek countered, hardly able to contain himself. 'There were more. You said so. More bodies, for Truth's sake. Who were they?'

'Sir, they had been dead for a while. I couldn't be certain.'

The man's stupidity was starting to annoy Dritsek. *How could he not know? He was sent with one task!*

'Who else was there? What about Sentenza? Did you not find him?' Agitation edged its way into the intermediary officer's voice. It took a great deal of concentration to not bellow at the man.

'Sir, the bodies had been found by animals before I got there; some were half eaten and the rest were so bloated by gas that they were difficult to recognise. I was able to find identification tokens on three of the bodies.' He reached into a pocket and produced several wooden discs, each dyed green and imprinted with the details of the dead soldiers. 'If the colonel was there, sir, he too must have been killed and no doubt his was one of those bodies that was mauled.' He placed the wooden coins on the desk one at a time, facing up so that the details of each could be seen. 'I guess that his token was somehow lost in the attack or was possibly eaten some time afterwards. I found only these and this one other.' He finished by placing a final broken and chewed disc down on the table. Both the dye and the imprint had been chipped away, leaving little to indicate what had once been etched upon its face. His report finished, the man came back to attention, his body tensing into an almost unnaturally straight posture and freezing there as he waited to be dismissed.

Dritsek slumped, his eyes transfixed on the tokens arranged in front of him. He was unsure whether to scream or laugh. *Even in death, the fucker mocks me*, he thought. *Is he even dead? He must be—surely he must be. He would have been back by now if not.* A noise, or the feeling of a noise, reminded him that the clerk was still stood to attention opposite him. 'Get out,' he snapped without ceremony. His hand moved across his brow as if it could wipe away the ache that was quickly forming there. He did not look up as the man left, instead choosing to close his eyes and focus on breathing slow, deliberate breaths. A knock came at the door. He filled his lungs deeply, holding them full and taut for a long moment. The room was silent again. If he could just stay as he was now, not even the sound of his own breathing to interrupt him... The knock came again, loud as a battering ram. He exhaled.

'What now?!' he shouted at the door. Had the man remembered some vital titbit of information? Was the colonel dead after all? Or—and at this Dritsek felt cool fingers coil round his spine—was Sentenza back, waiting behind the door wearing that derisive smile of his?

The door opened and a flush-faced private saluted badly before stammering, 'Sir, they sent me to find you. It's the hand, sir, and Adherent Al-Eldar. He's back and they're not, sir. Dead, all of them.'

The healing rooms of the barracks were old and tired. They had not been used in many cycles, and Dritsek wasn't even sure whether there were any Church healers here to run them. He guessed not. The most any injured man could hope for here was a butcher or a vet.

A man sat on a bench, two aproned soldiers fussing over him like whores around a cock. They stood to attention upon seeing the intermediary officer enter. One of them made to speak but Dritsek raised a hand, cutting him short. He eyed the man on the bench: Al-Eldar. He didn't appear injured in the slightest. Dishevelled and road-weary, but definitely not injured.

'My Lord, it was terrible,' the adherent began. His voice was dry and hard, wrung of all moisture. The priest was milking it, Dritsek knew. He looked to one of the soldiers, who immediately scampered away to bring refreshments. It gave Dritsek some short time to appraise things.

'What happened, my friend?' asked Dritsek smoothly. The adherent met his eyes, cool dark pools that first seemed devoid of life, but suddenly were touched by a slight brightness. *He enjoys this*, thought Dritsek. *It's as though he's an actor and we, his audience. This is a dangerous man.*

'The people were full of filth and depravity,' the cleric started, a thick film of white spittle forming about his lips, his earlier show of hoarseness forgotten. 'Even as we first arrived they had, all of them, gathered together in false worship. They called on idols and made offerings in the name of the perverse and the improper. They cast totems into a great fire as if summoning from the after-world, calling on the power of heathen deities and false gods. They scratched the clothes from their own backs and threw these too into the inferno before offering their nakedness to these impious fallacies. Then they stood, unclothed and impure in direct violation of the Goddess, as if to mock her and spit on her altar. Their lust and wickedness was as clear in their eyes as in those of a rapist.'

The officer had returned with the drinks and now stood, duty forgotten, gaping. Dritsek scowled at him before snatching a cup for himself and offering another to Al-Eldar, who took it eagerly.

'Continue. What happened with the finger? Did you receive any word from Colonel Sentenza?' Dritsek asked.

'What?' the adherent responded, spraying wine from his lips as he did so. 'We received no word from anyone. We were alone in that vipers' den. It was Pioneer Sergeant Braga who undid us. I counselled him to advance the hand onwards that very minute.

Instead, he ordered our withdrawal back to the camp, even as the apostates writhed naked and sinfully, neighbour against neighbour, husband against sister-in-law and worse. Then the pioneer sergeant rode in with only Sergeant Joyne to meet the heathen. We waited until well after the sun had reached its zenith but, when they did not return, I mobilised the rest of the hand and entered the town.' He paused for another drink and the two soldiers leaned forward, hanging on the man's every word.

He's every bit the showman, thought Dritsek.

'The town was eerie. Eddies of wind whipped up dirt from the road as we filed into the town. Little did we know that each step was designed to draw us on to our doom. That must have been the object of their prayer the previous night: that dark and evil forces rise up against us. Like idiots, we marched ourselves to the very core of the town, only for them to spring their trap.' He looked at each of the listening men, wiping his mouth with the back of his hand, then launched off again into his story, only this time his voice was sterner, louder than before. 'The doors to the town hall were flung open and armed men appeared. Taken by surprise, we turned and rushed to form ranks, but from the side streets and the myriad alleys that linked the rat-runs of the town, more men sallied forth, trapping us where we stood. There was little room to manoeuvre into fighting order and even if we had, we had but half the men they did. They made short work in cutting us down, blood soaking into the dry dirt about our feet.'

Dritsek felt that the man had overdone it with this last unnecessary piece of imagery, but a quick look to the two soldiers revealed faces both disgusted and engrossed. 'You two,' he said, 'leave us. I need to speak to the adherent alone.' He waited for the men to leave and close the door behind them and then stood quietly, taking in the image of the man before him.

'Such a terrible incident. You must have been both very unfortunate to have been party to such things and yet so incredibly fortunate to be reciting your tale here to us today.'

The adherent made no reply, instead fixing his gaze upon Dritsek.

'I am very aware, adherent, that you must be the Premiero's man,' Dritsek continued, heavily emphasising the man's title. 'In fact, by strange coincidence, I arrive here straight from an audience with him.' Dritsek was gambling, he knew, but he recognised the slight twitch in the man's eyes at his words.

'I am adherent to these barracks, Intermediary Officer Dritsek. I am as ever the Church's man.' Al-Eldar nodded his head. *Mock reverence*, Dritsek thought.

'And in Doarson and the Citadel, Irmao *is* the Church,' Dritsek finished for him. 'What is the next move in this game? The City-Lord's council will not just stand back and do nothing. There must be reprisals; the town must be secured...'

'The town will be secured, my lord. I have, in fact, already secured it. There is no threat left in Baile Soar any more than there is here in this very barracks, and to ensure ongoing security I suggest we send a further hand of men to stand guard there. Rest assured, my lord, that only the information *we want* will be coming from the town.'

Dritsek looked at the man, incredulous at his boldness, but decided to say nothing.

'Colonel Sentenza will mobilise the rest of the barracks and man the city defences against this unprecedented threat,' the adherent continued. 'You as intermediary officer will provide the order. He would not be so bold as to refuse an order with the strength of House Aargau behind it.'

'Colonel Sentenza will do no such thing,' said Dritsek, a gleam appearing in his eye. 'I am afraid I too have some terrible news.' Now it was the adherent's turn to look at his opposite with a sly expectancy. 'Colonel Sentenza was killed in a terrible ambush by a ragtime band of rebels and deserters while on his way to or from the Southern Estates, we cannot be sure which.' Here Dritsek took his turn bearing the mantle of showman, pausing for effect and taking the cup from the adherent's hand before finishing his wine for him. 'So, as you will understand, that leaves the barracks under the total control of... well, me.'

The adherent silently raised an eyebrow. Pleased with himself, Dritsek smiled widely.

By the next day, the barracks had erupted. Intermediary Officer Aargau delivered the sombre news detailing the unfortunate demise of the finger that included both Captain Susurro and Colonel Sentenza to a packed parade ground shortly after daybreak. Adherent Al-Eldar then delivered the even more sobering news of the massacre at Baile Soar, leaving nothing—neither the awfulness of the scene or the cunning and bravery of his own escape—to the men's imaginations. If the gathered troops had been near to rowdy in their indignation at the deaths of the two highest-ranked officers stationed at the barracks, Dritsek had not been prepared for how loud and desolate the silence that followed would seem when Al-Eldar concluded his second announcement. Even the wind appeared to stop blowing, as if the Goddess herself was holding her breath. The silence finally was broken by the sound of a solitary voice, distant on the parade ground. Strong and smooth, it sang a song at once mournful and yet triumphant. It called on the Goddess to guard the brave young souls as they marched on through the skies, to guide them through their everlasting battle, to shelter them in her glory and pay honour to them with their song. The words hung on the air without seeming to dissipate, until at last the gate horn blasted twice, cutting through the unending note and sounding the opening of the gate for the spirits of the fallen. None wanted them trapped among the living.

'It is with a sad and grieving heart that I must enact the constitution and declare myself intermediary commissioner at this tumultuous time,' Dritsek announced in the silence, bowing his head slightly to the assembled men. He touched two fingers to his forehead, his lips, and his chest, and then turned and made his way from the parade ground. In the near distance behind him, he could hear the men being dismissed and the thunderous response of feet marching. Al-Eldar joined him as he walked to the carriage that awaited him. Climbing its steps, Dritsek paused before sitting, the footman waiting to close the door behind him. 'Adherent, I met a man last night in my office who did me a service in bringing me some news.'

'Yes, my lord?'

'You will find him and show him my... gratitude.'

'My Lord?' said Al-Eldar.

'He must not be allowed to speak of the meeting nor of its contents to anyone. If he has spoken to anyone, then they too must be silenced.'

'Of course.' The adherent responded with a bow, touching his fingers to his ear. 'May you only hear Truth, my lord.'

The footman closed the door and Dritsek took his seat. The carriage-man spurred the horses and Dritsek Maldosu, second son of House Aargau and now self-appointed intermediary commissioner of Barkathet Barracks, smiled to himself. He had come to receive some information and, though it may not have been quite as definitive as he would have liked, he was leaving with enough power to bring a city to its knees. *Premiero Irmao himself could not have foreseen this course of events*, he mused. *Even he must take note of me now.*

Even in times of difficulty, hide not from the Truth. Turn your face with light and optimism towards it. Those who hide away in the shadows of lies turn their backs on the Goddess and shall be forever removed from her presence.

—**From the Tenets of Truth**

CHAPTER SIXTEEN
BRAGA, MAYOR PREFEITO, AND TERVAN

The road to Barkathet

The small company made slow time toward the barracks. Yet even at their sedentary pace, Braga was happy to be putting some distance between them and the grisly sights they had seen at Baile Saor. The old bear had been a fighter before he could walk and a soldier before he could talk, or so he had been told. He had risen through the ranks by giving his blood and sweat to the dust beneath his feet in the name of the Goddess, the king, the Church, or whatever House-Lord or City-Lord had paid for his services. He had known battles and he had seen death; he had put many to the sword in subduing rebellious estates; he had whipped a chain-gang of thieves, murderers, dissidents, and even just free-thinkers till their backs were little more than pulp. But he had not before seen such wanton carnage as he had in that town. Had he not seen it himself, he would have denied its possibility. It was one thing for the townspeople to have been massacred—a simple command to his men would have seen to that easily enough. But to eliminate a group of well-trained and well-armoured professionals, leaving no trace but their corpses? Braga shuddered. He would weep if he were not a soldier, if he did not feel responsible.

The three road-weary men—Braga, Mayor Prefeito, and the wandering tinker who'd finally given his name as Tervan—had taken a short pause, seeking shade from the hottest part of the day. Braga looked over his shoulder, shielding his eyes from the dazzling sunlight, and assessed his companions. The mayor was a poor rider, but he understood the need for good husbandry and he took care watering and feeding his mount. *A good job too*, Braga thought to himself. They all needed to keep busy.

Picking up the tinker had added considerable strain to their journey and, although he switched between the two horses, his added weight meant they were travelling far more slowly than the big man cared for. On top of this, they were eating through their rations too quickly, and had to supplement them whenever they could, sometimes stealing from estate lands as they passed through. Even the mayor's lamentations, intense and heartfelt to begin with, had withered away. Now he was silent, his words having evaporated in the oppressive heat alongside his energy.

Images plagued Braga. He saw again and again the twisted and torn faces of his men, their butchered and roasted bodies. The tinker proved an invaluable distraction. He was no longer a threat as far as Braga was concerned, but he was certainly a conundrum. They had wasted almost an entire day searching for the tinker's camp and papers—a deliberate ruse, Braga suspected, designed to lead them away from something. Either way, the captain would get all the answers they needed once they were safely back at the barracks.

Braga walked to where the tinker sat. Although he was for all intents and purposes their prisoner, there had been no need to bind the man; he travelled with them willingly, even eagerly at first as if he too wanted to be away from the place. Maybe the talk of slaughter was reason enough to want to move on; Braga could hardly blame him for that.

'Drink,' Braga said, holding out a canteen.

Tervan remained silent, just looking up at Braga, his hand covering his eyes from the glare of the sun as if expecting Braga to say something more. Eventually, he moved his hand from his face and took the canteen, taking a draught.

'You look tired,' Tervan said.

'Tired!' Braga half-laughed, half-barked the word.

Somehow, he wanted to say more to the man—he could hear the invitation in the man's voice and, strangely, he could almost hear the words flowing from his own mouth in response. He bit his tongue and took back the canteen before turning away and striding back to his horse. *Tired, he says. Of course I'm tired. Tired of all this talking*, the big man thought to himself. *He sits there expecting conversation at a time like this. I should tell him. I should shout it in his smug face.*

Decision made, the pioneer sergeant stopped in his tracks. He turned sharply and strode back the few paces to where the stranger sat, still smiling up almost hopefully.

'Yes, I am tired,' said Braga in a dangerous growl. He turned back on his heels and stalked away from the man.

The following morning seemed much brighter; the air lighter

and easier to breathe. Braga was happy to have cleared the air. He was happy too as an old familiar mark in the distance grew steadily, looming into view. It was all Braga could do to resist forcing the horses into a gallop. They were nearly there. Nearly home. Only, *they* were not. Only *he* was returning. The largest loss of men in his memory, and all on his watch! Suddenly, he no longer felt like racing to get there.

The three travellers continued towards the western gate of the barracks and by mid-afternoon Braga could see that the barracks was on high alert. There were more sentries posted around the perimeter than usual and many wooden carts could be seen drawing up to the gates before dishevelled-looking peasants dismounted and were quickly marched inside. It seemed like the forces stationed at the barracks were being strengthened from the estates. Were they raising the militia?

Braga brought his horse to a stop, the mayor and Tervan coming up alongside him.

'What is it?' asked the mayor.

Braga grunted in response.

'Is it trouble?' asked Tervan.

'I don't know. Something isn't right. It's...' Braga cut himself short, silently reprimanding himself. *What is it about this man? How does he loosen my tongue so?*

Two figures struck out at pace from the barracks to intercept them. They had been spotted.

'Do we run for it? asked the mayor.

'If we do, they will come after us with more than just two men,' reasoned Tervan.

'What then? What are you going to do? Are we safe? We are surely safe—we haven't done anything wrong,' said the mayor, the panic clear in his voice.

'Just be calm,' responded Tervan and, strangely, the mayor did exactly that, visibly relaxing at the simple instruction.

The two soldiers from the barracks covered the distance in very little time, pushing their horses hard. There was certainly something wrong—both men had their swords drawn. Braga was suddenly more concerned. What was going on?

One of the soldiers recognised the pioneer sergeant, though Braga could not return the courtesy. He sheathed his sword and leapt from his saddle, bounding over to Braga and grinning broadly.

'Pioneer Sergeant Braga! It *is* you. I cannot begin to say how relieved I am.' The man looked to his companion, who seemed more cautious, though he too sheathed his weapon.

There was something familiar about the first man's face, but Braga could not find his name. He nodded a curt greeting.

'The name is Ajuda, sir,' the man said, still grinning. 'But tell me, sir, how did you manage to escape the massacre? We were told that everyone was lost except the captain-adherent, Al-Eldar. He told us how he hid among the bodies, sir, and escaped that way. Did you do that too?'

The words rung in Braga's head. Al-Eldar—alive? It couldn't be. Surely no one could have escaped Baile Saor. The whole town and his hand wiped out except for one priest? It didn't make sense.

'Who?' asked Braga slowly, not wanting to believe what he had heard.

'Captain-Adherent Al-Eldar. He thought he had been the only man to escape from the town's rebellion, sir. He and Intermediary Commissioner Aargau are raising the militia to protect against the town of Baile Soar and resist all forces hostile to the City-Lord.'

The mayor gave a half-incredulous, half-hysterical cry. 'What?

Town's rebellion?'

'That's what they are calling it,' the man said. His words came quickly, almost tumbling over each other in their eagerness to be out in the open. 'The captain-adherent reported that our forces were overpowered'—he turned to Braga—'including you, sir. We must inform them straight away of this good news.'

Braga's blood froze in his veins at the young soldier's words and he shot a look to the mayor for him to hold his tongue. He was unsure whether the man understood the meaning, but Tervan gave his riding companion a sharp shove in the ribs. The mayor frowned but remained silent.

Braga needed time to think. Too many things were new and shocking to his ears. *Captain-adherent? Intermediary commissioner?* He had never even heard of such positions. Now this, a massacre led by the townspeople, all of whom lay dead, their bodies heaped and burning in the gutted hall. What happened in Baile Saor that day? Could the townspeople have first overpowered the hand and then put them to the spike, before themselves being wiped out? By whom? It was all too much to take in. He needed to seek the advice and comfort of trusted allies. 'Where's the colonel?'

The man's face fell. 'I'm sorry, sir,' he said quietly, 'Colonel Sentenza and the captain were both lost when the finger they led was ambushed almost five days ago.'

Braga felt the wind ripped from him. It couldn't be true. He must have been imagining things. The heat of the day and the intensity of recent events. Had he banged his head somewhere?

'Let me take you and your friends back to the barracks, sir,' the soldier said, brightening once again, 'and we can get you some food and some rest.'

'No,' said Braga, sharply. 'Tell no one. I have things to do.'

The man frowned and seemed about to argue, but after one

look at Braga's face he closed his mouth, nodded to his companion, and mounted his horse.

For a moment, it was all that Braga could do to sit and watch the two soldiers canter back to the barracks. Thoughts floated dimly around his head, echoes of ideas and fears swaddling all external noise. The adherent had known that he and the mayor had followed Dreban into the tunnel, yet he had reported him dead. Was it possible he had simply been mistaken and in the confusion of whatever had happened to the hand he'd assumed Braga dead? Yet the more he thought on this, the less it made sense. He walked through the scenes of carnage in his head. The faces distorted in agony. The stench of the burning bodies. The skewered meaty corpses. The soldier said Al-Eldar had hidden among the bodies, but there had been no bodies on the ground. All the dead had either been impaled on wooden spikes or piled and burned in the hall. No. It did not add up.

Braga glanced at his companions. 'We need to go,' he said, his voice sounding distant and foreign in his ears. He knew that they would not be safe in a place where lies and misdirection seemed to be taking hold already. It was unlikely that the two soldiers would keep their silence for long. No, the safest option was to be swiftly on their way.

'Come,' said Braga, bringing his horse around and passing his companions. His mind now set, he felt all action. Gone was the self-doubt and self-interrogation of earlier. Now he had a puzzle to solve and a mission to carry out.

'What are you doing?' the mayor snapped, face red and swollen. 'You great fool! What is going on?'

Braga did not pause. He touched his foot to his mount and spurred it on.

'To get answers,' he called without turning back.

Weep not for the dead, for they have returned home to the Goddess,
who, just as a mother might welcome back a child to her bosom, so
too does the Goddess welcome her children back into her care.

—From the Tenets of Truth

CHAPTER SEVENTEEN
SENTENZA

The Citadel

Light lurked in this place as though embarrassed to be there. The
Last Light Tavern was little more than a room in a crumbling
section of the old fort, set high on the cliff in the western-most
part of the Citadel. It was a hovel only ever visited by disreputable
types, and even they came infrequently. Ironic that a once proud
martial building serviced only those wanting to stay hidden from
the watchful eyes of the city guards. Now only the eyes of whores
and vagabonds peered from the dark corners of the barroom—and,
of course, those of the dishevelled-looking Colonel Sentenza.

He sat away from the main entrance, well clear of the room's
only window and dashing distance from a half-hidden serving
hatch. A dozen or so tables lay between him and anybody who

might happen into the place, and then there was the added security of the tavern owner being an old friend of his from what now felt like a former life.

A group of men sat nearby were drinking and playing some card game that he was not familiar with. Another sat smoking a pipe on his own, as he had been doing since before Sentenza arrived. No one had so much as looked at him since he entered except for the boy who had been sent to mind the bar. He had since disappeared with an order for food and brandy, a tiny hand clasped around Sentenza's coin. Sentenza wondered whether either the order or the boy would make it back.

A thin and frail-looking man eventually emerged from the doorway on the room's far side, a clay jug and cup balanced in one hand and a bowl of food and wooden spoon in the other. He placed them down in front of Sentenza.

'You better eat this,' the man said. 'You look like shit and you don't smell much better.' Kuljet had never been a big man—wiry and wily was a more apt description—and now the cycles had begun to take their toll. Lines creased his face and tugged at eyes as alive as ever, the youngest thing about him, glittering pools that darted like rabbits about the room, never seeming to miss a thing.

Sentenza smiled at the old smuggler. It had been too long—he'd not seen him since the colonel had brought him in for profiteering and selling moonshine. Surely he'd have forgiven him for that by now.

'You're not looking so spry yourself, Kuljet.' Sentenza snatched the bowl and spoon with a wink and began to eagerly shovel the rich, potato-filled broth into his mouth. Kuljet grinned before placing a cup down and filling it with a strong-smelling ruby-red brandy that promised sweetness and warmth. The colonel took a long and satisfying gulp before returning to the broth with a happy slapping of his lips.

'It's been a long time,' Kuljet said as he watched the other man eat. 'I know that you must be in some serious trouble if you find the time to remember your old friend Kuljet.'

Sentenza scooped up the last of the potato, using a grubby finger to help the morsel onto the spoon. He kept his eyes on the old man's face.

'And you do remember old Kuljet, don't you?' the elderly man continued. 'Yes, yes, of course you do. I can see it in your happy smile now that you have eaten. I thought you had forgotten me, it has been so long. And of course, I remember you. Yes, I am not so old that I could have forgotten my old friend Sentenza. How could I forget the happy fisherman who saved me and then sold me as a slave to our mother Church?'

Kuljet leaned closer, his bright eyes seeming to bore into Sentenza.

'Oh, what? You think that unfair of me?' he went on. 'Yes, you do, I can see it in your eyes. And all for what, do you recall? A pittance, a meagre living scratched out here among the thieves and whores, a trouble to no one. Certainly no reason to spend more than a cycle hunting me and setting me up. Do you know how much I have to do for the Church these days? There isn't a month that goes by that a priest doesn't arrive with more jobs for old Kuljet.'

Sentenza swallowed, the smooth liquid burning in his throat, and slowly lowered his cup to the table. He knew that he could easily deal with the man across the table from him, if it came to it. In fact, he was already feeling the presence of magical energy, searching it out, ready to form and bend it at a moment's notice. It would be nothing for him to use that power to strike out at the old smuggler, and at such a close range (taking into account the apparent frailty of the man) it could quite possibly kill him, even if he did not concentrate the strike on one of the body's weak spots. He glanced quickly around the room, trying not to let his eyes move too much lest he alert the Kuljet of his concern. He had hoped that he would be able to rely on his old acquaintance for help. It seemed a foolhardy idea now.

'I could have had you sent off to the labour camps like any other criminal, if that's what you'd have preferred,' Sentenza said. No one around them seemed to be taking any interest in their squabbling, and he was sure that they would not stir, even if he were to kill the man right here and now. 'In fact, I'm sure it's not too late, if that's what you want.'

For a moment, the man said nothing, instead taking on an impassive look and fixing him with a cold stare.

It's now or never, Sentenza thought.

Then, as if reading Sentenza's intent, the older man's dispassionate face opened suddenly up into a broad smile that pulled his eyes into dark and narrow pinholes.

'Ha!' he said with a throaty chuckle, 'I've little doubt you would do exactly that to an old man, you dog. You're more of a crook than I ever was. Come, let me have a drink with you, my old friend.'

Sentenza sighed a short breath. He'd been enjoying sitting and eating in relative comfort—and at an actual table no less! He certainly had not relished the idea of having to take flight once more, and certainly not so soon. He laughed: a short, honest bark, relief washing over him.

'You stupid old fool,' he exclaimed, 'do you know I could have killed you?' The light-heartedness of his tone and the moment washed away any venom his words might have held.

Kuljet fetched another cup and filled both his and Sentenza's with more of the thick, pungent brandy.

'Now, what can an old friend do for you?' the old tavern man asked once their mirth had subsided.

'There is some trouble,' Sentenza said, taking another sip of brandy, 'and I need your help.'

The old man rolled his eyes. 'Well, of course you do, or you would not have come to see old Kuljet, would you?'

'I need information. I need everything you can get me on House Aargau, and I need to know where this came from.' He plucked up his saddle roll from the sawdust-covered floor, placing it down on the table and unwrapping it to reveal the bodkin head he'd picked up after the ambush.

Kuljet looked in silence at the metal fixing for what seemed like a long time, scratching at its engraved markings before rocking back slightly and offering a short guffaw. 'Ha! You don't ask for much,' he said. 'I don't know who you think I am, my friend. Smuggling information is very different to smuggling alcohol.'

'Not to you it's not,' Sentenza said dryly. 'You have all of the connections. You even have contacts in the Church here in Doarson, for Truth's sake.'

'The last I remember, you were pretty well-connected to the Church yourself, my friend, and I doubt that you would not have a well-placed man or three about the city as well.'

'Yeah, well, it would seem not, *my friend*. Someone set me and my team up, and that kind of thing can only be done with the knowledge of someone at a high level. I need to find out who and why. I can't get back to the barracks without drawing too much attention to myself, and I don't know who I can trust in the Church in Doarson. That's why I need you.'

His position laid out, Sentenza sat back. He only hoped he had not misjudged the smuggler's affection for him—Kuljet had ever been a cautious old fox. There was silence for a time as the barman considered. He took a final drink from his cup, draining it before setting it back down on the table.

'My friend,' he said, 'you come to me with this all too late, it seems. You are already in too deep for old Kuljet to help you.'

A shadow moved in the tavern, drawing Sentenza's attention. Two men had appeared at the other side of the room, blocking out whatever light still crept through the window.

'I'm sorry, old friend,' Kuljet whispered. 'As I said, you come to me with this all too late.'

Sentenza tensed, reaching for magic, but Kuljet shook his head slightly, looking first into his eyes and then quickly glancing to the hidden serving hatch. Without any further word, Kuljet turned, spreading his arms wide and welcoming the two newcomers with loud shouts.

Sentenza took his cue and dived quickly, hoping that he could either get to the hatch without being seen or that the old man could delay them for long enough for him to get outside. He reached out with his Wielding, pushing the hatch open before his body reached it and allowing him to pass through seamlessly. The hatch slammed shut.

He was surprised to find himself in a dark and bare room. Grime and dust covered the floor and the only window was blocked, leaving nothing but shadows and a tense air of foreboding. It was hard to see and harder still to get his bearings. He had a sinking feeling that the room had no other door. He would be trapped in here with those two men outside. Oddly, there was no noise coming from the tavern. No yelling or commotion. Had he been jumping at shadows?

A noise from the darkness drew his attention—it was like a foot dragging across bare stone. He spun, readying himself to fight. A faint whistle and a pop sounded from the blackness, and he felt a chill spread through him. A small glow appeared in the corner of the room, a tiny bead of light. It offered little illumination but, just as he'd expected—just as he'd observed before—the glow grew quickly into a flame that appeared to be held in the pinch of a man's fingers. It bloomed red and yellow, casting ghostly shadows back and forth like spirits dancing in twilight, before the hand touched it to the taper of a lamp. The flame settled and spread its light about the room. A thin grey hand, with fingers that Sentenza knew had to avoid the heat of the flame, withdrew quickly from the lamp and disappeared into the sleeves of a black robe. It belonged to a pale and gaunt-looking man with drawn and ageing features deepened by the warm glow of the lamp. A lizard basking in the sun.

Sentenza knew the face well.

'The light of Truth be on you, my child,' the old man said. His voice was unexpectedly shrill; it trilled in the air like birdsong, completely at odds with his decrepit appearance.

Sentenza crossed the floor to the old man and knelt before him. His old teacher reached out and touched him lightly on his bowed head and, as the hand withdrew, Sentenza caught sight of the strange fire-tube that he understood to be the source of the magical flame. There was none of the usual tingling of magic in the air, not even a crackle. This, Sentenza thought, had always been the most disconcerting thing about the man. The thing that scared Sentenza the most.

'Eminence Sakani... What are you doing here?' Sentenza said, his head bowed.

'Not who you expected?' Golya Sakani asked, almost reproachfully. 'It appears that you retreat here looking for answers when you do not even know the questions.'

Even standing, the old man was a great deal shorter than Sentenza, yet the colonel still felt like a child being chastised.

'Eminence, I am here to resolve who is conspiring to kill me. I—'

'I am fully aware of these things, Sentenza,' Sakani said. 'I seem fully able to recall, however, that you receive your orders from the holy Truth, and not from some flight of fancy of your own—a fact that you seem to have lost sight of these past days. I may be an old man, but it appears my memory is much sharper than yours.'

'Yes, Eminence. However, I cannot complete this task whilst someone is trying—'

'You need not immediately concern yourself with these things.' There was a moment of uncomfortable silence. Finally, Sakani took a step forwards. 'I am aware that you provided Kuljet with an arrowhead that you say was used to attack you. He in turn will leave it with me, and I shall make my own inquiries. You will continue with the task I left you with some cycles ago—a task that remains incomplete, might I remind you. Tell me, what did you discover in the Southern Estates?'

The question took Sentenza off guard. How had his former teacher known about that? He assumed that Dritsek Aargau had engineered that mission as a way to set him up for an ambush. Could it have been Sakani all along?

'Do not worry unnecessarily. If I wanted you dead, Colonel, I would have summoned you to Togat Bai myself and told you as I executed you.' Sakani gave a slight chuckle, the sound like a drowning man's last gasp. Not for the first time, Sentenza wondered whether the old priest wasn't a Cognator after all. Surely the old man would need contact to use mind magic, and he would feel the tingle in his bones—but, then again, he never felt that flame wand of his. 'It wasn't my men that met you on the road. That is but a trifle,' Sakani continued. 'I am more interested in what you found at the estates.'

It seemed that the old man had spies everywhere, keeping an eye on Sentenza even though he had been the priest's sworn man since his testing in the Misty City. He probably had just as many hidden eyes at the barracks. Still, Sentenza knew Sakani's statement to be true. If the old priest had felt the need for it, he could have easily summoned him to the Misty City and dispatched him there himself. It would have been a trivial matter to engineer some story to conceal the deed. Sentenza knew there were many darker things than routine murders hidden within those mists.

'We found nothing, your Eminence,' Sentenza finally responded, fearing he had given away too much already.

'Nothing, you say?' echoed Sakani, his tone both admonishing and accusatory. 'No heretics? No stories of miraculous healings? Come now, Colonel, I might be old and frail, but I am not senile and blind.'

The old man's watery eyes stared unblinkingly at Sentenza. Again, he found himself wondering if the priest could see directly into his mind.

'Half-baked stories from the minds of the ravaged and tormented. Sick people getting well again, that's all—there's no mystery in that.' His voice carried a confidence he did not entirely feel. 'And as for heretics, just goodwives and wanderers. Gypsies and tinkers trying to sell trinkets and fake heirlooms. Nurse maids sharing brews. If I had come across them, I would have had them pilloried for not submitting their tithes and left it at that, I assure you. Petty crimes and nonsense. The Estate-Lords in the south simply work the peasants too hard, your Eminence. Nothing more.'

'Then you must continue your search, my child,' the old man said dryly, after a momentary silence during which he seemed to consider the report. 'In the meantime, however, there are other matters here. Matters, which I might add, you should have been able to control.' Again, Sentenza felt abashed at the old man's admonishment. 'There are some, even within the Church, that overreach themselves and fall away from the Truth,' Sakani said. 'A fog is forming in Doarson and, given time, all of Lacustria may be consumed by it. I have long held my suspicions, and I fear that things have possibly escalated even beyond our grasp now.' The old man trailed off, his gaze drawn into the near distance and lost momentarily within the orange-tinged lamplight. 'I sent a young man on an errand and now I fear we may have lost him,' he finally said.

Why does this sound familiar? Sentenza thought.

'A young man who you were to have retrieved for me. Instead, I find you have been gallivanting around the countryside,' Sakani continued, more force and conviction in his voice now. He fixed the younger man with a reproachful glare, as if the blame were all his. 'Now matters are worse and my initial fears have been vindicated. Many have lost their lives already, and this will not be the end of it. There are those who will see this as a chance to strike out for power. Our holy Truth that I love and serve is being subverted by lies and misdirection.' His last comment was made much more matter-of-factly, as if he had once again steeled himself. It seemed strange to Sentenza that his old mentor should be acting in such an uncharacteristically sentimental manner. What was a single young priest? When he had known Sakani, he had been a hard and brutal master, not prone to regretful remembrances or concern over the welfare of initiates. Sentenza had himself been sent out on his master's instruction to strong-arm people over debts owed to the Church or even to Sakani himself, and it was not uncommon for him to settle a petty grudge or slight by use of violence.

Maybe he has grown soft in his old age, Sentenza thought, before recalling the last instruction he had carried out on his old master's behalf: the hunt for Old Ballir. This mission had ended with the deaths of two men and the certain ruin of a family. He had meant to collect a debt: the Golya's, not his. To return a girl and keep an old promise. Only he had been too late and found her gone. Reported her dead. Killed by raiders, along with the rest of the family. Though he knew this to be a lie. So too, he suspected, did Sakani. Sentenza had never truly stopped looking for the girl, still hoping he might still find her. And discover the power he sensed that fateful day at Ballir's farm. So too, he suspected, did Sakani. Still slightly fearful that the old man *could* read his thoughts, he focused his mind on other things.

'You will put an end to this charade—cowering in the shadows like some milksop—and find this young man, if he is still alive,' Sakani said, 'and you will see that he is reunited with the Church. I owe it as a favour to an old friend.'

'Yes, Eminence,' Sentenza replied, knowing full well that both 'Church' and 'old friend' meant Sakani himself in this context. Strangely, he felt a momentary and unexplained pang of jealousy. As soon as he had the chance, he needed to find Braga and the boy. Then he'd see why Sakani was so interested in him.

Be ever watchful. Search for the hand of the Goddess in all things and be thankful of her touch, for there is no place where She does not preside, no act that She does not see, and no heart in which She does not live. For as the shepherd tends to his flock, so the Goddess will tend to Hers, guiding and guarding them from the wicked forces in the world and those who might turn them from her righteous path.

—From the Tenets of Truth

CHAPTER EIGHTEEN
SOLATTA AND DREBAN

The road from Baile Saor

Dreban writhed. Each time Solatta dared think he'd turned a corner, he'd take a turn for the worse. Every time she gave him one of her tonics too, no matter which type. Tonics with herbs, with spices, with berries, with honey... they all seemed to make him scream. Well, not all, she thought sourly. Plain boiled water and ordinary teas he seemed to drink just fine. It was just those that took *effort*.

'Ungrateful,' she scolded him, 'That's all it is. You're almost as stubborn as...' but the words trailed off.

'*Why have you left me?*'

The words were not hers, though they gave voice to her thoughts. It was the man again. He'd called out for someone several times now, his body thrashing in his fitful sleep. A mother? A lover? She knew not which. *Kareti*—a woman, at least. She took a cloth and mopped his brow.

'You're all alone,' she soothed, 'just like I am. Two lost fools, lonely but for each other.' He seemed to calm at her words. As did she. He was her responsibility now; there was no time to fret.

He had a kind face, she decided. Not exactly attractive, but he had full lips that looked like they would find smiling easy. She found herself staring at them before lightly brushing them with her cloth. His eyes flicked open. Pale blue. The flash of a clear winter's sky. She jumped back, suddenly flushed and flustered. What was she thinking? But they closed as quickly as they'd opened. She straightened herself, fixing her skirts and mopping at her neck and cheeks.

'What nonsense,' she scolded herself. 'If Tervan were here...'

But, of course, he wasn't. She was alone with nothing but a sick man and ghosts. She felt suddenly cold and empty. Nights were always the worst. Her dreams these past nights had been full of pain and fire and faces—some she'd seen in the town, some she'd imagined. His face. Tervan leaping through flames, their tongues lapping around him. She tried not to sleep. She drank teas to keep her awake, willing dawn onward, stoic by the dying fire, watching Dreban's chest rise and fall. Whenever she could, she kept herself busy with chores around the camp. She kept moving and, when she could move no longer, she looked after her patient.

Days had passed since she'd visited the town. Four, five? She hadn't counted. Nor had she taken much note of which way they were travelling. Away from there was enough. Now, though, there was no denying that she was lost. She kept the vardo on the river road, following it as it meandered towards the sea. 'All rivers flow to the sea,' Tervan had told her once.

'I've never been to the sea,' she'd replied.

'I'm not surprised,' he said, a mischievous look in his eye. 'That's where all the giants are.'

'Don't tease.' She punched his arm. 'There are no such things as giants.'

'Of course there are. Why else do you think people are weary of us?' He looked at her seriously. 'When we arrive somewhere new, it takes time for people to warm to us. That's because they think we're giants.'

'What? Don't be so ridiculous,' she said. But his face had grown still, free of any trace of humour. 'I'll prove it,' he said at last.

The next day, they arrived at a little town. Instead of beginning their usual search for the sick—'The Mother's work,' as Tervan called it—they climbed to the top of a huge hill, which took them all morning. As they neared the top, she began to hear it: a rumble like thunder, but the sky was clear. It came again. And then again, over and over. It didn't stop. Sollata grew afraid. Were these the giants Tervan had spoken of? That's why they'd come, after all. Suddenly, she no longer wanted to know if they were real. In fact, she wanted nothing more than to turn back. No wonder the villagers were always so scared if this was the noise that giants made!

'Don't worry,' Tervan said, taking her hand. 'There's nothing to be scared of. I won't let anything hurt you.' He took her hand, and they both crested the hill.

It was the most glorious sight: a glistening lake of blue that went on forever and ever. She had never imagined that there could be so much water anywhere. Unlike any lake she'd seen, this great mass of water threw itself at the shore again and again, as though desperate to be free. Thump after rolling thump. It was both magnificent and terrifying.

Solatta laughed. 'So this is the giant!'

'No,' he said, smiling at her gently. That mischievous glint had returned to his eye. 'This is just the sea. I wanted you to see this, but the giants come later.'

They sat together on the top of the hill, watching the sea. Tervan told her about the tides, and Solatta kept her eyes fixed upon the waves that crashed upon each other hour after hour. Each time the line of waves fell and retreated, a strange formation was revealed: a huge column of glistening black rock, then another, then another. Each was honeycomb-shaped. There were hundreds of them, thousands maybe, each thicker than a tree and at least as tall.

'There you have it,' announced Tervan, 'one of the many causeways made by the giants thousands and thousands of cycles ago. They hammered them like pegs into the ground to make a secret bridge.' He smiled, pleased with himself.

'But a bridge to where?'

'To the other side. To where all of the giants live now. Somewhere where they are safe and where they can't scare anyone.'

'But the sea goes on forever,' Solatta complained. 'You could never walk to the other side.'

'Maybe not us with our little legs,' he replied. 'But for a giant with huge great legs the size of a tree? Well, I bet it would take him but a day to get from here to the farthest point you can see.'

As was often the case, Solatta was uncertain whether her guardian was teasing, but she was happy in the moment they shared. She smiled and rested her head on Tervan's shoulder. With a contented sigh, she watched the sun begin its slow retreat below the horizon.

The memory brought a warm but empty feeling, a steady numbness. *He was a good man*, she thought. *And a good friend.*

He still is a good friend, answered a little voice in her head, unfamiliar and unsettling. She often spoke to herself around the camp, but it had only ever been her own voice that answered. *He is not dead*, the voice affirmed.

Dreban was alone, perhaps for the first time since he had entered the seminary—or, at least, so it felt. Even in the darkness of the tunnel he'd had his unwanted companion, but now even she had abandoned him. He cursed Kareti inwardly. Thanks to her, there was a confusion inside him. His world had somehow shifted. The life he had known and the Church to which he'd felt he belonged had been built upon lies and mistruth. Then, like everyone else, she had left him.

For what might have been the first time in cycles, he opened his eyes. He was swaddled in blankets, surrounded by the unfamiliar. Gaudy colours and bric-a-brac, bottles and trinkets, boxes and pans, herbs and potions... All were arranged in rows and racks or hanging from joists and nails, everything messy and strewn and yet at the same time seeming strangely ordered, as if everything had its place. It was a tired old caravan of sorts. Why was he here, wherever 'here' was? He remembered the cave, the pool, and the two exits. He recalled the choice he had made. The first exit had initially seemed so easy: a simple return to normality and back to the life he knew. Yet the path had been dark and desolate, leading him close to death and then into... into what? He blinked in the low light.

His head ached and he rubbed at it, hoping he might somehow wipe away the dull pain that throbbed there. His whole body felt as though it tingled and fizzed. Gingerly, he stood and walked past an empty wooden pallet upon which sleeping clothes had been neatly arranged and folded. He moved his hand to open the door and felt a buzz of energy, and for a moment it seemed he was a boy again, alive to the vibrance of it all. He recoiled in wonder just as the wooden shutter flapped open with a bang. There was no one there; just the sudden light, unbearably bright and rich, and the colours and sounds of the world. He brought up his hand to shield his eyes, but found they adjusted quickly; light leaked between his fingers and he peered out at the world, seeing it as if for the first time. Birds called in delight as they took insects on the wing. Trees swayed pleasantly in the breeze. He felt awake—truly awake. Alive. He breathed in the smells of the day. Kareti had forced him to look at what he was becoming, at the life he had chosen for himself. Deep down, he had been carrying shame and regret. He knew this now. He had transferred that into anger, both at his mother and himself. It had blinded him to the Truth. It had been too easy to accept the lie of her madness. Really, he had been too ashamed to admit that he had turned his back on her in her time of need. He had allowed the priests to take advantage of his weakness. Never again.

Only, there was no one left. All of the people he loved had gone. The thought brought him crashing back down. He felt spent and tired. Strangely, he realised he missed having Kareti's voice inside his head.

Stumbling down the wooden steps, he found a campsite with a little kettle sitting neatly atop a smouldering fire. He pulled the blanket tighter around his shoulders, protecting himself against a chill that he did not actually feel. Was it... loneliness? He heard the plaintive whinny of a horse. He could almost feel it. He found the beast nearby: an old bay workhorse grazing in the meadow. Dreban walked to it, the old familiar smells filling his nose. It was a comforting feeling. The horse looked to him expectantly. Dreban gently stroked its muzzle. The animal was lonely; somehow, he could tell. He patted the animal's shoulder and neck, speaking to it gently. He felt the hair rise on his neck and a warm tingling sensation down his spine. The horse snorted, and Dreban was transported to his father's stables. He was a boy again, watching as his father tended to the horses. He wished he had spent more time with him. He would have been a horse master himself by now, happy in his work. The horse flicked its head and Dreban's memories scattered, to be quickly replaced by a low fear. The lonely feeling he had sensed before washed over him. He fought back, forcing himself to feel calm. He focused on the meadow and the warm sunshine. Memories followed: an image of golden meadow stretching to a distant tree line; a fragrant breeze tugging at his hair; the soothing trickle of cold water as he drank from a stream, the intoxicating aroma of sweet summer grass in his nostrils.

A branch snapping him back into reality.

A young woman was moving through the camp, her arms laden with branches and twigs. She piled them with the other firewood. She had not seen him yet, though she saw the vardo's open door. She seemed alarmed, rushing to it and checking inside. She turned back, distress etched across her face. Dreban felt the sudden flare of her fear, an echo of sensation.

She began to call his name, but fell silent when she spotted him beside the horse, watching her. She looked at once relieved and peevish. 'There you are. I saw you were gone and was worried you might have...' Her voice trailed off. She pulled at her skirts absently before snatching back her hands when she realised what she was doing. He smiled at her. It seemed to ignite a spark. 'And just what are you doing wandering around? You could have fallen or hurt yourself. I've not spent all these days looking after you only for you to go injuring yourself again like some clumsy fool.'

'Hello,' said Dreban lamely, unsure of what else to say. After a moment's taut silence, he added, 'I am Drea, son of Bhan, or Dreban, as you already seem to know. But I am sorry, I do not know who you are.' For some reason, his words came out stiff and overly formal, as if he were speaking to an elderly relative. She smiled at his words, and now it was his turn to feel embarrassed.

'Oh, of course,' she said, still smiling slightly, 'I am Solatta, daughter of... well, I don't know who I'm the daughter of, but I'm pleased to meet you all the same.'

They stood in a strange silence that meandered painfully on, until Solatta finally cleared her throat. 'I was about to make some tea,' she said, her hands fetching a bunch of dried twigs and wildflowers from a pocket. 'If you would like to join me?' She brandished the bounty like a posy of flowers.

'I would like that very much, Solatta,' he answered. It was an old name; from the south, he guessed. It held the promise of sun. She led him to the fire and he sat while she fetched her brewing paraphernalia from the caravan. She returned with a battered old box bound in leather. Dreban reckoned it twice as old as she was, if not more. He felt his skin tingle, the feeling like especially intense gooseflesh. *Strange.*

Opening the box, Solatta took out some bottles and pouches from an array of colourful tubules and phials and laid them on the ground next to her. These were followed by a beautiful glass bowl, which she also set on the ground. It seemed to Dreban that the bowl collected and amplified the light around it somehow, making it almost difficult to look at. Yet he could not help but stare, feeling his eyes being drawn to its smooth features. The intensity of the light soon faded, and he could see that where he once thought it to be smooth, it was in fact intricately etched with detailed miniatures.

The bowl sang out to him and his ears were filled with a wondrous humming. His skin began to itch all over and he found himself becoming light-headed.

'Dreban?' Solatta called, her voice echoing as if through a deep, dark cave, 'Dreban?'

Then a hand on his shoulder, so calm and soothing, so present and firm. He felt it like waves rushing through him.

'Are you okay, Dreban? You looked like you were about to faint.'

'No, I'm fine. Thank you,' he said, forcing a smile.

She did not look convinced. 'Well, in that case,' she said, 'please could you pour some hot water into the bowl while I get some cups?'

He had been so engrossed in the swirling patterns that he hadn't noticed her mix dried herbs, bark, and flowers in the bottom of the bowl. He lifted the hot kettle using a rough cloth that had been folded over the handle and poured some water over the woody arrangement. The aroma was rich and earthy, carried quickly by the hot steam. Solatta returned with two cups and sat back down to stir the brew.

'Well, tell me, Dreban,' she said after a short and intense silence, 'who are you and where are you from?'

'I'm sorry, how did you... how do you know my name?' he asked, hoping he did not sound rude. Distantly, though, he felt that he knew her; her figure was indistinct like an old memory, only an outline really, but he felt sure that she was kind and gentle and that she would not try to hurt him in any way. He knew that she had been embarrassed earlier and that her embarrassment had irritated her. It felt that he had always known her, and yet he had no memory of her—or indeed of how he'd come to be here in her care.

'You really don't remember do you?' she asked. She bit her lip.

'It must be awful for you. I found you.'

'You found me?' He tried to remember: crawling out into the air, the sounds of life all around him, the drink from the canteen... water from the pool. He'd thought it would kill him. He heard his own scream in his mind. Then blackness.

'Yes, I found you in the river,' she said, bringing him back. 'You were floating by the rocks. I dragged you out but you were so cold that I thought you were...' She struggled against the last word, not able to say it, but it was clear what she meant. She'd feared the same thing he had.

'In the river? I don't remember.'

'Yes, as I said, you were in the river,' she went on. 'I dragged you out and brought you to the camp and kept you warm by the fire. I was hoping to ask you how you happened to be washed up there. You gave me such a fright. And then I was worried that I'd done something wrong because you started screaming. So I hitched Cobb to the vardo and went to search for...' She trailed off again.

He felt her pain. Could sense the ghosts that stalked her.

'I'm sorry,' he said, when it was clear she would or could not say more. 'I don't know how I came to be in the water. I must have fallen.' It was a weak explanation, he knew. Still, he did not want to add to her burdens with his own.

'Well, then,' she said sharply, 'that certainly clears things up.' She thrust a cup of tea towards him.

Dreban felt abashed, but it was necessary. How could he start to explain what he'd been through? That he'd been spying for the Church and had been caught and imprisoned? That he'd thought he'd gone mad? That he'd chosen to deny his Church and his faith and that now he even missed the voices he'd been hearing in his head? He was hardly sure that he believed it all himself!

'Are all men so damned stubborn?' he heard her mutter to herself. He could sense the pangs of guilt and regret that followed the comment. 'You should drink your tea; it's good for you,' she added.

Dreban sniffed at the hot liquid in his cup. It smelled heavily of blackberries mixed with something else that he did not recognise and, while the aroma was strange, he found it oddly comforting. He copied his host, blowing on the surface before taking a sip, and, finding that he liked the flavour, he drank more deeply.

He opened his mouth to say something but, as he did so, he found his head engulfed in pain. It was sharp and intense, as if an axe had struck it from the inside. He dropped the cup, doubling over and falling from his stool. The world began to flicker around him and black edges flashed ever thicker. There was something cold rising from beneath him: an abyss from which he instinctively knew that he may never climb out. His breath came in desperate gasps. His heart hammered, trying to break free. For some reason, his mind flashed back to the bowl. He saw the surface of it crackling as though ablaze with tiny storms.

He felt something touch him, at first on his shoulder and then his hand. It was a feeling like nothing he had experienced before—at once soothing, warming, and sharp. Where it touched, the sensation radiated outwards, spreading across his body and penetrating through his skin. With it came an overwhelming feeling of concern but, strangely, not panic. He could hear calming words and noises that softly eased away the cacophony that was raging inside his head. He felt himself being pulled close to someone. Solatta, he realised. He closed his eyes, allowing himself to be consumed by the feeling. He was overcome by a torrent of emotion: compassion and sympathy, worry and concern, hope and anticipation. In his mind's eye, an image began to form, strange and unfamiliar to him, but immediately comforting. Cosy by a fire, laughter, sitting on the ground at the feet of a loved one, leaning against a man's legs as he stroked a woman's long hair. The pain in his head began to subside.

'It's okay, Dreban,' Solatta was telling him. It sounded like there were two of her: one inside his head and one outside.

He opened his eyes, confused. She was holding him in her arms, gently rocking and speaking to him. He looked up into her face, but the image in his mind's eye was different. From that angle, he was looking down at a child wrapped in a blanket. A hand—a pale and familiar hand—comforted the child. Fear and confusion grew. How could this be? *He* was the child.

The image was as fleeting as it was disturbing. Dreban shook his head and pulled away, feeling dirty somehow, as if he had seen something he shouldn't have. He felt a physical shiver. It was Solatta's, he realised, not his; a draft was creeping up her spine. She looked at him strangely as though she sensed something but wasn't sure what. He wanted to say something to her, to explain that he was sorry—but he wasn't sure what he was sorry for. He opened his mouth to speak.

'There you are, Dreban,' said a familiar voice in his head. 'I've been waiting for you to find me. I didn't realise it would happen so quickly. You've changed so much already. Too much. Something else has happened.'

'What?' Dreban exclaimed. 'Where are you? What wouldn't happen so quickly? What are you talking about?'

Solatta looked shocked, hurt almost. 'Dreban,' she said, backing away from him, 'are you okay? Are you still in pain? What is it?'

'You chose your path, Dreban,' said Kareti. 'You opened

yourself up to the change.'

'Opened myself up to what?' he demanded. 'What path? What change?'

'To a powerful gift. You are becoming—'

Solatta stood up, putting space between her and Dreban and moving quickly back to her chair. The anguish in her face was clear. Immediately, the voice inside Dreban's head disappeared, and he slumped down to the ground, exhausted and suddenly terrified.

Just as the Church is wed to the Goddess through her holy covenant, so too must the family be wed to each other in unity with the father and mother in their rightful place. You should honour your parents and the love that they share for each other, for in honouring their holy unity, you honour the holy unity of Church and Truth.

—From the Tenets of Truth

CHAPTER NINETEEN
DRITSEK AARGAU

The Citadel

Dritsek sank further into the bath. Hot water flowed over his hair and face, cleansing him of the day's dirt, and he wallowed in it, his breath leaving him in one long, laboured sigh. It felt like a great weight was being lifted from him, washed away with the dust and grime of the barracks. *His* barracks, he corrected himself. He had ordered the heavy wooden tub to be carried into one of the upper viewing rooms of the Black Tower. From here, he could look out over the Citadel and imagine all of those small and idiotic people rushing busily about their idiotic little lives. Meanwhile, here he was: a mere stone's throw away from the Palace Tower, the City-

Lord's symbolic seat of power.

Black hair swam happily in the water, cascading around his shoulders. Black as coal, his mother used to say, in reference to the ore that had brought unexpected wealth back to the family. Now they were one of the richest, thanks mainly to a deal struck between his father and the Church. The Premiero's hand at play again. Goddess alone knew what he or the Church wanted with so much coal, but they were welcome to it as far as Dritsek was concerned, especially at the prices they paid. In any case, he was glad to see the back of it. Coal did little more than leave its filthy footprint all over the place. Even the peasants who handled the stuff were left covered in heavy black soot. No amount of bathing would rid them of that grime. He closed his eyes and grinned at the thought.

On any other day, he would have had a house servant wait upon him while he bathed, maybe even more than one. Today, though, he was happy to be alone with his daydreams. And what daydreams they were. Granted, the Black Tower was not the closest to the Palace Tower, nor was it as tall as those of some of the other House-Lords, but soon, he thought. it would be the most powerful. More so than the City-Lord himself. More powerful even than the Premiero. He felt himself stirring. He wished for a moment that he hadn't dismissed the servant and, as if in response, he heard a door open and close followed by soft footfalls. Their padding echoed around the chamber.

Maybe his command to be left alone had been ignored. The servant would have to be scolded, though all in good time. 'Top the hot water up, and then you can start by lathering my hair,' he demanded.

'Good afternoon, Lord Aargau,' a woman's voice responded, soft and smooth. The way velvet would sound, Dritsek thought, sumptuous and sweet.

'Oh, forgive me, my lady,' Dritsek said. 'Had I known it was you, I would not have been so wasteful as to suggest starting with my hair.' He smiled at his own wit.

The lady came to stand next to the bath. The tub was large and made of wood, held together by huge metal hoops that pulled the panels into shape. The sides reached almost to the chest of a fully grown man, and it was only by benefit of a wooden chair placed inside that the bather was able to relax without their head becoming submerged. Slowly, the woman reached into the bath water, allowing her hands to be covered in the soapy suds floating on the surface, and then began to stroke her hand through Dritsek's wet hair, building up a thick lather.

'It seems you have been a busy boy,' she said.

'Oh? How so?' he asked, a knowing smile creeping over his face.

'Please, you do not have to be coy with me, my dear. You know that I make it my business to know exactly what is going on, especially when it concerns the men in my life.'

'Well, there seems to be so many of them that I'm sure you must find it difficult to keep track.'

Her soap-slick hands yanked suddenly at his hair and he winced, opening his eyes.

'Ow!' he said, and was about to protest further when she splashed soapy water in his face. He sat upright, rubbing his eyes and scowling.

'My Lord, how careless of me,' she said with mock sincerity. 'I can be so clumsy sometimes.'

'I suppose I deserved that,' he said, relaxing back again, having relieved his face and eyes of suds. 'Now, please, tell me what you have heard.'

'Oh, very little in truth. Just whispers and the clucking of idle tongues,' she said. 'I hear that the City-Lord's council has not stopped bleating about the dire report you presented. The loss of a hand of men is quite shocking. The High-Lords are sat shaking in their towers; those who have not already skulked away to their estates, that is. The council might have demanded the colonel be stripped of his rank and privileges had someone not already deprived him of his life.'

She paused for a moment, gauging his reaction. His smile, however, remained fixed. He enjoyed this game. She stopped stroking his hair, allowing her hand to ripple the water, pouring it gently onto his chest. He tensed as the drops tickled first against one nipple and then the other. Her face was impassive, as difficult to read as ever. Was she enjoying it too, or was it truly a game to her? He could never tell.

'There is great fear in the air,' she continued. 'Even the small folk feel it, them more than most, in truth. A whole town massacred. That is not something anyone can afford to take lightly, especially following your report. The risk it poses to the Citadel was so expertly emphasised by you, my dear, that the council was beside itself with panic. Where might they turn to stabilise the army and organise their forces? The king was the natural choice. I mean, who knows what the attackers' motives were. They could easily target Doarson next.'

Dritsek blanched. Such an attack would be a disastrous for his plans.

'But then,' the lady continued, 'the answer was presented to them in the form of the report—there was already provision for such an eventuality. Besides, it would be the City-Lord and his representatives that would come out worse if the king were to become involved. Who would have known that the office of a go-between could actually assume complete control of the army in the event of a serious threat to the Citadel? With the condition, of course, that all higher-ranking officers had been deployed elsewhere or had otherwise been... removed. Of course, this unexpected opportunity for power would only begrudgingly be grasped by that go-between—out of a sense of duty, of course.' Again, she paused to gauge his reaction.

This time he smiled wider, this time feeling more than just his pride begin to swell.

'Only as a temporary measure, I assure you,' he said, trying to sound humble—unfortunately, it was not a disposition to which he was naturally inclined. 'I never expected such circumstances to ever present themselves. Anyway, the authority only transfers until the council has been able to convene and appoint a more suitable person to the role,' he added, hoping that he might claw back some semblance of meekness.

'Oh, of course. They wasted no time in doing exactly that, I assure you.'

Now his smile faltered and, for the first time, a glimmer of worry stole across his face.

'So, you didn't know that yet, at least,' she said with self-satisfaction. 'Well, isn't this fun?' She playfully swished her hand through the water, allowing it to stroke across his chest and down to his abdomen.

'Tell me,' he implored.

'La, la, la,' she replied teasingly. 'Swoosh, swoosh, swoosh. Oh this is a dangerous game you have been playing, my lord. And with such little certainty. I did not know you were a man to gamble with such high stakes.'

He grabbed hold of her hand, his grip tight and almost threatening. 'Tell me what happened,' he said. Realising that his teeth were clenched, he softened his tone. 'If it would please my lady.'

'Very well,' she said, shaking free her hand. 'After your report was received, the council was assembled. City-Lord Phaedra was not in attendance, as is usual these days, due to his health. Nor was your lord father, the Goddess preserve him. House-Lords Leytold and Brishen, however, were there along with the Premiero, among others.' Dritsek fancied that the Lady's voice tightened a little at the priest's mention. He stored it away for another time. 'I am not sure who turned the palest of them when the report was read, but it was quickly moved that you, Dritsek Aargau, should be appointed permanently to the post of commissioner of the army. You are to take whatever measures you see fit to ensure the safekeeping of the Citadel, its citizens, and the estates of those citizens. The motion was swiftly ratified by Premiero Irmao on behalf of the Church of the Righteous Truth.'

This time there was no hiding the joy in the smile that threatened to overwhelm Dritsek. He snatched back her hand in order to kiss it delicately.

'Such unexpected news you bring, my lady,' he said. 'I am in your debt as ever. How could I begin to repay you?' His eyes gleamed with suggestion.

'I am sure you will think of some *small* token with which you can clear your debt,' she replied, once again snatching her hand from his.

'You could stay a while and help me bathe while I come up with something suitable,' he teased.

'Alas, I have another engagement to occupy my time,' she said. 'I must attend your father in his prayer room.' Her voice had a new edge to it; he was being admonished, he knew. 'You should arrange to see him too. It has been noted that you have been avoiding him. He may not fully be the man he was, but he is no fool. You would do well to remember that.' She took her hand from the water and shook it dry. 'In the meantime, I shall send a servant who will help you wash your back. With any luck, you may be able to get them to help you out with that erection of yours, too. Remember, you are not the only member of the family that has duties. Only, whilst I am constrained by my sex, you seem intent on pressing yours against the world for all to see, like some dog in heat.' With that, she padded from the room.

Her parting words left him feeling slightly cold. He glossed over it. 'This water grows cold. Bring more hot water,' he called into the distance. 'Oh, I do so enjoy your little visits, Mother,' he added, very much to himself this time. With that thought, Dritsek sank further.

The Goddess is Truth, and the Truth is pure, unsoiled, unsullied. Like a freshly blossomed flower, it is clean and new to the world, whole and unadulterated. The Goddess teaches us to remain pure and honest, not to offer up our purity like a wanton whore, for those who are lustful and lascivious sin against her Church.

—From the Tenets of Truth

CHAPTER TWENTY
DREBAN AND SOLATTA

The Old Road

They had lost the river, and with it, Dreban felt he had lost his sense of security. At least on those lesser travelled paths he'd felt like he had a connection with something. Now, he felt adrift and purposeless. The river had marked their passing with a fresh sense of wonder, each meandering twist bringing with it trees and rocks, birds and insects. Here, their path was marked by a change from scrubland and disorder into manicured fields, all neat little rows and regular lines. He had much preferred the sense of freedom the Waipera had brought. Then, at least, he'd been able to happily imagine their solitude: that there was no one else, and that he and

Solatta would simply wander forever.

Crops and peasants toiling in the fields marked their route forwards. Estates and their workers; they signposted the end of things, Dreban knew. They told of rules and of authorities to enforce them. They told of the Church and a life to which he had to face up. It screamed of choices made and to be made, of unavoidable consequences. He felt the knots in his stomach twist tighter still. These things were more easily done at a distance. Now that the truth of it was in sight, he felt overwhelmed. Naïve to think that a decision could be made so lightly. He hoped it would not foretell the end of the little friendship that had blossomed between him and Solatta.

The villagers stopped as they passed. Shielding their eyes from the sun, they hid their faces, pushed their children behind them, and touched their fingers to their foreheads. Dreban wondered at these rituals; who were they calling on to guard them from the passing of these strangers? And who could blame them?

'They think we're giants,' Solatta had said. Her voice was bright and playful, but he was in no mood to join in her jollity. She looked as downtrodden as the field hands, and he felt the more guilty for it.

His travelling companion—and, he admitted, nurse—was a confusion. Just being with her made him feel warm and comforted, but he supposed this was normal; she had saved his life after all. And yet, he was worried. Frightened, even. When they had touched, he had seen through her eyes. Or, at least, he'd imagined that he had—he could not tell for sure. He had grown uncertain about a great many things. And then there was the voice. Kareti. Seemingly returned to him, though she too had since disappeared. Solatta had kept her distance since then. Three days had passed during which she'd seemed fearful to approach him, making sure not to allow herself too close. Could he blame her? After all, who in their right mind would ask someone they'd just met if they too could hear a voice inside their head? *Maybe I should just ask her if she's mad too!*

For all that, however, he might have wondered at the connection himself. Was it a coincidence that Solatta had found him? He had no memory of the deed; he only had her word. She could be part of it. It was her tea that made him feel wretched, after all, and Kareti had only spoken to him after they'd touched. No, he admonished himself, the thought was unfair. Still, the uncertainty of it all made him feel yet more subdued. In truth, her touch had made him feel human; as if he was a person, not just a tool. She had cared for him and he worried that his reaction had pushed her away. Now, he found that he craved her comfort all the more.

'Do you even know where we are?' he asked. His words were harder and more bitter than he would have liked. He felt her following silence in much the same way he'd come to feel all her moods, as a very physical thing. Ever since their touch, he had sensed her all the more intensely, like she were an extension of him, or he of her. Though, he thought, even a stranger might have read the following silence for what it was.

By midday, they were both tired, hungry, and sullen, and Dreban was uncertain whether the relief at them stopping for the afternoon was hers or his own. When she climbed down from the driving platform, however, he knew that he wanted to reach out to her. It would be a simple thing for him to say sorry, but the word seemed to stick on his tongue. His mother had always told him that he was as stubborn as his father.

Their meal was simple and polite, all *please* and *thank you*. Still, Dreban couldn't help but find Solatta's company pleasant. It had been too long since he had been content enough to simply share a space with anyone. Most pleasing of all was that he knew Solatta felt the same. She was happy to be there, safe with him. She too had lost someone, though she did not speak of it. He felt it like a great emptiness swelling within. She felt as adrift as he did, lost in this great wilderness with no aim or direction. She was holding onto him as much as he were holding onto her. It was almost laughable. He wanted to let her know she was not alone—for a little while, at least.

'I am grateful for all you've done for me, you know. I may not show it all of the time. It's just that things are very strange and difficult for me at the moment,' he managed, his voice low and eyes fixed on the ground.

He glanced up to catch her smiling at him.

She reached a hand towards him before remembering herself and drawing it back warily. The memory of their last touch was clearly fresh in her mind too.

'I think we're both struggling to come to terms with things at the moment. But at least we can try to help each other.'

Dreban felt the empathy in her words and knew that she meant what she said. Hers was a uniquely kind and pure heart and he was relieved and thankful that it had been her who'd found him.

'I'd like that very much,' he said.

Again, she smiled, her hazel eyes lit golden by the afternoon sun. The moment stretched and still her eyes lingered.

'Well,' she said, breaking the spell, 'what I would like is some tea.' She rose and went to fetch her box. With it, she brought the usual sensation. Dreban could hear it calling to him—that mysterious crystal bowl. Its voice was soft and sweet, its lure intoxicating. Somehow, he didn't quite trust himself to be around it for too long. He rose with the intention of seeing to Cobb, yet he found his head spinning as a wave of energy spread through him. The bowl, he realised, was drawing him towards it. Before he knew what had happened, he was on the ground, having fallen. As ever, Solatta was there.

'Dreban,' she called. 'Are you okay?' She was kneeling by his side. He looked up into her face. Slowly, tentatively, she reached out to him and gently stroked the hair from his face. He flinched, unsure of what to expect. Since the last time, they had been careful not to come into contact. Here, though, her touch was soft and delicate, unburdened by the voice of Kareti. Finally, it seemed, both had been released by their ghosts. He gazed into her perfect eyes. Infinitely slowly, she moved her face close to his—so near he could feel her breath on his cheek. His nostrils filled with the smell of her: herby and floral, like one of her teas. Her fingers traced the contours of his face with almost no pressure at all as if she were only some kind of phantasm. She seemed to glow, gold and bronze and copper. Her lips were full and glossy, like cherries. She moved inexorably closer. Powerless, he held his breath; the taste of her was in his mouth. She touched her lips to his, slow and soft, yet with a force of determination. He couldn't have stopped her even if he'd wished to. He closed his eyes.

His world exploded into hers; the pleasure and the power of the moment felt so intense that he was sure he must have died then and there. At once, he was aware of everything. Her lips. Her taste. Her hands moving to touch him and the feeling on his skin, their two bodies merged into one. As elation rode across his body, a warm yet cold shiver ran over *her* back. He could somehow feel the hair on *her* neck rising. The sensation rippled across his skin and into hers, multiplying and resonating through them both. They were the only two living things in the whole world—or, rather, they *were* the world and everything in it: the seas, the mountains, *everything*. With each touch, he felt he knew her more and more. Colours, lights, and images flashed in his mind, but nothing distracted him from knowing her. He wanted to explore more. To know more. To dive deeper and deeper into her body. He was aware of her wanting the same; he could hear her in his mind asking for it.

Eventually, they lay next to each other, quiet and still, with just the tips of their fingers touching, aware of nothing but the visceral feelings that they now shared. Without her even speaking, he knew everything that she could possibly say. A gentle breeze caressed wherever it touched against their nakedness, and he could even feel her skin blossom into gooseflesh.

'I knew you'd find your way back to me,' Solatta said in a voice that was not her own. Kareti. He felt anger rising—this was the ultimate intrusion.

'Why are you here? Why can you not leave me alone?' he asked out loud, forgetting himself. Even as the words were out, he knew that they were wrong. These were not delicate truths to give to a lover; not the sweet pillow whispers to be shared after such intimacy. He felt torn and exasperated. These past days he had longed to hear her again, fearing that she might be the only person who could help him understand what was happening to him. Now, he realised that Solatta could help him find his way, his truth. Why had she chosen *now* to come back to him?

'Who is Kareti?' Solatta asked, looking at him. He opened his mouth but realised he had no idea what to say. Who *is* Kareti? A name. One he had never given voice to.

He looked deep into her eyes, finding them full and bright and knowing. For a brief moment, it was as though he was not seeing Solatta at all. Her face had been replaced. Gone was the young woman he was just beginning to know. Now there were blue eyes where there should have been brown. Greying auburn hair instead of black. A stern-faced woman—a ghost. As he recalled the innkeeper's wife, he was somehow aware that Solatta saw her image too.

'You know her,' he said. It was not a question. 'You've seen her.' He sat up, disentangling their fingers. Immediately, the notion was lost.

Solatta looked at him, confusion in her eyes. She didn't know what to say, he knew, and he didn't know what he even *wanted* her to say. Did it matter? He let out a sigh. 'I don't know,' he admitted, dropping his head into his hands. 'A week ago, I'd never laid eyes on her. Now, I can't stop thinking about her.' He looked up guiltily. 'Not like that,' he added in a rush. 'It was never—'

He didn't get chance to finish. Solatta leant forward, taking his face in her hands and kissed him, deep and wet and full, slamming into him with all the colours of the world. It took his breath away. He felt as if he was falling from some great cliff—and fall he did, right into her arms. He felt both powerful and miniscule, like a child just become a man.

The snort of a horse tore through the silence, bringing them back to reality. Three horsemen stood a short distance away, watching them from the road. Panic spread through Dreban. He had forgotten where they were, happy in the ignorance that nothing else existed. Now he was painfully aware. He felt his nakedness acutely, though it was not his body that the men's eyes raided. Dreban struggled to his feet, placing himself between her and the intruders. She gathered up her strewn clothing quickly, fumbling herself back into them as best she could. A horse pawed impatiently at the ground. The sound annoyed him. What are they doing here? The uniforms—all three wore the hardwearing grey livery of the city patrol. At least they weren't bandits; these lawmen would be less inclined to raping and killing. Or so he hoped.

One of the men climbed down from his horse. He was older

than the rest, grizzled and with angular features. A dark grazing of stubble giving him a road-weary look. 'Get dressed,' the man instructed Dreban, though his eyes never left Solatta.

Dreban stepped forward, suddenly brave or suddenly stupid. The sound of steel rasping free from its scabbard rung in the background. 'I won't say it again,' the man repeated. This time he did look at Dreban, and his eyes were full of spite and venom.

Dreban did as he was told, though by the time he had pulled on his boots, the patrolman had led Solatta back to the vardo. He felt panic and bile rising. One of the other two horsemen leered forwards in his saddle, tongue agog, straining to see what was happening. Dreban heard them chuckle as he rushed to catch up.

'Of course, sir. I have it in the vardo,' Solatta was saying.

'I see. A vardo is it? Travelling folk then. That make you special, does it?' His tone was condescending.

Solatta disappeared for a moment before returning with her travel chit. The man took the papers and pocketed them, hardly glancing at the details.

'And his?' he asked, nodding towards Dreban.

'Ah, well,' she started. They had lost his papers—blown away, perhaps, or burned up in their campfire. 'I, erm. I mean, we don't have them at the minute.' She flushed. 'Not that we don't have them, you understand—it's just that we need to replace them.'

The patrolman looked at her, an eyebrow cocked, before grunting and walking them back to the other two men in silence. He climbed back into the saddle and some unspoken signal seemed to pass between the men. Dreban thought he caught the suggestion of satisfaction, though it was fleeting at most. 'You, girly,' the officer called to them. 'Go pack your things away, climb back on your *caravan*, and follow us.'

Solatta turned, giving Dreban an encouraging smile. *See*, it seemed to say, *we might just get away with it after all.* He turned to follow.

'Not you, shit-face,' he heard the officer saying from behind. With incredible swiftness, one of the other patrolmen had slipped from the saddle and Dreban felt a burly arm wrapping around him. In a flash, a gloved hand held a dirk to his throat. Cold steel stilled his struggle, yet it was not the feel of metal that worried him. An overriding sense of disgust filled him, hitting him like a wave of nausea. Lust for blood and other things besides—things deep and sordid and base.

Almost distantly, he heard Solatta scream a protest.

'Listen, go easy now. Both of you.' It was the lead patrolman.

'What are you doing?' Solatta screamed. 'You've seen my papers, we haven't done anything.'

'Wrong, missy. I've seen *your* papers right enough, and good and proper they are. I haven't seen his.'

'I told you, there was a problem, but we are going to get that fixed.'

'That you did, you did,' the man agreed. 'But I don't take my orders from little traveller girls, and there's been enough trouble in these parts without strangers romping on the roadside. So, if you don't mind, we'll just be making sure that this little cock-stand can't get into any more mischief than he has already.'

Dreban felt the rasp of rope around his wrists. The man pulled it tight and he winced as the fibres bit into his flesh. He felt like a pig being trussed. What an idiot he'd been! They should not have stopped, never mind the rest. They should have known there would be patrols now they were among the estates. No doubt the workers they'd seen earlier had reported them.

'Be a good little girl,' the officer called. 'Climb back into your caravan all nice and quiet like and follow us back to the Citadel.

If you're good then your little cockerel here gets to travel nice and tucked up inside. But if you're not good and you make a fuss then we'll tie you up inside and shit-face here gets dragged behind. We'll see how far he makes it. Your choice.'

For once, Dreban thankfully couldn't feel her anguish, though it was plain to see in her face. He flushed, furious. He might have struggled, but he felt the rope bite deep and hard, as though the man had read his intentions. There was no choice: hopefully they could sort this mess out once they reached the Citadel. He felt his stomach lurch. There was no telling what would be waiting for them there. He could be sure that an arrest like this would attract the attention of the Church. Like it or not, it was time to face up to his new reality, his new Truth. He only hoped that Solatta would still be some part of it.

Truth. Love. Honesty. Openness. These are the attributes we must achieve to truly be one with the Goddess. Only through these virtues can we find happiness and the true love of the Goddess. Learn not to keep secrets hidden in your heart, for there is nothing that can be hidden from her and her Church. Allow yourself to open to the interrogation of her Church, for if you are true in your heart, then you need not fear the Truth.

—From the Tenets of Truth

CHAPTER TWENTY-ONE
SENTENZA

The Citadel

Sentenza stuck to the dark places and kept out of sight. He might have become a shadow himself for all he knew. It had been many cycles since he had lived like this, though how quickly the art returned! Shifting from place to place, dealing in rumours and titbits of information that he could buy or glean or force. In some ways, he felt free. Only in some, however. His audience with Golya Sakani had disavowed him of that notion. Freedom was somebody else's Truth: a story that parents told their children or a fantasy that people told themselves. In the barracks, he had been happy to imagine that he was in charge, that his men would move to carry out his command. In reality, they'd all been watched and monitored. Each and every one of them had been someone else's puppet. Church or council or City-Lord, it mattered not.

Here, among the hovels and the gutter dwellers, he was unsure who had the greater freedom. The visit of his former teacher had left him looking over his shoulder at the slightest of sounds. He should be hunting from the shadows, not hiding from them.

'I am not cowering,' he told himself for the umpteenth time, 'I'm biding my time.' Had he the resources of the barracks available to him, he might have been better placed. Yet the Golya's mind was set and he would brook no argument.

'Besides,' Sakani had said, his voice crackling with apparent mirth, 'you forget that Colonel Sentenza was reported dead. Perhaps it would be best for you to leave the notion or returning to Barkathet behind, Malak.'

Sentenza almost choked at the memory. He had not been called that for a long time. Not since the first cycles he'd spent at the Misty City and, even then, only had a handful of people had known his mentor's pet name for him. *Little Malak—my little angel of death.* Back then, Sentenza had been excited, proud even, to have been singled out by the Golya. Little had he known how literal the name would become. He felt the familiar well of resentment growing. He'd hoped he had outgrown the moniker, as he'd thought he had outgrown the Golya. It had been naïve; the daydream of a fool. The work he had done for Sakani bound him to the priest in the same way as a man is forever bound to his failures or the dead to their ghosts. Sentenza had more of the latter than he wished to recall, though only one failure—one the old man was apparently unwilling to forget.

'Truth be with you, Malak,' Golya Sakani had said. His voice had been reedy even then, almost ten cycles past. Sentenza dropped respectfully to one knee in front of his teacher. 'Do not be so formal, my child. We are safe and quite alone in here.' Sakani waved his hand expansively around the room. It was sparse, as all of the Golya's quarters were. Others might surround themselves with finery, rich tapestries and hangings, but not Sakani. A single desk stood towards one end of the room, covered in papers and scrolls. There was not even a chair in which to sit.

'You sent for me, my lord?' Sentenza stood full-chested and erect. He was still considered young and strong and formidable. Sakani's rock; his little angel. It was Sentenza's first visit to the Tagot Bai since his posting with the army almost five cycles past. Not that the Golya had not kept him busy during that time; there had been hardly a season past without some kind of task, no matter how small and irrelevant. Sentenza might work for the army now, but he always belonged to the Church— and, more importantly, to Golya Sakani.

'How are you finding things at the barracks? I trust it has not been too difficult a transition.'

'No, my lord. It has been a very smooth and easy move.' Any other man might have relaxed, even allowed themselves a smile. Not Sentenza. He had grown too accustomed to the ways of the Misty City, even after so long away. These people were not cordial by nature; they smiled only when it suited them.

'Of course it would be. What are you? Lieutenant? Captain?' said Sakani almost absently, his voice as close to syrup as it ever was. The question was rhetorical. 'But then, without my patronage, you might not be an officer. As easily you would be a soldier or a stable hand or a cleaner or anything else I might deem appropriate. You might be a whore selling yourself to cadge a meal.' He had lost all charm. Sentenza held his place while the priest pressed his point, moving his face close to the younger man's. 'Would you like that, my child? Would you prefer to sell your pretty little cock?' Old and watery eyes searched for a response, a flicker of reaction. Sentenza would not give him the satisfaction.

'No matter,' Sakani continued. 'I have a task for you, my dear little Malak.' And there it was: there was always a task. It must have been an important one for Sentenza to have been summoned in person. 'I have lost something. Or, rather, I have had something taken from me. Stolen, would you believe? I desire you to retrieve it for me.'

'Of course, Lord Golya,' Sentenza responded automatically. He'd have rather screamed his refusal at the old man, but where would that have got him? He was powerless here. In truth, when it came to the reach of the Church, he was powerless *anywhere*. Easier to submit than attempt to resist. With any luck, it would be a simple matter.

'Good, good. Such an obedient boy. You have been my most promising pupil. I cherish the day that I found you. To think, had I not—had another Golya completed your testing...' The priest shuddered then rose two fingers to his mouth, warding against his own words. 'No matter. I have you now.' He smiled, a thin and mirthless thing that did not touch his eyes. 'There was a girl. Little more than a babe if truth be told. I had procured her from—well, that does not concern you, I suppose. She was brought here, to this room.' The old priest circled Sentenza as he spoke, watching for a reaction, the slightest deviation: tightened lips, flared nostril, the flicker of an eye. Any of these might betray Sentenza. Finally, the Golya paused in his pacing and leaned in tight, mouth so close behind Sentenza's ear that he felt the spittle land. 'You think the worst of me. You imagine that I brought her here for low and base reasons. You jump to impure conclusions because you too are impure. No better than the rats with whom you shared the gutter I found you in. I should have left you with them to fester. Understand that I do only the work of the Goddess.' He resumed his pacing. 'The girl submitted to a testing.' It was a challenge, Sentenza knew, and he kept his face blank. Still, testing a girl? It was unheard of.

He remembered his own testing: the extreme physical effort and exhaustion. How old was this girl? The Golya had said she was just a babe. It must have damn near killed her. She had not submitted to the test, Sentenza knew; the old fool had submitted her to an ordeal!

'You think me cruel,' Sakani said, cutting into his thoughts and examining his face.

Could he read minds?

'You have not been brought here to give me your approval, only your obedience and your service. You owe me at least that, don't you agree?' He did not wait for an answer. 'The girl failed, as I had suspected she would. I thought her worthless, like the rest. In a pique of anger, I disposed of her. Only afterwards I realised that she still had worth in... other markets.' It seemed he luxuriated in the telling, prodding and teasing. Sentenza held his face firm. 'Only, when I went to retrieve her, she had gone. Not of her own volition, of course; she had been too ruined for that. Someone had taken her from me. And not only that—some horses, clothing, and a box had also been taken. Theft, here in the sacred city of Togat Bai! Stealing at the very heart of the Church! A blasphemy. A mote in the Goddess' eye. These things cannot be left unanswered. Such sacrilege must be met by swift and unflinching justice. That is why you are here. You will leave straight away and track down those responsible. Of course, I would consider the return of these items a blessing from the Goddess, and, as ever, I turn you to, my Malak. You must mete out justice in the name of Truth. You must be my angel of death once more.'

It had taken him time and expense and energy, but he had managed it where he feared he might not. It had been Old Ballir. One of the untouchables—the men that clean the waste and the detritus from the holy city, the dead included. Considered unclean, no one else went near them. They were a small army of invisible soldiers, dutifully sweeping away the city's sacred shit day after day. Ballir had two sons already, as Sentenza later discovered, but his wife had long desired a daughter that they couldn't have. When he found the girl tossed out with the trash, he didn't have to think twice. He took the clothes and the horses and the box and the girl, and he took his family too. High into the hills, they went, where they hoped to be forgotten. No one challenged their travel. No one questioned the untouchables. Usually, no one even saw them.

By the time Sentenza had finally found them up there in the Mata Mountains, it had been too late. Dead, he'd told the Golya on his return, but Sentenza wasn't convinced. It was too neat, too convenient. For one thing, there had been no grave or shrine. It was the lack of things that had preoccupied him that day: lack of remorse, lack of guilt, lack of evidence, lack of snow, and lack of magic. *That* had filled his mind ever since. It took great power to strip a place of magic. Was this what the Golya had been looking for all along? It couldn't have been a simple coincidence—there was no such thing, not where the Church and Sakani were involved. Sentenza had returned with the horses, some robes, and the box, which turned out to be a cash box. He hoped it would be enough and, sure enough, it had served—for a time, at least.

Sentenza shook his head free of memories just as something crawled over his foot. He jumped, then felt the flow of magic through his arm and pounded down into the ground. A pillar of air solidified, crunching bone and gristle. 'Damned rats, and damned Sakani.' Had the priest not turned up to haunt him, he would have been spending the night in a tavern bed rather than its cold cellar.

'Do not look at me like that, old friend,' Kuljet said. 'Do you think that I had any choice earlier? If I had told you who was waiting for you, either you would have killed me or he would have.'

He took a bottle and two cups from a cabinet and joined Sentenza at a small table. He uncorked the bottle and sniffed at its contents, face twisting, before pouring a good measure for himself and his guest.

Sentenza took a heavy draught. The hot wash of alcohol hit the back of his throat before slowly engulfing him like a hot, damp blanket. Like the Golya's unexpected visit, it left a bitter taste, and not one he was likely to dispel easily. The vapours hit his nose, spreading a fog and flushing his face. He bared his teeth in a rictus grin.

'Ha! Siaurinus blood wine,' Kuljet barked. 'That will sure put hair on your chest.'

'Dissolve them more like,' Sentenza replied with some difficulty.

Kuljet joined him in knocking back his drink before pouring them both another.

'Tell me, *old friend*,' Sentenza said, 'who were those two goons earlier? I didn't see anyone leave with Golya, and it isn't like him to travel with an entourage.' *It isn't like him to travel at all*, he might have added.

'No, they were not with him,' Kuljet answered. 'They were City Patrol.'

Sentenza looked up. 'Things have certainly changed. What

are patrolmen doing around here? You been forgetting to pay your taxes again?'

'A shock for us all, yes. But do not worry, old Kuljet knows how to keep these things sweet. Besides, bribes are always a surer thing than taxes. It would not pay for the squirrel to kill the oak tree, would it?'

'Still, squirrels don't talk. Patrolmen do.'

'Where have you been hiding, my friend? Patrols are everywhere these last days. Patrols are up, taxes are up, quotas are up, and bribes are up. I have to sell twice as much to afford the taxes, else I have to hand over as much again as bribes and quotas. They are bleeding us all dry. Now they even have your soldiers in from Barkathet. At least they don't come expecting bribes. You teach them well out there, eh?' Kuljet smiled as though he'd made a good joke. Then he scratched his head with an exaggerated, bewildered look. 'But then, of course you would know all of this. Where *have* you been, my old friend?'

Sentenza did not answer, but drained the rest of his wine.

'And that patrol earlier,' Kuljet continued, 'you thought that they were here to find you? You, the big-shot army man and all that? Ha, my friend, what have you done?' He sat back in his chair and gave a laugh that was so loud it belied the thin and frail frame it rose from.

'Best not ask. Only, when you find out, I'd be obliged if you didn't tell your little squirrels I was here.'

The roads around Westip amounted to little more than dirt tracks between shacks and lean-tos. The hovels amid the alleys and walkways made as much a home for rats and vermin as they did for the peasants. It was not uncommon to find three generations sharing a four-foot shelter, all of whom thought themselves fortunate to share a sleeping pallet. At least the rats made for a decent meal. Ragtag structures of old wooden frames patched together with whatever could be found lying around stretched on across the grimy space, making it hard to see where one home ended and another began. Space was very much at a premium, and it was not uncommon for newer homes to be built on top of the older ones below. They stretched precariously skywards in a grotesque emulation of the immensely wealthy House-Lord's towers only a short distance away. These were among the poorest suburbs of the Citadel, and were most ignored and forgotten by all but the hardiest tax collectors. Those who lived here were, technically, one step up from slaves, or so the Great Emancipation Edict dictated. It would be difficult to explain that to the people themselves.

The last light had already fled by the time Sentenza emerged from the tavern. The air was thick and heavy and fetid, much like the people who scurried in the dark recesses. Thieves and prostitutes and sell-swords: hard people. He almost felt at home. A voice rang through the night: a priest calling the tenets, he knew. A call to prayer for the illiterate and the loose-willed, reminding them of the rules to live by. It felt like a warning. 'Remain plain and obvious in the eyes of the Goddess!' the voice proclaimed. 'Scheme and plan not, for she is ever present! Those who plot and obfuscate her holy Truth will forever be blinded from her grace and eternal favour.' Despite the heat, Sentenza pulled his collar a little closer. All of a sudden, the Citadel felt very small. There were too many eyes and too many tongues.

Torchlight grew nearby, emerging from around a corner. Two men in the livery of the city patrol wandered out, their uniform looking almost black in the night. They seemed young and bored and green, disinterested and out of place. Perfect. Sentenza sank further into the shadows, disappearing between the makeshift shacks. He followed them at a short distance, keeping to the dark.

Ahead, they stopped. One leaned back against a wall, all laughter and teasing, while the other took a piss, deliberately urinating onto a pile of rags—someone's worldly possessions. Rats ran. The other patrolman laughed. Sentenza felt a surge of energy wash over him. He stepped from the darkness and the first man jumped, piss-leaking cock still in his hand, and spun. Too late. The solid block of air hammered into the man, catching him in the gut, and he collapsed into the pile of sodden rags. The second man stood gaping, apparently too stunned to even draw his sword. Sentenza grabbed him, dragging him back into the shadows, and, in a single move, had his dirk at the man's throat. The man opened his mouth—to scream, to shout, to cry, it mattered not. The slightest pressure of the blade convinced him to close it again.

'The next sounds from you will be the answers to my questions or they will be the last you'll ever make,' Sentenza growled at the man.

Nervous eyes searched for an escape.

'If I think you're lying or stalling, I'll kill you. If I feel you move in a way that I don't like, I'll kill you. If I think you're holding something back, I'll kill you. In fact, you're going to have to work very hard to get out of this alive. Do you understand?'

The man nodded, eyes wide and afraid.

'Okay, let's start with the easy stuff. Do you recognise my face?' Sentenza asked.

'No, sir,' came the answer.

'Why are there so many patrols? Who are you looking for?'

'The whole city's on high alert after the hand and the finger were all killed. We're meant to stop anyone we see out and check their papers.'

Sentenza swallowed, his next words disappearing from his head. The hand and the finger. Braga and his men? Surely not—

who or what could have killed a whole hand? He heard a noise behind him. The second patrolman coming to? He had little time. 'If the pioneer sergeant is dead as well then who is in charge of the army?'

'Adherent-Commander Al-Eldar and Commissioner Aargau are in charge.'

And there it was: the confirmation he had been looking for. It had all been a grab for power. Dritsek had arranged to have him killed so that he could usurp control. Still, he hadn't imagined that Braga and his men would be killed too. It was sad to hear. Braga had been a stalwart of the barracks; the rock upon which it was built. What a waste.

Sentenza felt a cold hand grip him. He'd make the Aargau boy pay. One way or another, he would look into his eyes when he died so that he knew who was killing him. He would pay with his own blood.

The noise behind him was growing louder: footfalls and voices. He half turned and, beneath him, sensed movement. At once, he bucked and twisted, rolling his body to one side. Clumsy fingers dragged at his dirk, trying to wrench the blade free. Steel sliced into flesh. The man opened his mouth to call for help. The sound was thick and wet and guttural. Sentenza had eased free the patrolman's own short sword, which now sunk deep into his belly. The colonel rose. Two new patrolmen were closing on him, swords drawn. Now a third with a pike. He spun but slipped in the growing pool of blood, stumbling to the ground. The men were on him before he had chance to regain himself. It was no use. Even with his abilities, he would be hard pressed to escape. Best to live to fight another day, he thought. For now, though, he was at their mercy.

Love one another as the Goddess loves you, for are you not her children? She loves us with a mother's love, pure and unquestioning. Would a mother beat and punish their child for making a mistake, or would she guide and teach her child not to make the same mistake again? In the same way, the Church is there to guide and mould her children to be the best and most Truthful that they can be.

—**From the Tenets of Truth**

CHAPTER TWENTY-TWO
BRAGA, MAYOR PREFEITO, AND TERVAN

The Citadel

Pioneer Sergeant Braga is definitely not an easy man to hide, Mayor Prefeito thought.

He was a big man, and difficult to miss. The mayor had told him so on several occasions, for all the good it did him. Braga stood out, and would even if he dispensed with the field hat and the blue tail coat. It was not just the uniform, but his whole deportment. Even after days in the saddle, he had too much of the soldier about him. All stiff-backed and proper. He attracted the stares of anyone they passed. There had been mercifully few of those since their encounter at the barracks, but only by design. They kept now to the small roads, avoiding the better travelled routes in an effort to avoid patrols. The conversation with the soldiers there had certainly worried Braga—that much was clear. Where earlier he had simply been quiet, now he had grown sullen too, dark of mood and even more easy to rile. The mayor had found this after mentioning his beard. During their journey it had grown longer and increasingly unkempt, like the nest of some oriole. Braga's response had been low and dangerous: a grunt like that of a bear and a look to his eye that reminded all to keep their distance. He was clearly a proud man, and the mayor's comments had chipped at that pride.

'You know,' Tervan said carefully.

'Hrrrmm,' Braga responded, as though he sensed a barb.

'I do believe you to be the most recognisable man I've ever met. That soldier, for instance, from how far away do you think he recognised you? Two, three hundred paces? You certainly must have made an impression. Did he serve under you?'

'Not directly,' Braga said, his voice rough as granite.

It's no wonder he hardly speaks, the mayor thought. *It sounds so painful each time he does.*

'Oh, I see,' said Tervan, dryly. 'I can't exactly say I'm surprised, though. I thought much the same when I first met you. "There is a man you would not forget in a hurry," I said to myself.'

'What are you trying to say?' Braga growled.

'Nothing,' Tervan said, 'only that you are indeed a noteworthy man. Distinctive and well turned-out. Your uniform, for instance. Why is it so different from everyone else's?'

'I'm a pioneer sergeant,' Braga replied, as though that were all the explanation it required. Tervan looked at the soldier expectantly. Braga sighed. 'A pioneer sergeant,' he expanded, 'is expected to do things that other soldiers aren't. You need a different uniform so that people can recognise you easily. It also gives you extra protection. The beard, for example'—he looked pointedly to the mayor—'gives better protection from a forge's heat.'

'And that great axe you carry with you?' Tervan asked, hardly letting up on the man.

'Have you ever heard the screams of a horse?' Braga answered. 'Ever had to silence those screams inside your head as well as on the field? I have and, believe me, it is not something you shake off easily. Now, if you have a point to make, make it.'

'My point is that you stick out like a great ship in a little port,' Tervan said matter-of-factly. 'No sooner than you drop anchor will people see you and gawp. Gawpers talk and the patrols will pick you up before you know it.'

The big man shot Tervan an angry look but said nothing. He seemed to mull the comments over before giving another low growl and spurring his horse on ahead. Clearly, the conversation was over.

'If it were not for the fact that you get more out of him than I could ever seem to dare, I would tell you to stop riling the man,' the mayor commented to his riding companion.

'Yes, I have something of a gift for that,' Tervan replied. His voice was melodic, friendly—a far cry from Braga's feral grunting. It was very easy to forget that they had no idea who this man was. A stranger they had met on the road, a man with no papers and a flimsy story. Despite himself, the mayor was beginning to like him. He had an easy way about him that somehow managed to soothe and calm things, especially Braga. Even so, the mayor could not shake the feeling that Tervan was hiding something. He had led them a merry dance when searching for his camp, all just a short distance from the town and the horrors that had happened there.

The memory threatened to engulf the mayor, and he fought hard to shake those dark images from his mind. Best to remain in the here and now; dwelling in the past would bring no one back and no one to justice. He hoped that, once they reached the Citadel, they could do just that. Since the barracks, though, both Tervan and Braga had seemed more apprehensive. He knew the feeling.

They approached the great city from one of the low roads, skirting the towns and districts beyond the main walls. Braga kept them clear of the gatehouses, not wanting to be stopped by patrols. Only Braga held a valid chit, though he had been reported dead. It made them all nervous and tensions were running high as they approached the city. They used little-known and unused dirt tracks and passages that brought them close to the huge outer wall. From there, Braga led them to a small and rusted gate set deep in the stone wall. It screamed in protest as the big man huffed and heaved it open, but they were too remote for anyone to have heard— or so Prefeito hoped. Squeezing impossibly into a small alley, the pioneer sergeant disappeared, leaving the two men to hold the horses.

Before long, he reappeared with a short man who could easily have been a miniature Braga. He had a weathered face, cracked and craggy beyond belief, though his eyes were quick and bright. The pair exchanged some half-whispered words before Braga gave an uproarious laugh and slapped the other man on his thickset shoulders.

What was that all about? the mayor wondered.

'Come,' called Braga, beckoning to him and Tervan.

'But, what about our horses?' Prefeito protested, looking at the gate. 'They won't fit through that.'

The newcomer crossed to the two men and quietly took hold of the reins. He smiled at the mayor, all crooked teeth blackened with age.

'They ain't your horses anymore, boy,' he said with a dangerous chuckle. 'They're mine.' Prefeito struggled against the man as he took the horses, uncertain what was happening. It felt like they were being robbed, but the sound of Braga's laugh softened the moment.

'Come on,' Braga said again.

Prefeito turned to Tervan. 'I don't suppose we have much of a choice then.'

They both gave a last bemused look at the animals, who were being led slowly away by their new owner.

'After you,' said Tervan, ushering him towards the gate.

'You sold the horses?' Prefeito called after the big man, but he had already disappeared beyond a turn in the alleyway. They hurried after him, not wanting to find themselves lost as they went from one short and twisting walkway to another. The air was dense and thick as they scurried, though the sun was hidden behind the high walls. Each breath felt hard and heavy with the dust and grime of the city. No sooner would they catch a glimpse of Braga when he would duck beyond a corner, leading them deeper into the labyrinth of enclosed alleys. Here and there a small doorway led away through a wall, and the stink of bucket slop permeated the air.

Beyond a final corner, Braga had stopped and the mayor walked into him. It was like hitting a wall. 'What are you doing, man?' he called, annoyed and winded. 'Why won't you stop still and tell us where we are going?'

'He *has* stopped,' called Tervan from behind, with more humour in his voice than the mayor cared for. He shot him a look.

The three stepped out of the alley and onto a great square bustling with the sights and sounds of the city. A bazaar of workshops teemed with people, and the air rang with the heavy pounding of hammers striking metal and huge bellows being pumped. It had a rhythm all its own, and was like nothing the mayor had ever experienced. There were easily more than a hundred smithies and forges scattered around the crowded square, each one bustling with its own team of workers. Huge, bare-chested men seemed lost in their own fiery worlds, while carters delivering goods and hawkers calling their wares circulated among them. The noise and the heat hit Prefeito like a blast. How could anyone work in this inferno? All fire and flame and soot, orange and red and black swirling and colliding in a great whirlwind of activity. It was tumultuous.

'Where are we?' Prefeito asked, an edge of wonder to his voice as he took in the sight before him.

'Smithston,' replied Braga simply.

'We had a smithy in Baile Saor,' the mayor responded, 'but it was nothing like this.'

'This is not a smithy,' said Braga sharply. 'This is Smithston.'

'But what are we doing here? We hardly need a smith now that we have no horses,' the mayor complained.

'Smiths don't only work metal,' said Tervan. 'They also trade livestock, like horses. That's probably what he was doing earlier—selling the horses to one of these smiths.'

A boy trundled past with a barrow, but he caught an uneven stone and spilled some of his wares. The mayor bent to help him collect the things that had fallen. He pulled his hand away when it touched something sticky and wet and recoiled further when he saw a bloodied and severed hoof. His stomach churned. The barrow boy grinned at his reaction, waving another amputated limb up at him before continuing on his way.

Again, Braga laughed before clapping the mayor on the shoulder. 'Come on,' he said and, before Prefeito had chance to respond, he started off again, offering nothing more by way of explanation as to where he was heading.

'What in the name of the Three was that?' Prefeito asked Tervan as they made their way after the sergeant.

'Well, I don't know about smiths,' Tervan said, 'but animal horns or hooves, and even teeth, can be ground down and used in tonics and potions for healing. We use filings and clippings from my draft horse to make a tincture to treat all kinds of maladies.'

The words tugged at the mayor's mind. 'We?' he asked.

'I mean, uh, the horse and I. *We* used to make tinctures,' Tervan stammered. Shooting Prefeito a nervous smile, he hastened after Braga.

Prefeito watched him go. What wasn't Tervan telling him? Could he have had something to do with what happened at the town? It was hard to believe. The man just didn't seem to have it in him.

Begrudgingly, the mayor followed his two companions, not wanting to be left behind with the bloody hooves. He didn't much like this place; there were too many eyes for one, and the city represented everything he had worked hard to move away from. Baile Soar should have been a free town, cut away from the ties of the Citadel and its priests. That was what he had paid so much for, what they had all paid so much for. That was what they had been promised. He remembered the pomp and the fanfare, the quick green eyes of the king's emissary. Square jaw and angular features. Silver tongue and silver words. No more taxes, no more tithes, no more militia; freedom from the Church, freedom from the City-Lord. Freedom from anyone but the king himself. They'd thought that Baile Saor would grow to be the biggest and most profitable market town in the region. Traders would flock from every corner of Lacustria to sell their wares at low costs. It had been a simple decision. Who wouldn't have agreed? The whole town had been abuzz with excitement.

'We need workers for a cycle or two. Specialist work—requires small hands and tiny fingers. Delicate and gentle. A small price to pay, I think you will agree,' the emissary had said, green eyes sparkling and perfect teeth beaming a perfect smile for a prefect arrangement. The deal was struck, the parchment sealed. A small cost, or so it had seemed. The children would not be gone long, and they would be treated better than ever; fed and watered and even educated while they were away.

The seasons had turned and a cycle passed. Then the priest returned, demanding tithes and taxes, but the children did not. Angry, the town protested, but the priest did not listen. The people pleaded, but he showed no pity. They rose up their voices in prayer, but he wouldn't hear them. Even now, Prefeito wasn't sure what had broken them—anger? Pain? Guilt? It mattered not. They had carried the priest to the Knap. All along the way, he'd screamed the things that would happen to them—the Goddess would strike them down, the Suers would fall upon them and tear out their very souls with hot irons... all manner of wicked and evil things. More than two weeks later, he was still in the tunnels. Or, at least, his body was, slumped behind the huge stone. By then, his eyes had bulged and his swollen tongue lolled over his chin. He hadn't even gone one step. Where had his Goddess been?

Almost a cycle went by before the next priest arrived. He met the same fate. And then there had been a third, Dreban. He'd been young; the same age as some of the children might be now. It had not been lost on the town. It had felt different than the others; less certain. Too many saw their own Truth in his face, their own sins reflected in his eyes. Had he too called to the Goddess for vengeance in the tunnels? Had she answered? Was that why the town had been massacred?

Ahead, Tervan was calling something to him. Prefeito blinked, surprised by the light and the buildings around him. He felt as if he'd just woken from a terrible dream.

Braga was there, stood beneath the canopy of yet another workshop. It was filled with iron and coal and heat, and the smells of tar and soot and burning forced their way into Prefeito's nose. An apprentice boy worked the bellows tirelessly, legs pumping as he climbed his eternal staircase. He was shirtless and covered in soot. *Old beyond his cycles*, Prefeito thought. The contraption roared as it fed the flames of the smithy, sending the temperature soaring oppressively. The mayor wondered how the boy could bear it. Braga shared some words with the lad, who pointed inside without missing his step. It was mesmerising.

'If you're here for your quota, I told you that it would be ready tomorrow,' called a hard and threatening voice from further inside. A thick-shouldered man came to the door, wiping his hand on his heavy leather apron. His eyes fell on Tervan and the mayor. Despite the heat, there was no warmth there. Not for the first time, Prefeito wondered what they were doing here.

Braga clapped a large hand on to the man's shoulder—though, for once, it looked normal-sized. The smith dropped a hand to his belt, a blade flashing crimson in the glow of the furnace. The smith spun, but Braga met the man's fist with his own hand. For a moment, the two seemed locked in a struggle. It seemed the entire world stood still, and the mayor realised he was holding his breath.

A broad grin spread over the smith's face. 'Braga, you great barrel,' he laughed, dropping the blade. He pulled the soldier into an affectionate embrace. 'What are you doing here?'

Prefeito exhaled, letting the tension ease from him.

'I could have killed you, old man,' the smith went on, 'just walking in here like that. What? You don't send me word that you're coming these days? I would have brought ale, or at least drawn some fresh water. And who are your two friends? Come in, come in!' He beckoned to them all. 'Any friend of Braga can take embers from my fire. I'm Kovack, by the way.' His hands were big and rough and hard, and he shook theirs with evident glee.

Kovack ducked into the workshop and brushed off a worktable with a huge arm, sending piles of wood and metal clattering to the floor. He ushered Braga onto a stool before dragging one over for himself. He disappeared before sitting, however. 'It's been months, Braga,' he called from the next room, before quickly reappearing with a pitcher and four metal tankards. He laid the mugs on the table, sloshed some dirty-looking liquid into each of them, then handed them around. 'Why have you not been by in so long, then?'

Prefeito exchanged an uncertain glance with Tervan before shrugging and taking a sip of the curious liquid. He waited for a reaction to whatever it was to develop in his mouth, but was much relieved to realise that it was only water. Warm and gritty and earthy, but water, and much appreciated. It was the first hospitality they had received since leaving Baile Soar, and he found the simplicity of the act almost humbling.

'Now, tell me,' the smith continued, 'when are you going to take my little sister from my hands? You know that you like her. She is an excellent cook and can run a house for you.'

Braga laughed.

'Of course, of course, there is no need to take care of a house when you live in the barracks,' the smith conceded, 'but now that most of the soldiers are virtually living in the Citadel, you can take a house here, can't you? And tell me, what's with all of the demands they're making of us to up our work quota? Produce more axe heads and swords they say one day, more arrowheads and bodkins the next. They work us too hard and harass us even harder to arm the militia.'

Braga stopped laughing. He placed his mug on the table and leaned in conspiratorially towards his friend, inviting him to say more.

'What, you don't know this?' Kovack said disbelievingly. 'Of course you know this. You're stationed at the barracks, you must know—it is all over the Citadel and must be the talk of the soldiers.' He looked into Braga's weary face and sat back. 'But that's it, isn't it? You're not at the barracks anymore. But if you're not at the barracks, where are you?' He looked to Tervan and the mayor, taking them in. Bedraggled and unkempt, covered in dust and grime. 'Not on the run, old friend? How could *you* be on the run? Wait a minute, something has happened. Something serious? Is it anything to do with this business in the interior? The town?'

Braga's hand had been absently stroking his beard, but the smith's words seemed to still him. His eyes stole to Prefeito. It did not go unnoticed.

'The massacre, Braga—you were there?' Kovack said, leaning back. He looked at the mayor, his suspicion growing. 'I know that you weren't involved in any massacre, not our little bear. You may be the meanest bastard in the barracks, old man, but I know that you wouldn't hurt the innocent. What happened there? Who are these men you bring with you?'

For once, the smith let the question hang in the air.

Braga looked mournfully down into his cup and drained the water it held.

'An ambush, a trap, I guess. I don't know,' said Braga eventually. He sounded tired; not the gruff and angry man from the road. Here, he sounded almost soft.

'An ambush?' asked Kovack. 'Of course, an ambush, but you got away—not alone, though?' His eyes once again drifted over to

Prefeito and Tervan. 'I mean, the three of you survived.'

The smith stood and walked to a small cabinet, bending slightly to open it and taking out an earthenware flask from inside. He returned to his chair, stopping to half-fill the four tankards with a dark caramel-coloured liquid, thick with the smell of anise and other spices.

'This calls for something stronger than water and I have no ale,' the smith explained, 'so it will have to be black brandy. I warn you, it is strong.' He smiled at the other men and took a small sip from his mug, smacking his lips and exhaling loudly. 'If you three survived, that makes at least three more than the official stories are saying. Who knows what other lies they are telling, eh?'

Braga sipped his drink. Whether his reaction was a snort, cough, or grunt, it was hard to tell.

'They're bringing soldiers from the barracks to protect the Citadel and the people. They say it isn't safe after an assault on one of the City-Lord's towns—a barbaric attack that left only one adherent alive. And—get this—he only survived thanks to his *prayers*. It was the Goddess and his faith that saved him.'

This time Braga did snort.

'You know what this means though, Braga, if they are spreading this truth?'

'The *truth* is that everyone there that day died,' the mayor said in the following silence. 'We returned to the town afterwards, and not one person remained alive in that place. Soldiers, men, women. Everyone had been slain. Some of the townspeople had been cut down where they stood. Others, it seemed, had been corralled into the main hall like cattle before the building was torched with all inside. We don't even know what took them first, the flames or the smoke. For the soldiers and the rest, it was just as gruesome: each one was spiked from the arsehole to the chest or throat. There were too many in total for us to bury, so we burned the bodies. We surrounded them with faggots and set them alight. We filled the town with the smell of burning. People I'd known all my life. Neighbours, friends—everyone, gone.' Prefeito's voice trailed off, and when he looked up, his face was flushed. 'No one could have escaped from there, faith or not. There was no Truth that day. I have prayed and I have searched for the Truth, and I don't know if ever I have heard it—not from the mouth of men, not from my own mouth, and not from the damned Church. The truth is that something terrible and unforgiveable happened that day. The truth is that we are punished for the choices we make in our lives. The truth is that we two'—he motioned here to Braga and downed the rest of his brandy—'we two survived that day. We picked him up'—a nod to Tervan—'on the way back from there. The truth is that everyone I have ever known is either dead or lost to me now, and these two are the only people that I know for certain had nothing to do with it all. That is the only truth that matters anymore.'

The mayor banged his empty mug down on the table and walked back out into the sweltering day. It had grown late, and what sun there was left was already being stolen by the height of the city walls, though the sheer number of fires and furnaces in the square created a false daylight. Shadows of orange and red danced around the walls and floor, making the place itself feel alive. Ghosts, perhaps, having come to be remembered. The mayor felt stiff-legged and tired. Whether it was the days of travelling catching up with him or simply a heavy heart, he wasn't sure. He sank onto a nearby bench and closed his eyes, letting the rhythm of clanging hammers lull him. The mechanical draw of air echoed the rasp of his own breath. He focused on it, losing himself in the pattern.

When he finally opened his eyes, he saw the apprentice boy still stepping his bellows. Sweat soaked into the rough salamander trousers he wore to protect him from the heat, their grey fabric scorched and blackened. It looked like backbreaking work. Prefeito's mind drifted to his own son. He wondered where he might be now and whether he would ever see him again. Was he somewhere like this, working from dawn 'til dusk and beyond? The thought made him feel sick.

'Are you all right?' asked Tervan, though the mayor hardly heard his words. He stared at the boy, lost among his thoughts. The familiar self-loathing spread slowly through him.

'I lost someone too that day,' Tervan continued. 'Someone close to me. In fact, someone who I guess meant the world to me, who gave me the strength and will to carry on day after day. The world can be such a large and lonely place, and I had been alone for such a long, long time.'

The mayor felt the light touch of Tervan's hand on his shoulder. Finally, he turned to look at his companion. There was so much that they didn't know about each other; so much that people kept hidden from others. *Everyone has their own truth*, Prefeito considered. *One truth they show to the world, and another that they hide away inside, known only to themselves.* Would Tervan be so easy with him if he knew what he'd done? Still, the man's gesture eased the tension he felt. Just knowing that he shared his pain gave them a common bond. He knew then that he'd been too harsh with Tervan when they'd first met. The man had a kind heart.

The sound of a painful hacking distracted the two men, and they looked up to see that the boy had stopped working his bellows and was instead bent almost double in a rage of violent coughing.

Tervan crossed to the apprentice and, without thinking, Prefeito followed him. Up close, the boy's face was pallid, blue under the skin. His skin was covered in nodules and his brittle skin was cracked and riddled with warts. His cough worsened, intensifying until he began to produce globules of rust-coloured sputum that he spat on the ground. With each rasping hack they grew darker and redder.

The mayor could only watch, not knowing what to do. He felt helpless. Tervan, on the other hand, immediately began soothing the boy, patting at his back as though he might free him of some imbalanced humour lying heavy on his chest. It didn't work, and the boy wretched and coughed and gasped until the floor was thick with bloody phlegm. It seemed to pass and, exhausted with the effort, the boy lay on the floor, still. The mayor feared him dead, but Tervan continued to speak to him gently, calmly stroking at his hair and face.

'Could you please bring some water for him?' Tervan asked. The mayor did as he was bidden, quickly dashing back into the small room and taking the water pitcher and a tankard from the table where a bemused Braga still sat talking with the smith.

'Here,' said Tervan when he returned. 'Help me lift him a little.'

The mayor put the mug on the ground and assisted in raising the exhausted boy's head and shoulders. He reached out to grasp the mug and, as he did so, his hand brushed against the rough fibres of the salamanders. Immediately, he felt it burn with an angry itching as the skin turned bright and pink. 'What in the Mother's name?' he hissed.

The strong voice of the smith sounded as he and Braga emerged: 'Try not to itch it,' he said, 'it won't burn long. Scratching at it will only make it worse, and like as not set it bleeding.'

'But what in the name of the Goddess is it?' Prefeito asked, alarm thick in his voice.

'I told you, don't worry,' said Kovack, 'it is from the trousers. The fibres used to make them cause a strong reaction on the skin when they are first worn, but after a time the body grows tolerant and doesn't react—unless you bloody scratch at it!' he said, seeing the mayor scratching at the mark on his hand. 'Don't say I didn't warn you if it warts—but, if it does, try crushing blister beetle onto it.'

'Blister beetle?' Prefeito sounded horrified. 'Does that really work?'

'Some say it does,' the smith said. 'I don't know so much myself, mind. Now, what is wrong with young Vrat here?'

Tervan had been helping the boy drink a little. He set down the cup and first placed his palm on the boy's forehead and then on his chest. He closed his eyes as if concentrating while the other men looked on, somewhat bemused.

'It feels like he has the coughing sickness,' said Tervan, opening his eyes and lifting his hand from the boy's chest.

'Like shite he has,' Kovack argued. 'Nothing wrong with the lad that can't be cured with black brandy and broth.'

He bent down, trying to help the boy up, but he was met with resistance from Tervan. The tinker was resolute and immoveable, even for the burly smith.

'The boy isn't well,' insisted Tervan, 'and he will only get worse without the proper help. Believe me, I have seen it before. His flesh is out of balance and the miasma of this place has turned his chest sour. It will continue to eat away at his lungs until they can be of no more use, and at that point his body will give out on him.'

The smith seemed not to listen and moved once more to try to lift the boy, but Tervan laid his hand on the other man's. The tinker looked deep into his eyes, holding the smith there. 'You must trust me,' he said calmly in a way that brooked no argument. 'It is the only way. I have seen it before and treated it.'

Kovack stopped and looked to Braga and the mayor, who both

looked back at him expectantly. 'Very well,' he acquiesced. 'Tell me what you need us to do.'

At length, the smith was sent to retrieve a list of ingredients, most of which he had either little knowledge of or had never even heard uttered before: Althea root, lobelia, velvet plant, and wild cherry bark. The smith couldn't read, so they had him repeat the recipe to be certain. A table was brought and Tervan had Braga lift the boy onto it. Prefeito, meanwhile, was sent to find candles, and returned with three thick torches.

The commotion brought onlookers. The worried and the curious gathered round, vying for the best spot from which to watch.

'I asked for candles,' Tervan barked at the mayor.

'What's wrong with torches?' he asked, a little irked at the rebuff.

'Torches and lanterns are not what I require or asked for. Besides, they help to set the scene, my dear gi—' Tervan's voice cut off suddenly. 'I just want them,' he finished lamely, looking abashed. Annoyed, the mayor went off again in search of candles. 'And if you can find them, make them brayberry candles at that!' Tervan called after him.

Prefeito managed barely a dozen candles; most were tallow and none were brayberry. Tervan begrudgingly accepted the fruits of his efforts and instructed him to bring a large bowl or jug into which he could place some water. He returned with a heavy metallic basin that rang noisily as he set it down on a small side table they had found. Tervan inspected the offering with a heavy look of dissatisfaction, but seemed to accept that it was the best Prefeito could do.

When the smith returned, he had to force his way through the small group of onlookers, who kept having to be ushered back by

Tervan as they crept ever closer. The air was strangely calm, yet the candles, which had all been burning straight and still, began to sputter and dance about their wicks.

'Did you find them all?' Tervan asked the smith.

'Did I find them? Of course I found them! There is a woman I know who provides flowers to some of the House-Lords and to the Church itself, so she tells me,' he said with pride before adding more meekly, 'although, of course, I wouldn't know these things. I attend only the small church here in Smithston.'

'Good,' Tervan said, 'as you will need some more items once we are done here.'

'More?' Kovack croaked. 'I am not made of coin, man.'

Tervan and Prefeito looked angrily at the smith, though it was to Braga that he looked to for confirmation. 'I suppose it can be set against the boy's earnings,' Kovack conceded.

The mayor watched on as Tervan took the items, mixing up this and crushing sections of that into the metal bowl, and all the while seeming to whisper to himself under his breath. At one point, Prefeito was sure that he heard him singing softly, but he could not make out the words. The man seemed lost to his work, pouring hot water into the mixture he had created and then swirling the steaming contents around and around.

To the mayor, the meticulous process seemed almost religious in nature, although it was not at all like the sombre rituals he had witnessed at church. Instead, this had the free feeling of celebration that he had come to recognise since he had lost faith in the Church and returned to the old ways of worship. He watched Tervan closely; he seemed almost in a trance as he mumbled away to himself, although it seemed that he was very conscious of the people around him at the same time. In fact, the mayor suspected that the man's actions were more of a performance for those gathered than anything else.

Surely all of this is unnecessary, Prefeito thought. *Whatever it is he's made will be growing cold by the time he's finished*. Tervan mopped at his brow and gave the mayor a look. His cold glare made Prefeito feel like he'd been caught doing something wrong. He looked away to the small crowd once again, meeting the eyes of several of those gathered. Tervan did not speak, but nonetheless an understanding seemed to pass between him and the crowd, as though each person knew that they were somehow contributing to what was happening. Finally, as if breaking some spell, the healer called out.

'Mother,' Tervan called. 'Help this child. Bring him to your breast and suckle him with your nourishing love. Even though I do not hold your tear, see his tears and our own and let them wash away his pain.'

Holding the bowl at arm's length, Tervan tilted the metal to the boy's lips and helped him drink from it. Slowly, he moved back to the table and replaced the bowl before walking to each of the candles and blowing them out one by one. Finally, he disappeared into the shadows of the square behind the smith's rooms.

The crowd remained for some time, half-hidden in the comparative darkness, mere outlines glittering in the orange glow of the furnaces, until eventually even these faces began to thin and escape into the dusk. Finding himself stood within the clearing they had created, Prefeito went to the boy and used a damp cloth to wipe away the congealed and flaking blood from his chest and body. His hands moved slowly and methodically, and for a strange moment Prefeito felt that they belonged to someone else. Without warning, a great welling sadness settled upon him; tears filled his eyes and the air seemed to close in around him, bearing heavy against his chest. A cough from the boy cut through the silence, bringing with it a fresh glob of spittle, this time clear of blood.

'Maybe there is something to that healer of yours after all,' the smith said from the darkness.

The mayor had not even realised that anyone else was there. The surprise of finding that he was no longer alone helped him bite back the tears that had threatened to overwhelm him.

'I hope so, for the boy's sake,' he managed with a croak. 'Where is Braga?'

'Off to see my sister,' the smith said. 'I dare say that he will be a while. Is the boy cured? Did your friend say what we are to do with him?'

'No, he didn't, and I don't know where he's gone either.'

'Well, you can stay here in the rooms if you want. You can use the bench to rest while you wait. I will take the boy back to his lodgings to sleep and recover. I will need him back to his duties as soon as he is able.'

'He has no family?' Prefeito asked, 'no mother to take care of him?'

The smith's face didn't change, but the mayor thought he saw something like sadness come into his eyes. 'Few of the boys working on the square have anyone to take care of them, my friend. This is no place for a mother's care—it is a place of men and work. Even mothers learn that lesson quickly.'

With that, the smith crossed to the boy and slid his thickset arms around him. He picked him up as though he were nothing more than a bundle of clothes and carried him away into the near darkness. Exhausted, the mayor dragged himself to the workshop and collapsed onto a bench. It was not long before the warmth and the events of the day combined to overtake him, and he drifted off into a fitful sleep.

A noise roused Prefeito several times through the night, and he finally awoke to find that Tervan had returned and now sat with his back to the room, huddled over a metal stove in the corner. Orange light skittered playfully about him as he tended to a small fire burning beneath a metal pot, which bubbled as if near to the boil.

'Did I wake you?' Tervan said without turning. 'Sorry, I didn't mean to. I find it difficult to sleep after I work.'

The mayor sat up and rubbed at his eyes, which somehow felt even more raw and tired than they had the night before. 'What?' he said drowsily. 'Oh, yes, I must have dropped off. I wondered where you had gone to.'

'Just needed a walk to clear my mind. Where is the boy?'

'The smith took him to his rooms to rest. Will he be okay?'

'It's difficult to say. Things are never quite as easy or as accurate without...' Tervan's words slipped away. If he did finish the sentence, the mayor did not hear. He leaned on his hand and the action caused a stab of pain where the salamanders had rubbed him earlier.

'You really should put something on that, you know,' Tervan said, again without turning.

The mayor reflexively pulled his hand back and shoved it into his coat; a child caught stealing a treat from the kitchen. 'What? Oh, yes, the hand?' he said. 'It's nothing, it will be okay. Just a little... How did you...?'

The pot on the stove gave a shrill whistle. Tervan stood, picked it up with an old rag, and carried it over to the table. He poured some of the boiling water into two waiting cups and began swirling the contents. Finally, he brought them over to the bench and handed one to the mayor.

'Here,' he said, 'drink this.'

'What is it?' Prefeito asked, sniffing at the brew.

'Just a tea. Mostly cherry bark, but there was still a little velvet plant left over. I'm afraid that I am a little out of practice at mixing teas these days. I used to be much more proficient, but it should taste fine.'

Watching his travel companion as he sipped at the steaming brew, Prefeito was struck by how lost and mournful Tervan now seemed. It was as if he had suddenly been made aware of a great tragedy and loss.

There is much more to this man that I gave him credit. He wondered if he should go to the man and offer him comfort, but the sound of boots on stone and shouting rose suddenly from outside. Tervan showed no signs of having heard. Prefeito tried to look from a small window, but saw nothing. Even at this hour, the square hummed to the rhythm of the bellows and the chime of hammers. More voices rose in the early morning, sharp and angry.

Something wasn't right.

'Quick,' Prefeito said, placing down his cup and gathering together their things, 'I think it's time that we find Braga and be on our way. We have drawn far too much attention to ourselves.'

Tervan did not move. He seemed to be far away, absorbed and preoccupied. It was not the time. The mayor dragged at his arm, but it was like trying to rouse a drunk. 'We don't have time for this.'

'What? What are we doing? Where are Braga and the boy?' Tervan seemed dazed and befuddled, suddenly very old and uncertain.

'I don't know,' said Prefeito. 'That's what we need to go and find out. Most of all, though, we need to be away from here.'

The sounds grew louder. The mayor swore under his breath— the men were directly outside. Rough voices barked and shouted. He held his breath, trying to keep as still as possible. Maybe they weren't looking for them. They might leave if they just stayed quiet. A heavy hand hammered at the door, which swung slowly open. The square outside was filled with men in dark uniform. Eight, Prefeito counted, maybe ten. Two carried something between them—something dishevelled and bloodied and crumpled. A life-sized doll, perhaps. No, Prefeito realised with sickening certainty—it was a man. The smith.

The guards dragged him into the smithy and let him slump to the floor. The mayor stared at him, uncertain what to do. The guards stiffened and straightened, each of them clicking to attention. A dark figure moved through the doorway, his pace slow and deliberate, his black robes swirling around him as though they were made of shadow rather than fabric. A heavy black cowl covered his face, all features lost to the darkness within. All warmth seemed to evaporate. The mayor watched, transfixed, as the man removed his hood, revealing pale eyes that seemed to stab into the gloom of the place.

'The Truth of the Goddess be with us all,' the man said, his voice crisp and clear, with a singsong cadence that made light of the otherwise tense atmosphere. He was full of his own self-importance.

No one spoke, and Prefeito didn't dare move. He looked to Tervan, then back to the stranger. The silence grew, spreading its icy tendrils throughout the smithy, and the mayor felt all the more uncertain. Fear and dread stole through him. Whoever and whatever this man was, he was not good news. Just look at what he'd done to the smith! The mayor considered making a dash for it, but quickly decided against it. Even if he made it out of the room, there'd be more guards outside. Plus, he had no idea where to run. It was Braga who had brought them here and was nowhere to be seen. He only hoped that the big man hadn't ended up like the smith.

'Allow me to introduce myself,' the man said coldly. 'I am Adherent-Commander Al-Eldar.' He paused for effect, allowing the gravitas of his name to soak in. The adherent's mouth twitched when no one showed any sign of recognising his title.

Al-Eldar stepped further into the room, moving slowly and assuredly towards a wooden chair. He turned it to face the two men before settling into it. He was silent for a time, allowing the unease to spread as he slowly examined the room. He looked deliberately to the smith and beckoned one of the assembled guards with pale and slender fingers.

'Remove our friend now, I think,' he said. The man did as he was told, grabbing the insensible man underneath the arms and dragging his limp carcass from the room. 'We live in very dangerous times, gentlemen,' Al-Eldar observed at length. 'The enemies of the Goddess and her worldly Church are amassing. I myself have seen the perils that await the impious with mine own eyes. I have witnessed the torments and tortures that will afflict the bodies, and no doubt the souls, of those who align themselves with heretics— the fires that must consume the flesh of the wicked and the pain that purges the sinful.' His pale eyes seemed to stare emptily into the room, looking at but not truly seeing its contents. They seemed to focus instead on some distant object beyond the confines of the walls. Absently, he seemed to realise that he was still holding out his hand after beckoning his men. He looked at it as though seeing it for the first time, surprised to find it there. He slowly folded his fingers into his palm, creating a loose fist, as if he were closing a fan. The man seemed deranged, the mayor thought.

'The Church shows us that the pagan beliefs of the heretics from bygone eras were falsehoods,' he continued, 'used to deceive the people and lead them away from the Truth. It is only right, therefore, to expunge these lies and treacheries from the world with the sword of Truth and the hammer of righteousness, much in the way our friend there used his hammer to beat out the impurities from his metal. There can be fewer trades than that of the humble smith that symbolise so vividly the Church's eternal struggle against those elements that would seek to lead the people astray. Yet here we are, we four, and at least one of us holds untruths in their heart, and I have my suspicions about the other two.' His eyes came to rest first on Tervan, and then moved to Prefeito. They flickered a fiery red in the lamplight like the eyes of some monster from a children's story.

He looks every bit as insane as he sounds. 'What did you do to the smith?' Prefeito demanded. 'And what do you intend for us?' In truth, his voice sounded less demanding than he had hoped, but still much more forthright than he had feared.

'My dear friend, I have not done a thing to the smith,' Al-Eldar said, unfurling his fingers to indicate the limp pile of flesh at the door. 'I am a man of righteousness, albeit a soldier of Truth able to bear arms in the protection of the Goddess and her Church. I do so only in periculous times, when the pious children of the Goddess are threatened by the wickedness of those with lies and wickedness in their hearts.'

'I thought you said that these *are* dangerous times, full of impiety and peril,' Tervan interjected, his voice barbed and angry.

'Ah,' the adherent replied, 'so I did. Nevertheless, I assure you that I am not responsible for the unfortunate condition of our friend here. No, rather it is he himself that is responsible—oh, and of course, my excellent and most indefatigable compatriots outside. It is they who ask the questions to which the Truthful heart will sing out loud in joyful response. My humble responsibility is merely to recognise and hear that Truth.' He stood, his face twitching, and it seemed to the mayor that the very sound of the healer's voice

301

pricked at the adherent. Al-Eldar began to slowly pace about the room.

'Of course, you wouldn't want to dirty your hands with the blood of others, would you?' Tervan remarked. 'You are much better as the father confessor, arms open and ready to embrace the foolhardy back into the treacherous bosom of the Church.'

Mother protect us, Prefeito thought. *He's going to get us all killed.*

The adherent spun on his heels, arm outstretched with the heavy black robe framing the pale finger that pointed at Tervan. 'You dare speak of our sacred and benedight Church with such shamelessness?' he barked. 'You are a most foul and wicked snake. I knew you for the spawn of the beast as soon as I heard you speak with your forked and Truthless tongue. When I heard that a girl from the smith's church had been sent to search out herbs and ingredients that could only be used in some evil communion, I knew that you lay in wait. You, who fornicates with jezebels and harlots, who gives himself freely to obfuscate the worthy and pure of heart, selling your lies and filth to others just to benefit your own ends. I had the girl followed,' he said with satisfaction, 'which led us to the child whose innocent soul you tried to steal as the whole community watched, including the poor sinner at our feet, whom you ensnared with heresy and miscommunication. A fool who believed not in the blessed Truth of our holy Church, but instead in the depraved ravings of your lecherous mouth.'

The adherent seemed at once possessed by a great zeal and the lamps seemed to flicker and spit in reaction to his fervour. He rested for a moment, slightly out of breath and stifling a cough.

Tervan had also risen, standing tall and proud and meeting the pale eyes of the adherent with his own. They seemed to glow strong and green against the orange hue of the lamps. The intensity thickened, though neither man spoke. Prefeito felt like the whole room had begun to ache. It seemed to him that Tervan was somehow growing in stature while the adherent shrank into himself.

'Guards!' the adherent shouted, breaking the spell.

Two of the uniformed men came hurriedly into the room, short swords in hand.

'Take them both.' He motioned with his hand before lifting the cowl back over his head. 'We will have need to speak with them further. Leave the smith,' he added as he stepped over the prostrate body and through the door, touching his fingers to first his forehead, then to his ears, and finally to his lips.

Open yourself to the Church as you open yourself to the Goddess.
Allow them into you and your innermost places, the places you keep
only for yourself. Only then can you know Truth. Keep these places
pure and clear of the pains of the world. Be directed only by the
Church and your love for the Goddess in deciding who may share
these places, be that by choice or otherwise.

—From the Tenets of Truth

CHAPTER TWENTY-THREE
SOLATTA

Viytorren

Orange lights flickered in the near distance. It looked for all the world as though the wind had just blown hard onto a bonfire, stirring up a swarm of embers that glowed bright against the night sky. Only, instead of dying out or blowing away, they lingered in place, growing in size and, seemingly, in number. Solatta found it terrifying and mesmerising in equal measure.

She'd roamed far and wide during her travels with Tervan, but they had always kept to the smaller villages and hamlets. Tervan would venture alone into the larger towns to sell their goods and trade for food, but he'd always leave her behind. The soldiers called this place Viytorren and named it a town, but it was so big that she could not help but wonder if it was not really a city.

They'd travelled without stopping since the soldiers had found them that morning, and her body creaked and groaned from the journey. Her backside felt like a slab of stone, and she fidgeted in the wooden riding seat of the vardo, trying in vain to find some relief.

The leading patrolman—the sergeant, she remembered—had brought his horse up alongside the vardo at some point and, after fiddling about in his saddlebag, offered her a small blanket. Solatta had been reluctant to take it from him, embarrassed by the prospect of accepting his gesture while Dreban languished, but had eventually politely accepted. When she'd asked to go inside, the officers had agreed, but only if Dreban was brought to sit outside with them. It seemed a harsh thing to force him out of the comfortable caravan, and they had promised to remove his bindings if she was good, and so she opted to remain in the increasingly cool air as night drew in around them. Besides, this way she was able to see where they were heading.

The soldiers had not been cruel or mean to either her or Dreban, for which she was grateful. It was a difficult position, and she was very aware that Dreban could be in a lot of trouble for not holding his papers or the correct travel chit. It had always been so easy with Tervan—he had always taken care of these kinds of things. 'Just typical of him to leave me alone to deal with everything,' she found herself saying absently. 'I wish you were here, you stubborn old goat. You'd know exactly what to do.'

'Pardon, miss?' asked the sergeant. She had forgotten he was there. She felt foolish talking to herself in front of him.

'Nothing,' she replied hastily. 'I just wondered if you know what they'll do with me and Dreban.'

The sergeant kept his eyes on the road. 'I don't exactly know. We just pick 'em up and bring 'em in. That's our orders. What happens after that is out of my hands. Believe me,' he said, meeting her eyes, 'if it were up to me, miss, I'd much rather you been in my hands.' He smiled warmly and, despite herself, Solatta actually found herself warming to the man. He at least seemed genuine and had gone out of his way to make her comfortable. His two companions, however, made her feel uncomfortable. Their cold and hungry eyes followed her wherever she went. She felt them on her even now, gazing from somewhere behind the vardo. It made her flesh crawl.

Maybe if she just did what the guards wanted and didn't cause a fuss then they could sort everything out once they arrived in town. They could find someone to replace Dreban's papers and would be allowed to go on their way. The thought comforted her though, in truth, she had no idea who they needed to speak to about chits and papers. She frowned.

Night drew in around them, swallowing them up in the dark, though the air remained thick and sticky. Their path had driven them further south, away from the river, and west, towards the coast and the sea. A part of her longed to sit atop a hill and watch the waves crashing onto the shore, as she had with Tervan. The other part of her wanted to run away in the opposite direction. It dawned on her that she would never just sit and watch the world go by with her guardian again. *What is it with people and leaving me?* she wondered with a wry smile. *First my parents, now Tervan—who's next? Dreban?*

The thought had come unbidden. She had come to feel a great deal for her charge. He had come to her as a patient and she had given him her maidenhead. She'd taken his as well, she suspected.

She smiled a cheeky smile, all teeth and dimples. It felt like a release, until she felt the eyes of the guards on her again. She shrank back into her clothes and focused on the road.

The town loomed heavily, burning embers resolving into blazing torches. There seemed to be too many for one place. It must be huge. And it was. Everything about Viytorren was on a bigger scale than anything Solatta had seen before. The daunting walls and gates, even the roads and the square they led to—all were grand. The town heaved and moved to the pattern of the people that gathered there. The square seemed alive with a writhing mass of hawkers and traders. Peasants carrying tall wicker baskets filled with all kinds of goods weaved their way through, some hauling fruit, others cloth, and yet others small objects that looked like stones. Solatta's eyes grew wide and fat as she tried to drink it all in. She felt like climbing down and running among them. But would she ever be able to make it back? She thought of Dreban, trapped inside the vardo, and burned with guilt. It was a childish dream, she knew, and she was a woman now. She sighed heavily as a young girl stretched towards the vardo, hand offering an apple. Solatta took the fruit and searched about for a coin to give the girl in return. Before she had chance, though, the sergeant was there, forcing the peasant girl away. She fell, spilling her little basket onto the floor. Solatta looked back for the girl, but she had already vanished. She took a bite of the apple and immediately spat. The flesh was rotten and black and worm-eaten. It made her stomach turn and she retched over the side of the caravan. Behind her, she heard one of the two guards laugh.

The sergeant rode ahead, forcing a path through the crowd. Those who didn't move by choice had their minds made up for them. A borrow of nuts went tumbling from a basket and the crowd erupted: screams and shouts rose as dirt-stained children dived for the tasty treats. Birds dived and squawked, fighting for their own share of the booty. Solatta revelled in the mayhem. Around her, hungry hands took advantage, stealing meats and fish and spices from stalls of all descriptions. Nothing, it seemed, was off the menu.

The commotion was short-lived. Before long, the two patrolmen joined their sergeant, setting to with arm and riding crop to beat down into the crowd. The people scattered, carrying whatever they could away with them and disappearing into the shadows. Solatta was almost disappointed once they were on their way again.

Beyond the walls, the town transformed. Here, things were clean and ordered. Light danced from an army of wall sconces that seemed to wait on parade at their passing. Tall houses lined narrow cobbled streets, all of them silent; only the slow rumble of the vardo echoed through the night.

They passed beneath a bridge that, it looked like, supported another road that stretched above them. Solatta had never seen the likes before. Even further above that, the orange glare of lights skittered as if somehow suspended in the night sky. Fireflies tethered into place. She gasped, breath catching in her throat. It was beautiful. The sergeant looked at her, puzzled.

'There are lights,' she pointed. 'Up there. Hanging in the sky!'

The sergeant cocked an eyebrow at her. 'They aren't in the sky. They're in the windows.'

Solatta frowned. 'Windows? Up there? How high are the buildings?' She'd seen big houses before; indeed, some of the estates had huge houses with three storeys, even four, but none of them would make you crick your neck to see them.

'Towers, miss,' the sergeant answered. 'They're towers. Not just an ordinary building. Some of these are as tall as three or four normal houses.'

'What? Why would anyone need houses that tall?'

The sergeant gave a gruff laugh. 'I'm not sure they need them at all. They belong to the House-Lord. They say there is one tower for each seat on the council. Five in total, going all the way back to the Succession War.' He seemed to sit taller and straighter as if proud of the achievements of his benefactor, as though these gave him and his position credence. She supposed they did. 'It's even on the family crest,' he added. He pulled at his jerkin, twisting it round for her inspection. It shone in the torchlight, orange and amber. She had to squint to make it out. Some kind of bird and rat dancing around five sticks. She had no idea what to make of it or what it was for, but the sergeant seemed so pleased that she found it hard to say anything. She just smiled.

The road became steep and narrow and twisted, passing under yet more arches, though these were covered with coloured cloth that fluttered prettily in the night breeze. She longed to be able to share the moment with someone other than her guides. Guards, not guides, she thought, and her mind drifted to Dreban, stuck inside the vardo all alone. Suddenly, the high walls and buildings seemed to loom over her. These too were a prison, she realised, with no need for guards. When they stopped at a huge studded gate, the image was complete. The sergeant called ahead and they waited while the sound of heavy bolts and latches were pulled and moved on the other side. The door slid slowly open, allowing them access to a large, cobbled courtyard. Here at least there were people, busy about their tasks: young boys brushing at a yard and men tending to horses. They drew up to the stables, where the sergeant called for them to stop. He stepped down from his saddle and held a hand out to Solatta. It was a gallant act, and for a moment she was a highborn lady being helped from her carriage. She felt elegant. 'Thank you, sergeant,' she said with a blush. He smiled, eyes twinkling in the light.

Orders were barked into the night and a boy came rushing forward. With the agility of youth he bounced into the vardo's riding seat and, with a flick of the reins, the brightly coloured little caravan trundled away from them.

'Wait, no!' called Solatta, but the sergeant pulled her hand, moving her out of the way.

'It's okay,' he cooed. 'My men will sort everything out.'

'Dreban,' she managed.

'Yes, yes. They'll see to your friend. You just come over here with me.' He pulled her hand more insistently.

'Where are they taking him?'

'Don't you worry about that. They can help him with his papers.' He was all smiles again, and he loosened his hold on her without quite letting her go. Still, it was enough to give her some relief. 'I thought I could show you something while we wait.'

Solatta felt uncertain, but his grip was so gentle and he looked so earnest. It was difficult not to trust the man. After all, he was a patrolman. They walked to the far side of the courtyard, away from the stable hands and brush boys. The noise of them became faint in the background, overtaken by the sound of water. The sergeant led her to a small wall and through a little doorway, and Solatta found herself struck by a blanket of sound. Little pools were arranged at various heights all around the walls, cascading from one to another. The sound echoed around them, amplified in the intimate space. It was beautiful. She had never seen anything so opulent, and the sight almost stole the breath from her lungs. She twirled on the spot, trying to savour it all at once.

'It's a water garden,' the sergeant offered, his voice soft and low, almost reverent. He took her hand again and drew her to the centre of the garden. Here, there was a large central basin fed by the trickling waters of all the other pools. Light shimmered, reflected not only from the constantly undulating waters but also from myriad crystals and bright stones that ornamented the blue walls.

Ever so slowly, he moved both their hands, delicately dipping them into the crystal-clear waters. Solatta felt the icy chill spreading up into her. Cool and refreshing—and sensual. She bit back a gasp of delight. He cupped her fingers in his and lifted them out, drawing them up to his face. His eyes fixed on hers and, with infinite slowness, he lowered his mouth and drank from her palm. Solatta was taken aback. It felt wrong. It was too much and she felt herself flush.

'No,' she said, and tried to withdraw her hand. 'I'm sorry, I...'

He held her hand fast.

A wave of panic spread through her, the hair rising on her neck. 'I shouldn't,' she heard herself say. It sounded weak and pathetic. She hated herself for it.

He smiled, wicked and wide. Dirty rivulets of dust and grime smeared his cheeks as the water ran through his whiskers. He moved their hands to his chest, pressing her palm there. She could feel the beat of his heart: short and sharp thumps. They stabbed into her head like a warning.

'What are you doing?' she shouted, or at least tried to. She thought she was shouting, but the words might have been stuck, trapped somehow behind the panic and the fear.

'Shush. It's okay. It's okay.'

But it wasn't okay. He pulled her in towards him, reaching his own hand out to touch her hair. She did not want this. She had told him that she did not want this. Why wouldn't he listen? It was as though he could not hear her and, in her heart of hearts, she knew he could not—or, at least, he didn't want to.

All too quickly, he was upon her. She could feel the heat of his breath and smell the foulness of him, like sour apples, and she recoiled from it and from him. The action made him angry. He pulled at her all the more. She turned her face away. His mouth became a snarl, made animalistic by the beard.

He twisted her round, spinning her like a top. Then she was pinned, his great weight on top of her, forcing her into the stone surrounding the pool. She could feel it hard and unyielding, grinding against her. She tried to struggle free, to buck and twist and wriggle, but it was no use. He was too big and strong and heavy for her. She felt his hand in her hair, his dirty fingers clawing at it, dragging themselves through. She wanted to scream, but could not. She wanted to cry but the tears would not come. She wanted to push him away and run, but she felt small and weak and feeble and pathetic. Only earlier that day she had thought herself a woman, but he had made a child of her again, and she hated him for it.

Hard hands began to stray; first the neck and then lower. Rough and hot and wanton. They tugged at her dress and pawed at her curves.

'No!' she cried. Her words echoed around the walls and swam inside her head. She felt a blow strike her head, quick and sharp and heavy. He dragged at her hair.

'Shut the fuck up, you little slut,' he sneered. 'Don't think that I didn't see what the pair of you were doing when we showed up.'

She felt a sharp tug, yanking her head backwards. It shook the scream from her mouth even before it was out. He leant against her, forcing her further into the basin. It was her own face that stared back from the pool. It judged her harshly. An arm wrapped around, groping and grabbing, a hip, a breast, a thigh. He pawed at her like meat. She opened her mouth, hoping for some protest. He seemed to sense it. He slammed her head forward and into the pool. Water filled her eyes and nose and mouth. The icy chill stole the scream from her lips. She pushed her head clear, gasping for air and felt the air hit her thighs and buttocks, her skirts lifted. The cold splash of water against her skin. She lay open to him and his weight shifted. He groaned in anticipation.

A moment stretched on and Solatta's mind went blank. When the world snapped back, she thought he might be gone. Was it over? Had he finished? Please let it be over.

'I'll fucking show you, bitch.' Fingers digging into her hip. 'You won't be screaming for your little friend anymore.'

She tried to drown out the sound of him with the roar of the water. She felt her eyes glaze as she stared into the blue depths. Slowly, as if watching herself from very far away, she pushed herself forwards, her body slipping inch by inch into the pool. The cold water welcomed her, icy and calm. It was her friend. She leaned in further. She wanted to climb down to the bottom; maybe there she could find release. She would give herself to the water—not to him. He could never have her. Calmness spread through her. All she needed to do was open her mouth and lungs. The world disappeared, taking her fear with it. His hot hands disappeared. There was nothing.

Until, suddenly, there was something again. She lifted her head. The heat of the night hit her hard and she gasped, pulling air into her lungs. Her fingers gripped the stone basin, holding her there as her chest heaved. She was too afraid to turn around. She didn't want to see him standing there, waiting for her.

It was a woman's voice she heard, confident and rich and velvety. It was the sweetest thing she could imagine. It was hope and deliverance all rolled into one.

'Look at me,' the voice demanded.

Solatta turned to face the woman, though it was her back she found. She was tall and dark, her silky hair cascading over lush and well-cut robes. Cobalt, to match the gardens. Solatta thanked the Goddess—was this a vision? She realised that it was the sergeant the woman was speaking to. She towered over the man, who lay crumpled on the floor, whimpering at her feet. His face was pale and twisted, pain and fear and confusion each wrestling for control. What had happened? What control did this woman have over the man? It was then that Solatta saw the blood: a scarlet puddle spreading in this place of pools. A macabre reflection.

'How dare you defile the serenity of my garden, Sergeant.' The woman's voice echoed about the place, the sound rich and melodic, almost musical. Solatta felt frozen in place. She wanted nothing more than to find the vardo and Dreban. She longed for comfort, for warmth. The morning felt a lifetime ago. Tears filled her eyes and her body shook from shock or cold or relief, she knew not which.

The sergeant spat. His eyes were angry flames, full of hatred and spite and tears. He opened his mouth, perhaps to moan or shout, but no words came out.

'Get out of my sight,' the woman said to him—hard words for such a soft voice. Slowly and painfully, the man began to move, shifting awkwardly along the ground, leaving a snail smear of blood in the sand. Two guards stood beyond. They eyed the prone man impassively, disdain writ large upon their faces. They looked to the woman, waiting on her word. 'Take him away,' she ordered. 'I never want to see him again.' They moved to collect the man, but one of them paused, distracted. Solatta followed his gaze. Something fleshy and red and wet lay on the floor. A poisonous little thing, once, but now it was small and ruined and pathetic. It was then that Solatta saw the knife.

'Leave that where it is,' the woman said. 'The rats can have it. Let that be a warning to anyone else who cares to violate either gardens or guests.'

The woman turned her dark eyes to Solatta, sharp and knowing and bright. They flickered over Solatta, eyebrow raised. Her lips twitched. 'Fix yourself, child. I will not have anyone see you like that in here. It is not the place.' Her words bounced around the garden. Solatta was uncertain whether she was being scolded. She flushed and straightened quickly, flattening her skirts and trying to muster herself. She tried to calm her frantic heart but her knees betrayed her, shaking and knocking. Wet hair fell flat against her face.

'No,' said the woman, shaking her head. 'I cannot have you walking my streets in such a state. Come with me.' She left the garden in a swirl of fabrics, crossing the courtyard in several long strides. It was as if she owned the place, thought Solatta. Who was this woman? Did it matter after what she had done, what she had prevented? Solatta looked to the ground at the offending mass of flesh and gristle, dangerous no more. It would never threaten anyone again. Still, it gave her chills. She skipped to keep up.

The woman led her through a small door of worked and filigreed metal. It led to a walkway, covered from above by lavish blue canopies and made pretty by flowers and lemon and roses and jasmine. She was struck by how lavish it all was. It seemed as if they had entered an entirely different town, one removed from anything else. It felt calm and safe—and false. A million miles from only moments ago. Just through that gate, a minute more and she might have been... No, she would not think on it. She would not be the small and helpless girl that he'd made her. She would be strong and proud like the woman had been. She forced herself taller, made her stride long and confident. She watched the back of the woman, how it moved with such effortless grace. She tried hard to emulate it.

They passed other gardens and decorative gates and many-floored buildings that protruded into the night, and yet it was at a large and rather plain wooden door that they eventually stopped. It opened smoothly at their approach. They were expected, then—or, at least, the woman was. A courtyard awaited them, tiled and cool. Four floors reached up above them on all sides. Windows and balconies looked down upon them and the night sky stared down upon it all. A small pool stood opposite them, water trickling noisily from the marble mouth of a carved face. It was rich and opulent, laden with silk hangings and soft cushions, intricate decorations, and plump settees. Solatta had never seen the likes. She was suddenly very aware of how torn and tattered she must appear. She found her fingers pulling at her skirts.

A door closed behind her and she turned to find herself alone. 'Hello?' she called, but there was no response. She waited for a moment, uncertain and nervous. Nothing. 'Now what I am supposed to do?' she asked of no one. The sound of water was a comfort, familiar and soothing. She crossed to the pool and perched on the ledge. It was warm and tempting. She wanted to wash away the dirt and filth and depravity of the day, to find Dreban and start afresh. It wasn't so much to ask, was it? And yet it was difficult to know how to even begin. She slumped her shoulders with a heavy sigh. 'Well,' she said with forced brightness. 'I can only start here, with me.' She took another look around to make sure she was alone. Quickly, she slipped from her clothes, tossing them into a pile, and slipped slowly into the pool. Almost immediately, the waters melted away the worst of the aches and pains. She let it wash over her, ducking her head beneath the surface. It was a blessing from the Goddess herself. She rubbed at her face, scrubbing herself clean. The water churned and roiled and clouded grey. She rubbed at her hair, tussling and running her fingers through it. Hers and someone else's. She froze, uncertain. They did not. The fingers scrubbed at her hair. She swallowed and felt her muscles tense, images of the sergeant flashing in her mind.

'It's okay,' came a girl's voice.

Solatta twisted slowly, covering herself as best she could with her hands. The girl smiled sweetly. She was younger than Solatta, and prettier. Her smile was broad and bright. Big brown eyes met her own.

'What are you doing?' asked Solatta. 'You gave me a start.' There was more ice to her voice than she might have intended, but it had been a traumatic day.

'I'm sorry, miss. I didn't mean to startle you.' The girl flashed another impossible smile.

'There it is again,' Solatta bristled. 'My name is not "miss",' No, 'miss' was what the sergeant had called her. 'My name is Solatta.'

'I'm sorry, Solatta. My name is Varshied.' She raised two fingers to her mouth and bowed her head.

Solatta flushed, disarmed by the action, and felt the poorer for her hardness. 'Well,' she said. 'I didn't realise you were there. You might let someone know before you start to interfere with them while they bathe.'

'Of course. Though this is a house of leisure; that is what we are here for.'

Solatta frowned. 'What?'

'We are here to help you to relax,' Varshied explained. 'Why else did you come here?'

'I didn't come here,' Solatta blurted. She wasn't really sure what a leisure house was or even what she was doing here. It had been such a difficult day and now she felt stupid as well. 'I mean, I didn't mean to come here. I just. I just want...' Her tears came unbidden and she covered her face with her hands.

'Here,' said Varshied and, when Solatta looked, the girl was holding a robe out to her. Solatta climbed from the pool and stepped into it. Careful arms wrapped her in it and gently rubbed her dry. It was a comfort. Together, the women moved to a settee where another girl appeared, a tray of food held in her arms: bread and fruits and cheeses. She placed the tray on a table and sat with them. Two hands became four, light and tender and tantalising. Solatta's skin felt alive. She didn't think she had ever been touched with such delicate attentiveness. Then there was a third girl, bearing a tray of tea and milk. It joined the other tray and the girl joined the others. Solatta's head spun. Each touch was amplified, rapturous. She was hot and yet her body shivered and flushed. She grew incredibly aware of and yet somehow distant from herself, as if she were looking down at the four of them. The room was spinning. She wondered what was up with the girl, why the others were making such a fuss of her. Not to worry, she thought. All will be well again, after some tea. The room drew in and she watched the light wink out into darkness. Sleep washed over her.

When she woke, she had forgotten where she was. She was warm and cosy and coiled up in sumptuous blankets. Sunlight streamed through the silks and hangings, filling the space with colour. A fresh tray of tea, fruit, and bread had been left for her. With a satisfying stretch that tugged at her shoulders, she helped herself to a mouthful of each. A pretty troop of finches charmed themselves by the pool, frisking at the water's edge. She stood and watched them. If only she were a bird; then she could fly away from everything. She would fly until her little wings couldn't carry her any further. And what would that get her, besides lost? She thought of the things she'd be leaving behind. Cobb, the vardo, Dreban. It felt hard not to include Tervan in that list. She gulped at her tea.

At once, something flew at her—a shriek of black feathers and cold black eyes. The crow flapped at her, squawking. Solatta cried out, dropping her cup, which shattered against the tiles. Varshied was there almost immediately, shooing the bird away. She hurried and fussed about, drawing Solatta to a settee.

'Are you okay?' she asked.

In truth, Solatta wasn't sure. Her heart raced and her nerves tingled.

'Wicked bird,' the girl called into the morning. She touched her fingers to her forehead and eyes, warding away evil. 'Truth protect us, but they bring nothing good with them. Nasty little things.'

'What has happened here?' The woman's voice, soft and rich and unctuous. Solatta started; she hadn't heard her approach.

Varshied jumped up and curtsied. 'Sorry, my lady. I was just clearing things up.'

'Indeed,' the lady replied. 'Well, see that you do.' An edge crept into her voice, not cruel but commanding. This was a woman who expected to be obeyed. Varshied scurried away, pausing to take some of the broken pieces of cup with her. 'I see that they brought you clean clothes. Good. Stand now, child. Let me take a look at you.'

Solatta looked down. She hadn't even noticed. Someone had dressed her in a fresh dress; not fancy robes as those that the lady wore, but a practical dress, blue, neat and with plenty of pockets. She stuffed her hands into them to stop herself from fidgeting. It struck her that the poppet she'd carried was gone. She couldn't remember the last time she'd had it. Her spirits dropped. It had been Dreban's poppet. The thought of him, lost and alone or, worse, with those awful men while she was bathing and sleeping made her flush with guilt.

'That is much more suitable. What were you thinking? Surely you know not to be out alone at night. Which family do you work for, child? I shall have someone return you.' The lady looked expectant.

Solatta bobbed an awkward curtsey, trying hard to mimic Varshied. 'Please, my lady, but I don't work for any family,' she said.

'Nonsense, girl. Show me your papers.'

'I don't have them,' she said, hating how weak and uncertain she sounded. She wanted to shake herself: Stop being such a little girl! But it was no use. The lady was so imposing that she couldn't help herself. She found herself becoming all muddled and flustered until it all came flooding out, even though a little voice warned her not to give herself away. She explained all about being found on the road by the guards, about being lost and racing to get away from the town, about the smell of fire and death and the fear that she'd lost Tervan forever. About the vardo and Cobb. About how she had found Dreban and nursed him back to health. And, most of all, about how much she needed to get back to him to make sure he was okay. By the end, she was crying again.

The change in the woman was immediate. She was like a cat in the aviary, her eyes narrowing as if seeing Solatta for the first time.

'Indeed, child,' her voice was syrup. 'What an interesting little song you sing. Tell me, have you sung it to anyone else?'

Solatta frowned. How could she have? She didn't know anyone; the only people she'd met were the guards, the lady, and the girls from the leisure house. All she wanted was to get back to Dreban and be on their way. It wasn't so much to ask, was it? 'No, my lady,' she said.

The lady's eyes flared in the sunlight. Suddenly, Solatta regretted being so open. What was it Tervan used to say? 'Be careful who you speak to, girl, and what you tell them. The Church is likely to roast a man over a fire for trying to mend a candle.' Now it was too late. Her stomach churned. Was the room spinning or was it her? Her eyes, already sore from crying, began to fill again. She slumped to the floor, ashamed at her stupidity. There was nothing to do now but wait for the priests to arrive.

'My, my. Look at me, child.' Soft fingers lifted her chin. The lady looked down into her face, an excited sparkle in her eyes. 'A pretty girl with a pretty song. Who would have guessed? I forbid you to repeat what you have just told me. Do you understand?'

Solatta nodded.

'Good.' The lady released her chin and clapped her hands. Varshied reappeared, as though from nowhere.

'My lady?'

'Wine for me and my guest. I feel the need to raise a toast to our little healer.' She smiled broad and full, but something about it made Solatta feel even more unsettled. She couldn't shake the feeling that the cat had set her sights on her and there was nothing she could do to fly away. 'But first, it would be nice to have a demonstration of your talents, child. Go with Varshied and fetch whatever things you need from your little caravan.' She crossed to a table and scratched some words onto a sheet of parchment before handing it back to Varshied. 'If anyone stops you, hand them this. Go now. Hurry.'

They wasted no time and, had she known the way, Solatta would have raced ahead, her feet light with the excitement of seeing Dreban. When they reached the courtyard, however, the vardo had gone. A stable hand pointed the direction but, when they eventually found the caravan, they found it open and empty. Only a grumpy Cobb was there to greet them.

'He's not here,' she murmured.

'Who?' asked Varshied.

'Dreban. Dreban!' she called in frustration. Why had everything become so difficult? There was a time when life had been simple, when she had known what was expected of her. These days, she hardly even knew herself. She sat on the step of the vardo, head in her hands. I will not lose Dreban as I lost Tervan, she pledged to herself.

Her new friend tugged at her arm, anxious to be away. Their entrance had attracted unwanted attention: several guards were watching them from across the yard. One of the men pulled away from the others and strode purposefully towards them.

'You girls,' he called to them. 'What are you doing here?'

'Quick,' said Varshied, 'please, let's just get your things and leave.'

Solatta nodded tersely and quickly grabbed her potions box. Lying next to it, she found the poppet and wondered how it had got there. She snatched it up and pocketed it. There was something oddly comforting about it and, in a strange way, it was a link to Dreban.

The guard was waiting for her when she climbed from the vardo, his face stern. He glowered down at Varshied, who seemed to crumble away from him. Solatta's anger flared. How dare he? She would not let herself be threatened by these men again. She would not become that weak and terrified girl. Solatta took the parchment from her friend's hand and thrust it at the guard.

He stared at it, suddenly unsure of himself, and Solatta smiled. He can't read, she thought. It was strange to feel the power shift. Now it was his turn to feel small. She opened the parchment, revealing the seal embossed into cobalt wax. Even without the words, it was enough. The guard stiffened in recognition. Usually, it was the words that held the power; for some, though, symbols were enough. The guard told them to wait there before crossing to his colleagues and sharing some hushed words with them. They turned to look at the two girls almost as one. Solatta felt

Varshied's hand take hers. To her shame, she shared the younger girl's uncertainty. Maybe she had misjudged things. Two of the men ducked out of sight. They emerged moments later carrying a litter of sorts. They brought it to the girls and a third guard fetched a set of wooden steps.

The girls looked to each other. Solatta smiled. She had never been carried before. She'd never travelled in anything other than her vardo. It was a different world, and she almost felt embarrassed by the idea. Varshied obviously didn't, however, and hurried inside, grinning. It was padded with thick curtains and comfortable cushions. I could get used to this, Solatta thought. When they started to move and the little cabin began to rock and sway, however, she realised she wasn't so certain.

Fear, then, our wrath, says the Church, and cower before the thunder of our vengeance, for the Goddess has appointed us with her own words as absolute judges and executioners of all. Peasants and kings alike will submit to our authority when by their words or actions they sin against the Truth and bear false witness in her name.

—*From the Tenets of Truth*

CHAPTER TWENTY-FOUR
BRAGA, PREFEITO, AND TERVAN

The Citadel

The smell of sweat and sex filled the air, hot and sticky and salty-sweet. Braga looked at the woman lying next to him, amazed at how peaceful and serene she appeared after what they had just done. *Here I am, sweating like a hog on a spit*, he thought, *and she looks merely warm to the touch. Sometimes, I think I will never tire of looking at her.*

It had been too long since he had last seen Sirle, never mind lain with her, yet she had not aged a day. She smiled as she slept, knowing and cheeky, as though she still dreamt of the previous night. He almost stiffened at the thought. She didn't change, despite the months they spent apart: same hair, same skin, same smell, same taste. He wished he could say the same about himself. Every time he returned he felt the cycles all the more, though each night with her was like an elixir. She gave him the energy and the fire to be himself. She renewed him. He reached out to touch her perfect face but held back, not wanting to sully her with rough and tired hands; he'd done enough of that already. It was enough to just watch her sleeping. He leant forwards and kissed her lightly on the forehead. To him she remained the youthful, vibrant, and joyful woman he had fallen in love with. From the first time he had met her, long ago when he'd first visited Smithston, he hadn't been able to get enough of the woman. In fact, she was the main reason he'd returned here again and again over the cycles. The barracks had its own smith and forge, but there could only ever be one Sirle.

Slowly and regretfully, the big man carefully extricated himself from the tangle of legs and bed things, trying his hardest not to disturb the resting angel beside him. Unfortunately, he had never been known for his deftness of touch and, despite his best efforts, Sirle stirred.

The day was young, but the heat of the night had never truly escaped. It hung in the air like a blanket, smothering and oppressive. It felt apt for the times. Despite the heat, she tugged her bedclothes up higher as if his body had been the only thing keeping her warm.

Her eyes cracked open, though only slightly. Maybe she thought she might trick her body into thinking it was still asleep. 'You're going already?' she asked, her voice dry and hoarse.

Braga made no reply. Instead, he finished winding the red silk cummerbund about his waist and then leaned over the bed to kiss her. She accepted the brief kiss as though it was all the answer she needed, then rolled onto her side, facing away from him. The bedclothes fell about her, revealing the damaged skin of her back.

He had long hated the sight of those long, erratic stripes: jagged and criss-crossing red lines that told of beatings and whippings delivered by men that he would dearly love to meet one day. His hand moved to her back almost reflexively, as if his touch could somehow erase them. One seemed more pronounced and darker in colour than the rest. Sirle flinched at his touch.

'What's this?' he growled.

'Oh, Braga, you've been away too long,' she said, pulling away from him. 'Things are harder here these days.' She kept her back to him, the warmth fading from her words. It was an age-old frustration.

'What?' he growled again, his voice lower, more dangerous. What use was he if he couldn't protect her? Though that lay at the heart of it, he knew. She didn't want or need his protection; she was not a problem for him to fix. She could handle things herself—after all, she handled him well enough.

Now she rolled over to look at her lover. 'What, Braga, what do you want me to say?' Was it anger at him he found there, or at the way of things? 'You want me to say that it is easy for me? For any of us? You wander back here after how many months and you only now think to ask what happens while you are gone? Do you think we all sit around and wait for the day when the great Braga comes back to us? Well, we don't. We work, Braga. We work and we sweat, that's what we do. We work to meet demands so that we can earn enough to live.' She was scowling now, a red blush blossoming across her cheeks. 'And you know what? Sometimes, that isn't enough, because sometimes they want more and take more, and if we say we can't deliver? Then yes, they hit us. Do you think it would be any different if you were stood next to me?' She paused in her tirade, almost challenging him to say something. Wisely, however, he held his tongue. 'No, Braga, it wouldn't,' she finished. 'You're not here. You wouldn't know.'

He reached out to her, his fingers touching hers, but she pulled away.

'No, Braga. I love you, but you don't see it. You don't see the women being dragged from the streets. You don't see the children being whipped. You don't know how it makes a person feel. The anger, the frustration—but, most of all, the fear. You've never been afraid in your life. But we are. I am. I'm afraid that if we don't make our quotas then they tax us even more. I worry that if I get sick then I'll fall behind and find myself in the tower. It's that easy. I know an old man from church who was taken only last week. He was seventy-two, Braga. Seventy-two and half-blind. He'll die in that place, if he hasn't already.' There were tears in her eyes, but they weren't for her, Braga knew. She pulled her fingers through her hair, tying it back as though readying herself for action, the bedclothes falling away and exposing her nakedness to the world.

He felt useless—but, despite it all, proud. He felt it welling up inside him. He stared at the woman before him, beautiful and tender and compassionate, and with a lion's heart. 'I—'

'No,' she interrupted. 'Don't say it, Braga, please. I can't hear it again. I know. It's unfair. You have your life, your barracks, your men. You have responsibilities. Well, you know what? You have your battle scars and so do we. Only our battle is called *life* and we fight it every day.'

The big man reeled as if each of her words had been a blow to the gut. He had wanted to tell her how much she meant to him, to let her know that, no matter what, he would be there for her. He looked long into her face and felt a sharp pain in his heart. He knew what she said was true; if he'd said those things, he would be a liar. He was *never* here, *never* there for her. How could he be? He was a soldier. He had his role and that was the way of things. He wanted to somehow make her understand that he wanted to be here for her, to hold her each night and to keep her safe. He had coin to spare, he thought suddenly—he could send that to her. But no; it was not enough. Her brother's words came back to him. Maybe he should marry her. But how could he? Their lives were so different. He had his duty. Besides, they would need the permission of the House-Lord, just the same as anyone else, and he was unlikely to consent. Braga wasn't even certain which House-Lord was responsible for the barracks anymore.

He reached his hand to her face, touching her lightly on the cheek, his thumb rubbing away a stray tear. He wondered who it was for. She pressed herself into his palm, then turned away. 'Fuck, Braga. Why do you come back?'

He sat on the bed and pulled her to him, wrapping her in his huge arms. He held her there, wishing the moment might never end, and they could stay like that forever.

'I miss you,' he confessed softly. 'That's why. I come back for you.'

The door opened abruptly, breaking the moment. Sirle's uncle stood in the doorway, looking dishevelled and out of breath.

'You haven't heard then, I take it?' he said, taking in the intimate scene. He didn't look abashed. He had other concerns.

'Heard what?' Braga rasped back at him.

'It's Kovack,' Uncle Temir said gravely. 'A priest and some guards took him.'

Braga sat up. Kovack had been a good friend of his for many cycles. What could the Church want with him? He was no criminal. He recalled the smith's words—he'd have the quota ready tomorrow, he'd said. Had they come to collect through the night? 'When?' Braga managed after a moment's thought. *I left the mayor and*

329

Tervan at his workshop, he realised. *What has happened to them?*

'Last night,' said Temir, 'not long after you left. I'm afraid they worked him over pretty good.'

'Where is he?' asked Sirle, her face a mask of barely contained rage.

'I saw him at the workshop and he was in a bad way. They took your friends too, Braga.'

'Where?' the big man growled.

'The Rose.'

The words quietened the room, and Braga felt himself sink.

The Rose was a square, a tower, a killing ground, and a sentence. Few people left that place and fewer still of their own volition. It was the Citadel's main jail and, if recent months were anything to go by, it was getting easier and easier to gain entry. Stories abounded of the rank and overcrowded conditions. If the rats didn't eat you, so the rumours went, the starved inmates would.

A great square serviced the area, a grandstand to the grim and macabre spectacles that had once been held here. In cycles gone, it had been an execution ground, a warning to all of what might befall lawbreakers. The tower was not the tallest in the city—those were reserved for the ruling elite in the central old district—but it was the most imposing. It was adjoined by a red sandstone wall some four storeys high. At some distant and sinister point in its history, the City-Lord had ordered more than a thousand metal spikes inserted into the wall. Ironically, it was the smiths who had been employed to fashion them. Three-foot metal rods, each honed to a brilliant point and bent at a right angle: these had come to be known as the Rose Thorns. Braga understood their purpose well enough. Once a person had seen the thorns in use, they were not eager to see such a thing again.

More blood had been spilled here than anywhere in the Citadel and, to Braga, even the sand and dust still clung to its sinister past. It was darker than elsewhere, a deeper tell-tale red. Now, as the shadows grew long and slow, the square came alive with hues of terracotta. Red ghosts for a red square.

There had been a time when the people had flocked to the Rose for sport. They would cheer and call out at the sight of a banner announcing a coming spectacle, but few recalled those days any longer. Only tales remained. Back then, the square had been lined with taverns and inns, each bearing a suitably wicked name: the Tickling Thorn, the Weeping Wall, the Ripping Rose, and half a dozen more besides. Only the Bloody Boy remained and even that was now a ramshackle place held up only by the buildings on either side. Though it had fallen into disuse, the Rose had never lost its reputation. The pioneer sergeant had seen a great many things in his life, but he hoped he would never be called to bear witness to death paraded as some kind of sport or spectator event.

He and Sirle dressed quickly before joining Uncle Temir outside. They hurried through Smithton's central square towards the looming shadow of the Rose. In its surrounding square, a crowd was already waiting. Men, women, and children buzzed with nervous expectation, gossiping and chattering like drovers at an auction. Braga recognised the faces of smiths in the crowd, all wearing anxious and worried faces. Sirle clung to his arm.

Notices had been affixed to the great sandstone wall. Banners, each twice the height of a man, pronounced the details of a crime. The three pushed their way through the crowd to get a better look.

All of you who are Truthless in their deeds shall know the full force of the Goddess when she calls to you. Those who do not hear her Truth will be cast into the pit and be made pure through suffering, for there is no pain given that is not of Truth, just as there is no relief from pain that is not found in the Truth.

'It's a passage from the Tenets,' Sirle said, confused, 'but why?' She looked to Braga, as if he might somehow have an answer for her, but he did not. He turned to Temir.

'What happened?' he asked.

'The patrol dragged Kovack's body from his workshop,' Temir said. 'Old Jarlssen thought he was already dead, he looked so broken. With the soldiers was a priest dressed in formal blacks. He left and took your two friends with him. No one has seen anything of them since, and then this.' He nodded towards the sign.

'What does it mean, though?' Sirle asked. 'The passage is about healing and suffering, but Kovack would never do anything like that. He is a smith, not a healer. A smith, for Truth's sake, not a fucking heretic.' The words seemed to strike Braga like a hammer blow, and he felt stupid for not having seen it before. 'A heretic healer,' he mumbled absently.

Healers were common enough in the army: each barracks held one or more depending on their size and standing. Barkathet had two, adherents both, fully authorised and ordained into the faith. It hadn't occurred to him that, last night, he'd watched a healing. He'd stood by open-mouthed as the tinker had performed. They all had. Had they been so caught up in the moment that they'd simply not noticed? He didn't even know what had happened with Vrat, whether he had lived or died. Maybe that was the difference. Had the lad jumped back to his feet and danced a merry jig they would have shrieked and screamed and ran to the priests for absolution. But nothing had happened. It had been an anti-climax that left him feeling empty, yet less concerned for the boy's welfare. Tervan had soothed the lad, nothing more.

In the short time they had been stood outside the Rose, the number of people had swelled dramatically, and Braga could feel himself being jostled forwards. There were easily a thousand now, all eager to get a better view of whatever it was that was happening, with more coming all the time.

They heard the crack of bolts and the crank of winches. Slowly, deafeningly, a rusted portcullis upon the wall drew up into its housing and the great gate beyond groaned steadily open. As the great slabs came to rest, a lone figure emerged from the shadows. He wore the heavy black robes of the Church, Braga saw, and seemed to float as he went. The crowd was silent now, a thousand eyes transfixed. The priest stopped before the gatehouse, surveying the assembled crowds. From behind him came two soldiers, a ruined man dragged between them. It was Kovack.

Sirle gasped, hiding her face in Braga's chest. He held her tight, as if he could somehow protect her from this malignant mummer's show. But what, really, could he do? Two more prisoners were pushed out behind Kovack, a guard following them, his pike held ready. Braga knew them both. Vrat—Kovack's cough-racked apprentice—and the mayor. He swallowed, feeling his palms dampen.

The priest held his hands out to the crowd, raising them slowly like a puppeteer about to perform. Obligingly, the sway of people stilled.

'I am light. I am good. I am Truth. So sayeth the Goddess.' The priest's voice rang out across the hushed square. 'Those who come to me will always know Truth; those who listen to me will always hear Truth; and those who spread my words will always speak Truth.'

In unison, those gathered touched their fingers to their foreheads, their ears, and then mouthed in time, 'Our holy Church has ever taught that in the Goddess we can all find Truth.'

'Truth of mind, Truth of soul, Truth of heart, Truth of body!

The Goddess gives this Truth freely, with the joy and happiness of a mother. But it is only through the Goddess and her holy Church that this Truth can be found. That is the very simple and clear message that we find in her scriptures, which She handed down through the Church—*her* Church. Before you, you will see written out those very teachings, that we may better know and understand her. The teachings are clear: only through devotion to the Goddess can we truly be free from lies, and thus from the pain of being blind to and hidden from the Truth. In turning our back on the Truth, and by acknowledging lies, we turn our back on the Goddess.' The priest paused, his hard eyes searching the crowd. Braga could have sworn the man looked directly at him. 'It is this act—the sin of those lies—that creates the pain that torments our souls and our bodies. Only by accepting the Goddess and her holy Truth into our hearts can we ever be freed from pain.' He fell silent, seeming spent, but soon peered out again. He seemed pleased to see a large number of those gathered nodding their understanding and approval. 'The foundation,' he continued, 'of all our confidence and understanding is found in our holy mother Church and in her teachings. The Goddess herself has entrusted to her Church the safekeeping of all good and sacred things in order that everyone may know that through her alone is found Truth and hope and salvation, and in these three things is a world free from lies and torment. It is not for mere men to attempt to second-guess or better the Goddess and her workings. Anyone'—and here he raised both his voice and his fist—'who attempts to pervert the Goddess and her blessed Truth sins against the Truth and is guilty of a terrible heresy. Those people must be purged without pity.' Here, the man's cowl slipped from his face. Braga drew a sharp breath as the wind was ripped from him. The man was paler, thinner maybe—darker around the eyes, certainly—but it was him. Adherent Al-Eldar.

The priest stopped once again, testing the crowd. His mouth dragged thin at the edges as though he was trying hard to hide the pleasure he found in his own words. If he hoped to find the crowd hanging on his every word and baying for the blood of the condemned, however, he was left wanting. The lines of pleasure that edged his eyes slowly gave way to darkness, and Braga watched him glance anxiously towards the guards. The crowd was quiet. Sour, almost. Braga allowed himself a grim smile.

'You have heard of the massacre in the market town,' the adherent spat, voice higher now, the words sounding for all the world like an invocation. It was a call to arms, Braga knew, an invitation to share in his disgust and disbelief, as though this would whip those gathered into some righteous crusade. 'You will know, therefore, the evils and dangers that lurk so close to our great city. We must stand against those who would tear apart our community and attack the very foundations of our faith. We must not be weak against those who practise heresy. We must show those that would do ill against us that we will stand strong and resolute against them.'

Still the crowd remained silent, and Al-Eldar's eyes narrowed into black pin pricks. He took a stride forwards and threw his hands into the air. 'Fear, then, our wrath, says the Church!' he cried, 'and cower before the thunder of our vengeance! For the Goddess has appointed us with her own words as absolute judges and executioners of all. Peasants and kings alike will all submit to our authority!'

He swept his hands down and spun away. At this cue, the guards dragged the sickly apprentice boy, Vrat, forwards, and threw him over the edge of the towering sandstone wall.

The boy seemed to linger in the air as if gravity had not quite taken its grip. Then, after a moment, his scream reached the crowd. It broke the spell. He dropped like a great weight, straight and heavy and hard. His back hit first, thumping into the face of the Rose and bouncing free, careening down the slanted wall. Braga had heard that the uneven width of the wall was by design; its tapering height gave a clear, gentle slope from top to bottom so that anything thrown from the ramparts would bump and spin on its way down. As such, no two executions were ever the same: each victim landed, bounced, and twisted differently.

Vrat spun, his body lurching. He hurtled face-first down— though, now he was clear of the wall, Braga hoped that, impossibly, he might escape its clutches. The whole crowd seemed to hold its collective breath.

And then the Rose showed its true nature. The boy's foot caught first: snared on a vicious metal thorn. It tore through flesh and tendon as the boy's momentum pulled him down. A scream cut through the air, though whether it emanated from the crowd or the apprentice boy was hard to tell. The next thorn took him directly in the face. Metal plunged through his open mouth and bit deep into his skull and, with a sickening crack, the boy's neck broke. There the body swung, its descent cut short.

The crowd howled in disbelief. All around Braga, men and women surged forwards, many reduced to tears. Unbidden, a vision of the staked bodies littering the square in Baile Saor shot through Braga's mind. The boy—his skull split like a ripe peach, eyes wide and bloody—stared down at him.

Al-Eldar stood atop the wall. Had he expected a cheer, Braga wondered, the bloodlust of stories? If so, he would be disappointed. Gradually, the crowd quietened, their eyes turning on the high priest. There was a terrible silence.

The priest seemed stunned. He stared back at the massing crowd, black eyes glancing from one face to the next. Even from here, Braga saw him swallow. Al-Eldar turned back to his guards as they pushed the mayor forward. Braga felt his throat go dry. His companion lashed out feebly, but one of the guards slammed the butt of his spear into his midriff. The mayor stumbled, dropping down onto one knee. The guards dragged him up.

'Do not trust this man!' the mayor bellowed down to the crowd. He pointed his tied hands towards the adherent. 'He is the one who lies! He is the one who spreads falsehoods and deception! I know; I was there in that very town! I saw the truth of what happened that day. Don't listen to his lies—' A second strike took him hard in the crook of the neck and he dropped to his knees once more. The sound reverberated around the square, thick and meaty—a butcher's work. It echoed in the face of each man and woman, and Braga felt the strength of their silence. Like them, he felt disconnected, as though he wasn't even there. He couldn't be; if he were, after all, then it would all be real. Then he would *have* to do something.

But what could he do? What could any of them do? This was just the way of things. People who broke the law had to be punished. But that was his friend up there—Prefeito, the mayor. For the second time that day, self-disgust swept over him. He'd not been there for Sirle, and now he wasn't here for the mayor. This wasn't justice. This wasn't how the law should work. This was an abuse of power. Maybe the king could overrule the Church, but that would be as unlikely as it would be too late. Who is there to keep the men in power in check? What had the colonel said? "They exercise their political and cultural power to control us," and "the barracks are responsible to whomever the City-Lord appoints." Well what if someone took that control away and it was no longer up to the City-Lord to choose?

The mayor picked himself up, standing taller than he had previously. Braga stood taller too, pride for his friend swelling in his chest. The crowd felt it, growing murmurous around him. And, at long last, the priest recognised it for what it was. What little colour remained drained from his face, and he marched to the mayor and kicked him, shoving him forward and over the lip of the wall.

Unlike the apprentice boy, the mayor did not linger. He dropped like a stone. The first impact rolled him like a barrel. It narrowed the trajectory, forcing back into the waiting thorns more quickly than before. He struck hard, metal tearing at cloth and an ample amount of flesh. The thorns snagged at him, holding him there for too long—until at last he tore free, great gouts of angry red flesh spraying behind. The mayor's screams struck Braga's heart, and he became dimly aware of a single tear rolling down his cheek. He almost retched. Memories of his own men flashed into his mind, each one atop their own spike. The mayor had stood with him. Had honoured the dead alongside him.

He didn't deserve this.

'This is not justice,' he growled to no one. He twitched, body aching to do *something*, even only to catch the broken body as it fell. Sirle grabbed at his arm. He felt her nails sink deep. He clung to her, not wanting to let her go. He knew what she wanted— he wanted it too, but not like this. Not this way, in blind fury. It would be futile. Even if they could somehow get to the top of the wall, it would be swarmed with guards before they ever reached her brother.

The mayor bounced from the wall and dropped, true and straight this time. A line of thorns waited for him. He met them with silence, even as the air was ripped from him; even as metal sliced deep, splitting his leg, arm, abdomen, chest. He twitched there without a sound. Eyes open, staring. Mouth gaping.

Braga did not allow himself to close his eyes. He watched,

keenly hoping his friend was dead. It was a terrible thing to think. But better that than the crows and the vultures. Blood soaked the wall and dripped down to the sand below. Another victim to nourish the Rose's roots.

Sirle sobbed, beating her hand into the pioneer sergeant's chest. It meant only one thing: the final man being dragged into position was her brother, Kovack.

It was thankfully quick. His lifeless body clung to the wall and slid more than bounced. It made no spectacle but met the first line of thorns and held there. No scream, no gasp, no movement. He was dead before the thorns took him. It did not make it any easier on Sirle. She buried her face even deeper into Braga's chest, struggling for breath. He closed his eyes, not wanting to see her agony. Her body shook in his. How could he even begin to understand? If it were him and he had watched her execution, how would he react? With a great heaving gasp, she pushed away from him. He expected to see tears, but there was no room in her eyes. They burned with a fury he had never seen in her—a raw and unveiled heat. She tore at her shirt and struck her hands upon her chest. She called down the ire of the Goddess and begged all kinds of injury and disease to befall the priest and his guards. In another time and place, it might have been a blasphemy, but here it seemed a call for justice. None of the people around her and Braga seemed to question it. They knew her grief intimately—it was plain for all to see. She turned to Braga, beating at him, though the fight was finally leaving her. He caught her when her knees buckled and pulled her close, but Sirle roused herself, standing of her own volition. There were tears in her eyes, yes, but the fury remained. She would not suffer this indignity, not here, not in front of them. He could see it in her face: the tight clench of her jaw, the incredible resolve. His lioness.

The ordeal was over but the crowd remained, staring back to the wall's summit. The guards, at least, had the good grace to appear nervous. Al-Eldar looked to them and then back to the people below, his expression dark, lips twisted into a sneer. Slowly, the guards backed away, distancing themselves from the priest. His figure lingered for a time and Braga wondered whether he'd dare try to address them again, to somehow attempt to give credence to his grim exhibition. Thankfully, he did not. Instead he scanned the crowd, contemplating, seeming to take the measure of them. For a fleeting moment, his cold eyes connected with Braga's—and then they were gone. And so was he, following his guards back into the tower.

If he had expected to win over the masses then he had failed miserably. Instead, the muttering of disquiet and disbelief grew around the pioneer sergeant. Angry and frustrated voices echoed his own feelings of guilt and emptiness. But what could they have done differently? The question tormented him. They should have done something, he realised. They could have walked away. Just by being there they lent the grim spectacle a validity of sorts. It made him feel sick. They had all played their part in this show, had allowed themselves to be used. It wasn't right. Those men didn't die in the name of Truth and justice; they died so that the Church could continue to subdue and dominate. They'd been a statement of power.

Other angry voices grew around him as people arrived at their own conclusions, none of them happy. He knew a great many people here: faces from Smithton he remembered, friends, allies. He looked to Sirle. Family? She should be.

There is something to be done here. He knew it in his bones. But what? What would Sentenza do? He'd rally people to him, use those eyes of his. *They always forced me into action.* But no, Braga

340

realised, it wasn't the eyes. It was what he said and how he said it. It was his words.

Braga looked to the crowd, to the restless and agitated and angry many. They were on the cusp of something great, he knew. Whether that be riot or out-and-out rebellion, he couldn't yet be sure. They needed something to galvanise them—or *someone*. He looked at Sirle, the woman he loved, a woman who had just witnessed her brother being killed in the most brutal of ways. He looked back to the wall and to the lifeless bodies that hung there. They would cling there for days to come. His old friend Kovack, beaten and broken even before they threw him to the thorns, and for what? The mayor, a man whom he'd been coming to know and like, even growing to trust—killed to keep him silent. He saw the apprentice. Little more than a boy, for all the good it had done him. Heretics all three. What kind of church would advocate that? One full of zealots and hypocrites. Not one he wanted any part of.

He realised there was a man missing. Where had Tervan been during all of this? Why wasn't he one of those now adorning the wall? Wherever he was, Braga was glad he'd not been there. The realisation seemed to galvanise and stiffen him further. It was like the tinker was there with him, silently and patiently waiting for him to speak. He turned to the crowd.

'Friends,' he called out tentatively, still unsure of himself, and yet his deep voice resonated around the square as if this had been his calling all along. 'Look around you. See the faces of those you love and have lived with all your lives.' He watched as people turned, suspicious and sad eyes finding his before swivelling to do as he'd bid them. Some of those gathered tugged each other close, maybe to guard against the horrible scene before them. Braga swallowed, pushing down his swelling doubt. He was no great speaker; in fact, he didn't think he'd ever said so many words all at once. He looked to Sirle and saw the light in her face. She shone, a burning beacon of pride. For a fleeting moment, they were alone among the crowd. He was her bear, and hers alone.

Suddenly, he realised, the barracks and the army were not all he had. They were very far away, an almost-distant memory. This was his place, his home, and she was his family—the only family he needed or wanted. She smiled at him and he felt himself grow somehow, as if he was only now filling his great frame fully. The crowd would hopefully see him as an excuse or an answer or a leader; she, though, just saw him, and it was all he needed.

'Do you not see Truth in their eyes?' he called to the people, 'in their smiles and in their hearts? Is our love and our respect for one another not a form of Truth? Now look to the sky above—see it reach out in infinite blueness, touching the heavens themselves, spacious and empty. A solid ceiling of blue. Now feel the ground beneath you, secure and honest, holding and supporting you and your family, yet kick at it and see it is made of mere dust and dirt scattered by the winds. Then feel that wind upon your face, warm and gentle. That same wind could take the roof from your house. Is it not in these simple things that we see the Goddess? Is it not in the simple sounds of a babbling brook or a gurgling babe that we hear her Truth?'

He watched the faces. He could see them considering his words, and he knew that he was reaching them. He could see that they *felt* what he was saying, and it told him that they were coming with him on this journey. They were not just listening; they were hearing, understanding what he meant and projecting his imagery onto their own lives and experiences. Something welled up in the big man, something rich and new and pure, and he felt tears bubbling in his eyes. What was this feeling? In fact, was he speaking at all? He wondered distantly whether he'd become possessed by the Goddess herself, or could these really be his words?

'Does the Goddess not dwell among us always?' he asked, the words coming easily now. 'Is she not in the hearts of the righteous? In the radiance of each wondrous morning and standing vigil over us through the darkness of night?'

People were nodding now, some going so far as to mutter their agreement.

'Look then, again, to that spectacle before you.' He pointed towards the wall, deserted now except for the dislocated and punctured bodies that clung to them jealously. 'Look upon the perverse face of the Church and what it calls justice. I ask any of you, do you see the Goddess in that montage of madness? Do you see the mother tending to her children? I, for one, see nothing except the threats and wickedness of greedy and treacherous men. Men who have forced their will upon us all in the name of Truth.'

He waited for a moment, surveying the entirety of the crowd. He peered from face to face, challenging each man and woman to look away. Not one did. They held the eyes of the great man, urging him on, daring him to push and rouse them further, almost begging him with their own eyes for permission to do the unspeakable. He looked back to Sirle once more and found her looking up to him with a new and invigorated face, full of respect and trust and love, and Braga found that, at last, he was inclined to give the crowd what they wanted.

'The time has come,' he growled out to them. His voice had become grit and thunder.

'It has!' one man called in response.

'The time for action on our part. Will you be slaves to those tyrannous men?'

'No!' came the scattered response.

'Or will you, as true children of the Goddess, defend your

religion?'

'Yes!' More took up the call.

'Your hearths?'

'Yes!'

'Your rights, your very lives, and those you love?'

A thousand voices roared their assent.

'Then march,' Braga growled, 'we will defend them.'

Open yourself to Truth. Let the light of the Goddess touch upon your inner self and leave nothing hidden from her or her Church. In the darkness of deception and obfuscation hides despair. Only through the blessed Truth can her holy light dispel the wickedness of what lies cloaked behind the thin veneer of falsehood.

—**From the Tenets of Truth**

CHAPTER TWENTY-FIVE
SENTENZA

The Citadel

The wall was covered in thick mucus. To Sentenza's prying hand, it felt like a particularly disgusting slug. The floor was little better, but at least there were dry patches. His cell was little more than a deep pit hewn directly into the bedrock, set deep beneath the towers of the Citadel. There was at least a stool, but it gave little comfort—Sentenza's back ached already. It was hard to say how long he'd been down here; two days, maybe three at a push. Sleep had taken him a half dozen times already, brought on more by boredom than tiredness. At least it was quiet and free from vermin. Even the rats didn't want to be trapped down here.

A guard had dropped food to him twice, a feast of hardtack and sour wine that he wished he wasn't hungry enough to consider. As it was, nibbling at the tough, dry biscuits was one of the only ways to pass the time. That's what an oubliette was for, he supposed. A place to put people you wanted to forget about while they forgot about themselves. The boredom was numbing. He wondered how many people had been left down here to rot and go slowly mad. He had no way of knowing what tower he sat beneath or, by extension, which House-Lord he was visiting. It certainly wasn't the Rose—he'd seen that before and knew the cells. He'd delivered men there himself. The conditions were filthy—rife and rank and overcrowded—but it had no pits. His own cell was old and secret. Most others had been filled in, he knew; it had been written into law. Too many people had been lost to places like this. Political enemies were silenced, feuds settled, and even disobedient brides lost forever. Once, oubliettes had been seen as status symbols among House-Lords, almost to the same extent as tower height. The depth of the cells was never discussed in polite company, but it was often hinted at. The Great Emancipation edict had supposedly put an end to it all. That and slavery. Sentenza scoffed.

He had expected an interrogation, or at least some kind of softening up with threats and fists, but the guards had been surprisingly light-handed. Instead, they'd seem bored and disinterested. He was evidently not the first person they'd brought down here. They must not have known who he was. They would never had been so easy on a Wielder, nor so relaxed around him. As it was, they hadn't asked him a thing. Just prodded him into his cell before lifting away the ladder. It had given him all the more to think about. It was a good thing too, as it was about all he was able to do.

The sound of movement disturbed him: heavy doors swinging on reluctant hinges, grinding and screeching a lazy protest. The noise thundered above, amplified and distorted by echoes. A procession of torches gave brief illumination, a bright red flare skittering across the green slime. Footfalls bounced and turned and bounced again. One, two, twenty? He couldn't tell. Voices stole into the dank. Men, strained and annoyed. The sound of a scuffle, of someone being dragged against their will. A muffled gasp and stifled shout. Someone with their mouth bound and gagged, struggling against the inevitable. Sentenza might have felt sorry for him, but something else was tugging at his senses. A familiar feeling: a slow itch spreading over his skin. It developed and grew, the hair on his body standing to attention. Stronger, closer. A warm buzz of energy danced all around him, setting his senses on edge. A gentle stroke of nettles. He'd felt it before and knew its meaning, but never like this, never this intense. It was the sensation of someone using magic, only magnified, intensified almost beyond recognition. It was bright and fierce and magnetic. He was on his feet, straining for a glimpse, a sniff, an indication of who it was or what they were doing. All in vain. A man fell, yelping in pain. A guard perhaps? Sentenza heard him cursing. There was a sickening crack, wood on flesh and bone. The struggling stopped. The feeling dissipated, leaving him cold and numb.

'Hello, hello. What's all this shouting? We'll have no trouble here.' The voice clattered around the space above, challenging the newcomers.

'Here's one for a pit,' a second man answered.

'He hardly looks anything. Why's he getting a pit?'

'I don't really care how he looks, I'm not taking any chances. For the time being, any bastard that comes in goes in a fucking pit. You heard what happened to that town.'

'I heard it was nonces,' a third man chipped in. 'That's why there ain't any children any more. Took 'em all into the woods and had their nasty little way wiv 'em.'

'Who told you that?' asked the second man. 'Some dirty ol' prick with his cock in his hand, I bet. Anyway, stop talking with all that shit, you're gonna frighten the poor lad before he finds us that pit. He can't be more than tuppence old himself.'

'I bet he's too young to 'av even seen a tuppence. Pretty young thing though, ain't he? Probably got a pretty little tuppence of his own. Sweet and tight and pink.' There was the rustle of cloth and leather, as though they were wrestling, ribald laughter and the slap of a hand being swatted away.

'Get your dirty hands off me,' called the first voice, flustered. 'You can both fuck off and then fuck off some more.'

The other men cackled a response.

'Listen, you gonna find him a pit or not? We ain't got all day to wait while you bat your eyes and shake your derriere at us. The streets won't clean themselves.'

'What,' said the third man, 'you mean just like his tuppence?'

They broke down into heavier fits of laughter.

'What's he in 'ere for?' asked the first guard.

'Rape, kidnap, sniffing yer mother's small clothes, whatever, it doesn't fucking matter. Came in this morning from Viytorren. Just put him in a pit and shut up.'

'I know, you carry on like that and I'll find your fucking pit, even if I have t' dig it myself. Only it won't just be for him. As it happens, though, I haven't got no pit for you or him or no one, they're all full. Send him up to the Tower. I heard the Rose is back in bloom—maybe he can help water its roots.'

Grumbles. Assent, dissent, he couldn't make it out. He didn't care. The feeling had gone. The aftertaste gave him a shudder, the memory of it wrapping around him like a blanket. It had never been like that before. The strongest reaction was usually a warm tingle, a slight itch, a fleeting feather down the spine. Nothing like that. His hands were shaking. He found he needed to sit down. What he wouldn't do to have that kind of strength.

The sound of feet receded into the background and he was left with naught but echoes, possibilities, and pipe dreams. He had to find out who that was and what they were capable of. Could he somehow tap into their reserve, use it somehow? Steal it? It was a ridiculous idea. He'd never heard anything like it, but he had to try at least. He had to do something. That kind of power called to him. It would do the same to any magic user. It was too intoxicating to ignore. One thing was for sure: he couldn't do anything from down here, except maybe rot and die and wonder. There was only one thing for it. He had to get out. *Easier said than done*, he thought.

Sentenza paced his cell. A simple hole in the ground. No door, no way out, and only accessed from a ladder. The guards had taken that. He had been marched through the streets of Westip with sword and dirk and bow all trained on him. They'd taken no chances. No one had paid attention to their sombre parade, or at least they'd been careful not to be seen to. Eyes and faces turned from them as they passed. It didn't always pay to see what was in front of you, Sentenza knew. The tower door had opened at their approach, slow and steady. Were they expected? He had the feeling they were always being watched, hidden eyes following their every move. They passed into a corridor lit by torches. There were no trappings and hanging here; no little touches of softness or hints of colour. The cells themselves were small, simple, crowded. Cold and desolate eyes stared out. They had been so long in this place that they had lost all hope and grown disinterested. He could see it in their faces, distant and lost. He pitied them. He didn't doubt that someone missed them: a child, a mother, a lover. Would anyone miss him, he wondered? His parents were dead, though, in truth, they'd been less than interested in him when they were alive. He'd sired no children, left no lovers. His was an empty life he'd grown to filling with himself. Sometimes, he wondered whether that was enough—only sometimes, though. He pushed the thought from his mind. It was beneath him; self-pitying, even. He didn't need anyone. He was better off that way.

The guards stopped at a metal gate. Two kicks brought a shout from the other side. The rattle of a key and then it was open. From there, he was shuffled to his pit. And there he paced. The walls were more than twelve feet high, too high for anyone to jump, even with the stool. He continued his circuit, round and round. He walked so much he felt dizzy. It was no use. He banged his hand onto the stone and immediately regretted it. He pressed his head against the wall, forcing his forehead into the cracks and crevices. He pulled away, cold and wet and frustrated. He could smell the damp and stale water where it collected in tiny pools, could even taste it. He fingered one of the puddles. Flicked at the rivulet that fed it and traced its tracks. A delta of rivers and canals born of hammer and chisel; tributaries feeding miniature lakes that clung to the stone. He wondered if he could do the same. Was there a way he could use them to clutch onto the wall and climb his way free? He tried, groping and feeling his way around. He found purchase, lifting himself up six inches, a foot, two. He searched for the next hold. Wet fingers clicked into place. He slipped and fell, crashing back to reality. He sat there, arse bruised and temper flaring. It would not defeat him. There must be something he could do. He was a Goddess-damned Wielder, after all. The wall was full of miniscule indents, maker's marks from the pit's construction. If he had planks or poles then he could wedge them into the gaps, creating his own scaffold or staircase. He looked to the stool, felt the power build, and struck out at it with his Wielding. It felt good to see it splinter apart, to have some kind of effect down in this place of forgotten things. He took the shards of wood and tried wedging them into position, but they didn't hold and kept falling away. It was then that he thought of it. If he could reach up and get at least a little purchase with his hands, he could use his Wielding to create his own plank, force it into place, and each time lift himself higher and further towards the top.

The progress was slow and deliberate. The task would have been beyond most other Wielders—they would expend their stores of energy in no time, but that had never been a concern for Sentenza. The skill came easy. All it took was concentration and will, and he had plenty of that. He marked out each anchor point as he climbed, pulling himself up an extra step. He formed the image in his mind and a slab of air condensed at his feet, opaque and cloudy. It looked like a layer of ice and creaked and groaned like one too. He slammed it into place beneath him and it shimmered prettily in the torchlight. Then, using it for stability, he clawed his way higher and higher. The chamber above was a panopticon: it used a centralised guard to monitor all of the cells. He'd seen the type many times before, though only from the other side. It was his first time as a resident, and he was hoping it would be his last.

The cold wall caressed his skin. He returned the gesture, hugging it close as he sought out the next notch. It was slow progress. The air crunched beneath him like fresh snow. Sweat beaded on his brow and stung his eyes. He slowed further at the top, each fresh push to compress and drag the air taking more and more from him. His breathing grew heavy. He could hear the rush of blood running through him.

Tentatively, he pushed his head above the lip of the pit, edging up as smoothly as possible, not wanting to draw attention to himself. The warm air hit him, hot and dusty compared to the dank of his pit. The chamber was lit by both torches and, higher up, hanging braziers. There were no guards in sight. Still, he kept low, stomach to the ground, a worm hiding from circling birds. He dragged himself clear, edging onto the flat, stony ground, rasping at his hands and wrists as he slid. There were other pits to either side, each with a worm of its own, he knew. None of them stirred as he slithered past.

The guard was lazy or asleep—either way, he raised no cry. Sentenza thanked his luck. He was closer now, almost at the door. He took a deep breath, sprang up, and kicked the door open. His flesh was alive with energy, the Wielding power surrounding him like an aura. The crash of wood bounced around the chamber, screaming an alarm for anyone to hear. The shack was quiet, though. A chair sat empty, while a lonely fire crackled in a brazier. It was all too easy—not that he was complaining. Now all he needed to do was find the keys and...

There was an angry growl from behind. A door stood ajar across the room—a privy perhaps? It mattered not. The scowling guard lurched at him, a knife slashing at Sentenza's face. He leant back just in time, feeling the warm rush of the blood-coloured blade's passing. The guard was young and scared, yes, but quick too—a cornered animal. He kicked out before Sentenza had time to react, sending the colonel crashing into the wood-plank wall. Old and part-rotten wood gave way beneath him and he cursed as he fell, blinking in the dark. He rolled to the side just as the guard grabbed a short-handled crossbow, pre-loaded and wickidly curved. The man feathered the tickler just as Sentenza pushed out with his Wielding. At this range, he stood no chance of stopping the bolt, but he managed to push the shrieking quarrel off-course. Metal bodkin chinked off the stone. The guard hesitated, wide eyes staring in disbelief at the smoky panel of thickened air. His thick fingers fiddled desperately at the crank—too slow. Cursing, he threw the weapon at Sentenza. The colonel ducked and the guard lunged for a sword, desperately grasping at the hilt. Sentenza slammed down with his Wielding, holding the blade in place. The guard's eyes bulged. He slashed out again with his dagger. Sentenza switched his weight, forced the Wielding up and into the guard. It took him in the chin. Bone crunched. Teeth and blood spattered onto the floor. Sentenza took a quick stride forwards, swept up the guard's sword from where it had lain on the table, and plunged it deep into the lad's chest. The guard looked surprised. Sentenza almost felt sorry for him and, almost tenderly, he let go of the hilt. The weapon would be too large to hide on his person anyway. He took the guard's dagger and turned away from the still-gurgling man.

His blood up, Sentenza felt primed. His instinct was to run, but he would not forget his mission. It had been another pull that had dragged him from the pit: the draw of magic. 'Take him to the Rose,' they'd said. Well, it was a place to start, he supposed. Across the room, a wooden door was wedged open onto a dark corridor. From atop a shadow-shrouded staircase at its end, light flared. Voices and torches drawing closer. The only other exits were the metal gate he'd come through and a third heavy wooden door. He snatched a spluttering torch from its sconce, swung the door open, and hurried through.

He froze. Three men sat in the room beyond, dicing at a table. Past them stood a bank of cells. Dull faces turned to stare at him. For a long moment, no one either moved nor spoke. And then, at once, the spell broke. One man shot up, drawing his sword, but Sentenza was faster: he thrust the torch at the man, driving him back. The flames licked his chest and he fell back, his yell rousing his colleagues like a battle cry. As if stirred from a deep sleep, they staggered to their feet. Sentenza threw the torch beyond them, where it nestled neatly among the floor rushes. As the flames took hold, Sentenza pulled the door closed and slammed the latch into place.

Guards emerged from the stairway, drawn towards the splintered wall. It left only the metal gate available to him. It was locked. Could he force it? Not without making enough sound to alert the whole place. As quietly as he could, he pushed against it. Nothing. He scrambled for the thin dagger and slotted it into the keyhole. Maybe he could somehow lever the mechanism. He struggled with the knife, wasting precious time. He would have been better with a stiletto. The voices behind grew louder. They'd found the body. He glanced backwards. Smoke was leaking under the door he'd just slammed. It would only be a matter of time before the men came to investigate. *Damn these old man's hands!* He pushed his weight into the dagger's hilt, twisting and turning, but the thin steel only buckled. Useless, even as a weapon. He felt his frustration grow. Some Wielders, he knew, could delicately control their power. They might have been able to intricately persuade the lock, worrying the mechanism to and fro until the barrel clicked into place. Not him, though—he lacked the finesse. One of the guards—a big man with a crossbow held ready—was coming. Sentenza cursed inwardly, trying to shrink into the dark. *Come on, old man. You can take them.* There couldn't be more than four. *In here—but what about in the next room? What about upstairs?* A patrol, a finger, a hand, a whole garrison? Where would it end, except with him back in the pit or—worse—in a grave?

He focused his thoughts, trying to block out the noise and the smoke and the fast-approaching guard. He poured everything into his Wielding, felt the power buzz all around him. He could almost *see* the force coming slowly together, wispy tendrils swirling round him like soup. He didn't care about the noise anymore; he wouldn't wait quietly for them to stumble upon him. He brought everything he had swelling above his head and hammered it down into the lock like a battering ram. Metal and stone split and crumbled and, with a shriek of twisting iron, the gate swung and buckled. Without a second look behind, Sentenza ducked through the opening, the voices of the guards hounding him, and ran along the corridor beyond, passing rows of cells as he went. The prisoners were on their feet, suddenly alive and excited. They called to him, a mix of keen and hopeful voices. They begged and cajoled, prayed and threatened. How many of them were innocent? Victims of circumstance. It could have been him. Did he have time? Did he care? He faltered. Something tugged at him. Something alien. The plaintive cries of the doomed pricked at a conscience he'd not known he had, or at least had thought he'd successfully supressed. The guards were squeezing through the gate behind him—he could hear their curses. It wouldn't take long. Besides, it would be a further "Fuck you" to his captors. He smiled inwardly as he got to work on the nearest lock.

True prayer and honest toil are key to living a righteous life. Keep Truth in your words when you commune with the Goddess and each other, and be honest in all your travails. Lies and schemes are aberrations in the eyes of the Goddess.

—*From the Tenets of Truth*

CHAPTER TWENTY-SIX
PREMIERO IRMAO

The Citadel

The morning air was cold. The frost seemed to come earlier each cycle. Premiero Irmao could feel it in his bones, even with his heavy black robes. It clung to his body and chest in a damp embrace that left him almost sodden. The gardens of the Mother's Palace were known far and wide for their beauty; he himself had overseen their expansion and development for almost a decade, ever since he had been appointed to the Holy Seat in his home region, the youngest Premiero in memory. It was not an appointment he had wanted or sought out; frankly, he would rather forget this place, just as it had forgotten him. It was fit to be nothing more than an entry in a family chronicle. A footnote, in fact, neither remembered nor recognised. His appointment to Doarson had unsettled him. Old fears and bitter resentments had resurfaced. His father had ever been a distant man, never investing his time or energies in his firstborn son. He had seen it as a waste of time. Why bother with a child that you didn't see as your own? That was unfair, Irmao realised. The old man had been just as aloof with and disinterested in his younger brother too, though, he had at least been allowed to remain at the family seat. Not so for Irmao—he'd been the property of the Church even before he was born. Few recognised him, he had changed so much since his childhood, and the short, intense cycles of the Misty City seemed to have aged him prematurely. Strangely, now he was here, back among the gossip and the intrigue, he found that he lusted for control and retribution. He touched his fingers to his forehead, striking away the notion. It was not seemly for a man of his position. He was above the petty schemes and squabbles of the House-Lords. Yes, they lusted for the power and control, but they lacked the vision. Not him. He held influence in the Citadel now, at least while the City-Lord was *unavailable*. A strange convenience, that. For any man to lose their sight so early in life was a worrying thing, but to happen to someone who could show no weakness, admit no failing, lest his position be challenged by some upstart... well, that must have been terrifying. *Another foible to take advantage of.*

The Premiero stopped in a section of the Summer Gardens that he particularly enjoyed. Flowers stretched around him, reaching for the blossoming branches of trees that were themselves busy with bees and other flying things, darting in among the leaves. Amaryllis and anemone, begonia and crab-blossom, yellow carnations and hyacinths. His hand reached out to his favourite, the white chrysanthemum, and plucked a head. He brought it to his nose, inhaling the earthy, herby aroma. A smile stretched across thin, pale lips. He had planted the garden himself, grown each flower and tree from seed and bulb. They struck a rare peal of joy in his heart. These plants were simple and uncomplicated—just how he wished his life could be. Instead, he felt the constraints of how it was: stiff and claustrophobic. It felt like a garden overgrown with weeds, the life choked out and the colour extinguished. At least he had his belief in the Church. It was a crutch, even if it did sometimes feel flimsy and uncertain. Though, what was faith if it went unchallenged? Blind obedience to doctrine was the same as none at all, in his eyes. Still, his was not a position widely promulgated by the Church. There were those within the Misty City who would have liked nothing better than unquestioning devotion to the Tenets. The Premiero thought them childish and insecure. They held the Church back, stopped it from achieving its full potential. He would show them. He would create a shining beacon of what they might achieve with the right guidance. Here in Doarson, he would eventually marry the clerical and secular. One holy overlord, one universal Truth, mighty and sacred and beautiful. His hand had closed in his reverie, absently balling into a tight fist. Long, wiry fingers stretched open. Irmao was saddened to see the crushed and ruined shape of the chrysanthemum in his palm. *Such a shame*, he thought, and, surprised at himself, he bit back a tear. *Ridiculous. It's only a flower.* And yet, it seemed to symbolise something more.

Collecting himself and feeling cold, he pulled at his robes, tugging the thick collar about his neck, casting his face further into shadow. The days were growing cooler. A sure sign that Urah Satti, the hot and arid month of the lion, was surrendering its stranglehold over summer. A haar had risen up from the harbour, warm air from the sea condensing as it met the river breeze. The fog lay thick and heavy like a soup, and almost as salty. It would be a matter of weeks until the mountain snows melted and swelled the river, and then would follow Samu Satti, month of the monkey, and with it the rains and the fading of his sun-loving plants. It reminded him to speak with his gardener. It was high time to ready the winter gardens.

The chime of a gong punched through the solemnity of the terrace. A visitor. Irmao turned back to the palace, dropping the crushed white petals to the floor and wiping the residue against his robes. A serving boy approached bearing a delicate silver tray. Even with the fog, light played on the intricate design. The Premiero paused to rinse his hands in a copper bowl, and the boy handed him a cotton towel. The water was colder than he liked, especially for the weather. On another day, he might have scolded the youth, but, like the morning, he fancied himself shrouded in a fog of melancholia.

'Illustrious,' said a young woman. She had been waiting in an antechamber and, upon seeing the Premiero, came rushing forward, prostrating herself at his feet.

For the life of him, Irmao could not bring her to mind. Some eye he'd placed somewhere, surely—there were too many to remember. 'Rise, child,' he said in response, holding his hand out before him as if he were reaching out to pet an animal. She did not, much to his annoyance, choosing instead to remain with her head to the floor, arms outstretched as though clinging to the ground for grim life. 'Get up, girl, for Truth's sake,' he ordered more sharply. 'Am I to go on talking to the back of your head?'

'Apologies, Illustrious,' she said, lifting herself up onto her haunches. She remained there, face bowed, addressing his knees.

These blasted peasants are little better than cattle, he thought with irritation. *Subservient to the last. Even free, they just ask to be dominated.* 'What is it, girl?' he snapped, 'why do you disturb

360

my morning?'

'I am sorry, Illustrious. I only mean to serve the one True Goddess—and you,' she added quickly. 'Your Holiness and our holy mother—'

'Yes, yes. Get on with it,' he interrupted, exasperated. 'I do not have the patience for your sniffling.'

'Yes,' she said, bowing her head lower, 'it is House Aargau, Illustrious. You told me to report if I saw anything out of the ordinary. Strangers and the likes.'

That Goddess-damned fool Dritsek. As reckless as he was stupid.

'I did, child, I did,' he said, trying hard to smooth his tone. 'Now please, go on.'

'Two travellers arrived. They'd come from the estates. A man and girl, I heard.'

Irmao rubbed at his throbbing temple. 'And how exactly is this extraordinary? Why does this concern the Church of the Righteous Truth?'

'They matched the two heretics, lord. Two what was seen in the estates that said as they could heal the sick an' all.' The girl touched fingers to her lips, disgusted at such blasphemy.

And rightly so, Truthless heathens.

'Really?' He had grown distant, lost in the import of her news. An interesting titbit. What was Dritsek doing with healers? The Premiero had thought his talk of healing and heretics all part of the young lord's ruse, a smokescreen to draw out the colonel. Maybe a couple of mummers he'd hired for the role—but why bring them to the Citadel? He surely had no further need of them.

'Yes, Illustrious. They had a tinker caravan an' everything, just like the rumours said. Her, the girl, she had papers saying she's a traveller. Kellawayan, they reckon, but him had no papers at all.'

'Interesting that you bring this news to me, child, and the honourable house itself does not. Where are the two *healers* now?' he asked with a sneer, as if smelling something foul.

'The Lady Aargau has the girl, Illustrious.'

'Ah, has she indeed?' Irmao murmured. *So she is involved, too? I should have known Dritsek wouldn't have the wit to cook something up on his own.* 'And what of the man?' he asked.

'He was detained, Illustrious.'

'*Was?*'

'Yes. He's disappeared since, Illustrious.' The girl sounded embarrassed, as if she had lost the man.

'Indeed? How so?'

'There was an *incident* when they first arrived. A guard was, uh... cut, Illustrious.' The girl began to flounder, somehow unnerved by the conversation.

'Well, child, there is no mystery to it,' he said. 'Your mysterious healer has obviously been disposed of after cutting this guard. It is ever the way of things and no doubt it was well deserved. There is little of worth in this.'

'Beg your pardon, Illustrious, ' she said, 'but it wasn't the man who cut the soldier.' The girl seemed abashed. 'It was Lady Aargau who—unmanned him. Afterwards, they went looking for the man, but he'd gone. Disappeared into the night, like a spirit.'

The priest stiffened, and the girl looked down again, hiding her eyes. *Superstitious cretin.* 'This *is* of interest,' he said absently. 'You were correct to bring this to me. Return to your mistress in Viytorren and attend her well. Do not let her know that you have been here to see me, but recall everything that you see and attend me again when you have anything new. I will have my clerk give you new papers and a reason for travelling to the Citadel. You have done well, child. May the Goddess shine upon you.'

The girl spread herself low again, a joyous smile on her face, but Premiero Irmao paid her no further attention. He strolled from the antechamber, passing through the vaulted cloister. There was much to think on. The day's long fingers stretched over the grounds but struggled to burn away the fog, which lay thick and still and stubborn, masking the central courtyard behind its gently glowing cloud. An unseen fountain lent the place a ghostly ring.

The Premiero made his way through the otherwise silent and empty stone archways, his own footfalls chasing him around the imposing limestone garth. Not even the birds seemed to sing; maybe the fog had somehow smothered and swallowed their voices. Reaching the corner of the quadrangle, he pulled on a heavy rope. A bell tolled in the near distance, clear and sharp like a call to prayer. He alighted himself upon a stone bench that sat against the wall and gazed into the foggy interior. On any other day, he might have rested here and watched the comings and goings of the palace. Today, however, the world was hidden in a shroud of secrets.

The mist swirled, dancing apart in little eddies. A tattered old man in tattered old robes emerged, so slight and frail that the Premiero worried that the fog might eat him up whole. The man bowed, the frayed cowl of his robe falling over his face. He pulled at the dress with ancient fingers, all twisted and bent by age. 'Truth of the Goddess, my prince,' the old priest said in reverence, touching two fingers to his forehead. It was a historic title, used almost solely by the Church and its clerics. The old priest delivered it complete with the sibilant sounds of the aged, and Irmao found it much to his liking. It made him lament the title's passing. Now, only those holding the position and the old even remembered the term, and that was on a lucid day.

Irmao beckoned the man forward. 'I have reason to speak with House Aargau,' he said. 'Send word.'

'Lord Aargau has been excused from the council, my prince, on grounds of poor health. He is abed with ague,' the old priest replied, evidently confused. He bowed deeper than he had before.

'I am aware of this. I too sit on the council. Truth, with the City-Lord in ill repair, *I am* the council. Just send for Lord Aargau.' He could feel the bile rising in his stomach. *Must I suffer so many fools in one day?*

The old priest dithered, hovering in place. He glanced up at his Premiero as if fearing his superior had made some error.

'Lord Dritsek Aargau, son of House-Lord Aargau,' Irmao said coldly.

'Of course, my prince, forgive my impertinence.'

Irmao touched two fingers to his forehead, ears, and lips, dismissing the older man, who bowed once more and backed away a couple of steps before allowing himself to turn and shuffle off on his errand.

A quick wind had picked up. It whipped at the fog that still clung stubbornly, swirling the yet-heavy plumes and bringing with it a chill. Irmao rose, thankful for the warm robes of his position, and stepped into the thick of the mist towards the central fountain, inviting the haunting wisps to dance around him as he moved. The mist did not clear, but it mattered not; even if he had not walked these floors a thousand times before, the sound of the water splashing playfully would have been enough to guide him. The outline of the feature formed ahead, looming out from the surrounding murk. A broad footplate of stone rose up in the centre of the square, housing a central shaft that elevated a decorative flower. Water spilled down from its carved petals and, today, there was something more. A dark figure rested upon the footplate, crouched, waiting or watching or both. The Premiero paused, for a moment unnerved. He had expected no audience, had not called for anyone to attend him. Who then, would have the temerity to ambush him here, in his own sanctum? Was nothing and nowhere sacred?

'My Lord Irmao,' a rough voice said, all croak and crackle. It did not sound natural, though he recognised it nonetheless. A shiver crept over him. *How did he get in here?* 'You are mistaken. There is no House Irmao,' he said with some pomp and irritation. 'I am the representative of the Goddess here in the Citadel. I need no house to attach a title to.' He smiled—inwardly at least. *That should be enough to put him in his place.*

The visitor laughed, a hideous sound that caught and rattled in the man's chest. It made the priest think of death-adders and other things that slither and crawl, all of them deadly. 'Lord, priest, or whore, it matters not if a man has the coin,' the visitor said. 'The events have begun. Within the month, the Council will have need either to appoint a new City-Lord or to execute the incumbent for incompetence, or maybe I'll do that as well. Either way, the Goddess will appoint her own representative.' His tone was wry and suggestive, tawdry in its own way. It irked Irmao to the quick.

'I pay you for your services, not your blasphemies,' the priest snapped back venomously.

'But you do pay, my lord. That I must admit. And handsomely too.' The intruder dragged the title, making it sound like an insult or an accusation.

He thinks me a petty thief. He calls me lord and thinks to assume I covet the City-Lord's chair for myself. 'You forget yourself. Lesser men might think before they speak, lest they earn themselves a spell at the Rose.'

'That's true, but lesser men do their bidding themselves and wash away their own shit and piss and blood. Lords and ladies and

City-Lords have other men do that for them.'

Irmao fixed the intruder with a stare. The man was unreadable, hidden deep within the shadow of his cowl. The priest couldn't recall ever seeing the man's face. He'd thought it a blessing at first, but now he wasn't so sure. You could tell a lot by looking a man dead in the eye.

'Are you sure?' Irmao asked, breaking the silence. 'About the City-Lord, that is. It must not appear to be anything other than natural.'

'It is tried and tested. The City-Lord will answer to the Other's call. I shall see to that myself if needed. You won't need be there, not even when the Other comes to claim his soul.'

The Premiero did his best to mask a slight gasp at the flippant use of the blasphemous name, turning it into a deep barking cough even while touching his fingers to an ear to ward off the evil. He felt foolish, as if fumbling to mask his superstitions like a green girl or some milksop youth. Here he was, Premiero Irmao, the Goddess's own appointed priest within the Citadel, equal to City-Lords, a prince among men with the ear of the Golyas and the Grand Tuk himself, and yet somehow this man was able to unsettle him in his own grounds. 'No,' he forced himself to say, thankful that his voice did not quiver or falter, 'it would not be proper if I were absent.' Then he was struck by an idea—an opportunity of sorts. 'We have needs of a decoy and it just so happens that I have the very vehicle we might use.' And there it was. He had committed to his very own blasphemy. *It is only for the glory of Truth and Church and Goddess*, he told himself. The breath caught in his throat and he coughed once more.

'You'd better be careful, Lord Irmao,' the intruder said. 'I hope that you are not suffering from the same ailment as our dear City-Lord.' The shadow laughed his rattling laugh once more. The man rose and took a step back. The fog roiled and swirled. It seemed to condense and thicken and, when it cleared, the man was gone. The Premiero was alone at last, but for cold and the fog and the faint rasp of the lungs echoing around the garth.

The roles of men and women are distinct yet equal. Though the Goddess alone created the world and all things, She too created men and gave them their place in her creation. Trust in men as you might trust in women, for though the power of creation is inherent in women, men must play their part.

—*From the Tenets of Truth*

CHAPTER TWENTY-SEVEN
SOLATTA

The Citadel

The sound of trickling water filled the little courtyard and drove Solatta to distraction. Her fingers needled the fabric of her skirts, tugging and toiling at the hem. It gave little relief. Her stomach was in constant turmoil, tossing and turning like a butter churn. The vardo had been empty. Everyone had gone. Her parents, her guardian, and now her—her friend, she supposed, scoffing almost bitterly at the word. Friends did not lie together in that way. A friend did not run. Had that been his plan all along? She flushed, both at the memory and the harshness of her thoughts. It had not been like that at all. He had just been the man she'd needed. First the patient, then the companion, and next the lover. She had chosen him to make a woman of her. Her stomach turned another somersault. 'I wonder if he made a mother of me, too,' she whispered. A sadness swept over her, lonely and distant and fearful. What would she do now? Where would she even start to look for Dreban? She was lost in this maze of narrow streets and hidden alleys, of secret gardens and base men. She shuddered at the thought.

Day had long since drifted into night and bats dived through the courtyard, making a feast of the moths and flies drawn by the torchlight. Solatta pulled her potions box close, the wooden smell warm and familiar. A welcome connection to Tervan. An owl hooted her lonely question from somewhere above but, as hard as Solatta strained, she could not see it. Curious, she followed the bird's call up a vermeil staircase potted with snugs and alcoves. The passage traced the outline of the building, splitting off onto balconies and corridors, a complex of rooms and quarters. It led her up over four floors until she reached a final filigree gate covered in jasmine. She pushed it open, the smell of the plant filling her head, giving her a boost. She picked a handful of the blossoms to use in teas and tonics; they were a wonderful relaxant and helped to treat all types of yellow sickness and fevers.

The gateway opened onto a wide roof terrace filled with all manner of pretty little plants and flowers. A fire crackled happily in a brazier and torches sat ensconced on a low wall. All of Viytorren lay before her, a tapestry of walls and lights and roofs stitched together by a golden thread of streets and alleys. It was a beautiful sight. Not for the first time that evening, she wished someone was there to share it with her. She deposited her box onto a table and edged to the wall, gripping it tightly and peering over the lip of the building. The entire town going about their business below, oblivious to her watching from her perch. She was the owl, head swivelling from light to light and from one scurrying little shape to the next.

'It is beautiful, child, would you not agree?' It was the lady. She had been sat watching from a cushioned settle hidden in a recess and Solatta had not noticed her. The lady stood and sauntered across the terrace, her eyes flaring blue against the torches. She stopped at the table and allowed long and elegant fingers to idle at the straps of Solatta's box. 'Ah, I see you recovered your accoutrement.' Her smile was full and wide and sweetness itself. Solatta felt the warmth of it as she joined the lady at the table. She looked in turn to the box and then to the lady. 'Of course,' the woman said, removing her hands from the leather. 'It is such an intrigue.' Blue eyes shone, fixed upon the box.

'Here,' said Solatta, reading the hunger in the woman's eyes. 'Let me show you.' She undid the clasp and let the straps fall free. The leather was worn with age and warm to the touch. Solatta lifted the lid. The lady held her breath. What did she expect—dragons and giants and griffins? Solatta stifled a chuckle, biting her lip to hide the grin that was forming there. The contents were dull and ordinary, exactly as Solatta remembered. She heard the breath escape her companion; she'd doubtless wanted lightning bolts and fire and brimstone. Instead, there were phials and tubes and a bowl. The lady raised an eyebrow. 'That's it,' said Solatta. 'Not very exciting, I'm afraid.'

Feeling a little awkward, Solatta took the bowl from the box and placed it on the table. It caught in the light, orange and red and gold, spinning and shining and twisting in the patterned surface. She took the jasmine and placed it into a compartment at the bottom of the box then reached to replace the bowl, but the lady shot out a hand, catching Solatta's wrist. Her fingers were soft and smooth and cold.

'Such a delightful bowl, child,' she remarked, her eyes fixed on its intricate designs. They played and danced across the surface. 'Where did you get such a wonderful thing?'

'Thank you,' Solatta answered warily. The woman had a house filled with such beautiful items, and she was worried that she had her eyes on her bowl, too. 'It was my guardian's, before he...' The words were gone, lost in painful memories.

'I see. It is a recent loss. You have my sympathy.' The lady turned as though to leave.

Solatta felt the itch of loneliness stirring. 'No,' said Solatta, more sharply than she had intended. She looked abashed. 'I could show you. If you like, I could brew a tea or mix a tonic?' She tried to keep the desperation from her voice.

The lady stopped, turning slowly. Her eyes seemed sharp, almost menacing. They held Solatta's for a moment, considering. Suddenly, Solatta felt small and silly, a mouse frozen in place. She chewed at her lip, anxious fingers clawed at the fabric of her skirt.

'I think not. The night grows dark and you must be tired. It would be unfair of me.' She half turned to leave, but paused. 'Unless,' she ventured, 'if it were more than simple brews and potions.' She left the words hanging in the air, waiting for Solatta to take them up.

'It is more. We—I,' she corrected, 'use them to help people that are feeling sick. I can help. If people are unwell, then I—' *I what?* she thought. *I did nothing. It was all Tervan.* What about Dreban, though? That hadn't been Tervan. The realisation gave her confidence. 'That's what I do.' She held her head that bit higher, pushed her chest out and puffed up her feathers. 'I help to heal people.' There, it was out. It felt good to say it. Empowering.

'Well, I am sure that there is a certain soldier who would benefit from a healing touch,' the lady said with a mischievous smile. There was a pitcher of wine on a table next to the settle. The lady fetched it and several cups before pouring for them both. 'But no, I think not. That man deserves his lot and I am sure he would not savour meeting you or I again.'

'I can search the taverns and alehouses or go to the villages? That's where we find most sick people.'

'Certainly not!' The lady was aghast at the suggestion. 'I have no intention of letting you out of my sight, and even less intention of trawling through endless lines of peasants and winesinks. Besides, I have a thought of someone much closer to home.' She smiled warmly over the lip of her cup. 'Now drink,' she commanded.

It was Varshied who woke her. Thick, embroidered curtains were opened and bed covers pulled back. Solatta's head swam and her sticky eyes struggled to shut out the light of the morning. She turned away, burying herself deep into impossibly soft pillows, but the girl was deaf to Solatta's protest, her voice swallowed up in feathers and silks. The servant's touch was not light or gentle, and she rough-handed Solatta out of the bed and into her tunic. Sweet bread and hot tea helped clear the fog from her mind before she was bundled down to the courtyard, where the lady was already waiting on her. It was Varshied who remembered the box.

The pair left without a word. The lady seemed impatient and distant that morning, and Solatta trotted behind her, trying to keep up without stumbling over her own feet. She was not used to the wine, but it had felt so grown up and sophisticated. They had drunk far too much, though the lady seemed as elegant and graceful as ever, dressed in sapphire brocade and with her hair pulled back to reveal smooth and flawless skin.

They passed through a maze of internal corridors and chambers, a labyrinth of twists and turns. Each new room seemed more elaborate than the one before, each hung with stunning tapestries and with artworks painted directly onto the walls or else draped in vibrant curtains or fabrics that softly rippled as they brushed past. Servants stopped as they passed, variously bowing or bobbing in deference. It was a whole new world, one that Solatta found alien and uncomfortable. *It's not for me*, she had to remind herself. *They don't even see me. I am nothing to them. They only see the lady.*

Eventually, they came to a large hall with vaulted ceilings. Colourful scenes were delicately painted onto the roof spaces between the arches, drawing the eye upwards. Solatta strained her neck so much that she almost tripped. The lady glared round at her. 'Come, child, we are almost there,' she said, taking her by the arm and leading her briskly away.

They finally arrived at a long room that was quite bare in comparison—its walls were of dull brick and there was neither embellishment nor even a glimpse of daylight. It had a sullen and sombre feeling, seeming to shun colour or laughter or joy of any kind. A range of candles smoked heavily at one end. They were tall and burned a garish orange glow, casting short, spectral shadows across the hall. The smell was cloying, bitter and almost rancid, as if the candles were made of butcher's fats, though they looked anything but cheap. A gaggle of men lingered in their glare, huddled together in their stark black robes. *A murder of crows*, Solatta thought, all whispers and hushed voices. A metal canister swung above their heads trailing thick grey smoke that hung in the air and settled in sickly sweet layers, clinging wherever it touched. Every now and then, the canister would slow and stop, and one of the men would detach himself from the group and renew its vigour by tugging on a dangling rope.

The men turned at their approach, tongues stilled, eyes

narrowed and untrusting. The silence stretched, only the sound of the lady's footfalls breaking it. Solatta rushed to keep up. A plump little man, hair cut down to the root, stepped forwards to meet them. He looked like a pudding, Solatta thought. The man lifted his hands out to them in welcome, loose sleeves flashing red trim like a warning. 'My Lady Aargau,' he said with forced cheeriness, 'it is an honour and a shock that you *women* come to join our vigil.'

The group of men behind renewed their whisperings.

'It is my lord husband that I come to see, Adherent Al-Kartoo.'

So that's what this place was, Solatta realised. A chapel. It was bigger than most churches she had seen. She felt the priests' eyes rest upon her, each full of suspicion.

'As is your prerogative,' he responded, though his expansive smile was stiff and unflinching, as if it had been painted on. 'And yet...' he added, stepping beyond the lady to pace about Solatta like a cat around a mouse. She felt herself shrink away from him. Priests were always to be avoided, she knew that much. Tervan had told her so many times: 'Priests are fearful and terrible people. Jealous and self-important. Quick to judge and quicker to convict. You should always have a healthy fear of the Church and its priests, and healthier still to have nothing to do with them at all.'

'The girl is mine.' Lady Aargau stepped between the two, gently pushing Solatta behind her. 'I have the beginnings of a headache—'

'Blessed be the Goddess,' interrupted the adherent. He touched fingers to his forehead. 'I trust the pain she sends helps to focus and shrive you, my lady.' He bowed his head to her meekly. 'Though, this is most improper. His lordship requires rest and prayer in order to recover. We are his priests, ordained to watch over him and call upon the blessed Truth of the Goddess to restore him to balance as only She can command. I am concerned that for this *girl* to disturb him...'

'And I thank you for your tireless vigil, my faithful adherent,' Lady Aargau replied tersely. 'If you will kindly ensure that we are not disturbed while we attend my husband.'

'But, my lady,' Al-Kartoo protested, 'I insist, this is most irregular. It is the place of the Church to minister to the sick, and that is why we are here.'

'And what good has it done so far? Each time I attend my husband, you tell me there is some improvement. Then, after I leave, it seems that he suffers a setback. No, I thank you, Adherent, but I will attend him for a while myself, along with my servant girl.'

'My lady, the sick bed of a lord of the Council is no place for a *girl* of such sorts, I am sure you will agree.' The adherent stared hard at Solatta, making her feel almost unclean.

'Once again, I thank you,' the lady said, 'but I will keep my own counsel on the matter. The girl is here to bear me tea and wine. I am sure you would not begrudge such a simple pleasure, my dear adherent?'

Al-Kartoo chewed his words, uncertain. He eyed the box suspiciously. It would be unseemly for him to insist on inspecting the contents. The priest conceded with a stiff bow, waving the pair through the door. The other men clucked and crowed as they passed between them, none of them moving to ease their passage. The door was stiff and Solatta had to help the lady open it. The room beyond was even thicker with the sickly, cloying fog of smoke. It burned from tables and niches all around the room, choking and suffocating. It was a small antechamber, ill served by too few candles. Banners lined the walls, dense with written words, letters a foot tall—holy scripture and passages from the Tenets. The effect was imposing and Solatta felt a shiver ripple through her.

A bed stood at the centre of the room, richly covered in blankets and pillows. They dwarfed the man who lay there, whey-faced and pallid, thin wisps of hair lying wet and slick against his aged skin. The lady crossed to him, towering over her lord husband, and stared down at him, head held away at an angle, almost haughty. She reached out a hand, her fingers tracing the set line of his mouth. It seemed such an intimate thing, and Solatta looked away. When he sighed heavily, the lady snatched her hand away as though frightened he might bite her. His lips were wet and discoloured where they hadn't been before.

'Oh, you poor man,' said Solatta. How sad to see someone fading away in such a cold and unwelcome place as this. She stepped to the bed, placing the back of her hand against his forehead. He had the smell of disease about him, all decay and soiled bedding. He had been left to fester in his own feculence for too long. What in the name of the Goddess were those men outside doing? Not tending to their lord, that was for sure.

The lady stepped away, skulking back into the shadows of the room. 'Can you help him?' she asked, lowering herself onto a chair in the corner. Her voice sounded distant and disinterested. It was sad to hear her so disheartened; she must have tried everything. It made Solatta all the more determined to breathe new life into this man.

Solatta placed her potions box on a table. It was so hard to know what to do. She had no idea what was wrong with him— the sweating sickness? Yellowing fever? Or a dozen other things besides? Her face burned at the thought of letting the lady down. Maybe, if she couldn't cure the man, she might at least be able to ease his suffering. It was worth a try. 'I can make him a drink,' she said, trying to sound confident, 'to ease his pain, for a start. Then there are other ingredients that may be effective...' Though, in truth, she couldn't imagine which.

Her fingers shook as she rifled through the contents of the

box. Should she brew a tea or mix a tonic? It made her head spin. *What would Tervan do?* He'd perform, she knew. He'd play to the crowd and drag them along on a wonderful journey. *Well, I can't do that,* she admitted. *So, I'll just have to do what I know I can do.* She lifted her bowl from the box and lay it on the table, taking some powdered centipede and pangolin scales to cool his blood and some roots and berries to ease the pain and help his breathing. She took some water from a jug and poured it onto the contents, swirling the mixture around in the crystal bowl. Silently she said a prayer, though she wasn't sure who to. Maybe the Goddess, maybe Tervan, maybe even just to herself.

At once, the room seemed to grow brighter, the air less oppressive. Solatta watched, wide-eyed, as tendrils of smoke lifted and weaved around her and the bowl. Lady Aargau sat forwards, suddenly interested. Solatta brought the bowl to the man, allowing a little to dribble between his slack lips. He coughed, face twitching. Solatta poured more of the liquid, allowed it to splash over his face and chin, soaking his bed clothes, but he swallowed more than was wasted. It was done. Solatta had no idea whether it would have any effect.

'Very good, child.' Lady Aargau was beside her. 'I think we are done here.' She placed a hand on Solatta's shoulder. Cold, yes, but not unkind. They turned to leave. The man groaned: a deep and guttural sound. They looked back at him. He bucked, arching his back, his body shaking. His face pulled and twisted, his eyes screwed shut. It was difficult to watch him spasm and splutter. Panic began to spread through Solatta.

'Good,' said the lady, almost cooing. She seemed unworried by her husband's reaction. Solatta wished she could share her calm disposition. She shrugged away from the lady, poured some fresh water from the pitcher, and carried it to the stricken lord. She soaked some fresh linen and used it to mop the man's brow and face and torso—slow and methodical strokes to help ease and soothe. The lady settled back into her chair and, when Solatta finally looked up, she was asleep.

It was a commotion from beyond the door that finally ended her vigil. Voices called from outside and fists began to pound the thick wood. Lady Aargau's eyes shot open and she rose, frowning, just as a man Solatta didn't recognise entered, his face stern and officious. He wore the same uniform as the patrol guards. His eyes never left the two women, but it was to the House-Lord he made his obeisance. 'House-Lord Aargau,' he said, bowing to the waist. 'Lady Aargau.'

'What is it?' she demanded. 'Why do you intrude upon me while I attend my husband's bedside?'

'Lord Aargau has returned from the Citadel, my lady, and he begs an interview with you if it pleases.'

'You mean those fools outside have run crying to my son, who now wishes to appease them?' she said dryly.

'My lady,' the officer said with another bow, as if that was somehow an answer. Neither spoke. The room grew stiff and still and tense. Solatta wanted to say something to break the spell but thought better of it.

'Very well,' Lady Aargau said finally, 'you may advise my son that I shall attend him shortly.'

The man bowed and backed from the room. A hassle of black crowded his exit, priests straining and jostling to see into the room. The sight was almost comical.

'Come, child,' said Lady Aargau, rising, 'I am tired of this. Let us leave him with these fools. They can wipe his backside and pray to the Goddess for it to smell better. Besides, I think that my son and I might find further use for you. Bring your things. I think they may come in very useful.'

Love your mother and father. Keep them true in your heart and in your thoughts, and honour them in your words and in your actions.

—From the Tenets of Truth

CHAPTER TWENTY-EIGHT
DRITSEK AARGAU

The Citadel

Huge dark nimbus clouds streaked the horizon far out to sea, spitting distant flashes of lightning and foretelling the turbulent weather to come. Young Lord Aargau stood at the window to his apartments and looked away from the gathering storm to gaze upon the great Citadel below. He had returned from the barracks only this morning and, while he still ached from the journey, he feared that he was a long way off being able to rest his weary bones. He massaged his aching temples, hoping that he might stave off the oncoming headache—though, just in case, he poured a drink. He savoured the wine, a dark red from one of the family estates (he could not recall the name)—strong and fruity with a lasting heaviness that lingered on the palate. He inhaled the cup and helped himself to more.

There was a knock at the door. He bade the caller enter before dropping onto a heavily upholstered chair, over-cushioned in the modern style. It was maybe the only thing in here that could be considered truly his. The rest had been chosen for him—like much of his life. He sank uncomfortably into it, spilling his drink. He sighed. *Typical.*

A servant announced Lady Aargau. He stiffened against the chair. Her footfalls were neat and measured, ever graceful. She seemed to glide over the marble—even the *sound* of his step-mother's walk was elegant. She was his opposite in almost every respect. He looked away from her, not wanting her to see the jealousy that bubbled beneath the surface. She reminded him of everything he was not and too much that he had long desired. 'Mother.' He feigned indifference, offering but the slightest of bows as he stood, lazy and petulant. She waited upon him as though for a welcoming kiss, but instead he crossed back to the window. It was difficult to see from this height, but he imagined all the people below—peasants, priests, High-Lords, all of them—going about their insignificant lives. He wondered what they might be thinking, what little thoughts filled their little minds. Before long, it would be soldiers filling the city streets. Days or months, Dritsek thought, depending on how well the adherent handled the situation. *His* soldiers fulfilling *his* dreams. Only, there was still a great deal to be done, and all of that depended on the people around him not standing in his way.

He turned to look at his step-mother. She wore her mask well, all smiles and courtesies, but he could tell that she secretly seethed. Had she been born a man, she would have risen high with her easy looks, her charm, and her guile. His own attachment to the barracks had been her idea, he knew. He had resented it at first. It had felt like he was being sent away, much like his brother before him and his half-sister. He'd thought it her way of punishing him for being the only one who'd remained. Second-born and all the privileges that held—if you could call them such.

Lady Aargau crossed to the console and poured herself some wine. She was not wont to wait on his permission or invitation. He side-eyed her, wary of the confrontation to come—and yet, when she turned to him, her face was light and pleasant. Her council face, Dritsek thought. The one she kept for the politicians. *So, she intends to smother me in her loveliness.* Suffocated with sugar and sweet-smelling spices. *There are worse poisons.*

A smile touched her lips, thick and luscious, painted delicately with some kind of berry grease. 'My lord.' She dipped low and raised her cup to him, her voice like syrup. 'How delightful to see you. Had I known you were here, I might have attended you all the sooner; however, I was called away to tend to my poor, unfortunate lord husband. You may recall him: House-Lord Aargau. I believe you are acquainted.'

He returned her toast with a raised cup and a sarcastic smile of his own. *So, it is this game she wants to play. Very well.* He stood, bowing beyond courtesy. 'Lady Aargau of House-Aargau, I bid you welcome.'

She stood in silence, a well-defined eyebrow raised in admonishment.

'Oh, come on Mother, share a cup of wine with your youngest son.' It was an old joke, worn thin over the cycles. He had little known his true mother; she had not returned from her last trip to the estates with his father. The victim of some unfortunate accident or other, apparently. A bite or a sting from a snake or a wasp or a spider—he had heard so many variations. Thrown from her horse or fallen from a boat. His lord father had never been too interested in the details. The peasants had their own versions: a wolf in the night had stolen her away from her chambers, or she had happened upon a nightcrawler while walking in the gardens. He'd even heard that she was stolen away by a witch woman. All Dritsek knew was that one mother had gone and a new one had arrived, complete with a big round belly.

'My only son,' she corrected. The truth of it was bitter and cold: his elder brother had been given over to the Church. An ancient rite, though seldom followed anymore. Only his lord father seemed to hold true to the old traditions. It was supposed to reflect the ruling hand's personal commitment to the Church: their firstborn offered to the Goddess to consummate their ties to the faith and bestow good fortune. In more barbaric times, before the Expansions Wars, it had been a blood sacrifice, but these were not such barbaric times. Only, it had not worked: the family's standing had not risen. House-Lord Aargau had looked to Dritsek, but there was no precedent to offer up the second-born son, so his eyes had turned to his sister. The firstborn daughter and only child of his young new wife. The resentment had festered and grown between them.

Dritsek replenished both their cups and joined his mother at the window, his eyes catching her mournful reflection. He touched his hand to hers. It was a simple gesture; an honest connection between a mother and child, even if it was not the actual truth. 'I do think of her, you know. Wonder what she has made of herself.' Her voice wavered and Dritsek frowned; it was not like her to show any emotion. Not unless she wanted something, anyway. 'It is the not knowing that is the worst.' She sniffed. 'They took her from my arms, dragged her from me. I still wake at night to the sound of her cry. Feel her little lips nuzzling at my breast. I would have named her for my mother, Amada. My beloved child.'

It was the most he had heard her speak of the matter, though he knew how much she brooded over her daughter's absence. He sometimes found her silently gazing from some window or sat like a statue in one of her gardens, staring ever eastwards, towards the Capital and the Seers' Tower, the seat of the White Woman and her cluck of sacred virgins.

'I would not recognise her now. Not even if she were to wait on me like some servant. Sometimes I think I see her in the face of some girl or other, and wonder...' She drained her cup and turned on him. 'Not like your brother, of course. I would know his features anywhere. I see them so often in your own face.' Her words had lost their plaintive tone and turned bitter again. 'It is a wonder that the rest of the Council has not yet found his eyes in yours or sniffed some scandal in that nose.' She smiled at his discomfort. 'What, did you think I would not notice? You thought yourself so clever, and maybe you are, but it is not hard to hide things from those who do not care to look, my son.' She poured more wine, a smug smile twinkling in her eye.

Dritsek fumbled, unsure of what to say.

'Do not overly concern yourself, Dritsek. Your schemes are not so far removed from mine. There is no love lost between your father and I; even the servants whisper about it behind my back. What does worry me, however, is your lack of duty.'

Dritsek felt himself stiffen at his step-mother's words. 'Duty?' He almost spat the word. 'I have been nothing but dutiful. When my mother died and my father's new wife replaced her, I was dutiful.' Now it was her turn to feel the sting of truth. 'When the older brother—my only true family—was torn from me, I was dutiful. When my lord father overlooked me for the family businesses, farming me off to Barkathet, I was dutiful. Alethyeia has seen nothing *but* the dutiful face of Dritsek Aargau.'

She stared at him, her face unchanged. 'And what of your lord father and the priests that attend his every waking hour? What face do they see? Or do they see your face at all?'

Her words struck true; he *had* shunned his father's sick bed, remaining aloof, though he was not entirely certain why. House-Lord Aargau had been a strict man, cold and indifferent to his only remaining child, and the fear of being sent away in the same way as his siblings had remained a constant threat in Dritsek's mind. Some of that doubt remained to this day, and he still desired to satisfy his father's whims and demands, even knowing that he never could. 'He has priests and adherents to comfort and pray for him—and you, mother. I hear you are a regular attendant.' He returned her smug smile with a knowing one of his own.

'And what wife would I be if I did not?'

'Of course, mother. I mean nothing by what I say. It is often talked about, how you spend long days and nights alone with our lord. Dismissing the adherents and priests, even, so that you might be allowed to pray alone together. Your devotion is admirable. Although,' he added, 'I fear that the Goddess does not answer your prayers.' He drank deeply and she maintained her silence. 'It is said that father's condition worsens. Every time the priests seem hopeful of a recovery, he falls back into a mysterious decline. It is most frightful and worrying, don't you think?'

'Make your point, Dritsek. I have things to be about.'

'Oh I am certain that you do, Mother. That is my point. Each period of decline fits a certain pattern. It is all too evident what you are up to; it is so unsubtly done.'

Lady Aargau's mask split, and she scowled at him, eyes blazing. 'You dare to lecture me on subtlety? You are the sow that has found the truffle glade: heavy-handed and desperate to be done. You may insinuate yourself onto the Council, but it will be clumsy and half-hearted at best.'

He roiled at the suggestion. How was she aware that his requests to replace his father had been refused?

She saw the flare of annoyance in his face and looked pleased with herself. 'If it is really so important to you, *son*, then I might be able to have it arranged. In the meantime, however, it would be prudent for you to visit your father. Questions might start to be asked in other circles otherwise, especially if you keep pushing to succeed him on the Council.' She smiled: a half-victory.

'I cannot bear to,' Dritsek responded, his voice quieter than he'd intended. 'The place is dark and dismal and reminds me of death. Besides, he stinks of shit.' The young lord moved away from the window and slumped into a chair. It was hard and straight-backed, all stiff angles and gold gilt. A gaudy and pompous reminder of his lord father.

'If I were a man, I would strike you for that obscenity,' Lady Aargau remarked coldly. She had never been enamoured of his coarse tongue.

'Oh, I am sure you would, Mother, but you can't help being so much woman, can you?' He grabbed at his chest in a crude gesture, but she did not see. It made the childish tease all the more satisfying. She sipped her wine and he drained another cup, then poured some more. 'Speaking of visiting our lord,' he said conversationally, 'I had an interesting message from one of his little nests of vipers earlier. It said that Lady Aargau'—he raised his cup in her direction—'prevented the adherents from ministering the sacred rites of the beloved Goddess to their lord. And in their own church, I hasten to add!'

'They forget whose money built that church. Whose lands and taxes keep them in their lifestyle,' Lady Aargau snapped.

'That is just it, Mother. The Church and the kingdom own the land. We merely own the licenses to it.'

She was well aware of the argument and made no reply.

'Furthermore, Lady Aargau entered said church with an unknown young woman. It is feared that, together, they tended to the critically unwell House-Lord.' He waited for a response, though his mother had returned to her vigil by the window. 'For Truth's sake, Mother, what were you thinking? Do you know how this will look? They may as well have named this girl a witch and burned her as a heretic, and you along with her. Truth knows they wanted to.'

'I know exactly how it will look.' She rounded on him. 'It will look like a desperate and devoted wife at her wit's end due to the profound lack of improvement in her dear husband. It will look as though she was so driven to distraction that she was taken in by the false promises of a heathen healer and allowed her into her husband's chamber. You think me a fool? Besides'—she fought to bring herself back under control—'whatever the fears and concerns of the priests, they will need to petition the Council before they can act, and who among them would blame a loving wife for trying all she could to help her husband? Especially,' she added with a smile, 'if one of the Council members also happens to be a loving son.' She raised her cup to him and drained it. She stared him directly in the eye, holding it until he was forced to look away. 'Now, finally, I suggest you do as I instructed and attend your sick father before it is too late. Your inheritance of the house estates may well be a formality, but if he becomes lucid enough to name you his heir and successor in front of a witness then it would save us all a great deal of time once he is dead.' At this, she rose. She placed her cup on the table next to her son and marched from the room.

Look to those less fortunate than yourself. When you come to the aid of even the lowest of her children, you honour the Goddess and keep her true in your heart. Know that when you turn your back on the lowly, you turn your back on her in turn.

—From the Tenets of Truth

CHAPTER TWENTY-NINE
DREBAN

The Citadel

The smell of urine was heavy and cloying. It ripped Dreban from a sleep that left him feeling groggy and unrefreshed. The room was cold and overcrowded, little more than stone box with a solid wooden door. He'd tried it when they'd first brought him here—beat at it until his hands were bruised and shouted until his throat was raw, but it didn't budge. There was no way out, though it did not prevent the rats from finding their way in. Damp, stale straw pressed hard into his skin, scratching at patches already red and sore. Worse, it moved with the evidence of things living among the stalks.

He was uncertain how long he had been here among the filth,

not all of it his own. Six poor souls shared his lodgings: four men and two women in a room hardly large enough for three. They were ragged and broken things, almost animal in appearance. The red eyes that met his were as scared and distrusting as they were discoloured. Rodent eyes. He could almost feel them ferreting over his body. His pockets had already been picked clean of what little they'd held, and his feet were bare of boot or sock. He half expected to see one of the wretched beings sporting them, but it was naïve to think that the guards had not taken their fill before leaving him here. Besides, of his new companions only one of the women wore anything that could be considered clothing, and even those were torn, as though someone had yanked them open. They watched him as he righted himself, the impassive stare of the downtrodden, determined to look but not see. Seeing was too dangerous in a place like this. Always best to remain blind. He looked again at the vacant-faced wights, the echoes of people who had once lived left now only to haunt their own bodies. The wrapping at what might be an arm or perhaps an emaciated leg moved, a rat crawling free. It scurried down the limb, pausing only to look to Dreban and sniff the air. It hopped down to the rushes and edged cautiously towards him, stopping to check the air every few steps. Dreban's fingers and toes already stung, covered in tiny little nicks and fresh welts from over-keen incisors. He kicked a foot towards the beast, causing it and his cellmates to shriek back in terror. He cringed; he'd not meant to scare them. He crouched, showing them his open palms, 'I'm sorry,' he told them. 'Look, I mean no harm.' The words hadn't registered. Blank faces stayed blank. He wondered if they saw or heard him at all. *How many cycles have they been here?* He moved closer, staying low and maintaining eye contact. 'I'm not going to hurt you,' he said gently. 'I'm stuck in here just like you.' He hoped his words were just platitudes; he couldn't imagine becoming anything like they were. He was sure that's what they'd thought when they'd first arrived.

The stench grew stronger as he approached: the overpowering perfume of rotting flesh. He forced back a gag, the smell searing his eyes. He feared them all diseased, though one was in a worse state than the rest. Perhaps he'd once been a man. Now, he seemed an assemblage of bones dressed in a badly fitting suit of welt-marked skin. 'How could this happen?' he asked no one, and no one answered. It was beyond belief. He had heard rumours of the conditions in such places, but never believed that they could be true—and the stories were not even as grim as the reality. This was some nightmare, he thought. Who would do this to another person? Six sets of eyes watched him, unsure and frightened. In one pair, he thought he saw a glimmer of hope. A hard-given tear ran a from single dry eye. It was a girl, he thought. The conditions had made an old hag of her, but he guessed her much younger, maybe half his age. How much of her life had been wasted in here? 'I'd like to help,' he offered, but even as he spoke he knew they were empty words. What could he do? He had no magic. He couldn't heal. He wasn't a Cognator or a Wielder. His only aptitude was for obedience and dim-witted belief. He ground his teeth. Only the Church could heal, and they tended only to other priests, nobles, and soldiers. These were ordinary people—who was there to help them? The Tenets said that suffering and pain was sent by the Goddess to scourge the wicked and the impure. Only by submitting to her holy vengeance could someone be made pure and true. Looking round, however, Dreban realised that this too was a lie. *How could this redeem anyone? What type of god would demand this in their name?* Dreban found himself wishing that Solatta was here. She would know what to do. The guards had seemed better inclined towards her, but he couldn't help worry that she might be in some other cell, living a similar nightmare. His tears came unbidden, running down his face and falling onto the man below, whose body flinched as though burnt. There must be something he could do! Slowly, his hands touched the man, moving as though on their own accord. In his mind, he tried hard to picture what Solatta would do, could almost see her fingers as they tended to his own sickness. She had been so delicate and caring—something the Church would see only as witchcraft. Healing, or at least trying, was tantamount to heresy. She had risked so much for him, all out of the goodness of her heart. Hers was a pure soul. That was her Truth.

Dreban lay his hands on the man, mimicking Solatta as best he could. He moved them slowly over the mortified flesh, though where she had washed Dreban clean with water from her bowl, he had only his tears. Before long, he was lost to the motion. The slow and repetitive actions were hypnotic, therapeutic even. They took him away from that horrible place. For a while, he was anywhere: in the vardo with Solatta and Cobb; running through the fields of the estate, chasing butterflies in the coming dusk; in the tunnels and the cave, staring at the reflection in the blue glow of the waters, only it was not his face that he saw... instead, a thousand different people looked back at him. He pulled his hands away from the man, feeling suddenly uneasy.

The man before him coughed. Angry red globules of spittle coloured his otherwise bland lips and dribbled down, disappearing into his lank and greasy beard. The disease had entered into him, he knew. The insides were no doubt as ravaged as the outside; possibly more so. Dreban felt small and helpless, his frustration bubbling over into anger. He placed his hand on the man's forehead, testing for fever. His flesh was too cold, the ice of it causing Dreban's skin to tingle and itch. A shudder ran down his spine before spreading throughout his body like ripples skittering over a pond. He felt the chill deep inside, spreading like fear. He fought against it, pushed it away in his mind. A warmth pulsed at the heart of him. He forced it to build and glow, like a brave flame trying to catch in a storm. He imagined it as a throbbing ball of light radiating outwards, pushing through his chest and down his arm, almost saw it pass from his hand and into the chest of the man. The man gasped and opened his eyes, the sudden movement causing Dreban to jump and break the contact—but, when he looked again, the man was the same. His breathing was shallow and weak and his eyes were as firmly closed as they had been before. 'Idiot,' Dreban chided himself. 'Stupid and superstitious. You're not a healer. You're nothing.' He sat back, shaking his head. What had he expected? This was his lot now; soon, he would end up like these people: a scared caged mouse waiting for the rats to swallow him up.

He sank back onto his haunches. The foulness of the air seemed to change, becoming more woody. He strained his head upwards, as if by tilting his head he'd somehow be better able to pick up the scent. There it was, just beyond recognition. He moved to the door; the smell was stronger. Wood and straw and smoke. Something was burning. He could hear the crackle of flames, the roar and rush of fire. Shouts and yells, people panicking, a terrorised scream that curdled the blood. *People are burning*, he realised. Dreban banged on the door, hollered for a grey to let them out. The effort was wasted. This was a place of death and desperation and his was just another terrified voice. The guards themselves were awash with panic; most were too busy saving themselves to hear, while those that did couldn't have cared less about the prisoners.

The smoke was thickening. Wispy tendrils curled up beneath the door and swirled around his feet, just waiting to claim him. He looked back into the room. The people had shifted, trying their hardest to move their thin and emaciated frames. He could see the strain of their wasted muscles, the agony in faces that wanted, somehow, to live. Dreban rattled the door, tugged and pushed and kicked as hard as he could. Panic began to spread over him, waves of nausea that threatened to unman him. He felt like screaming. It was hopeless. He could feel the weight of those eyes behind him.

'I *will* get you out of here,' he said through gritted teeth. Someone behind started to cough, the fumes heavy and choking. Dreban could sense their desperation; he shared it. He forced calm into his mind, tried to shut away all other thoughts and focus only on the door. He ran at it once more, throwing all of his effort into it, his shoulder ramming into the wood, sending a searing pain through his arm. He bounced away, falling to the filth-covered floor. The door remained closed and impassive. Dreban slumped, feeling useless and pitiful. His hope was fading. His hands clenched, balled into tight fists, shaking with the tensions held within. He washed away all thoughts and feelings, becoming an empty shell. He drew upon the last desperate vestiges of hope. He pulled at the feeling, twisting and melding it into something else, something pure; not desperate, but honest and true. A desire to help and protect not just himself and the faded people in the cell with him, but everyone. He saw Solatta smiling down with encouragement and knew somehow that she was thinking of him in return. It lent him strength and greater purpose. He punched out again, his fists cannoning towards the door. They didn't connect; they didn't need to. He saw the ball of light flow from his hands: a brilliant burning force. The room seemed to shake, ruptured by thunder. Splinters of wood and stone and metal erupted, peppering his skin. Pinpricks of blood puckered his exposed flesh, then formed over and healed as he watched, astonished. The heat of the fire hit him. Flames surged and roared, dancing in through the newly opened doorway, then shrank back down the corridor. Dreban could hear the sounds from outside through muffled ears made numb by the blast. The shouts of people running and those who were being left behind. Guards fled, carrying whatever possessions they could, not one thinking to help the inmates. But Dreban had no time to wonder and marvel. He dragged the nearest of his cellmates free, carrying them along the corridor and away from the fire. He left the first man at the bottom of a staircase and went back for the next. He did this again and again, lining the prisoners up like dolls against the wall. His eyes stung and his chest burned with every laboured breath, but he forced himself on. He opened latches on other doors, dragging free those who could not walk and spurring on those who could. Six, eight, ten—the parade of poppets grew. There were more, he knew, but the smoke was smothering those he had already moved. He picked up the first, hoisting a woman over his shoulder like a sack of potatoes and carrying her up and out into the blessedly cool night. He lay her there in the dust before returning for the next. His legs screamed a protest and his lungs longed for the taste of clear air, but he forced himself on. Two, then three, then he felt the hands of someone behind him, huge and strong and helping. A bear of a man nodded down at him, head wrapped in the cloth of the northmen. He smelled of sweat and fighting, and there was concern in his brown eyes. 'Hey there, what are you about?' The man's voice sounded hoarse, maybe from shouting, smoke, or both.

'What's this? What's the hold up?' came another man's voice from further below.

The bear ignored him and kept his eyes on Dreban. 'Come, boy, has the fire struck you dumb? What are you, jailed or jailer?'

'For Truth's sake, Braga, what are you doing?' The speaker emerged—a slight man with bright eyes. He frowned at the bear—Braga, was it?—before glancing at Dreban. 'We need to get these people out before they burn and we choke to death.'

'What?' Dreban managed. 'I was in here. Jailed—jailed, I was jailed.' The words rushed out, a wave of relief washing over him. They were helping. At last, someone was helping.

'What do you mean asking him that?' a third man asked, a naked man hoisted over his shoulder, 'of course he's no jailer. Have you seen any of them helping people out?'

'No,' agreed Braga. His eyes held Dreban's for a brief moment and then he was gone, ducking into the corridor to snatch up two of the people Dreban had dragged there. The second man followed, then the third, and then more, men and women alike, all sharing the burden.

Submit to the Church. Be prepared to offer up your life and the lives of your family to satisfy the Truth. Faced with the choice, the truly righteous would rather lay down their lives than live as a liar and apostate.

—From the Tenets of Truth

CHAPTER THIRTY
DRITSEK AARGAU

The Citadel

The wind had turned, bringing cold air hard and fast from the harbour. Dritsek could taste the sea and the faint tang of brine sharp and salty on his tongue. It signalled the end of summer and the coming of shorter days. Still, these were not the only winds that blew over the Citadel; the foul hurricane of rebellion was brewing. He watched through the open window of his apartments as smoke rose over the city, the flash and flare of flames licking up into the night sky. News had reached him on his journey and given him a great sense of urgency. He had ordered the driver to let the horses feel the leather of his whip.

There had not been an open rebellion for generations and,

at first, Dritsek had found the idea intriguing. He imagined a small band of angry dissidents running through the streets and, perversely, he'd found himself wanting to be in the thick of things just to see what was happening. When he'd finally arrived, however, he found that things were much worse than he'd thought. Infighting between the peasants was one thing and even the death of a few guards could be easily swept over, but this had gone too far. The Rose itself had been attacked, buildings were ablaze, and there was even talk of looting in the central district. House-Lord Abosi had been forced to call the guards when a gang of filthy children had found their way into one of his apartments. Dritsek shuddered; the notion had him reaching for the brandy. The Council would demand that firm action be taken. How could any of them sleep soundly? He could almost hear the petitions from House-Lord Abosi: 'I could have died, my throat slit in the night by those tiny assassins!' There would be calls for retribution, of course. 'Such an outrage cannot go unchecked,' Dritsek would affirm. He found himself playing the part of the statesman, catching his reflection in a looking glass. He puffed his chest out, hand tucking into his shirt. 'We need a strong and permanent force within the Citadel to ensure its safety and security,' he told his mirror-self, chin rising by a degree. 'The barracks of Barkathet are too distant. In the times before the forced emancipation of the peasants, our forefathers lived sound in the knowledge that the city barracks could respond to any such insurrections. Since their relocation to the far edge of the region, we have become a fatted goose, and now the peasants are warming their cook pots for the feast. I will not sit idly by and watch the hard-fought fruits of my family's labour be ransacked under my nose. I vote for the return of the soldiery to our streets. I, for one, would rather hear the steel march of the army than the raucous screams of rape and pillage.'

Dritsek smiled as he took a draught from his cup. Speech or not, it would not be seemly to appear too eager. It had been deftly done thus far, and this next step could not be seen to be anything more than a reasoned response to an unfortunate situation. None of them could have predicted the course of events following the attack at Baile Saor. The uncertainty was stifling and terrifying for everyone. Of course, as figurehead and intermediary commissioner of the army, he would be duty-bound to accept the request of the Council.

A knock at the door disturbed his thoughts. He poured another drink and began to pace the floor. 'Enter,' he called. The door opened and Adherent Al-Eldar swooshed into the room, his clothes a ridiculous black mess of militaristic and monastic styles that struggled somewhere between crisp lines and draped seams. *Truth, he looks more like a turkey than any of them*, Dritsek thought.

'Commissioner,' the adherent called haughtily, making the title ring about the room.

'What the fuck is going on?' asked Dritsek, cutting the other man short. The adherent's countenance changed as the forced smile slipped from his lips.

'My lord?' The adherent looked somewhat bemused, almost wounded.

'Do not give me "my lord", you fucking imbecile. I want to know what you're playing at.'

Al-Eldar's eyes darted nervously about, assessing the situation or perhaps looking for a quick escape. Finding none, he gave a low, swooping bow. 'Forgive me, Lord Commissioner, but I have done exactly as instructed. I have steadied the ship, so to speak, during dangerous and uncertain times. The strength and position of the guard has been improved and the city arsenal is being reinforced.'

Dritsek found his hand balling into a fist and fought against his rising temper, stretching and fletching his fingers. Was the priest being deliberately obtuse? 'You were meant to slowly pave the way for the army to mobilise,' he said slowly, 'to spread the city guard wide and thin and poke at the populace.' Dritsek said through gritted teeth. 'Instead, you've created an almighty fucking shitstorm in shallow waters.'

'My Lord, I sought only to serve—'

'No,' barked Dritsek. 'You saw an opportunity and you overreached yourself. You were instructed only to fucking serve, but instead you gambled on promoting your own career. Increased fucking levees and tithes for the Church? You raised the number of arrowheads over 200 per cent.'

The adherent grimaced.

'What? Did you not think I'd know about that? Did you not think that, at some point, things, people, would fucking break under that kind of pressure?'

'But, my... my lord,' stammered the adherent, bowing so low now that he lost his balance and slipped fully to the floor.

'Executions on the fucking Rose Wall! For Truth's sake, man, what did you expect would happen? That the peasants would just smile and thank the Goddess? They aren't slaves anymore, you damned fool! They won't just stand back and take that shit now they have their fucking liberty. No, Adherent Al-Eldar, you sought only to serve yourself, and now you will have to mop up the mess that you've made. The only saving grace for you is that I may yet be able to convince the Council that the army is needed to help quell the insurrection. Elsewise, you are on your own.'

'I throw myself on your mercy, Lord!' The adherent threw himself to the ground, kissing at the other man's feet. The sight was pitiful, forcing Dritsek to step away. Had he pushed the man too far?

Did he have the stomach for what was needed? This looked like the action of a weak-spirited lickspittle—but when the priest looked back up at him, Dritsek saw something else there. A malice that he fought to keep hidden. *It's all an act*, he realised. A mummer's show to make him believe the adherent was his man, grateful for his support. *Dangerous*, he thought, *but very well. That makes the pair of us. Two actors on the same great stage.*

'Throw yourself upon my mercy? Maybe I should throw you on the fucking Rose Wall, eh? Maybe that will bring the people back under control.' Dritsek bent close to the adherent, letting his spittle fleck the other man's face. When the priest didn't respond, he straightened himself and turned away. The moon had grown full and high, spilling its light into the room through a lancet window. He watched the smoke rising over the city walls. *Just one more push*, he found himself thinking. 'There will be a reckoning for this, Adherent. People will have to answer for their actions, and not just to the Council. The Church itself will want to know what caused its holy congregation to rise up against it, don't you think? It would be best if the responses they heard were the ones that placed you in the best light. I have heard tell that the Suers can be particularly relentless where perfidious Churchmen are concerned.'

Al-Eldar's eyes became slits, narrow and malevolent. The threat had struck home, as Dritsek had known it would. The priest drew himself up to full height, a good foot taller than the young lord. Gone was the sniffling and pathetic face he'd worn only moments before. Now there was threat in those dark eyes, hard and cold and menacing.

Good, Dritsek thought. *That should put a fire under his arse.* 'I think we understand each other, Adherent. Go in Truth.'

The priest turned, black mood and black robes curling and snarling in the air around him. He slammed the door behind him.

Dritsek walked quietly back to the window, a smile of satisfaction eating at his lips. The sound of silk ruffled behind him as another man stepped from behind a screen. He too was dressed in black, though his robes were richer and more traditional, their red trim marking authority. He joined Dritsek, accepting a cup of brandy from the young lord.

'A little hard on him, weren't you? After all, he is a man of the Church.' The voice was cold, as it always was these days. Gone was the excited, youthful timbre that Dritsek remembered.

'Peasants have loose lips and servants are forever whispering in the ears of their true masters. Even in my household, I have no doubt someone will be paid handsomely for news of the conversation you just witnessed,' responded Lord Aargau.

'Oh, I have no doubt about it. You House-Lords are ever in search of the Truth in the wrong places,' said the man in black.

Dritsek looked at the man standing next to him. He was taller, thinner, paler in complexion, and older-looking around the eyes, but he had the same strong family nose and shallow forehead, now framed by rich, black hair that had the same tendency to curl as the young lord's. *Is he about to preach to me?* Dritsek wondered, suppressing a smile. 'Indeed we are,' he managed, 'and the *truth* that will be discovered today is the one we want them to discover.'

'Truth indeed. Things could not have gone better for us. That overreaching fool has stirred up more than enough trouble to draw the attention of the House-Lords and the City-Lord alike. They will have little choice but to have the Council ask for martial law to be enforced. Thanks again to our friend the adherent, we will see substantial troops return to the Citadel before the week is out. You have enough to reinforce your position if called upon?'

'I do—they're stationed at the barracks. More if we activate the militia, and more again still held in serjeanty should they be needed,' Dritsek responded.

'Forgive me; I am not familiar with your military terms Serjeanty?'

'Peasants indentured to serve in the army should they be called upon to pay off debts,' answered Dritsek. 'There is a small battalion.'

'Ah yes, yes, I have no doubt, though I should not imagine that they will be required. It is only a small group of peasants and subversives who need to be reminded of their position. I am sure that you can handle that, can you not?'

'Of course. And the City-Lord?' Dritsek asked the question tentatively. Even though he was unwell, the City-Lord was still the dominant power in the Citadel. If he had his wits about him, he could enact legislature to wrestle control of the military away from House Aargau with the support of the Council.

'Once again, our friend the adherent has inadvertently played a pivotal role in enabling us to take decisive action in that area too,' cooed the man in black, evidently pleased with the position he now found himself in.

'Really?' Dritsek's question was, this time, far more forceful, almost to the point of being disrespectful. His sombrely clad companion turned cold, dark eyes sliding over him for a moment, considering.

'I hope that you do not question my judgement, second son of House Aargau,' the man said. 'It would be disappointing if I were forced to reconsider my actions in these and other matters. Especially where your house is concerned. You recall, I assume, the incredibly profligate arrangements that the Church has made with House Aargau for its fine anthracite fields?'

'Eminence,' said Dritsek, bowing his head in deference, 'I meant not to question you. Rather, I am happily surprised at how well things are panning out.'

'Yes. Well, it would appear that House Lord Aargau is not the only person to cavort with heretical healers of some description—or, at least, he won't be soon. It would seem that the region is beset by them at present.'

'And I thought the report had been a ruse in order to send Sentenza on a fool's errand,' Dritsek mused aloud.

'Only a fool can fool a fool,' Premiero Irmao smiled back. 'Be that as it may, your ruse was surprisingly successful in drawing out and eliminating the erstwhile colonel. I had expected better of him.'

Dritsek cast a furtive glance at the Premiero, feeling uncomfortable at the uneasy turn in the conversation. Despite his best efforts, there had been no way to identify the bodies from the ambush he'd arranged. He prayed to the Goddess that his nemesis had been among those slain.

'Then it is agreed,' said Dritsek, 'we continue as planned. The Council will no doubt call for a messenger to be dispatched to the Capital to advise the king's court that we have been pressed to enforce martial rule. I will ensure that no such message leaves the city. The king and his court must not be warned.'

'Be sure that you wait for a formal proclamation from the Council. It would not be wise to pre-empt their decision on the matter, even if it is a mere formality,' Premiero Irmao warned.

'Of course, Eminence,' Dritsek said with another respectful bow of his head.

Premiero Irmao turned from his companion and strode across the apartment, leaving Dritsek to his window. The wind rattled at the shutters, making him feel suddenly cold. He poured another brandy and rang for a servant. 'A second healer,' he said absently, 'here in Doarson. Who would have imagined? A strange coincidence to find two heretics.' He crossed to a bureau, taking a moment to scratch a note on some parchment before sealing it with a heated blob of black wax. A short, sharp knock disrupted him from his pondering, and he turned to find a servant boy in the doorway.

'My lord,' said the boy with a respectful bow.

Dritsek eyed the boy suspiciously. That was quick. Had the boy heard?

'Who was just here, boy?' he demanded.

The servant looked blank and confused. 'My lord?' he said again.

'Never mind. Have a message dispatched to my lady mother to advise her that the City-Lord's Council will be in session and that my lord father should be called to attend. She is to return via the same messenger that my lord father is ill-disposed and unable to attend.'

'My lord,' said the boy once again.'

'Did you get all of that, boy?'

'Yes, my lord.'

'Well, get out of here—and see that the message is zreceived intact!'

But the lad had already disappeared. Dritsek yawned, loud and long. It had been a long and busy day. While he feared there would many more like it to come, he left his apartment with a spring in his step. He had the certainty that he would sleep well. *Things*, he thought with a smile, *are finally going my way*.

No man nor woman is to be exalted or raised up in equal to the Goddess.

—From the Tenets of Truth

CHAPTER THIRTY-ONE
BRAGA

The Citadel

Bells rang out across the city. They warned of fire, though none of the city officials answered their call. That role had been left to the people. *His* people. Workers and peasants, the lowly rabble. Their chimes sung loud in Braga's ear; he thought they might go on forever. Now that the flames seemed under control, however, it seemed to him that the tune of the bells had changed. They still sang a warning, only now their pealing was a warning of something more threatening and sinister. Threatening to the House-Lords, at least. Weariness had hit Braga like a hammer now that the excitement of the previous night had waned. Just like his tired body, he feared that the mob had expended its energy and was at risk of petering out into nothing. There would be reprisals for the rioting, he knew; jail would beckon for those caught and no doubt the Rose Wall would be called upon again now that its thorns had been reinvigorated with fresh blood. Pain and torment would follow in spades, and all of it ran the risk of being for no good purpose at all. What they were in dire need of was something to rally around. His words at the Rose Wall had been enough to inspire hope and self-belief in the crowd, but they would all break easily if they felt that there was no point to the fight. What we are desperate for, he realised, was a sign. If they stood any kind of chance of really making a difference, they needed last night to carry on, but not just as mindless destruction and not just in one district of the Citadel. They needed their words to spread, to somehow touch the hearts and minds of all the common people—and even those few House-Lords who might listen. Easier said than done, he knew.

Sleep took him unawares. He'd only sat down to take a deserved rest, but his arms and legs were felled logs, heavy and almost as lifeless. The smell of smoke was still thick in the air when he awoke, but was a blessed relief from the stench of putrefaction. The room had been a holding pen, a place for those left to rot. The broken forms of men and women had been crammed into the Rose Tower; far too many had been unable to stand and walk of their own volition, and the incensed crowd had turned from simple destruction to carrying the inmates out of the burning tower. Braga himself had carried out more than a dozen and now his chest felt like it had been burned from the inside. The light of day cut through the fog, slicing through the dark in crepuscular spears. He leaned heavily against the wall, his chest flaring with a deep rasping bark. The room was a pitiful sight. Those for whom rescue had come too late they had brought here: prisoners so wasted and rotted as to be less than waifs, brittle husks that snapped and tore when touched. He had felt it himself, bones that rubbed and crunched, even under hands that meant only to help. A few of the women had been trying to find names for the withered faces, and it promised to be a long and painful process.

The day had grown strong and the sun burned his eyes. Braga cursed the vermin that scurried underfoot for having found the place so soon. *We will need to be quick*, he told himself, *or they'll make a feast before we have chance to return them to their families.* But it was not the rummaging of rats that he heard as he closed the door behind him; it was a cough and a gasp of life. He burst back into the room, half expecting some ghost or ogre to await within. At first, the room seemed as quiet as the grave, but then he saw it: the twitch of a limb, some shit-caked foot in the corner. He crossed to it, digging the owner from beneath another corpse, scrabbling desperately to free whoever it was. How could they have been so careless? He cursed himself for not personally checking the bodies. He pushed the last of the bodies aside and peered down at the figure. It was a man, weak and frail, though wide-eyed and almost ruddy-faced. How could anyone have thought him dead?

The man sucked at the air like he'd never tasted it before. Braga lifted him up and leaned him against a wall. Voiceless lips moved, cracking at the effort. Braga nodded before dashing from the room, returning with a pail of water he'd filched from a horse trough, still thick with straw and the smell of animals. The man gulped it down greedily, spilling most down his chin and torso. Braga watched as it washed through the shit and grime and filth, his eyes falling at last on the debtor's mark. 'I know you,' he said slowly, the memories slotting together in his mind, 'I saw you last night.' He traced his actions, trying to place the man. There had been a young man on the stairs, carrying his own burden of bones. In truth, it had been the sight of him that had spurred many of Braga's rebellion into action. The smoke and flames had been welcomed and applauded at first; the shout had risen up, a happy chorus around a bonfire: 'Let the Rose burn!' and 'Down with the Rose!' Only when one of them had spotted a lone figure struggling against the inferno had they appreciated the suffering unfolding inside. They ran to help, Braga leading the charge. He'd almost knocked the lad over, him and the bundle he'd been carrying—a dirt-crusted skeleton with a debtor's brand. The same man that now stared back at Braga with fresh eyes and skin that nearly glowed. 'Impossible,' he murmured, a broad smile stealing over his lips. He laughed aloud, a hard escape of relief. It was exactly what he'd been searching for: a glimmer of Truth around which the city might rally. 'You, my friend, are a marvel. Returned from the dead, or so close as to make no difference. The Miracle of the Rose, they'll call you, and the boy who helped you. The pair of you will be the figureheads we need. The survivor and his saviour. They'll write songs about you both, and I will lead a revolution with its words.'

The man stared back, wordless.

The Church was built upon the words of the Goddess, passed down from time immemorial, unchanging and resolute. Let the Church be your teacher, your rock, and your family. Place the Church at the heart of all things, as you are at the heart of the Church. When you think of the Church, think only of good and righteous things; when you speak of the Church, speak only of the Truth it brings to all.

—**From the Tenets of Truth**

CHAPTER THIRTY-TWO
SENTENZA

The Citadel

Smoke vented from cracks and joints of doors and windows like steam from a kettle. The red glare of fire cast shadows that danced around the square like happy demons. Sentenza had watched the Rose in all its fiery glory from the safety of a wall, merely a stone's throw away, safe and sound and smug. It had been a disaster of his making, he knew, though only indirectly. A little-noticed building lay in ruins nearby, burned out already and eclipsed by the bright flames that lapped up around the Rose. The fire he had set in the small tower nearby had taken hold quickly and spread through the adjoining tunnels even quicker. The only downside was that he would get none of the glory. That honour would be likely reserved for the rebellious crowd. They had been baying for blood at first, hungry attendants of some grisly fete (complete with freshly skewered meat, Sentenza thought, barbecuing nicely on the wall); that had changed, though, when they'd realised that it was their own people's they were spilling. The mood had turned even more volatile and, as the sun began to set on the whole sorry affair, it appeared that the Rose was crying tears of blood in the fading twilight.

Sentenza left the party as the mood grew dark and sour and even more heated. Not that he wasn't intrigued to see how the night panned out, but he knew that the riot would provide a convenient excuse for the Church and Council to crack down. If he had the choice, he'd spend the evening searching for the source of energy he had sensed in the pit, but Sakani's warnings still weighed heavy on his mind. The Golya had always known how to play to his insecurities, forever making a child of him.

Sentenza skulked through shadowy overhangs and vaulted archways that lent the central district an air of claustrophobia. Stone-eyed statues and gargoyles added to the feeling of being watched, and dead and revered House-Lords stared down from lofty plinths. Something drew him to the tower of House-Aargau— instinct, intuition, or just a deep-seated dislike? He couldn't say. Carved stonework told of generations of ownership; animals rampant set against escutcheons, heraldic charges denoting history, ancestry, and entitlement. Sentenza paused. A newly etched shield, a rat with a shovel, and a flaming falcon stood guard beside the five pillars. He reached into a pocket, drawing out the arrowhead. Tired fingers scratched over the five lines he found there. *That's all the proof I need.* He began to imagine all the ways he could kill the young lord, the thoughts giving him great pleasure. A door opened in the near distance and he shrank further into the depths, away from the light at the approach of footsteps. He watched as a man passed. He wore some strange cross between military uniform and the black vestments of the priesthood. A heavy hood covered the man's features. Before Sentenza had the chance to follow, he heard the sound of the door again and held himself in place. It was a boy this time, dressed in servant's livery, red-faced and flustered. By the time Sentenza looked back, the priest had gone. He balled his fingers into a tight fist and watched the boy's quick feet rush to his errand, face set and urgent. The colonel fell into step behind him and the boy half-turned, eyeing him suspiciously. Sentenza dropped a few feet further behind. They turned a corner, then up a flight of steps. Along a narrow footway that spanned the street below, the boy hurried down several twists and turns and down a dim-lit alley and, before long, the colonel had no memory of which way they had come. The boy was leading him a merry dance.

He rushed a few steps, gaining ground. 'Hey kid,' he called.

'What the fuck do you want? Can't you see I'm busy?' the boy called back acidly. 'If you're some kind of peccadillo then you can go fuck yourself, it's my day off.' He turned to run, the sound of a laugh already bouncing in the tight space, but it was ill-timed. Sentenza reached out beyond himself with just enough force to send the kid tumbling down the steps. With a swift pounce, he was upon the boy, first pinning him to the ground and then dragging him from his feet and lifting him by the collar.

'Shouldn't have stopped,' Sentenza told him.

The boy wriggled and kicked, but Sentenza's grip was firm. The kid was all fury, hot eyes filled with anger and venom. Sentenza had to admit the kid had spirit; he almost liked him. The boy spat in his face.

'You little bastard.' He slapped the boy hard, an ugly red welt swelling already, but he didn't cry out. Sentenza felt the kid's weight shift and was only just in time to see the glint of steel that came racing from his belt. The slash was aimed at the colonel's throat but Sentenza tensed, energy tearing from him and slamming the boy's hand into the wall behind him. The knife clattered to the stone floor.

The child gaped, realisation seeming to hit him.

'Oh shit,' he said. 'I'm sorry, mister. I didn't realise you was a, a—well, one of them, honest.'

'Now then,' Sentenza said, 'did no one ever teach you to respect your elders?' He took a dirty cloth from his pocket and stuffed it into the boy's mouth. Satisfied, he backed into the darkness, carrying his bundle with him.

The smell of raw alcohol stung at the nose. Cheap wine mixed with moonshine tasted very little like brandy to an educated palate, but Kuljet's clients bought it by the bucket. The old smuggler had given Sentenza use of a warehouse in one of the seedier parts of town, famed for its cheap alehouses and rough women. It was perfect, even if the smell did take a little getting used to. The boy's eyes streamed, a mixture of fear and disgust. *Good*, Sentenza thought as he lit a candle. *Maybe now he'll be a bit more respectful.*

The boy sat quietly. Sentenza hadn't even needed to bind his hands. He was unlikely to try anything as stupid as the knife trick again. He took the gag from his mouth and the kid gulped loudly.

'What do you want?' the boy asked with a whimper, all swagger gone.

Sentenza didn't reply and instead lit a small torch from a candle and set it into a sconce. The light flared and flickered in the room. 'Please, mister. I'm sorry about earlier, I really am. I didn't mean it, honest. Whatever you want, I'll do it, just please let me go.'

'Oh, I know you will,' said Sentenza, leaning into the role.

'You're going to give me exactly what I want.'

'Of course I am, that's why you came to me. You want girls, I can find you the best and the cheapest. You want boys, well, I'm a bit more expensive.'

Sentenza gave the boy an icy stare.

The kid seemed to grow less sure of himself. 'Listen, I'm rich. I've got plenty of coin, if that's what you're after. Only, I don't have any on me, not here anyway. I've been saving all my wages—you can have it all, but it's back at the Black House. I can get it for you.'

'That's not what I'm interested in,' Sentenza said, stepping closer.

'What, then?' the boy asked desperately. 'I could suck you off—I'm good at that.'

By the Goddess, Sentenza thought, *what is it with young people these days?* He stuffed the gag back into the boy's mouth. 'Shut up and listen to me,' he said. 'You work for House-Lord Aargau, don't you?'

The boy nodded.

'They had a visitor earlier. A man in black. Who was it?' Sentenza removed the gag again.

'I don't know proper. It was some capercaillie that was meeting with Lord-Aargau.'

'What, all dressed in black? I could have guessed that myself. You need to give me more. What was his name?'

'I don't know, honest I don't.'

Sentenza sucked at his teeth and stood back, disappointed. He looked to the candle, lifting it from the table with his Wielding and moving it towards the boy, who froze, terrified.

'It was the one from the barracks! The one that escaped from that town where they was all killed.'

Sentenza's ears pricked up. Al-Eldar? He'd heard the story

about the priest: the sole survivor of the massacre that had taken Braga and his hand of men. None of those tales added up in the colonel's mind, and any association with Dritsek only confirmed his suspicions.

'See, you're getting good at this. What did they talk about, House-Lord Aargau and the adherent? And don't give me any nonsense about not having listened at the door,' Sentenza warned.

The boy sighed, closing his eyes. 'Lord Aargau was talking with Al-Eldar in his apartments.'

'But you said you didn't know who it was,' Sentenza said menacingly.

'Lord Aargau was shouting at the priest. Telling him off for messing things up while he was away. He said that he wasn't meant to go starting any riots and that he was supposed to be making things better, not worse. Aargau blamed him for throwing them people onto the Rose Wall and said it was his fault they torched the Rose. He said the adherent was greedy and bloodthirsty, and I think he called him an idiot or the like before he kicked him out. That was it, I swear, may the Goddess strike me dead if it ain't.'

'I'll strike you down myself if I think you're lying.'

'Did I say me?' he backtracked. 'I meant to say sister. A slip of the tongue.'

Sentenza considered the boy through narrowed eyes before making a show of turning to go.

'Wait, you can't leave me here!' the boy cried, suddenly worried he'd been caught in a lie. 'What about the other one?'

Sentenza paused at in the doorway. 'Other one?' he asked, turning back.

'The other man. I didn't see who he was, but it was another capper. It had to be. It went quiet at first and I thought he was

416

alone, but then Aargau called him "Eminence".

Sentenza's eyes sparkled in the torchlight.

'I couldn't hear everything, but they said they were bringing the army to the city and that no one could know, not even the king. There was something about using healers too.' The boy was running out of steam, but Sentenza knew he'd struck gold.

'Why would a man of the Church be talking about using healers?'

Sentenza hadn't directed the question at the boy, but he answered anyway. 'They're all at it,' he snapped angrily. 'Bastards don't let no one else do it, but Lady Aargau has one and they even said the City-Lord had one an' all.'

'What? You'd swear that on your mother's life, too?'

'Don't need to,' the boy said, proud of himself. 'I saw it in a message what she sent.'

It was Sentenza's turn to look surprised. 'You know your letters?'

Despite everything, the boy smiled. 'My ma makes the banners they use in the square. She's been teaching me how.'

Enterprising little rat, Sentenza thought, *reminds me of me at that age. Goddess help him!*

The Goddess is the light that shines within us all. Hold that light in your heart and keep it glowing through your words and your deeds. Let the pureness of Truth feed the fires that make it shine. Nurture her light as you would a fire, both in yourself and in others.

—From the Tenets of Truth

CHAPTER THIRTY-THREE
PREMIERO IRMAO

The Citadel

Memories stalked Irmao from the shadows, ghosts of a child long forgotten. Torchlight burned them away as he wandered deeper into the caves. Footfalls danced in the echoes, skipped and ran and played as they had when he was a child. There had been catacombs beneath the Citadel once, centuries ago, when it was little more than a bustling harbour town and the people held sway with other religions. The Premiero raised two fingers to his forehead to scourge the impure thought from his mind.

The fish folk had once been laid to rest in the caves and ceremonies had been held to honour their brackish god. The evidence was all around, if one knew where to look. These days, the signs were harder to find, but they were there: niches in the rock face that had once cradled the bones of the dead; scratched effigies of leviathan sea beasts, called upon to watch out for lost spirits and guide them home to shore. All manner of deviations and distractions from the one True faith. The Suers had cleansed the place decades ago; they exhumed skeletons and gave them to the ocean to be reclaimed by whatever watery spirits resided there. The power of belief had not been lost or wasted, and a great shrine had taken the burial ground's place in honour of the Goddess and her Righteous Church.

Even that had mostly been lost and forgotten now, subsumed by the city itself. Once, the Church of the Rock had been the focal point of the Citadel. Now, however, it served only as a foundation stone for the great towers above. Premiero Irmao lamented its loss as he made his slow and solemn procession. There had been a time when he was surer-footed and more comfortable in these surroundings, but that carefree child had long since passed on. These tunnels had made a happy playground known only to him. He had stumbled upon an entrance by accident while playing outside one hot summer day, and had made the place his special retreat, not even telling the younger brother who adored him. He would have proven too scared or too clumsy, either spilling the secret or hurting himself or getting lost, and then everyone would have found out. So he had lost himself in the bowels of the Citadel, far beneath the great houses, exploring and discovering its mysteries, following its tunnels and learning which set of crumbling stairs led to the personal crypt of which lord's tower. The young Irmao—Desistrir, as he had then been named—watched and listened at the cracks in floorboards and ancient sealed doors to the gossip and scandal. If only he had paid more attention at the foot of his own lord father's house! Then he might have anticipated what was to come. He could have hidden himself away down here. Instead, he had been blind. The priests arrived the day before his eighth cycle, old, sour, and black-robed. Rough hands had pawed him, brushing over his body and measuring him as if he was a horse at market. They smelled of mould and wine and corruption. Desistrir had thought they'd come to bless and anoint him on his name day, even as he was handed into their keeping and bundled into their carriage. Never had he thought that the historic rite of Munera would be enacted. Gifting the firstborn to the Church was a tradition almost as lost to time as the brine-soaked tombs and tunnels. The thought still made him angry. He felt the grip on his torch tighten. 'I would have stayed down here all those cycles ago,' he told the rats and spiders and ghouls.

A low rasping laugh answered him. 'It does not do well to dwell in the past,' said a cold and dispassionate voice. 'There are too many ghosts there that are like to bear a grudge.'

Irmao knew the voice, though had not expected it so soon. He'd thought he'd have at least a little time to pray at the ancient altar. 'You are early,' he told the man, shining his torch on the figure. The assassin wore the black of the faith, though Irmao doubted the man had ever set foot in a church. Now he sat lazily on the worn stone shrine of the Holy Sepulchre, a blasphemy that the high priest fought hard to tolerate. 'Remove yourself at once,' he spat acidly. His fingers glided to head and eyes and lips. 'This is a sacred site. You should show more respect.'

'Of course, Eminence,' the man said, standing and offering a low and affected bow. 'Had I known what we were about, I would have brought my prayer beads.' The man's smile was tight and mocking.

He enjoys this too much, Irmao thought.

'Is everything prepared?' the Premiero asked curtly.

'Of course, Eminence. They await in the upper chambers.'

'How will I know it is done?'

'Oh, don't worry. You'll know it is done when the screaming starts and bells begin to toll.'

'But what about you? How do I know I can trust you?'

'Bugger your trust, I don't want it. Trust won't put food on my table. I can't spend your trust. You can keep it as far as I'm concerned. You'll know it's done because of that nice fat purse you have for me.'

Irmao eyed the man cautiously, his hand faltering.

'Listen,' the assassin smoothed, 'if you must be sure, you can see him for yourself. Get up close and look into those milk-white eyes of his—if you have the stomach, that is.' The man laughed, a sound like stale water being flushed from the rushes.

'And what of the others?' he asked, fingering the collar of his hood. 'They'll know me for sure.'

'Then skulk in the shadows, as is your wont, and wait for my distraction. Do or don't. Come or stay. It matters not—as long as I get what I'm owed.'

Irmao removed a heavy leather purse from a hidden pocket and tossed it to the man. He caught it one-handed with a satisfied smile. 'Good,' he crowed, climbing from the altar. 'Let's go.'

The assassin led the Premiero through the tunnels and passageways as though it was his playground, though Irmao had told him of its existence only days before. *Rats are always at home in dark places.* They left the torch burning in a wall sconce at the top of a flight of time-worn steps and emerged into a vast chamber. Morning sun spilled through a great blue dome built into the roof and stung at Irmao's eyes, and he was suddenly glad of his heavy cowl. Water danced prettily throughout the Hall of the Saddler's Son. Eight great fountains fed a central pool. Around it, manmade stalactites hung from the ceiling, alive with the swallows, martins and saw-wings that nested there. They chirruped and sang and took their little drinks on the wing, making a racket as they did. *If this were my tower*, he thought, *the first thing I would do is invite all the noble lords to feast on bird pie.*

The assassin hurried them across the chamber and down a side-passage half hidden from view by intricate screens. Stairs led them up and around, spiralling back in tight little turns until they reached the eaves. Ahead stretched a labyrinth of narrow corridors and half-doors, suitable only for children and dwarves. He could only imagine their purpose. They came to a stop in a suspended gallery of sorts that circled the central dome, from which they could see the hall below in all its brilliant blue splendour. They walked a quarter turn, pausing at a wooden panel. The assassin turned to face Irmao, a stupid and childish grin fixed on his face.

The Premiero shivered. *I like this not one bit, and here he is as giddy as a goat. I will sleep all the better once this sordid affair is done with.*

A hidden panel slid open and a pair of blurry eyes stared out at them. The Premiero looked away sharply, cursing his footpad's lack of warning. The sentry seemed not to care, and a latch was heard being slid from within.

The room beyond felt dark, macabre even, and smelled overly sweet and perfumed. They stepped inside, feeling the glow of the Saddler's Son disappear as the sentry sealed them within. A brazier burned in the room's centre, casting the occupants in a fearsome orange glow. A range of House-Lords and their entourages stood arranged in neat little enclaves, clucking and whispering to each other. The glare of the fire served to distort their faces and most of the men gathered had chosen to remove their hoods as a result of the stifling heat. They were all there, Irmao noted, the great and the good. Council men and city leaders. The room was blessedly small, with columns and screens that offered him cover, and no one noticed as the priest manoeuvred himself into the shadows.

The assassin stepped forwards into the room and clapped his hands once. The atmosphere grew tight and tense and silent. Two of the Grey Guard rough-handed a prisoner into the chamber. The man was slender, on the verge of thin, and definitely older than Irmao; maybe fifty-five or sixty cycles. His clothes had once been fine but now they had clearly seen better days. Still, they suited the man's face, which was stubbled and tired and wary. Irmao wondered how the man was being treated. *It matters not*, he supposed. *He will play his part in this farce regardless.*

Here was an average man of little significance, and yet Irmao half-expected him to burst into flames or grow a second pair of arms at any moment. *So this is the heretic*, he thought with grim satisfaction.

The assassin beckoned for the man to be brought closer. He laid a hand on the prisoner's arm, turning him from the crowd and taking him into his confidence. 'The choice is simple for you,' the assassin told the man, loud enough for Irmao to hear. 'You are supposed to be a healer, we know this already, as do all these lovely people here. What they don't know, though, is that I don't really care if you are or not. I've told them to expect a show and that is exactly what you're going to give them.'

He could see the prisoner begin to protest, but the assassin grabbed his elbow tight, pulling him closer. 'Now, don't imagine that you can say no and just walk away. I've seen your precious little girl, see.'

The prisoner tried to wrestle himself free, but the assassin clung to him like a limpet. It was likely a lie, Irmao suspected, though the man in black was surprisingly well informed. 'I know where she is and I know that she is safe, for the moment. I can also see to it that she stays well, or that she doesn't. It makes no odds to me either way; I still get paid. So, I suggest you wiggle your magic little fingers, or whatever it is you do, and make these nice gentlemen here believe that you can pull magic beans from your arse.'

The prisoner considered the assassin, weighing over his words. Irmao could see the fight fading from his eyes. It was a wicked game to play, but Irmao knew it was necessary. The stakes were too high for niceties. After a long moment, the man nodded his consent, face sullen. The assassin smiled broadly and directed him back towards the centre of the room. He nodded to the guards and a second door was opened. Irmao strained to see a wheeled contraption being rolled slowly into the room. It was a heavy chair of sorts, with a low-slung back that propped its occupant in a lazy slouch. The guard left it near the fire. A man was strewn across it, stiff and unmoving. It had been weeks since Irmao had seen the City-Lord, and to see him so weak, so childlike and undignified, was a shock. The man's hands were bound by strips of cloth and tied fast to the arms of the chair, while his head was encased on all sides with cushions and more straps that prevented any movement. He looked pitiful. The sickness had ravaged him and stolen his strength. No number of prayers had rid him of the sickness and nor were they likely to. Irmao had paid good coin for the poison that ate away at him.

Some of the House-Lords looked away, as though embarrassed to see their lord in such a sorry state. House-Lord Tsin even wrinkled his nose and lifted a kerchief to cover his mouth. Brave, Irmao thought. Such a trifle was like to be reported back if the City-Lord ever regained his strength.

The prisoner had lost some of his nervousness. He peered

now into the faces of those gathered, lingering in particular on House-Lords Chiqae, Fetl, Qublis, and Loram, who watched each other almost as much as the man in front of them. A council of blasphemers, each knowing that even being here would be seen as an act of heresy. This was, after all, an unlicensed and unauthorised healing performed by a stranger, a simple layman. No wonder they seemed furtive. *Did they truly think that I would not uncover their plottings?* Irmao wondered. It was just as well he had. It would provide the perfect foil. The prisoner seemed to dare those gathered to say something, to challenge him in some way. They did not, though some had the good grace to look away, red-faced at the part they would play.

'I want to know that she is safe first,' the thin man said, his voice calm and surprisingly confident—not at all what Irmao had expected.

'She will be, as long as you are indeed what you claim to be.' It was one of the council members that answered, House-Lord Kariq. The Premiero had not seen him enter. His was the most noble house present. A man who most thought the natural replacement for City-Lord Phaedra. He seemed anxious. *As well he might be*, Irmao thought. Now, the cabal was complete.

A tray was brought to the heretic, and he looked down at the instruments available to him: a range of metal spikes and thin-bladed knives arranged neatly in rows, shining hot and red in the firelight. He closed his eyes and looked away as if their presence offended him. Instead, he stepped forwards to the City-Lord and placed a hand on his chest. A low murmur filled the room, reminding Irmao somehow of a hacking cough being stifled. It seemed amplified by the air of expectancy. A cloth had been inserted into the City-Lord's mouth. A gag? Or to prevent him from swallowing his tongue? It mattered not; the healer tore it free with disgust. The City-Lord gasped, as did the House-Lords at the sudden movement. Irmao edged closer, knocking a small screen. It clattered to the ground, drawing questioning eyes. He shrank back into the depths, pulling at his cowl.

The healer turned back to his patient, placing his palm on the City-Lord's head and sliding it down until it covered the sick man's eyes. The healer whispered softly, some kind of prayer for the sick maybe. The heretic paused, looking up at the ceiling. There was nothing there to be seen except dust and wooden panelling, but he seemed to focus there intently. He took his hand from the City-Lord's chest and raised it high, balling the fingers into a fist. There was a rush of wind and a sudden pop—the sound of wine being uncorked. The light flared, fire and torches spluttering and growing suddenly bright. House-Lords shuffled and whispered their discomfort. Was that a wisp of flame around the healer's hand? *No*, thought Irmao, *my eyes must be tired*.

Slowly, the healer lowered his hand towards the City-Lord's face. He held it there, then touched his fingers to the sick man's forehead. The City-Lord's body began to twitch and shudder and shake and, at once, he screamed, a hoarse and awful sound, like pigs being slaughtered. It was too much. Lord Kariq ordered the guards forward. They grabbed the healer by the arms and dragged him from the trembling man. 'This was ill-advised,' Kariq called, shaking his head. He nodded to the guards. 'Take him away and place him in the cells.'

The room erupted in noise: hens panicked by a fox. They clucked and crowed and flapped their wings.

Irmao felt a hand at his elbow. It was the assassin, pulling him from his hiding place. 'Now is your chance,' he whispered. His hand slipped a phial from a pocket and he dropped it to the floor, crunching the glass under his boot. Immediately, smoke began to fill the room, low and grey, enough to cause panic.

'Fire!' someone called, Irmao knew not who. The call spread, guards being hailed.

'Now, Eminence,' the assassin told him. 'Make your play and then let's be gone from here.'

Irmao stole forwards in the confusion, slipping between the bumbling House-Lords. The City-Lord had stopped writhing and instead appeared to be trying to say something, but it was lost in the folds of a mouth little used to speaking. Irmao used a cuff to wipe away some of the blood from his face and the City-Lord opened his eyes, gingerly at first, as if adjusting to the light. Irmao looked into those bright eyes, seeing a deep shade of green that had not been observed in some time. Gone was the calloused grey film that had clouded them for more than a cycle. There was a look of joy and great delight there, as though the City-Lord was seeing clearly for the first in many moons. There was recognition in those watery orbs, and relief filling the City-Lord's face. Irmao returned the smile. It would not do to have the man anxious or worried at this delicate moment.

Discretely, Irmao produced the phial from within his robes. It was filled with a thick and viscous liquid. He dipped a finger in and drew it out, finding it coated in something greasy and thick and tacky. 'May the Goddess bless you,' he murmured, with a shake in his voice that could have been mistaken for fear. He pressed his two fingers lightly to the City-Lord's ears, then to his lips, and then to his forehead. 'May you always hear Truth, speak Truth, and know Truth,' he intoned. With a final motion, he touched the same liquid-coated finger to the City-Lord's eyes, ensuring that they made contact with the moist and juicy areas so readily accessible to infection.

Irmao had been surprised to see those clear green eyes and the

428

recognition he found there. As he dissolved back into the shadows, however, he realised that it mattered not. Already, he could hear the crashing and banging of the City-Lord's body as it convulsed and thrashed in the chair. *I must remember to wash my hands before lunch*, he thought as he left the chamber.

Let the Goddess be your father and your mother. Let her Truth be ever-present in the unity of family, for who is anyone without a family? Who can truly know or love themselves if they know not and love not their family?

— **From the Tenets of Truth**

CHAPTER THIRTY-FOUR
SOLATTA

The Citadel

The carriage was slow and cold and uncomfortable. Solatta felt every bump and jolt from the uneven road.

She bit back her annoyance, unable to understand why they could not have just brought the vardo. She had seen it and Cobb for a brief second time, and Lady Aargau had afforded her little time to be certain that Dreban hadn't returned. 'No one has seen him at all,' Solatta had reported miserably.

'I have done some checking of my own, child, and I am certain he has been taken to the Citadel.'

The Citadel? Solatta wanted to ask. *But why?* Yet there had been something in the lady's tone that made her hold her tongue. It was as though something had passed between them. Some invisible barrier had risen since Solatta had ministered to her lord husband. She'd been wondering how best to tell the Lady Aargau of her wish to leave when a servant arrived with a message.

'This time, he goes too far. I am not some commoner simply waiting to be summoned at my lord's pleasure. "Lord Aargau demands my presence at the Citadel," she spat with pomp and venom. 'Demands! Who does that man think he is to click his fingers and think that I will come running like one of his cheap slatterns?' The atmosphere had been tense all day, and Solatta found herself creeping like some lizard, afraid that the slightest misstep might lead to some tirade. If Lady Aargau hadn't requested her company on the journey then Solatta would have stolen away in the night. 'I insist,' she'd said. 'If I am demanded to the city then the very least I can do is bring you with me. That way, you might continue your search for your little friend. Besides, I should like to show you off to my son before I lose you. Quite why I bother with him at times is beyond me, but I know that he will be terribly excited to hear all about you.' The lady had sunk back with a cup of wine, smiling like a fox who'd found the key to the henhouse. 'Now,' she'd added in a tone that brooked no argument, 'join me for some wine. If I am to attend *his lordship* then it will be at my pleasure and not his.'

The evening had not been pleasant, with the conversation turning almost as sour as Solatta's stomach felt now. Lady Aargau had drunk to excess and grown increasingly angry and embittered, complaining about everything, though the worst she reserved for her husband, her ingrate son, and men in general. Solatta had risen late the next day, the fog of the vine still haunting her. Lady Aargau had been waiting already, and Solatta had rushed out before breaking her fast.

It was the growl of her stomach that disturbed the silence

that had grown between the two women. Solatta looked down, first embarrassed and then angry. *Goddess knows why I should be embarrassed*, she thought. *It wasn't my idea to be driving around so early in the morning.*

'That shade of blue suits you, child,' Lady Aargau offered, her caressingly soft voice almost an apology for her frostiness.

Solatta reddened as she realised that the lady had been watching her. 'Thank you, Lady Aargau,' she responded awkwardly.

'Do you know that you really do have a considerable talent?' the lady asked.

'For wearing blue, my lady?' Solatta asked, trying to lighten the mood.

Lady Aargau raised a slender and perfectly shaped eyebrow in teasing reproof. 'I will admit that I was more than a little sceptical of your abilities,' she said. 'After all, my lord husband has been attended by some of the most promising and learned men from all across Lacustria, and not one has yet managed to achieve a small fraction of the improvement in him that I observed yesternight. I swear, there was a moment when I thought he even recognised me.'

Solatta smiled in return, but was unsure of what to say. She had been disheartened by the small response. Had it been Tervan, she thought almost bitterly, then High-Lord Aargau would have been awake and sitting up by now.

'It is a rare gift. A rare gift indeed,' the lady continued. 'Scholars, apothecaries, and even the adherents themselves—all have tried and yet all have so far failed to make the slightest bit of difference. And then you come along. I wonder what your story is, my girl. You and your box of tricks, your little caravan, and this *friend* of yours... it is all terribly intriguing, *exotic* even.'

Solatta smiled politely, but had the feeling that she was being humoured, or that some joke was being made at her expense.

Lady Aargau's voice had grown flat and disinterested, no longer the soothing brush of velvet, and it made Solatta feel even more uncomfortable. Still, she desperately wanted to find Dreban, and if she had to suffer some small ribbing then suffer it she would. Besides, how else would she get to the Citadel?

'Do you really think that he will be there, my lady? My friend, Dreban, I mean.'

'Oh yes, my dear. I am very sure. We can at least try.'

Solatta smiled at the offer of assistance. Maybe she had imagined the earlier frost. She feared she had judged her companion too harshly, and allowed herself to lapse back into an embarrassed silence, her eyes closing slowly.

It was the roll of the carriage that jolted her awake. For a moment, she was back in the vardo and travelling with Dreban while Tervan sat up front, driving Cobb on their merry journey. One happy little family. It was such a happy dream that it was difficult to drag herself away. Lady Aargau's eyes were closed, though Solatta didn't think her asleep; she held herself too stiff and proper.

Solatta turned to the window, only to be dumbstruck by the size and scope of the city looming beyond. It rose in the distance like some manmade mountain, all sheer walls and high buildings. She had thought Viytorren big, but the difference was like that of a dormouse and a horse. When she looked back, Lady Aargau was watching with a poorly disguised smile, all sly and smirking. Solatta felt her cheeks redden, embarrassed to think what a yokel she must seem. She folded her hands demurely into her lap and sat tall and straight-backed. The lady smiled warmly and offered a slight nod of approval.

Their carriage slowed, drawing into a gatehouse. Solatta saw the uniforms and felt a panic wash over her. 'Oh no,' she muttered.

'Don't worry, child. These aren't like the guard in the water garden.' The lady sounded exasperated, reproachful almost.

'It's not that,' Solatta said quickly, a barb to her voice. 'I don't have my papers. Without my travel chit, they'll arrest me like they did Dreban.'

'Child,' the lady laughed, 'don't worry yourself. They won't ask to see your documents while you are travelling with me. Besides, they are right there beneath your seat, along with your clever little box of *things*.'

'They are?' Solatta asked incredulously.

'Of course. I had your belongings brought aboard the carriage before we left.'

Solatta looked down beneath her seat and, true enough, in a cubbyhole behind her feet, she could see her leather box. She pulled it out and placed it on the seat beside her, opening it carefully and peering quickly inside. Just as the lady had said, her bowl and all of her potions and tinctures, as well as her well-thumbed travel documents and Dreban's poppet, were all there.

A thought came unbidden: a hidden memory of tiny hands and a doll of her own. The image flooded her mind and, with it, the smell of spices and cooking. She could pick them all out, garlic and paprika and cumin, heady and warming, and, above all that, the lingering calm of lavender. It was a revelation, a window into her past that she'd thought lost and closed for ever. A forgotten Truth.

Foof! The name came unbidden, almost as instinct. Her own doll, or a pet? She couldn't quite remember. It was a nonsense name, stupid and meaningless and infantile, but it was a little link to childhood. Possibly the only one she had. Her hand hovered over the poppet briefly and she felt an urge to pick it up, but she resisted, instead closing the box and placing it on her lap.

'You seem anxious, child. Is there something troubling you?' The lady asked, her voice regaining some of its charm.

'No, of course not,' Solatta responded, shifting the box back onto the seat beside her to demonstrate as much. 'Only, where are we going?'

'Of course, child. Is it the Citadel that bothers you? It is such a large and busy place, full of strange sounds and smells. It must be very different to where you're from. Tell me, where is it that you are from?'

'I'm not quite sure,' she admitted and, for some reason, she found herself opening up to Lady Aargau as if she were some kind of big sister. It all flowed from her like a river: her early life (from where she could remember, at least), being an orphan, living with Tervan. The towns they would visit and their talent for helping others. She, again, told of meeting Dreban and losing Tervan and then finally she described the horrors of Baile Saor and her flight in the caravan. It was as though someone had opened a sluice inside her and the words rushed out, building and gaining speed until it was a bubbling torrent. It was a tale soaked in sorrow, Solatta knew, but Lady Aargau listened with a sympathetic ear and an almost motherly interest. When she was finished, she felt exhausted but relieved. The weight of her struggle had been eased. Lady Aargau said nothing, but moved to sit next to her. Stiffly at first, Solatta allowed herself to be pulled into her arms, melting into the embrace; full of warmth and understanding, like a mother's.

The carriage drew to a stop and a troop of servants descended upon them. Doors were opened, steps were positioned, hands were offered, and bags were fetched. Solatta could hardly believe the treatment. *How do people live like this?* she thought. She stopped a man carrying her potions box and wrestled it away from him.

They passed through myriad archways and passages before

arriving in a great hallway bedecked with ornate carvings and exquisite tiling. Marble statues stood all to one side: a damning of judges glaring down. Lady Aargau directed them onto a spiralling staircase that seemed to continue onwards and upwards for such a turn that Solatta began to feel dizzy. A long hallway gave blessed relief, draped in many splendid cloths of rich colours and patterns. The sound of their footfalls echoed throughout like the chittering of birds in a forest.

They stopped in front of an imposing door, all dark wood that seemed to draw away both light and life. Lady Aargau lifted a hand to knock but seemed to check herself, suddenly doubtful. She tried again, steeling herself, but paused once more, seeming to argue with herself.

'Didn't Lord Aargau summon you?' Solatta asked.

The lady chewed on the words. 'You're right,' she said at last, the fire returning to her voice. 'And who is he to demand I attend his every call? I am his lord father's wife. Why should I be expected to always kowtow and bend to his whims?' She turned on her heel and led the way back down the hall. Solatta followed her through several lush apartments and through another small door. Lady Aargau did not pause to knock; she glowed with a quiet confidence. Once through the doorway, however, she faltered.

A man sat within, silently waiting. Solatta recognised him: the long, greasy hair raked hastily straight; the piercing eyes red and raw.

'My lord husband,' Lady Aargau managed, her voice tight with a forced cordiality that failed to mask her shock.

The man turned and glared at them. 'Never mind the pleasantries, woman. Who else might you expect to have summoned you to their side? Unless you have taken some new Lord Aargau in my absence. No,' he added, answering his own question. 'I thought not. Now, where the fuck is that little shit Dritsek?'

Ask not why the Goddess created the world. Ask instead how you can glorify and praise the Goddess for the life She has given you. Expect nothing from the Goddess and offer her everything. Neither the Goddess, nor the world, owe you anything, but you owe them both your existence. Life is given, honesty is bought through hard work, and Truth is attained by purity of heart.

—From the Tenets of Truth

CHAPTER THIRTY-FIVE
DRITSEK AARGAU

The Citadel

The Citadel seemed quieted. Eerie, even, as though all its inhabitants were hiding in the depths and holding their breath. Dritsek Aargau felt it like a smothering blanket as he walked slowly through the arched arcades and stone galleries that wound through the city's central district. His pace and the odd feeling reflected his mood—or, at least, the one he hoped to portray. 'Important news,' the messenger had told him, some portentous event for which Dritsek and all the other lords were being recalled to the Citadel, though the bells were not yet tolling. Dritsek had not wanted to hear anymore, had choked back tears that would never have materialised. It had been one of his finest performances, though he had needed to dismiss the messenger boy before his false emotion failed him.

He strode in a sombre and deliberate fashion, one he liked to think would look suitably respectful to anyone watching. After all, it would not be fitting to appear happy, not when you were arriving to receive news of the passing of your City-Lord.

The black robes of the priests greeted him, flapping and rising together like ravens. Just like the bird, Dritsek considered them an ill omen. Surely they had better things to do than crow and croon here in the low halls. Were there not preparations and prayers to be said, blessings to be made? A thought nagged at his mind, taking hold and growing in its unease. Why had there been no bells? *Please don't tell me he's drawing out the end*, he prayed. That had not been the plan. Quick and decisive, they had agreed. The more sudden the better. Anything slow and lingering would be a cruelty, and would give others the chance to scheme and position.

An unkindness of adherents flocked together outside the main council chambers, a small army of shadows spreading their dark whispers. 'Heresy' and 'murder'. The words made his skin prickle. What if they knew? They quieted as he neared, all sibilant shushes. Dritsek began to panic, his stomach churning like a wriggling bucket of eels. He paused at the door to the debating hall, suddenly frozen in place and unmanned. 'Fool,' he mumbled to himself. 'If they knew, you'd be staring at the metal thorns of the Rose, not drawing attention to yourself here.' He fought against the deafening drum of his heart. For now, he just needed to put his trust in the Premiero. His heart skipped at the notion.

He pushed open the access panel inset within the oversized

door, pale hand trembling against the deep ebony wood. It screeched its resistance, silencing the conversations within. Eager eyes watched him, poring over his flesh. House-Lords of the upper chamber, each of them with a seat on the Council. The air inside felt as cold and crisp as their greeting. They were surprised to see him, he realised. 'Gentlemen, please, I apologise,' he offered, affecting his most humble and respectful tone. 'I hope that I am not interrupting.'

It was House-Lord Kariq who responded. He gave a slight nod of the head, little more than an inflection, intended to show as little respect as possible without appearing overtly rude. 'Lord Aargau,' he said, nasal and thickly pretentious. It was a purple voice for a purple man. His clothes, his hair, his rings, and even his pallor seemed to carry a hint of the colour. His family arms held a purple beetle crawling over an iris, set against a lavender field. Dritsek had always thought it turgid. A leech of a man, swollen fat and slow on slavery, though it was to him that the others looked. He held sway here, and most assumed it would be him to whom they would soon kneel and call City-Lord.

I am sorry, Lord Kariq, he thought, *but I shall be only too happy to divest you of that notion.* The other House-Lords shifted uncomfortably in their lavish seats. The table, a huge mahogany thing, was raised on a plinth at the centre of the room. Only Council members, nominated officials, and members of the clergy were allowed to step there unless given special license by invitation. Dritsek approached, stepping brazenly close. 'Such a sad loss for us all, and a dark day in our history,' he said, trying hard to rise above the insult, 'I think we can all agree.'

'So, you have heard then,' said Lord Abosi in his small voice and grating accent.

Dritsek suppressed a smile. *Well, not officially.* He'd heard only

441

from his footpad, but he wasn't in the habit of trusting men he hadn't paid with his own coin. 'It is done,' the man in black had said, and that was all Dritsek had needed.

'Indeed,' Dritsek offered, placing a hand on his chest. 'A tragedy in my heart, heaping further upon my own family's suffering.'

'Oh? Your father fares no better these past days?' House-Lord Essee enquired. He was a fat and weaselly man, though his family was an ancient one of good standing and Dritsek held no contentions with either him or house.

'No, unfortunately not, my lord,' Dritsek responded, displaying a dignified solemnity that he felt marked the occasion. 'In fact, I fear the messenger's news referred to my own lord father. It weighs heavy on my heart.'

'Messenger?' enquired House-Lord Kariq. 'But I sent no word to yourself, only to your lord father.'

'And finding my lord in such poor health, the man must have sought me out in his stead.'

House-Lord Essee nodded his sympathies.

'But such trivialities are immaterial,' Dritsek continued. 'Please, tell me, how did City-Lord Phaedra die?' he asked smoothly.

'Not well,' answered House-Lord Kariq. 'He was attended by his adherents and, though they tried to heal his affliction, it would seem that there were... complications.' The man seemed to struggle to find the right words.

'Complications?' Dritsek pried.

'Yes,' House-Lord Kariq said, 'the procedure did not sit well with him, and some form of ill humour set in, spreading quickly through his body. He was in some great pain before all life escaped him in a final roar. In the end, his passing came as a blessing.'

'I see,' Dritsek said ponderously. 'You were present?'

'I was,' House-Lord Kariq confirmed, eyeing Dritsek with

suspicion.

'It is gratifying then, my lord, to know that he was surrounded by those who cared for him and whom he trusted,' Dritsek said with a bow of his head. He made to leave their company and then paused, thinking better of it. 'I heard, my lord, that he was attended by a healer of sorts,' he offered, allowing the words to ring in the ears of the gathered House-Lords. 'Not of the Church, but a stranger from the south.'

The other men remained silent, eyes flickering nervously from one to another as though some terrible secret had been revealed. 'Of course, that could not be so, could it, Lord Kariq?' Dritsek asked. 'Especially when, as you say, you yourself were present at that sad time. You know how people are—they can spread such malicious and hurtful rumours without even realising it.'

House-Lord Kariq looked momentarily like he had been slapped about the face; the colour visibly drained from him.

'I am sure it will all be made clear, my lords,' Dritsek said, again offering a deferential bow of his head. 'We shall talk more on this, I am certain,' he finished, and made to leave the men to their whisperings.

'Thank you for your kind words of condolence, but there will be no need for you to attend, *Lord* Aargau.' It was House-Lord Kariq who spoke, having regained much of his composure.

'My Lord?' Dritsek replied.

'Yes, Intermediary Commissioner Aargau, High Commissioner Aargau, or whichever title it is currently—it does seem to change so often,' House-Lord Kariq quipped. 'It is incumbent upon the *House-Lord* of those great houses that are members of the City-Lord's Council to attend such meetings, so there will be no need for you to compliment us with your presence.'

'Lord Kariq,' Dritsek rebuffed, 'as I am sure you and your

other lords are aware, my lord father has been so very ill of late.'

'Of course,' House-Lord Kariq said, 'and our sympathies have been passed on to your family. Have you attended him often during this time?'

'My lord, I have been attending to matters here in the Citadel while my father has been resting, too ill to move from our estate.'

'That is a shame,' House-Lord Kariq said dryly. 'It would have been gratifying to know that he was surrounded by those who cared for him and whom he trusted during such difficult times. I shall pass on my best wishes to him when I see him next.'

'See him, my lord?' Dritsek begged, unsure exactly what game was being played.

'As I say, when I see him,' House-Lord Kariq repeated. 'House-Lord Aargau sent word earlier today that he will be personally attending the Citadel and its Council. Did you not know, Commissioner?'

It was now Dritsek's turn to look like he had been slapped, and indeed, he almost felt that he had been. He almost wanted to do it himself to make sure this was not some hideous nightmare.

He gave a tight smile, feeling the blood drain from his face. 'Of course, my lord.'

With that, Dritsek turned and hurried away.

The Truth and the Church are universal. They exist for all, men and women, young and old, low and highborn. All are equal. As a woman cries through the pain of labour, a man will cry through the pain of work. As a child cries with its first breath, the aged will cry as they breathe their last. As the poor fall in desperation, the rich will be desperate to stop them.

—*From the Tenets of Truth*

CHAPTER THIRTY-SIX

BRAGA

The Citadel

Braga was a listener. He listened to all kinds of people with all kinds of voices. There was an art to it, he knew, though few hard rules. There were women with big booming voices, loud enough to scare the hardest soldier into action, and there were huge men who could manage only the slightest of sounds, mice afraid of their own shadows. Some talked sense while others spoke nothing but shite. It was not always the who and the what that made a person listen, Braga knew. Sometimes, if the right person was saying something in the right way, even if what they were saying was rubbish, it was all anyone could do to listen to them.

The army was full of these types of people: the ones who could stand up and tell their men that despite there being only five of them and twenty enemies, they would somehow win. They'd tell the men they were the best-trained and most disciplined group of soldiers they had ever known, and that each of them was worth four lesser men. Such speakers could make anyone who listened feel like a hero; could make them *believe* it. Soliders stood up taller and prouder, fighting with the fury of four men after all, all because at long last they actually believed in something. It wasn't the veracity of a given truth that mattered, Braga had long ago realised; it was who you could convince with it.

There were the other types too, insidious and haunting and dark: men who could force you into doing things. All it took were a few words and a touch. A hand, a foot, a wrist—it mattered not. Just the simple connection of flesh was enough. Then there were men like Captain Susurro, the Cognators, who could whisper into your ear and tell you you were blind and, like a candle being blown, the world would disappear. The pioneer sergeant found it hard to dwell on such men. Even the briefest thought of them made him feel ill at ease.

Over the past days, he'd found a voice of his own. Not the battleground growl of old, but something more pure and persuasive, honest even. Maybe it had been the shock of Baile Saor, or perhaps that damned tinker—either way, something had loosened his tongue. He was certain, however, that he had not seen Tervan on the Rose Wall or anywhere else. If he'd been arrested along with the mayor, why had he not met the same fate? The big man cringed at the thought.

Sleep had come unbidden through the morning, fitful and short. He woke each time in the arms of Sirle, their foreheads touching and her face the first thing he saw when he opened his eyes. Each time, there was a brief, dream-fogged moment where he was afraid she too had fallen victim to the night, dying while he slept, and he'd gape or even weep—when she stirred, however, as she inevitably did, he'd weep all the more.

He wondered dimly how many people had lost their loves to the Rose. Until the mayor and the blacksmith's lad, it had been a generation or more since the thorns had seen use, but Braga knew plenty had died within its cells. How many hundreds could have spoken out at what they'd seen there? How many had remained silent? The people were too fearful, too familiar with the heavy-handedness of the House-Lords and the priests and the guards. They held their silence where he could not. What good was a soldier if he couldn't protect the people he loved and cared for? That was what had loosened his tongue, he knew, not Tervan. He had spoken only a few words at the square and yet look at what it had led to. The crowd had listened and responded, striking at the very institutions that had kept the people in their place these many cycles. It was a start. 'It was a revolution,' he said aloud, though he had not meant to. He looked about, abashed, happy to find no one was around to overhear him. *You overreach yourself*, he thought. *It was barely a riot.* Still, there was a purpose to all of this. If he could believe that, perhaps he could convince everyone else of it. If not, what had it all been for?

Bells had been tolling throughout the city since just after midday. To some they sang a warning, to others a celebration. The streets that Braga had seen were full of people, all of them clamouring to know what was going on. Some called out to him as if he was some fabled warrior, desperate for a glimpse of their unlikely hero. He didn't feel like one. He was just a soldier trying to protect people; surely that was his job. No, he remembered, 'The Church supports

447

the king and the army is there to keep the king's peace.' Those had been Sergeant Joyne's words, and they were true. What did that make Braga? His sergeant had said something else that day: 'The Church has a poor record where the army is concerned and'—what was it?—they 'can't be trusted with power'. That too was true. Al-Eldar was an adherent, a priest of the Righteous Truth; he'd been there that day to support and guide the soldiery, not to assume control. He was a snake, Braga now knew, nothing but a viper in the pit. He was a rotten and pustulant limb, a symptom of richer, deeper rot. Braga realised his fists were clenched. It was down to him to cut the pestilence away.

The mood in Smithton was dangerous. The people were momentarily jubilant in their small success, but a deep-rooted undercurrent of anger and indignation still bubbled, threatening to reignite. Sparks flared here and there in brief tussles or heated exchanges, flashes of intensity that could easily spread and engulf the entire city if not controlled. The smiths had been the spearhead of what some were already calling the Rose Rebellion, though their numbers had been quickly swelled by workers from other industries and districts: crofters from Croitean, roofers from Mullaich, loggers from Luch-Loghaid... all united for one brief evening to vent their grief and horror and disbelief. What might have been spent as a shared outpouring of emotion, Braga had channelled into an attack on the Rose Tower itself. The priest and his goons had expected to find an unruly mob that they could appease with a bloody spectacle, but they had found people sickened and horrified by the deaths of friends, colleagues, and innocents. It had not taken much for their outrage to be turned to anger.

It was only by coincidence that a rising pillar of smoke had focused their attention on the tower. Had it not, their fury would likely have spilled up against the walls and shacks and taverns;

they'd have looted and burned their own homes like so many protestors before them. When the jailors were seen fleeing the flames, however, what might have just been a mob gained new purpose. They would not run and leave the prisoners inside to burn.

The next morning, the rich smell of roaring furnaces spread through the streets and alleys of Smithton, just as it would on any other day. Spirals of smoke rose into a sky already grey and dark, thick with the ash of the Rose, and somehow the air smelled all the sweeter for it. Braga looked around at the many smiths as they tended to their workshops and was warmed, almost amused, by their devotion to their trade, even in the shadow of what they had been responsible for. It had been an attack at the very seat of authority, a stake driven through the heart of power. They must have known that there would be questions to answer and settlements required, and yet no one seemed worried. Braga saw many men and women he recognised from the night before, as well as others he had known a long time, old friends and acquaintances. Most had been there, had raised their voices and hands in defiance, but not all. A great many had minded their own business, kept to themselves, and shied away from trouble. They were simple and honest people. It should not have been on them to shoulder the burden of rioting, but it was them who would pay whether they fought or not.

'Braga, what is it?' a tired-looking man asked. 'Why are the bells ringing? Do they ring for us? Are they coming?' The man was covered in a heavy layer of soot and dust. It clung to the wrinkles of his face, making him appear far older than he was. Beyond him, a crowd of bedraggled strangers lingered, peering at Braga through bloodshot eyes.

This man will be dead before the day is out, he realised. *They all will. Killed because they are covered in ash, whether from the Rose or a furnace. They will make an example of him and me and them, and more besides.*

'I don't know,' Braga told the smith, his low voice adding a weight to his words that he had not intended. It was a lie. He knew they would be coming, but it was not a truth he was willing to share—at least, not yet.

'What will they do?' a woman asked. A young girl clutched at her legs, and the woman part-covered the child in a ragged and dirty shawl that draped from her shoulder as if it could somehow hide them both. Braga could see the fear in the woman's eyes. Had that same terror been present in Baile Saor? Had his hand looked to him for answers that day? He would never know. He hadn't been there for them. Though this woman was afraid, she was braver than him. At least she'd turned up to protect her own.

It's now or never, Braga resolved. *I either bang their heads into order or I leave them here to whatever punishment awaits.*

'They will kill some of you,' he eventually answered matter-of-factly.

The woman crowed at his response, weeping for herself and the child she would never see grow to womanhood. People stared back at him, disbelieving. It was not what they had expected.

'Others will be imprisoned as insurance so that the rest of you fall back into line. All of you will be forced to increase production or pay higher taxes to pay for the damages and repairs.'

'What?' a man called out. 'How can they expect us to work harder? We barely sleep as it is, and only just meet our quotas.' More people now stopped to observe the growing furore, hearing the harbinger of doom that stood at its centre. Braga was a massive man, serious and unflappable. His huge frame looked large even set against the broad-chested blacksmiths. Many of those who gathered recognised him. He had ever been a friend to Smithton, having visited often during those early cycles he'd spent at Barkathet. He would pay some coin and, in return, he'd gain access to tools, an anvil, and a furnace, and would be able to lose himself in the steady, therapeutic rhythm of the methodical labour. After a while, when he had become friendly with some of the local smiths, his stays lengthened, and he grew to find comfort in the people as much as he did in the work. They were honest and easy to deal with, as if they had less to hide than many of those he met elsewhere, making them altogether less complicated—much like himself. Maybe it was because theirs was such a tiring and punishing trade, the smiths had no energy to maintain the lies and deceits that others seemed to relish. Those who watched him address the crowd in Smithton that day knew that he too was not a man to fabricate or stretch the truth.

'That won't matter,' he insisted. 'They will see it as a way to make sure that this doesn't happen again. If you are worked too hard to pay, you will not have the strength to rise up again.'

'They can't! It will kill us!' the soot-covered man shouted. 'How can they kill us? They need us.'

'They don't need all of you,' Braga answered quietly, sensing that his warning was beginning to take hold. 'How many people are there in the Citadel? They could easily train new smiths. It only takes one of you to teach a dozen others.'

'Stop it, you're scaring people,' another woman said, though she looked much like the others, dishevelled and weary. Braga was tired too, but he felt the blood rushing through his veins, heard it in his ears like the beat of a drum sounding the march.

'Good,' the big man called. 'They need to be scared. Listen to me: you saw what they did to Kovack and his apprentice boy. He was a smith, like many of you. That other man they killed on the wall, well, he was a town mayor. He was the first citizen of a town not four days' ride from here, and they had no trouble killing him, either.'

The people stared at him, some wincing in revulsion at the memory while others looked on, eyes wide.

'Many of you know me,' Braga said in a gentler voice, 'and have for many cycles now. You know that I am a soldier and not a smith. I know there will be death because I have been used by these people to kill before. It is nothing new. It has always happened and it always will. The strong stay strong by making sure that there are plenty of weak people beneath them. And to them'—he pointed towards the central cluster of towers in the Citadel, the Palace Tower gleaming amid them—'to them, *you* are the weak and you will *always* be beneath them.'

'Will they send in the army?' the first woman asked, her child still cowering beneath her shroud.

'If it's necessary to keep you in your place, then yes. Yes, they will.' Braga let the words sink in. It was difficult; he did not want to terrify these people, but it needed to be done. They needed to understand what was at stake here. 'You all saw what happened last night when the tower began to burn. Their first response was to save themselves. There were people in that tower—you might have known them. They might even have been relatives. Most were there for petty crimes—stealing to help feed their children, not carrying identity papers, or being unable to pay their taxes on time or meet their quotas. Had we not been there last night, they would have died horrible deaths.'

Some of the people stood the taller at his words, seeming to grow in stature. He was conducting them as if they were a regimental band.

'I myself dragged more than a dozen people from the tower,

most of them so wretched and thin as to rob them of their sex—you could not have said if they were man or woman. Only one man from inside the tower stopped to help anyone else. He dragged a weak and pitiful thing to us and brought him out. That man's fingers had been bitten away—either by him or by rats or by his cellmates. That is the truth of it. That is how they treat people.'

There were angry noises from the people around him, hisses and boos at the tale of terrible degradation as if Braga was acting in some mummer's play.

'That man thought that he was going to die,' he went on. 'In fact, for all intents and purposes, he *was* dead. Were it not for the courageous act of a complete stranger who thought to help rather than leave him to burn or die, he would not be with us today. That stranger reached out his hands and plucked him from a terrible fate. He made his choice and there is the evidence of that choice, right there.'

He pointed a little way behind the crowd, causing those gathered to turn, following his finger. Next to a workshop stood Sirle. Under her arm was a reedy little thing, more stick than man. She held him in place as all eyes turned towards her and her charge, murmurs and exclamations rising from the crowd. In the light of day, the man seemed somehow thinner and even frailer than before, like an evening shadow, stretched unnaturally long and rakish. A ghost of a man; a wisp or a whisper.

'Now, the rest of you have a choice to make,' Braga said, pulling their attention back to him. 'You can choose to be like the jailors from that tower, who turned their backs on one another and fled at the first sign of danger, or you can be like that stranger. You can choose to take the hand of those around you and stand together as one. Only, you won't be a stranger. You will be a neighbour, a friend, a brother, a sister, a father, a mother. And who knows, we might all one day know the surprise of the man you see before you—the surprise of seeing another day when you thought all had abandoned you.'

The crowd cheered. It was a glorious sound. Braga's words had carried clear and strong across the square, and hundreds had been there to hear him. There were men and women from all over Smithton and other districts besides. That message would spread, then, for others to hear. He felt the energy shine back from them, but it wasn't until he saw the smile on Sirle's face that he truly knew those had been the right words to say. He could almost feel her pride in him. *By the mother's love*, he thought to himself, *you just might have done it. There might be a chance after all.* He pushed his way through the crowd, wanting to share the moment with Sirle. He had almost reached her when a boy came running into the square. He was shouting incoherently, his face flushed scarlet.

'What is it, boy?' someone called to him.

'Guards,' he replied heavily between great gasps of air, 'more than I can count. They're sending in the city guards.'

No, not yet. It's too soon. Braga swung back to scan the faces of those around him. All too quickly, pockets of panic were rising, terror starting to spread. The crowd began to tear itself apart as people ran for cover, darting into houses and alleyways. They stood no chance, Braga knew, unless they stood together.

'Wait!' he barked. Dozens of people stopped in their tracks, caught like rabbits. Their fear was evident and understandable, but Braga knew he had to reach them. He only hoped their humanity was enough to hold them. 'This is it. This is your only chance. This is where you can stand together and make your mark, or else you can run and be dragged out of your homes like foxes from the den.

The Citadel can either laugh at the sound of your screams or cower at the roar of your fury. It can look scornfully upon you as you beg for mercy or it can shield itself from the brightness of your fires. They have kept you down and they have trodden you into the dust, forcing you to work and work until you cannot work any longer, but now let it be your turn. Let it be you that rises up against them. Let it be you that shouts "no more!" and makes them listen. Let it be you that feasts at their tables for once.'

He looked and saw that, somehow, the people had listened. Those who had a moment before been running like frightened rabbits turned back, faces resolute and determined. They were smith and crofter and father and mother and each of them had the grit and fire of a warrior. They banded to him, a great cohort of ordinary people. They answered to his call, responded to his direction. He could organise their will into defence—this was, had always been, his job. Already, he saw how some had broken away, coordinating barriers and barricades. These peasants had the making of soldiers. They would be his army.

A distant rumble drifted on the air, causing some to flinch. Little fingers of panic and doubt clutched where they could, grasping keenly. He could not let them take hold.

'Now, for Truth's sake,' he shouted, raising his trunk-like arms into the air, 'go get your fucking harrows and hammers and let's beat the shit out of them! If anyone needs me, I'll be at front, killing the bastards with my bare hands if needs be.'

The crowd erupted. Braga only hoped they'd live to see the evening.

In all things, be yourself and your own keeper. Do not be a false wastrel, who uses falsehoods and lies to hide away from others and have them do what your own hand should do. If the Goddess gives you a task to complete, it is your task. Do not offload it onto others through schemes and connivances.

—*From the Tenets of Truth*

CHAPTER THIRTY-SEVEN
SENTENZA AND DREBAN

The Citadel

It was a cold morning. The sun had been late getting up and, as a result, everything seemed grey: the sky, the mood, and the men filling the streets. Only, Sentenza fancied that he caught the occasional glimpse of green. It was enough to make an old soldier nostalgic. Still, there were too many uniforms on the streets either for comfort or for it to be coincidence, and he had no intention of getting picked up by a patrol or becoming embroiled in whatever was about to unfold. He'd already wasted enough time in the pits and he could almost feel the Golya's little spies watching him. At least from his vantage point on the inner wall he'd be able to see them coming—or, at least, he would if he had any idea who they were. It felt like the old priest had eyes everywhere, and Sentenza found himself suspicious of each hawker, whore, barrow boy, and crone he saw. In a city like this, that meant just about everyone.

He watched the final few Greys leaving the old stables, but it was the uniforms of the new men that interested him most, the green of Barkathet. Even if they were distracted by the unfurling events, it would be best to keep out of sight or to the other side of the Citadel, if he could help it. Two hands of lightly armed men marched in three tight columns through the narrow streets. They kept to the outer alleys and passages, slimming down to single file when it became too cramped. They were here as support, he guessed, a secret reserve meant only to push back if things became too much for the Greys. The men seemed at ease; Sentenza suspected they had no real expectation of being called upon. *We'll see about that*, Sentenza thought. He'd not seen the rebels since those few hours at the Rose Wall, and even then it'd been from a distance, but there had been more than a handful. Sentenza remembered a horde of big and burly silhouettes and, from what he had heard, their numbers had only swelled. Their success would lie in the industry hands they were attracting. These were not the usual tin merchants and streets traders; they were big men, loggers and masons and builders, some stronger and grumpier than even the smiths. The inevitable confrontation promised to be the most entertaining draw in cycles, but the colonel didn't have time to sit around and watch the events unfold—not if he was to get Sakani off his back.

Sentenza had heard only rumours of how the rebellion had begun. There'd first been sedition in the estates, where the farm-folk told tales of a sick boy being made well again. Now even Sakani was worried, and there was talk of healers bringing the dead back even within the Citadel. Sentenza thought of the failed attempt on his own life. *Too many coincidences.* A thought had begun to form at the back of his mind, an answer to a question he hadn't yet asked or even understood. That sensation he'd felt in the pits. Whomever it was that the guards had brought there—could it have been one of those healers? Perhaps even the same one he'd been looking for since his trip to Old Ballir's so many cycles ago? Another one of Sakani's damned projects. The man was always involved, pulling strings from the safety of his tower. Sentenza knew better than to think his involvement was coincidental.

He heard a call to order. The guards began setting their lines, a man in black at their head. That same strange uniform... So, he realised, Al-Eldar was leading this nonsense. He watched as the men of the army took up positions around the grey square, a ring of green steel, and felt a small pang of pride.

The city had grown surprisingly quiet, and an air of tension prevailed upon the fresh ocean wind. It was oddly peaceful, Sentenza thought, like a graveyard. Only when he heard the first screams of the day did he decide that it was time to move on. This was not the clash and furore of the battle still to come; this was the blind cry of an old woman. Just one of the innocents who would die as a prelude to the main performance. Joining her would be idiots and halfwits without the sense to mind their business, the slow-minded and slower-moving who weren't quick enough to flee. They would be the early victims of this folly, the first catch of the day. This was good news for Sentenza. The distraction of battle would be his smokescreen.

He made his way across the crenellated walls, dodging between parapets and skirting the main gatehouses. Wherever it was unavoidable, he waited for the guards to show interest in the streets below before skulking his way over or past or around. The boy had said that the mysterious priest had himself a healer, but then so too did House Aargau. No matter where he looked, that supercilious prig, Dritsek, was at the middle of things. So, while the world and her dog were distracted with the circus, he intended to pay a visit to the Black Tower himself.

He dropped down from the walls and into the upper district, where streets and alleys crisscrossed above each other on stilts and ledges. Distracted, he turned at the old traitor's gate and careened into two old men embraced in some drunken struggle. The smell of spoiled ale and stale piss hit him an instant before they did, though he was by far the younger and steadier. The gin-soaked squabblers teetered for a moment dangerously close to the edge before one lost his footing and, grasping frantically, managed to pull the other from the wall. Sentenza winced and heard the hard ground below quickly break their fall. *Serves them bloody right*, he thought as a moan drifted up to him. He turned to leave, not thinking to look, but was stopped in his tracks. He felt suddenly tangled as if in the arms of a dogwood tree, each of its thorny limbs pricking at his flesh. The magic washed over him, spinning him round. Surely it couldn't have been coming from one of those drunkards. When he looked, one of the men had gone, but the other remained. He was sat up and befuddled, though not alone. A young man, little more than a boy, knelt beside him, his hand on the drunkard's arm. The man mumbled and burped, then was lost to sleep.

Sentenza was down a level before the lad could move away. 'Hey!' he called. The boy seemed skittish, eyes darting for cover. 'Wait, wait!' Sentenza called, desperate not to let him out of his sight. 'It's okay, it's okay. I'm not here to hurt you.'

The young man hesitated, eyeing Sentenza warily.

'I only want to help.' The itching sensation had abated—gone almost as quickly as it had appeared.

'I didn't do anything,' the lad said, 'he just fell. I was only trying to...' He trailed off as though unsure what exactly he'd been trying to do.

'I know. I saw it all.' Sentenza scrabbled around in his head, trying to think what to say. 'The other one was trying to rob him, I think. It's a good thing you were to here to help, otherwise who knows what would have happened. Maybe I could help you move him somewhere safe. Do you have anywhere nearby?'

'No,' he said evasively. 'I'm not from the city. I'm just travelling through.'

Even better, Sentenza thought. *If I can get him back to the warehouse, maybe I can figure out what to do with him.*

'I was just looking for someone. After that I'll be leaving,' the boy added.

'I'll tell you what, if you help me get him somewhere warm and safe, I'll help you find whoever it is you're looking for. After all, the streets are a dangerous place to be today—both for us, your friend, and him here.' He turned to gesture to the drunk, but the man had gone, leaving nought but a steaming puddle of piss. 'Well,' Sentenza laughed, 'that was quicker than I expected. Shall we get looking for your friend?'

The kid was called Dreban—the same name as the priest he had sent Braga to find all those days ago. That was the last time he had seen the big man alive. *Another little puzzle to solve,* he reminded himself. *I'll add his murderer to the list.*

The boy didn't look like a priest and he certainly didn't sound like one; he was altogether too determined to find the young lady he kept going on about, Solatta. He knew under good authority that half the adherents in the Citadel had private tabs with the good-time girls of Westip, but this seemed different. If he didn't know better, he'd say the kid was in love.

Sentenza walked him through the city, keeping to the back alleys and side streets, and even doubling back from time to time over areas they'd already been. The kid had no idea and, apart from making them completely lost, it confirmed to Sentenza that he was telling the truth about being a traveller. Anyone from around here would have smelled a rat an age ago and either pulled a blade or simply run away. This kid was far too naïve, or else he was for more cunning that the colonel gave him credit for. One thing did worry Sentenza, however: the feeling had disappeared completely. Surely someone with so much power would hold onto at least a little of that energy if they were being led around the lonely back alleys by a complete stranger? He knew he would. Yet there was nothing, not even a gentle buzz. Maybe he had been wrong about the kid after all.

'So,' Sentenza asked. 'Tell me more about this girl of yours— Solatta, was it? Maybe if I know more about her then I might have a better idea of where to start looking.'

'Where do I start?'

'Usually the beginning is the best place. Where is she from, for example?'

'I don't know,' he answered, almost apologetically. 'She doesn't know herself. I think she was an orphan, so she travelled about a lot with a man, her guardian.'

'So, they're Kellawayans then? That's a good starting place; they're not exactly common.'

'That's what I said. They had a caravan, a vardo she called it, and they travelled helping people.' He looked suddenly sheepish and clammed up.

Sentenza guessed he thought he'd said too much. 'Helping people how, exactly?'

'Erm, nothing. I don't know. I just need to find her and then we're going.'

'That's fine,' he said, though his mind was working overtime. He had hit on a nerve there, he knew. *Now, should I keep prodding, or will that lose what little rapport I've managed to build?* It struck him then, like a bolt of lightning. Of course—why had he not seen it earlier? The kid had told Sentenza himself: he'd been trying to *help* the drunk. The old fart had fallen and then there he was, laying hands on him, flush with magic. They—Dreban and this Solatta, whoever she was—*they* were the blasted healers! For all these cycles, he had searched and cajoled and threatened and even killed, and here they were, right under his bloody nose.

'Don't worry, Dreban,' Sentenza murmured, eyes gleaming in the gloom. 'I know *exactly* where to find her.'

The Church is a guiding light, a beacon in times of desperation and a familial embrace in times of discomfort. However, just as a child needs to be held, so too do they need a strong arm to show them discipline when they have turned away from the Truth.

—From the Tenets of Truth

CHAPTER THIRTY-EIGHT

BRAGA

The Citadel

Braga peered over the ranks arrayed before him. A more motley group he'd never seen. All sizes and ages, short and fat and tall and thin, young and old, even women, bearing hammers and axes and spades and harrows and hoes, whatever they could lay hands on. Even so, they were a determined and fearsome sight. They would give any foe a fight, he thought. Still, that alone would not be enough. He needed the grit and ferocity of those who knew that losing was not an option. If they didn't defeat the guards, it would have all been for nothing. Many people would die this day, spill their blood on the sand and stones they had trodden all their lives. It could not be for nought.

Braga had dressed that morning in all of his finery, shunning the offer of breast and backplate, not wanting to be seen wearing armour where others had none. Anxiety was growing; even he felt it. It gripped at his stomach and drove it into knots. Feet slapped heavy against the stone from beyond the Black Gate. A single peal of bells tolled an ominous note in the distance. Braga joined the front line. A weather-beaten smith wavered at his shoulder, slipping away from the pioneer sergeant by a hand's span. They couldn't afford gaps in the wall—each of them relied upon the next. Braga looked at the man, half-expecting to see fear in his eyes, but, to his relief, he found only resolve. The smith had merely been securing a spare blade to his belt. The older man winked a grey eye at Braga. It may as well have been stone.

'Don't you worry none on my behalf, lad,' he said with a grim smile. 'Just be sure to keep your mind and your eyes ahead so you can see what's coming our way.'

Braga was almost embarrassed to realise how anxious *he* was. This felt different to any other battle he'd fought before. There was much more riding on this, more that could go wrong. The determination of the smith filled him with a hope that went some way to steeling his heart. That and the man's arms and back, broad and thick with muscle. If it were a battle of strength, it would be already over and won. It was not, alas, and he knew that beyond the gate a horde of trained and armoured men was forming ranks. He could already hear the clamour of metal-shod feet on stone. At least it was only the Grey Guard. Soldiers would be another thing completely.

While Braga had called on the rebels to arm themselves, he had not counted on the weapons that the smiths had been pressed to deliver as part of their quotas. Where he had hoped for harrows and hooks, he had expected only scissors and spades. Instead, he saw row upon row of spears and short swords and axes, though many of the smiths had opted for the familiarity of their hammers. They were heavy and fearsome things but, in the smiths' bulky hands, they looked light and agile.

The bell stopped, its final note bouncing around the square like a thunderclap. It called the ranks to order, bringing with it a hushed quiet. Shouted orders echoed against one another and escaped through the mouth of the gate before them. Braga wished he could hear what those orders were, but the words were lost. He had gambled on making a stand here and drawing the guards to them. This was the smiths' district, their part of the city. Any attack on this ground would feel like an intrusion upon their homes, and they were likely to fight all the more to protect it. He was gambling on the gate acting as a bottleneck against the attacking force, impeding the flow of men as they sallied through its gaping jaws, spitting them out in narrower ranks for Braga's assembled men to swallow up. Braga clenched his jaw, his whole body primed and ready. Strangely, after a moment he felt himself relax into it. This was *his* world. This the only thing he really knew how to do well. It was what he'd been born to do.

Time stretched on. How long had they been holding there? A minute? An hour? Braga's shadow had barely moved. He twitched at each creak and sliver of sound that rose from those around him. The air felt thick, as palpable as smoke from a furnace. There was movement above the gate. A small group of men, six, maybe eight, moved into position, spreading out along the wall's length, heads just apparent above the crenellations. The tension was too much for an apprentice boy on Braga's left. He broke forward in a charge all of his own, but a growled order from Braga stopped him in his tracks.

The men raised crossbows almost as one. Braga shouted a warning and the lad spun, dropping his spear. His eyes were wide and fearful. He was just a boy, Braga saw. An unnatural crack split the air twanging bowstrings snapped against their laths. The fluted song of bolts called out and the boy jerked suddenly, the muscles in his arms tensing, coiling, spasming... He staggered one lonely step towards his own line before crumpling into the sand. All noise seemed to fade as Braga watched the boy die. Dimly, he sensed the disbelief of the people alongside him.

Well, it's real enough now, he thought. Still, even he was surprised that crossbows had been deployed. He had hoped the soldiers' orders were to quell the rebellion using measured and proportionate force—take the town but minimise unnecessary bloodshed, allowing normality to be quickly restored after the fighting was over. This suggested not. Their orders seemed clear: stop them by any means necessary.

For a long moment, no one moved nor spoke, then a single voice rang out from the wall. Immediately, the crossbowmen atop the gate responded, ratcheting the strings back on their weapons and nocking fresh bolts into place. They returned their aim towards the square and Braga watched in dismay as they deliberately raised the pitch of the crossbows. *The bastards are going to shoot into our rear ranks*, he realised, anger rising. *They want us to panic, and either run in fear or because our own rearguard have pushed forward and broken our formation.* The time for waiting was over. Now, there was only action left. He thrust his sword high into the air. 'Forward!' he bellowed.

The mass of men moved in short response to the pioneer sergeant's command, taking up the call to advance, many shouting battle cries. All too soon, it felt, Braga heard the snap of strings and the unsettling rush of bolts through the air, thunderous and terrifying. He could not tell how many of those bolts found their mark and nor could he spare a second to look and survey the damage as he quickened his pace into a run, feeling the men to his left and right respond in kind. Within moments, he and a dozen of the men who had stood with him dashed through the gaping mouth of the gatehouse and spewed out into Rose Square. They were met by a holding line of swordsmen moving up to meet their charge.

The familiar sound of metal on metal rang a sweeter sound in his ears than that of the throng of strings, and inwardly he chided himself for holding fast while the arbalesters moved into position. Had there been more of them, the battle might have already been lost. At least on this side of the gate, they would be able to carry sword and hammer to the enemy. They might just hold the advantage of numbers and, at close quarters, crossbows would be useless. No commander would risk shooting his own men, after all.

He saw a blade orange and red in the afternoon light whip toward him, to be met by the hammer of the old man beside him. Braga growled a guttural roar as he thrust his sword arm forward and up, feeling both relief and an animal satisfaction as the blade dug deep into the scowling guardsman. Another darted forwards and Braga slammed his fist into his chin, almost lifting the man from his feet.

The rhythm of cut and thrust swiftly became almost hypnotic. Motion after motion, a lifetime of practised memory, and aside from when his sword bit too hard and become caught on bone or gristle, as it had now, Braga barely had to think about what he was doing. The older smith next to him took up the slack as Braga twisted his hand to free his bloodied blade, slamming the head of his hammer into the helmet of another guard.

Braga finally succeeded in tearing his sword free and glanced about him, taking a ragged breath. His rebels were doing well; they'd pushed a wedge into the swordsmen's ranks and were fighting stoically. He glanced down at his blood-covered sword. His gaze lingered for a second, and he swallowed. It had been easy to justify rebellion against the House-Lords and the Church, but it was different now that he could see the faces of the men he was killing. These were men like him, just doing their jobs.

No, he thought. These were the men who'd arrested Tervan and the mayor. These were the men who came to collect taxes and quotas and who carried those off those who couldn't pay. These were the men who'd added fresh stripes to Sirle's back. He grit his teeth and hurried onwards, following the path carved out by the eager old smith.

At times, it felt as if he'd become lost in the fog of his own rage. He was mechanical, like a cog turned by a mill, slashing and thrusting and gutting; he was an instrument, no longer a man at all. He thought distantly of the adherent pushing people to their deaths over the Rose Wall. The vision struck him, stunning him as much as any blow, and he checked his next thrust, bewildered.

No, he told himself, looking to the ragged men and women and boys around him, *this isn't the same*. Al-Eldar killed because he could; because he was protected from any consequence. *I led these people here to protect them*. He had to admit, however, that it didn't look much like protection.

Dimly, Braga realised he and a handful of men were alone, surrounded by armoured guards. He looked up as if waking from a dream, seeing above the heads of the men around him his own line scattered and unsteady. Despite the intensity of their collective will, his rebels were being pushed back. The guards, somehow, had held their position, as immovable and unbreachable as the Rose Wall itself. Looking now, Braga wondered whether the guards were simply biding their time, toying with their prey. *This could swiftly become a massacre*. 'A guard is less than half a soldier,' Sentenza had once told him. He wondered what the colonel would make of his own warriors. Should he call a halt to it all? Retreat or surrender? What would be best? Doubt and fear stalked him, crept about at the edge of his mind like a circling wolf. But he was a bear, and they had broken the Rose once already. Besides, the Greys weren't named solely for their uniforms; they were old and grizzled, well past their best. Surely they would tire soon. Braga could only hope so.

The old man next to him shouted, the sound tearing Braga back to reality a moment too late—the sword arced towards the pioneer sergeant. The blow never landed. Braga blinked. He felt the old smith's hand grasp his shoulder, felt something hot and wet dribble down his arm. A nicked blade was wedged in the meat of the old man's neck. The guardsman—grinning, teeth and lips stained red with blood—tore his sword free and, inexorably, the smith crumbled, bright eyes slowly fading. Braga's mind emptied and he took a single step over the smith's corpse, his own sword plunging into the still-grinning guard's open mouth. Another stepped up to fill the gap, sword in hand, and Braga reached to his back, fingers finding the binding of his axe. He brought it up into the guard's chest, taking him with the hook of the blade. He heard the impact more than felt it, even above the roar of the melee. Somehow, the act released him. Two and four and six more men fell within moments, yet more running to fill the ranks. The square was Braga's forge and the axe his hammer. His rebels swarmed behind him, pushing a thin wedge between the surging guardsmen, splitting their formation.

It was then that Braga saw it. There, beyond the buckling line of grey, a glimpse of green. A python watching from the trees. The breath caught in his chest and his bowels turned tight. He should have suspected as much.

His own bloody men. And beside that first green-clad soldier, twice a dozen more. Braga twisted but, everywhere he looked, hard faces stared back at him, grim and resolute. His rebels could not stand against the army as well as the guard. He turned back into the square. If he could somehow get back through the gate...

But an envelope of grey had sealed itself around them, blocking off any chance of withdrawal. Braga felt cold fear settle in his stomach, and something else besides: guilt. It had been a fool's errand to think he could lead these people to anything except a slaughter. Now, the most he could hope for was to keep his rabble alive. Perhaps he could negotiate a surrender of sorts.

'You, soldier. What are you doing?'

Braga brought himself to attention at the sharp command, suddenly back on the parade ground.

'Get back into rank.'

He turned to see the man, who stood just across the square before of a rank of green-shirted soldiers. An officer, Braga figured, tall and slender and too handsome to have seen much in way of fighting. He seemed nervous. Braga didn't know the man, but the lad next to him he recognised. The name came to him as though from a dream.

'Ajuda?' he called uncertainly.

The man stared, disbelieving. 'Pioneer Sergeant? What are you doing here?' The lad glanced at his officer, who was addressing a fresh column of arriving soldiers. 'Quick, sir! You need to pull back from the square. We're only meant to hold them here, not engage them.'

Other soldiers had spotted Braga too. Many he recognised— old friends among them—beckoned to him, calling for him to join them. Braga looked away. He glanced instead down at his own uniform: a pristine wave of green torn and scarred and peppered with bile and blood and dust. *They don't know*, he realised. *They haven't worked it out.*

It was then that he heard the call, sharp and sly above the clamour. A single shrill command and the sudden release of strings. Braga turned to see the first bolts hit home. A dozen of his fighters fell, some killed outright, others collapsing, shrieking into the dust. Confusion spread through the crowd like a contagion. The men atop the wall were already reloading.

Six more bolts whistled their song of death. Then another. Another. Six and twelve and eighteen. The crossbowmen were so close and their targets so plentiful that they could not miss. *Rats in a barrel.* Braga wanted to scream, to tear at the world and scratch the bolts from the sky. He felt so useless. This was not battle; it was murder. Surely the guards could see that too. Why were they firing on their own men? He saw the faces, men and women and apprentice boy and Grey alike, all skewered by feather and iron and wood.

Only, it was not their faces he saw. Instead it was Joyne and the men of his half-hand. He felt the anger anew, roiling like a torrent. They had been his men, his hand, just as these were his people. They were here only because they had followed him. He had been idiot enough to drag them into this and now he had to find a way out. At the very least, he would die trying.

'Braga, Pioneer Sergeant, what are you doing?! You're going to get yourself killed!' It was Ajuda again, his voice rising above the din. Braga felt like ordering him to shut up and leave him alone. And then an idea took him—one so stupid and foolhardy that it might just work. He ran to the alleyway, ducking low at the sound of yet more bolts. Six more lost.

'Corporal!' he shouted at the soldier standing next to Ajuda. 'Why are you just standing there?'

The man reddened, back stiffening in response. Braga didn't have time to worry about the man's pride, but he saw the corporal's eyes twitch. There was uncertainty there, confusion even. 'I want you to open up this alley for anyone trying to get through,' he pressed. 'Ajuda, you and five others with me.' Braga turned to lead the men back onto the square, but the corporal stuttered something after him. Braga rounded on him.

'Sir, my orders are—'

'Soldier!' Braga barked, 'I've just *given* you your orders. Did you not hear? Not understand? Or were you suddenly promoted while I wasn't watching?' He drew himself up to his full height until he towered over the other man. He stared down at the corporal with hard eyes, daring him to challenge his authority.

There was a tense silence. At last, the corporal nodded sheepishly before shouting a series of orders to his team to move the barricade aside.

Braga fought back a sigh of relief. If there was one thing he could count on, it was this: soldiers loved to obey orders.

The square still rang with the sound of fighting, a music all of its own. Strings added their own sombre sound, high-pitched and lethal, spreading chaos. Pockets of fighters struggled with soldiers, many trying to flee the carnage. Grey turned against green, but the soldiers stood their ground. Braga watched the men on the gate open up on one skirmish: two soldiers and one guard fell, clutching the bolts that protruded from their bodies. Ajuda and his men were incensed. If it were up to them, Braga knew, they'd run headlong at the gate. It took a strong arm to hold them back. 'That's not the way,' he growled.

He led them to the oak doorway at the base of the scorched tower through which they'd only yesterday dragged prisoners to safety. They burst through the door, Braga's axe making splinters of burnt wood, and hurried up the stairs, rising through the ashes and the stench of death past the now-empty cells. Braga burst onto the parapet, squinting in the glare of the day. He stared down at the hundred metal thorns shining up at him, eager and hungry. Ajuda and his troop careened into his backside, making more noise than a gaggle of geese.

Braga could see the crossbowmen up ahead, raining laboursome death down upon the fighters below. Draw and load and loose, slow and mechanical; as inexorable as the tide. They were not the only men there, flanked as they were by their own guards, one dressed in the black robes of a priest. Feverish-looking men, Braga thought, wild-eyed and demented. The Greys turned, saw Braga looming, and shouted a warning to his companions. They came running, swords drawn.

Ajuda and his five formed up around Braga, faces set and weapons ready.

'Here they come, boys,' Braga growled.

The Greys crashed into them in a ragged wave. There were desperate, uncontrolled, some swinging wildly while others screamed as if at terrors Braga couldn't see. Some even scratched at their own flesh until it ran red with blood. They fought with unbridled fury, zealotry even. Braga took one, then two, Ajuda a third and a young corporal a fourth. A fifth careened over the rampart, meeting his end on the Rose. The wall ran slick and rich in the sunlight.

A shriek in the air signalled the involvement of the crossbow men. Braga caught the blazing eyes of the distant priest as bolts arced towards the melee. One struck a soldier, the force shunting him over the wall. Two more sent a guard slumping into one of Ajuda's companions. Braga growled and tore away from the fight, leaving Ajuda and his remaining men to fend off the two frenzied

Greys. He charged along the wall, saw the crossbowmen scramble and fumble at the stirrups and strings and laths. They too seemed glazed and lost. One found his fingers, ready to slot a bolt just as Braga slammed into him, forcing him from the wall. He turned to the man in black, the priest, hunched and taut like a cornered rodent about to strike. The man brought his hands up as Braga stalked towards him, his cowl falling back. Sunlight hit the man's face. The eyes were sunken now, scared and angry and black as his robes, and his features seemed somehow distorted, as though bent out of shape, but Braga saw the truth of the man. There was no mistaking those eyes. Al-Eldar.

Braga roared. He lashed out, a huge hand grabbing the skinny priest by the throat. He lifted him as if the priest was only a poppet, his legs dangling and twitching like a hanged man's. Wiry fingers grappled against his grip, but Braga held the adherent tight. This was the man who had bloodied the Rose. He had kicked and pushed those men onto the spikes that had claimed their lives. Callous and cruel and craven, his actions had fanned the flames that saw countless dead. Braga would not let him get away.

A thin and mirthless grin scratched across Al-Eldar's face. Braga felt a rumble of something tickling up through the man's body and, at last, a chuckle tore from the priest's throat, dry and crackling. It sent a chill down the big man's spine, gooseflesh freezing along his arm. Silently, Al-Eldar's lips began to move. Braga found himself straining to hear, but the half-whispered words were too faint to make out. Anger swept over him with renewed vigour, animal and visceral in its nature, yet somehow alien. Faces and images sprung to mind, unwelcome and unbidden. Terrible sights of death and destruction. Smithton ravaged, forges engulfed by their own flames. Flesh melting from bodies like metal being smelted. People he'd known for cycles left broken and bent, features charred and distorted. Yet, somehow, they moved towards him. Heat-ravaged fingers pointed at him, reaching, admonishing, blaming. Their fate had been his fault, he knew. They hissed curses from mouths burnt free of tongues.

He saw a forest of young trees, scarlet leaves swaying in a storm. The wind rasped through the branches like a thousand voices cackling and wailing, full of scorn and blame. It named him a traitor and a deserter and coward. It mocked him and called him craven and, even as it did, the trees slowly turned, each one showing the face of one of the men who'd followed him. The hand that he'd left to die, their spikes now taken root, feeding off their mutilated corpses. The trees had grown around their faces, Braga realised, morphing with their features, their bark wrinkled skin ripe with knotted welts that glowered down at him. He turned away, not wanting to see, not wanting to hear the accusations on their wooden lips. Instead, there was Sirle, on her knees, crying into her hands. When she pulled them away, tears of blood drained from the fleshy pits where her bright eyes had once been. He reached out to her but she turned away, dashing herself onto the metal thorns of the Rose Wall.

It was too much. He felt his knees buckle and he crashed hard onto the sandstone wall. Numb fingers lost their grip, became weak and limp, crippled with age. Somewhere, he saw the glint of a blade, but distantly, as if it was the faded vision of some other man. It didn't matter. Nothing did or ever would again. A life alone and without Sirle was less than half a life, and less even still if she were to leave him through hatred and disgust. He almost welcomed the sweet sting of that blade. He would gladly open up his chest and allow it to nestle in his heart. He had no use for it now.

Then there were voices: shouts and the clamour of feet and men and fighting. The sound wrapped around him, deafening in its sudden, jarring ferocity. Light flooded into his world, replacing the gloom and misery, though still something leaden festered in his heart. It had been Al-Eldar, he realised—mind magic, like that of the captain. Braga could still feel the shadow of it inside his head, like the ghost of a headache.

Fresh hands grabbed at him, though these were hard and heavy and dark-skinned, not the sun-shy fingers of the adherent. 'Where is he?' Braga managed. He lurched to his feet, leaning into the arms of his soldiers, punch-drunk and unsteady. The priest had gone, leaving the last of his crossbowmen to their fate.

Ajuda patted him on the shoulder and peered into his face. 'He's gone,' he said. 'It was mind control. I've never seen it before. But when he drew his dirk, you just waited meekly. If I hadn't have been there ...' He left the rest unsaid. It did not do well to tell your commanding officer that you'd saved their life.

Braga did not need the reminder. The feeling of loss and shame at leading so many to their deaths, both here and at Baile Saor, lingered within him. That had been hard enough, but Sirle had been a step too far. 'Thank you,' he said, and realised he was blinking away the sting of tears.

Below, the clashing of metal rang through the square like a death toll, though with the adherent gone, there was fresh hope. 'Ajuda, find your corporal and tell him that we've been betrayed. He needs to take his men and convince the guards to stand down. Tell him to use force if he has to, but I hope it won't come to that.'

'What will you do, sir?'

'I'm going to help stop the fighting. After that, I'm going to find the adherent and kill him.'

'How will you do that?' Aduja asked, bemused.

The big man gave a grim smile. 'Simple. First, I'm going to walk down there and talk to them. Then I'm going to take my axe,

478

find the adherent, and smash it through his face.'

The Church is a rock; a foundation stone upon which the entire world is built. In times of instability, turn to the Church to provide support and bring order to chaos. Trust in the words of Truth, and trust in the Church to deliver and interpret that Truth.

—From the Tenets of Truth

CHAPTER THIRTY-NINE
PREMIERO IRMAO AND HOUSE-LORD AARGAU

The Citadel

A strong wind had risen. It raced in from the sea, whipping the bay into angry white foam and driving the small fishing fleet in search of the harbour wall towards the shore. Premiero Irmao looked wistfully out at the huge three-masted hulk bobbing perilously in the waves and wondered how different it must have once been. 'It would have been a sight to behold,' he said quietly, though no one was there to hear him.

Servants raced here and there attending to their assembled House-Lords while guards stood solemnly at their posts. Grey men protected by other grey men, Irmao mused. None of them took any notice of him. They were absorbed in their duties and their thoughts and their squabbles. 'Masts and sails as far as the eye could see. Cog and carrack and caravel. Each one heavy in the water with spice and sugar and cotton and rum and all the world's trade. All gone now,' he lamented softly, his voice melancholy as though it had been some personal loss. He wished he had been able to see it for himself. Those sights were gone, however, lost to the ages along with all the other deep sea-going ships. The king had seen to that with his sugar law. Now, only the green-water boats remained. They were small vessels, each with a hole carved into the stern to prevent them venturing too far out to sea. As a result, cargo was carried cross-country using the network of canals owned by the Crown Estate. 'High time to break that monopoly,' Irmao murmured, smiling to himself. He raised a glass to the intrepid boatmen.

'My lord?' enquired a small voice.

The Premiero turned to find a young servant girl attending him. It took him a moment to realise that he had spoken aloud. He shooed her away before thinking better of it. 'Girl,' he called after her. 'More wine.'

She scurried away. The elegant Debating Hall was growing busier, the great and the good all attempting to outdo their gaudy surroundings. Ancient tapestries and painted silks adorned the walls, doubtlessly hung to show a rich history of wealth and opulence, though Irmao just found them sun-bleached and lifeless. More than anything else, he thought, they reflected the need to sweep out the stale old traditions and usher in a bright new dawn. A metaphor he hoped to make reality very soon.

His footfalls sliced through the bustle of the room, cutting hushed voices short as heads turned to follow him. Even the solemn tolling of the city bells seemed to take note, becoming quiet and timed as though to miss each step. The men had been waiting on him, he knew, anxious and expectant in equal measure.

He stalked from the window, almost angry. Eight men awaited him on the raised platform, House-Lords each, though even they seemed to shrink back as his shadow loomed towards them. Irmao watched the assembled men fuss and fidget for a moment. *They think themselves so important, and yet they are nothing next to the might and majesty of the Church. And the Goddess*, he added. He imagined reaching out and squeezing so that his huge shadow self might squash them where they sat, their pompous heads popping like pomegranate seeds.

He stepped up onto the platform. They knew exactly what he was doing. It was not until he had joined them that their voices began to mean anything. Nothing they said—none of the votes they cast—would stand unless ratified by his presence. *See where the power truly lies*, he was saying to them. Now, they together formed the Council of Nine. Eight good men for honour and one man more for Truth. That was all they needed, though the city council often held more. Any House-Lord could attend if their house had been called by the City-Lord.

This day, however, was different to most, as a single pealing of the bells reminded them. It was the reason so many of them looked on edge. All, in fact, except House-Lord Kariq. Now *there* was an oily fish indeed, a shark circling at the edge of the reef. They had been called to appoint a replacement for City-Lord Phaedra, and Kariq thought himself the biggest fish in the harbour. *A pity for him*, thought Irmao.

Those gathered grew quiet, though this did not dispel the hushed voices of those in the gallery beyond. They—lesser nobles who could not sit on the Council—watched like the seagulls above the harbour, following their favoured boat in search of briny morsels. Their attendance did not worry Irmao. He welcomed them, in fact. Their eyes meant there was no chance the result revealed today would be misconstrued or misrepresented.

Slowly, he walked to the head of the oval table, hands stroking the carved edge as he went. The seat was reserved for the City-Lord, even on those occasions when he was unable to attend. There was only one exception to this rule, and this was it. The Premiero sat himself upon the dais, fighting hard to combat the smile that tried to force its way to the fore. Only now did the House-Lords take their places. He was surprised to find that House-Lord Kariq avoided the seat next to him. Instead, he opted for the other end of the table, settling down directly opposite. *So*, Irmao thought to himself, *this is how he wishes to play.* He smiled and nodded to each of them in turn, acknowledging their attendance. They returned his courtesies in varying degrees—some honest, some begrudging, and others outright challenging. It bothered him not. Though they might like to kick his arse, he knew full well that first, they would be required to kiss it. He intended to enjoy this.

'Your Excellency,' House-Lord Chiqae began, 'may I welcome you and offer our heartfelt sorrow at the sad loss of City-Lord Phaedra. It is during these sad and dark times that we look to you and the Church to show us guidance and reveal to us the blessed light of Truth that can only be found through the Goddess.'

Irmao dismissed the comment as clumsy and obvious. *If he thinks to serenade me with empty words and gestures, he is as naïve as he is stupid.* 'Thank you, Lord Chiqae. I am sure that Doarson and the Citadel will not forget the considerable efforts and loans you made to help grease the wheels of commerce and trade.' *And the usurious rates that you charge.* Irmao gave a small smile.

'I would like to echo those solemn words, Premiero,' offered the man sat to Irmao's right, House-Lord Tsin. 'As you are aware, House Tsin has ever supported City-Lord Phaedra and, in these difficult times, we would of course extend all support to you and the Church in appointing a new City-Lord.'

'Quite literally,' Irmao smiled. 'I've no doubt that half the cushions and furniture in the region comes from one of your workhouses. Though they are not so comfortable as others, I think.'

'Excellency—' interjected another of the Nine.

'Enough!' Irmao barked. He raised his hand, stealing the wind from House-Lord Fetl midstride. 'Gentlemen, allow me to save us all some time. No doubt you will all attempt to woo and gain favour with promises and vague notions of solemn loyalty to the Church, but I assure you it is not necessary.' He spoke with a clear, smooth tone so as not to be misunderstood. Eyes made wide fixed to his, uncertain and anxious in the face of this slip from tradition. 'The Church is simple, Lord Tsin, and lusts not for the glamourous trappings of your textiles.' He lifted his sleeve for effect. 'As you see, our clothes, as our desires, are simple and honest. No doubt, Lord Fetl, you were just about to remind me that your family has provided much of the grain that has been used to bake our bread for generations and explain how well placed you are to restore the granaries and still this disorder. Yet the body cannot live on bread alone.'

Irmao almost laughed when Fetl's face fell, but managed to contain himself before rounding on the two lords seated next to Kariq. 'You, Lord Qubis, Lord Loram, have both sat on this Council for as long as I can recall, and without your wine, Lord Qubis, the cycles would have been far much duller. Although, thanks to your Grey Guard, Lord Loram, we've been spared the wrong kind of excitement. No one doubts that each one of you is to be commended, and I am sure that you will continue to show your support to ensure our city's position in the world for generations to come. If we work together, I know that we can make Doarson great again.'

The assembled lords shifted uncomfortably. He had disavowed them of their opportunities to stake their claims, leaving them in unfamiliar territory. No matter the face they wore now—successor, sponsor, spoiler, supporter—in his eyes they were all usurpers or the supporters of usurpers. He and the city had suffered them and their like for too long. This was the fresh broom that he had dreamt of, the beginning of a new way that would see the Church sitting at the centre of the Citadel.

Lord Kariq opened his mouth to speak and Irmao watched the other men waver. No doubt they thought he would re-establish stability and return to the traditional way of doing things. Irmao almost snorted at the notion.

'The rest of you,' he said before Kariq could speak, 'Lords Noda and Terat and Lords Chiqae and Kariq. Yours are houses of historic heritage. Your families have held titles since almost the very founding of the great Citadel of Doarson, during which time you have been stalwart in your support of the City-Lord. You have helped build this city from its meagre foundations and your towers reach up to the heavens themselves, visible signs of your dedication. Lord Kariq, your family was instrumental in establishing the city as a great mercantile centre, shipping goods far and wide, and your support of the most honourable house of our dearly lamented Lord Phaedra during the revolts helped to safeguard their position for generations. Your own house has been the rock that helped solidify control in the region.'

House-Lord Kariq appeared ready to shed tears of pride, his full lips curling at one side in a sneering smile of satisfaction. He had clearly not expected Irmao to offer any words of support. Now, more than ever, he'd expect the mantle of City-Lord, the final reward for a lifetime of manoeuvring and positioning behind the backs of the other House-Lords and indeed the City-Lord himself. He puffed out his chest and sat a little straighter in his seat.

Irmao watched, amused. 'And so,' he continued, his sense of satisfaction growing, 'it is of no surprise to me, Lord Kariq, that I must pronounce'—he paused, looking into each face with a gleeful malice he no longer tried to hide—'your arrest.'

Gasps rang through the hall. Outside, the bells tolled and, at once, a dozen Grey Guard flooded into the room, surrounding the table. The House-Lords gathered erupted in displays of indignant fury, and none more so that House-Lord Kariq himself.

'What? Preposterous!' he blustered. 'Arrest? What is the meaning of this? If this is some kind of joke, Irmao, then I assure you, I will be the one laughing loudest and longest.'

The Premiero steepled his fingers. *Irmao, is it? Where are all your pleasantries and titles now?*

Kariq stood with a jolt, sending his chair clattering to the floor. The sound of steel being drawn rang hard and sharp.

'That was an ill-considered move,' Irmao told him. He turned to the nearest Grey, an older sergeant who quickly snapped to attention. 'Could House-Lord Kariq please be removed from the Debating Hall for his safety and that of everyone else here?'

Two Greys moved to flank Kariq. He tried tugging his sleeves free from their grasp, but they held fast.

'You cannot do this. What is the charge?' House-Lord Terat demanded.

The Premiero snapped his head around to face the man, eyes a blaze of fury.

'Your Eminence,' Terat added quickly.

'I demand to know on what grounds and authority you are having me arrested,' Lord Kariq called. The other lords murmured their assent.

You can almost smell their fear, Irmao thought. He sat back into his chair and called for a cup bearer. The wine was dark and fruity, and he took his time to let the liquid roll over his tongue, flavours developing almost as intensely as the unease around the table.

'Very well then,' he said, fixing Kariq with a cold stare. 'You are charged with conspiracy to murder our beloved City-Lord Phaedra and, foremost among your crimes, you are also charged with heresy.'

Kariq looked stunned, as if the Premiero had physically struck him. All those gathered quieted. Their faces turned to Kariq. Lords Loram and Qubis edged away from the condemned man, lest they too be tainted.

'What?' Kariq's voice had lost some of its bluster, and he seemed to visibly slump at the enormity of the charge.

'You, along with Chiqae here, and Fetl, and Qubis, and Loram.' Irmao indicated the other men with an almost casual motion of his hand. 'All of you conspired against the teachings of the Goddess and her most benedight Church of the Righteous Truth in bringing a so-called healer into the Palace Tower. You were present and took part in heretical practices, through which you allowed a farce— no, an abomination—to take place. This, this *healer* conducted a parody of a most sacred act upon the body of our embattled and beloved City-Lord, which ultimately resulted in his death.'

'That is absurd and you know it,' Fetl started. 'You weren't even there—' He stopped himself too late, biting back his own words.

Irmao leant forward, eyes glowing.

Kariq and the other lords sank, almost buckling at the knees. It was a death sentence, they knew. The most they could hope for was for their families to retain their lands and standing.

'Condemned by your actions and now your words. Only through the Goddess can we be freed from pain and suffering. You would all do well to think on that over the coming days. Pray to the Goddess for guidance and mercy. Only through her holy Truth will you find release from the depravity of your sins. When you engaged in these unholy actions, you not only turned your back on the Truth and the Church, but you turned your back on our beloved Goddess. Such a blasphemy is unacceptable, even for the lord of a great house such as yours. I will pray for your souls.'

Irmao's voice was a whip cracking through the room, taut and graceful and edged with painful retribution. Kariq, he realised, had actually soiled himself, and the smell began to creep over the table. With a look of disgust, Irmao dismissed the guards restraining him. Kariq did not struggle.

Dritsek Aargau entered, lingering in the doorway as Kariq was dragged past. It could not have been better timed, Irmao thought. The young lord wrinkled his nose before approaching the table.

'Lord Aargau,' the Premiero said, holding out his hand in a welcome, 'it is an unexpected pleasure to see you,' *let him deal with the fallout, this is the position he so craved, afterall.* 'The Council is in session, but we had expected your father and House-Lord.' There was an air of expectancy in the Premiero's voice, almost challenging those present to detect the underlying meaning. He smiled expansively at Dritsek. *Go on then, let's see if you really have the balls.*

House-Lord Noda stood and thumped his hand down upon the great table. 'I must protest at these proceedings,' he said. 'Premiero Irmao, Your Excellency, not only is it unsettling for guards to be standing over us and holding us hostage, but it is improper and against protocol for Lord Aargau to approach the Council session.

Furthermore, as there are no longer nine House-Lords sitting, I fear the session must be formally closed until we can sit once again to agree upon and appoint a successor to the late City-Lord. This has been an eventful day, and I for one wish only to retire to my estates.'

He was a venal man, Irmao knew, and no doubt wished to retreat to establish just how he might benefit or lose under these new circumstances. Still, his words rang true. 'You are quite right, House-Lord Noda,' Irmao said in a syrupy voice, 'this is indeed most irregular.'

Noda allowed himself a self-satisfied smile, his relief evident to all.

'Lord Aargau,' the Premiero continued, 'do you bring word from your lord father, House-Lord Aargau?'

'I do, Eminence,' Dritsek said with a deferential bow. 'Unfortunately, House-Lord Aargau, my own lord father, has been subject to a terrible and heinous crime.' More murmurs and uncertain voices swept the table. 'This very afternoon, a heretic, who had somehow managed to gain my father's confidence, attended his chambers. As you are all aware, my father has been an unwell man, and this heretic must have filled his head with evil words and lies, preying upon his weakness. In his desperate and weak-minded condition, he allowed the heresy of healing, during which he was coldly and brutally stabbed and robbed.' His voice cracked a little as he spoke, but Irmao thought he saw a brief smile touch the corners of the young lord's lips.

There was a long and pregnant pause.

'That is truly awful,' Irmao offered at last. 'We are, of course, sorry for your loss, my child, and we will pray for your father's soul.'

'Of course, we are all sorry for your loss, Lord Aargau,' House-

Lord Noda said. 'Your father was a great man and served on the Council for many cycles. He has ever been a vocal and respected member of this Council, even during these last cycles when, on occasion, you have attended in his stead. However'—he turned from Dritsek and back to Premiero Irmao—'this sad news, coming as it does so soon after the loss of our City-Lord, only serves to further demonstrate the need for the Council to recess until it has had time to grieve and acknowledge these great men's passing.'

'My dear House-Lord Noda,' Irmao said coldly, 'what this sad news demonstrates is the terrible suffering that can be caused when people choose to ignore the teachings of the Church. The heathens who take advantage of the weak and prey upon their doubts have brought both of these untimely deaths upon us. Two men have been lost to us, and you too have played your part. You also were present at this so-called healing; you too offered up false prayers and lies. Well, you will answer for your part, just as House-Lord Kariq will.'

In truth, Irmao couldn't recall whether the oaf had been present at the healing or not, but he had heard enough of his blustering for one day. He gestured to the guards, who took hold of House-Lord Noda and drew him from the table.

'Wait,' the Premiero ordered, remembering something, 'there was some truth in what you said, House-Lord Noda. Lord Aargau, it is with a sad heart that, with the passing of your lord father, I confer upon you his titles, styles, and estates. My office will register the death, and you can take this proclamation as receipt of the necessary licences on behalf of the Church, payment for which will be waived in lieu of sums outstanding against one shipment of coal from your estates. House-Lord Aargau, may I welcome you to the Council table. As you are now present, we number enough to declare the Council once again in session, at least until the removal of the criminal House-Lords already named. Shall we?'

There was a deathly silence. Each of the lords seemed too stunned to offer opposition, grown suddenly small in the shadows of the Greys that ringed them.

'Good,' Irmao continued, 'now, I think that the small matter of electing the new City-Lord should be attended to forthwith. House-Lord Aargau, please accept my nomination.'

Dritsek bowed low.

And there it is, Irmao thought. *A lifetime of dreams come to fruition.*

Dritsek looked to Irmao and inclined his head—a knowing and conspiratorial sign between siblings. 'I would be honoured, Your Excellency.'

'Wonderful.' And with that, the Premiero stood, nodded absently to the Grey sergeant, and strode from the dais. Only when he was safely across the room did Irmao allow a wild smile to stretch across his face.

* * *

Dritsek watched the high priest leave. Not once did his older brother look back. *No matter,* he thought, *this is my stage now.*

There were muted rumblings and murmurs from those remaining at the table, and the mutterings from the gallery were growing in volume, as annoying as they were disruptive. Dritsek ignored them.

'Gentlemen,' he said curtly, finding the remaining House-Lords' eyes fixed upon him, a mix of emotions wrestling across their faces. Some were pale, though there were several who could not hide their distaste, mouths set grim as though they were chewing wasps. Foremost among these was Lord Noda, who still hung to the edge of the table like a lingering fart. 'May I say that I am proud to join you today as the first of House Aargau to sit as City-Lord in Doarson, and I am pleased to know that I have your unerring support. As such, it is sad and regretful that my first duty shall be to have Lord-Noda removed and stripped of all titles and privileges. Guards, please remove Mr Noda from the hall.' There were more, he knew, but the Premiero had left without furnishing him with the detail. Besides, it might benefit to leave the others sweating. Let them fear a knock at their door in the night, it would serve to focus their attention.

Noda stood quickly, glancing left and right as if calling on unseen allies, but the other House-Lords avoided his gaze. The Greys descended upon him, dragging him kicking and squirming from the table, his protests quickly becoming little more than background noise. The action sent ripples around the table. Mouths fell agape and wide eyes were made suddenly sharp.

Dritsek turned to the nearest Grey. 'Clear the gallery,' he commanded. 'We are no longer quorate and as the session is closed, so too is the chamber. Besides,' he added, glancing over the men sat at the table, 'I have but one minor issue to raise with you all before you pledge to me your oaths.' He sat back smiling, a squirrel with all the nuts.

In the gallery beyond, several arguments flared as the Greys swept among those assembled. Some of the more arrogant lords had to be dragged away with bloodied noses. It was not a pretty sight, though it would serve to warn the others, Dritsek supposed. He beckoned the sergeant to his side and whispered into his ear. The older man bowed a confirmation and backed away from the table.

Lord Abosi was the first to offer tribute. 'Congratulations on your appointment, City-Lord,' he grovelled. 'We place ourselves at

493

your service.' He became distracted by the ugliness unfolding in the gallery, wincing as a man was struck down by the butt of a spear. 'Can you, in turn, assure the Council members of their safety? Not just here, but in the city as a whole. You may be aware of the recent infraction in mine own home? There are worrying reports of dissent among the populace, and we would not wish for it to spread. I for one could not sleep knowing the poor and unfortunate of the city were at the mercy of the mob.'

It seemed a popular question, with grumblings of assent from the remaining lords. Dritsek almost laughed. They were all the same, he thought: simpering old fools who thought only of themselves. 'You have no reason to fear, my lords,' he declared. 'I am fully advised on the situation and I assure you that the matter is in hand. The talk of rebellion is exaggerated. There have been some localised disturbances, yes, but these have been dealt with swiftly. As you will be aware, I was forced to take control of the forces garrisoned at the barracks due to the unfortunate demise of its commanding officers. Since then, I have taken steps to ensure that the army has strong leaders whom I trust fully. At this very moment, one of our adherents is leading the Grey Guard through Smithton, the source of the troubles, and I have released a hand of soldiers to him to offer what minimal support may be required. The streets will be safe by this afternoon.'

The House-Lords glanced at one another.

'A priest? In charge of the army, my lord?' House-Lord Terat asked tentatively. 'Is that wholly wise?'

'Of course not, Lord Terat,' Dritsek snapped. He was not so fool as that—even before the closing chapters of the Evulgation, the Crown had decreed that the Church would never again hold office over the army lest the king's own reign be stolen. The sacred armies were dissolved and the jurisdiction of the Suers restricted. 'That is why I will retain sole charge of the army. Adherent Al-Eldar will hold office over the Grey Guard.'

Jaws dropped.

Yes, Dritsek thought, *let's see how much you prefer black to grey.*

'I assume there are no objections? After all, I don't think any of us gathered here would be so unwise as to question the intentions and integrity of our holy Church now, would we?' Dritsek's words were soft, but there was no hiding their deliberate barb.

'Of course not, my lord. I only meant that... by the king's own decree—' Terat began.

'By the king's own decree, I, City-Lord Aargau, am head of the army here. Do you expect me to be able to attend this Council while also personally leading the effort to quell a petty squabble among the peasantry?'

Terat searched the faces of those other lords, hoping for some sign of support but finding none. They had retreated back within themselves, fearful of the wrath of their new master.

A guard bent at Dritsek's shoulder, begging pardon for the intrusion. Nervous and uncertain eyes flickered between the House-Lords before falling on the girl who stood beyond the guardsman. She was a slip of a thing dressed prettily in a blue dress. *My mother's influence*, Dritsek thought. She glared back at them, all anger and fury, though he sensed a good serving of fear there too.

'What is she doing here? Remove her,' Lord Loram called to the guard.

Why so interested? Dritsek might have responded. Instead, he said, 'My dear lord, I am sure that in the latter days of our late City-Lord Phaedra's life, when his health was uncertain, you were accustomed somewhat to exercising a greater range of freedoms and liberties in this hall. I, on the other hand, am neither weak nor feeble-minded, and my eyes bear not the fog of age. Therefore, I would respectfully remind you that, whilst at my table and indeed in my presence, you will kindly conduct yourself with a modicum of deportment.'

'Forgive me, my lord,' said Loram, flustered, 'it is just that, in all these cycles, and quite possibly in the history of the Council, I am sure that no women have been allowed to attend the high table.' He looked to the young girl pointedly, his nose wrinkling as if suggesting that her very presence poisoned the air. She glowered back at him, almost making him shrink back under the weight of her stare.

'And why is that?' City-Lord Aargau asked. 'Do we not serve a Goddess? Are women not represented by this Council? Are their welfares not dictated by the decisions we make? Is your wife mute, my lord? Does she not have a say in the running of your household? Were you born of a woman or of a man? Did you suck at the tits of your milk-maid or did you prefer your father's cock?'

The question rendered the room silent, the words echoing around the chamber as if they were the ringing report of a slap, leaving Lord Loram dumbstruck. Even the girl's face shone with embarrassment. Dritsek looked challengingly at the remaining lords. He'd had quite enough of them and it was only his first day.

'It matters not, my lord,' Dritsek continued with an exaggerated sigh. 'You may think of her as neither man nor woman, merely as heretic and criminal.'

Several of the lords shifted uncomfortably in their seats.

'Heresy is a grave and ugly word, my lord,' Lord Abosi said as diplomatically as possible, 'it brings ill tidings and troubling times.'

'And yet it is the truth, my lords,' the new City-Lord replied matter-of-factly. 'This very week, in my own estates, this girl blasphemously claimed to hold the power to heal. She preyed upon the desperation of my own sick father. She convinced my ill-advised mother to allow her to lay hands on my father, promising to take away his suffering. Instead, she took a blade and stole away what was left of his life, and with it the happiness of our home.'

Mutters and gasps rose from the seated lords. Even the accused girl appeared shocked by the terrible news. She opened her mouth, only for one of the Greys to close it again. She whimpered at the slap, sucking blood from her lips. Abosi squirmed in his chair at the trickle of claret that ran down her chin.

'Do not be fooled, gentlemen,' Dritsek said. 'She is a dark and malevolent force. Even as she stands here before you, she carries with her the very items that she would use on any of us. The hexes and poisons that would rot your insides as you sat pleading with her, much as my own father did.'

The girl's face contorted with rage, her hard eyes fixing upon the City-Lord, but she had better sense than to let her tongue run away with her again. Dritsek stood and crossed to her. Gently, he took a hand and lifted it to shoulder-height, as though readying for a dance. She inched stiffly away from him. His fingers found a strap and slipped it from her shoulder. He hefted the leather-bound box and carried it back to the table before spilling its contents for all to see. 'There,' he announced, smiling with grim satisfaction. 'See for yourselves, the trinkets and effigies of her trade. A dark witch.'

He peered around, gauging the reactions of the other men. Their eyes had widened at the display of phials and tubes that glistened wetly in the bright light of the room. A great crystal bowl rolled to a slow halt at the table's centre, spilling gems of refracted light glittering into the room. Powders and preparations swept from stray packets, dusting the wooden table. Most damning of all—and even something of a surprise to Dritsek—was the poppet. Knitted black eyes stared back from its twisted face, shocking all into silence.

'For Truth's sake,' Dritsek heard the girl bark, 'you can't be scared of a doll. Have you never seen one before?'

Dritsek's eyes shone dangerously. The final die had been cast and it felt like a winning score. Who, after all, would question the word of the City-Lord? He looked to the girl. A shame to waste something so pretty, but she was a convenient sacrifice. He smiled.

A guard approached the table and saluted Dritsek. 'My lord, there is an adherent requesting an audience with you and the Council.'

Dritsek nodded, half-expecting a delegation from the Misty City, but when the doors were thrown open, it was only Al-Eldar.

'Commissioner Dritsek!' he called. The priest was ragged and rattled and out of breath. 'My lord commissioner,' he added, hurrying towards the table and bowing his head gravely. He smelled thickly of sweat and panic and fear. Dritsek eyed him warily.

'You have not had chance to hear of my lord's new appointment, Adherent,' Lord Terat coughed, 'Premiero Irmao elevated our great City-Lord Aargau but a short time ago.'

The adherent stooped quickly to his knee and smiled conspiratorially as though he were somehow part of Dritsek's grand scheme. *I must disabuse him of that notion*, Dritsek thought.

'Congratulations, City-Lord,' Al-Eldar said, 'may the Goddess's Truth shine upon you and forever light your days.' His voice had changed over the last week, Dritsek noted. It had grown thinner and reedier, as if forced out by some great effort.

'We are glad that you are here, Al-Eldar,' Dritsek said, though nothing was further from the truth. 'You have arrived just in time to take this heretic into your custody.'

'Heretic, my lord?' The adherent was confused. He looked around, taking in the strange setting for the first time: the grey and shocked faces of the assembled lords, the strange collection of items strewn across the table, and the girl huddled beneath looming soldiers. He stood slowly, trying to piece together what was taking place, but Dritsek could tell his mind was elsewhere. He stepped to the girl, sniffing around her as a dog might, trying to somehow glean information from scent alone. He turned and took a pace back towards the table, eyes falling upon the poppet. He reached out his hand, fingers hovering momentarily before he dared pick it up. The air was split by his scream, shrill and piercing, like a cat wrestling with a hawk. He spilled the poppet to the ground, throwing it as far from him as he could muster. He pawed the hand that he had held it with as though it had been pressed against a scalding kettle.

'Witch!' Dritsek screamed.

'Witch!' Al-Eldar echoed.

The guard's hand closed around Solatta's shoulder.

The Church will lead you to Truth. You must place yourself and your trust in the Church and its ministers. Let no one stand against the Church, for only through the Church can anyone find Truth.

—*From the Tenets of Truth*

CHAPTER FORTY
SENTENZA AND DREBAN

The Citadel

The door was bolted from the inside, and no wonder—this was the inner sanctum of the Citadel. 'You can't just walk in there, kid,' Sentenza explained, though he may as well have been talking to the door itself. Dreban looked deflated, childlike almost. He truly felt for the girl. Somewhere, distantly, it warmed Sentenza. Maybe he could help him find his love and rescue her. It wasn't such a terrible idea. He felt it bloom like a tiny light fighting a wave of darkness. He snuffed it out. He had no place for such things; they made you slow and stupid and got you killed. Lady Aargau had told them where to find her. Sentenza had no reason to believe her, but there had been something in her face—she was *scared*. She had not appeared like the woman he remembered. He'd met her only once, maybe twice, and even then fleetingly, but there had been a

501

presence about her, and not just her beauty. She had a sharpness, both of spirit and tongue, which seemed absent now. There'd been a distance in her eyes.

The door to the family chambers had been unlocked and unguarded. Dreban had been ready to tear the tower apart—'*If they have harmed a hair on her head,*' he kept saying, and Sentenza felt a fire begin to ignite, as if the air itself was kindling. It was the proof he'd been longing for. This boy—barely of age—was the one he'd been searching for. He would have been only a child when Old Ballir had sold the girl as payment for saving his own skin. It didn't make sense, but then, nothing ever did these days.

What Sentenza wanted was for Dreban to direct that tremendous energy and anger at the Aargaus. He wanted him to become wrath, to tear every brick down one by one, casting them and Dritsek back into the sea with all the other eels. But they had found only the lady in the tower, her eyes as blank and glassy as her lord husband's. Beside her, he slumped in a low chair, blood pooling beneath him.

'Where is she?' Dreban had asked, the sight of blood beneath the chair panicking him. But the lady had merely stared through him. It took a strong slap to knock her near to her senses.

'Where is she? What has he done with her?'

She had not made sense. 'Such plans,' she kept saying. 'So many. They took her, you know. They took them both, but she was mine. No one else's. They had no right. No right.'

'Where?' Dreban shook the woman. 'Where have they taken her?'

'To the Capital, with all the rest. They never even let me hold her properly. I never got to say goodbye.'

Sentenza had meant to scare the lady out of it by drawing his dirk, but it was Dreban who flinched. In a flash, the room had filled with energy—it slammed into Sentenza, forcing him back a half-step, and Lady Aargau jerked as if struck, her pale eyes swivelling to focus on the kid for the first time.

'Who are you?' she said, frowning, 'how did you get in here? I'll call the guards!'

'Solatta,' Dreban asked again, 'what have they done with her?'

The lady hesitated, seeming to cringe away, fighting against the boy's grip.

'Her, it was her. She did this. She killed my lord husband.' Even to Sentenza the words sounded false.

Dreban stood. 'It's okay, I know where they are.'

Lady Aargau looked up at him with frightened eyes.

'How? Where?' asked Sentenza. Then it had been his turn to be led like a child—he'd followed Dreban through the maze of arches and galleries and vaulted ceilings, all the while winding inwards towards the Palace Tower.

Maybe there was another way to get into the Debating Hall, but he doubted it, not without more guards and more fighting. He wondered whether it was all worth it—not just for Dreban, but for him. What could he truly hope to achieve? He had little hope of stealing the boy's powers and, even if it was possible, Sentenza doubted he could do it alone. No, he realised with a sinking feeling, something like that would be the domain of the Misty City and its priests, and that meant Golya Sakani. He shook his head at the thought.

A scream from beyond the door shook him from his thoughts, a horrible, tormented howl, animalistic and rotten to its core. Sentenza felt it in his marrow. Dreban wheeled, anxiety and panic writ clear on his face, and Sentenza felt his skin begin to throb, alive with the itch of nearby magic. He watched, wide-eyed, as Dreban reached towards the door and simply pushed. For a second, he almost glowed. Then the world went white.

Sentenza blinked, his ears ringing, and realised dimly that he was on the ground. Where the door had once stood were shards of splintered wood hanging from ruined hinges. Beyond, the fog of debris clouded a distant cohort of shouting figures. He picked himself up, coughing, eyes clogged, the rippling of energy across his skin finally subsiding. He didn't know whether to feel awed or jealous—maybe both. What he could do with such power! Even if he couldn't take it for himself, maybe he could direct the boy, bind him somehow to his will... Either way, he knew he couldn't let him out of his sight.

Dreban stepped forwards, rushing into the hall, and Sentenza ran after him, laying a calming hand upon his shoulder. He recoiled almost instantly—the residue of magic bubbled across the boy like a torrent, raging and uncontrolled. *He doesn't even understand what he's doing*, Sentenza realised. The thought scared him.

As the dust settled, figures rose within the hall. Cries and shouts echoed past him: a call for guards. Two Greys rushed them. Sentenza drew his sword, meeting one of the men head on. Blades sparked, a pin of light in the dusty gloom. He lunged, the air pulling and coalescing before him, and struck out, thumping it into the guard's chest. Light bent and twisted, shining in the air like metal. His Wielding stabbed and slashed, leaving ribbons of blood in its wake. Sentenza almost lost his concentration. It had never done that before; his was a hard power, flat-edged and pounding like a hammer. He'd never been able to master more delicate shapes.

The second guard slashed at Dreban and Sentenza turned, willing the boy to repeat what he'd done to the door. Instead, Dreban ducked and fell, tripping over his own feet. He looked scared and lost, a little boy in over his head. What was he doing?

The guard bore down on him, scowling. Sentenza waited for a fizz of force that didn't come. The air was dead.

Sentenza threw himself forwards. Dust swirled into the air, forming a tendril that whipped from his arm, lashing around the guard's wrist like a rope. Sentenza pulled and felt the tension release with a snap. The guard screamed, broken bones tearing through muscle and fabric. He dropped to his knees, staring at the bloody stump through disbelieving eyes.

A woman's voice rang out: 'Dreban!'

Sentenza turned back into the hall. Dritsek Aargau stood, highlighted by crepuscular rays, a young woman held firmly in front of him. Sentenza saw recognition in the man's face, cold and dangerous eyes narrowing as they found the colonel. Dreban took a step towards him, but Dritsek pulled the woman tighter, his arms wrapping around her like a python. *So this is who he'd been looking for.*

'Step easy,' Sentenza muttered, 'he could snap her neck before you made it halfway.'

'I can't just leave her there!'

That's exactly what I'd do, he thought. *Better leave her here today and collect her alive tomorrow.* 'Perhaps not,' he replied steadily. 'But you can't just go running into things headfirst unless you want to get yourself into trouble.'

Truth, what am I now, his father?

A dozen Greys filed in from a door directly opposite, and the hall rang with the sound of swords rasping clear of their scabbards. The men formed up around Dritsek, protecting him. It made Sentenza feel uneasy. There had clearly been a development he was unaware of. A strum of strings sounded a warning and he threw himself backwards, trying to tug at Dreban, but he was too far and too slow. The bolt took the boy hard in the thigh, hitting clean and tearing straight through the flesh and out the other side. He dropped to the floor, howling in pain, and as though in answer Sentenza felt a wave surge through him—not the usual tingle of excited energy, but something deeper, visceral almost. It pulsed like an alien heartbeat, forcing its way through his very core. He thought he felt his bones itch somehow, as if pulling and tugging free of him. The energy was all around him, stronger near Dreban, but stronger still towards Dritsek. For a short moment, he thought he could see it: a flash of blue and indigo and violet. A vapour connecting Dreban and the table. It hung briefly in the air before vanishing. Had he imagined it? No. The adherent had seen it too. The man sniffed at the air suspiciously. He looked to Dreban, then back at Dritsek. The girl had grabbed a bowl from the table. She clung to it, struggling against the restraining arm of the upstart lord, desperate to wrench herself free. He threw her violently to the ground and she screamed, the bowl spilling from her grip. Dritsek struck her, a vicious back hand, then grabbed her by the hair, pulling her up onto her knees.

Sentenza hesitated. Beside him, Dreban stirred, lifting himself to his feet. He staggered forwards and, before Sentenza's eyes, the deep and angry wound began to knit itself closed. The colonel blinked. The skin had sealed, leaving only a red and angry patch on the boy's leg.

Slowly, it began to make sense. Ever since his journey to Ballir's place, deep in the mountains, he had been searching for whoever or whatever had created the old man's thriving farmstead amid the snow and rock and ice. The Golya had tasked him with retrieving a girl, but Sentenza had never found her. Sold to a travelling healer, Ballir had suggested, the price for saving his life. Ballir had got more than he bargained for. The healing magic had turned the land fertile, but it had stripped it of its inherent energy.

Sentenza had found that out almost at the cost of his own life. He looked back to Dreban. The young man looked pale and weak, but fury blazed in his eyes. He wasn't the source of power—*she* was. What had Dreban called her? Solatta? Sentenza looked back at her. She was young and pretty, almost as old as Dreban, he guessed. The Golya's little girl? So... was Dreban the travelling healer? Surely not; he would have been a child himself. Not only that, but he didn't even seem to understand his power, could barely even control it. It didn't quite make sense, but Sentenza felt like he was almost there. He just needed the final part of the puzzle to fall into place. There had to be something he hadn't seen.

Dritsek yelped—the girl had bit his hand. She tried to run but he caught a handful of her hair, wrenching her back to him. Dreban ran forward, his leg seemingly healed, but four guards blocked his approach, a wall of steel. Dritsek dragged the girl deeper into the hall, but the colonel had eyes for something else entirely: the girl's bowl. It was a small and unassuming thing; a decorative piece that would sit well in any House-Lord's parlour. Why was it here? The adherent had seen it too. He watched it hungrily and began to slink his way towards it, cautious and deliberate, a snake winding through the reeds. Ghost-white fingers reached out from the depths of his robe. He was almost touching it when he froze, uncertainty writhing across his features.

At once, all hope seemed to die, leaving Sentenza feeling desolate and alone. His head throbbed. More than five long cycles of searching. The longing and passion, the deep-seated desire to possess—all of it threatened to roil up within him. The world darkened.

The Church and the Truth are the only universal constants. While great trees topple in the wind and mighty rivers bend in their course, the Church stands firm, grounded in Truth. It neither retreats nor concedes in the eternal war against the false and the Truthless.

—From the Tenets of Truth

CHAPTER FORTY-ONE
BRAGA

The Citadel

Many lay dead, though more still were dying or injured. Braga knelt by the body of the old smith. The man's face was calm and still. It held a peacefulness that seemed incongruous in this place of death. Braga passed a hand over the smith's face, closing his eyes. He felt an ache, deep within him. He had seen death before, dealt with the bodies of his own men, but this was different. Harder, somehow. He realised he didn't even know the man's name. At least a soldier had an identity disc. Their names could be recorded and remembered. How many of the peasants and workers would be lost forever, without anyone to mourn for them? Braga promised that if he had the chance, he would replace the Rose's thorns with roses—

one for each of those who had lost their lives here today. He'd create a living wall of remembrance.

Braga stood. He would find the tinker, but first he needed to find Al-Eldar. He was a twisted and dangerous man, a wolf in sheep's clothing. Braga himself had only narrowly escaped his knife, though that was not the weapon he feared. Residual images and feelings still flashed in his mind, placed there by the icy hand of the Cognator.

'Sir,' it was Ajuda. The young soldier had been pivotal in turning the tide of the battle. Had he not called to Braga, mistaking him for an ally, they would still have been fighting now. *Or already dead*, Braga thought. 'We've searched everywhere, but the priest has not been found. He must have fled the square.' The soldier looked disheartened, as though he'd failed in some way.

It mattered not, Braga knew. There would be only one place a man like that would run to. 'Bring the healers from the barracks,' Braga said, nodding to Ajuda. 'They have work to do.'

The young man looked uncertain. 'Is that wise, sir? What if the Church questions us using healers?'

'I don't care what the Church says, soldier. It was a priest who started all of this.'

'But isn't it against the Tenets?'

Braga scowled at the man. It was Sirle who saved his temper from boiling over by stepping in with a knowledge of doctrine Braga didn't have.

'The Tenets also say that the Truthful will give without prompting or question and that there is no disease or illness that we cannot overcome. Besides, aren't your healers ordained in the faith?' she said quickly, crossing her arms. 'There's nothing in the Tenets that say you can't heal anyone, only that it is the role of the Church. For all intents and purposes, this will be the Church delivering on the promises made by the Goddess.'

Braga felt her words like a tonic. They soothed his aching bones and washed away his weariness. She was right—he'd never thought of it like that before. Braga turned to her, a smile in his eyes. It was not returned. She was still angry with him. He had asked her not to take part in the fighting and, while it had been hard for her, it would have been impossible for him. 'These are my people,' she'd argued. 'If we have to fight for our freedom, for our very way of life, then I want to be part of it. I need to, just as much as they need you to lead them.'

'And that's why you can't,' he'd said, his voice small and apologetic. 'I need to know that you're safe if I'm going to do anything. I can't do that if I'm constantly worrying after you. I can't be the man they need me to be.'

She had sulkily accepted, staying behind when so many others marched into battle: her men, her women, her people.

In another time and another place, he might have reached out to her, but not here, not now. He would be hard-pressed to find any softness now. Braga sighed. If she was all business, then he had his own to be about. 'I have to go. The priest escaped.' He was as succinct as ever, eager not to lose any time.

'Good,' she said in response. 'I'll be glad of the great Braga's company.'

The big man was confused, irked even. 'What?'

'Did you think I'd sit at home like some good wife while all the men went off to war?' Her eyes shone dangerously. She adjusted her belt. It was then that he saw the blade and the wood axe. There would be no refusing her this time, he knew.

'I watched from beyond the gate. I saw where he went.'

Braga raised a single eyebrow and opened his mouth to say something, but she had already turned and started jogging across the square.

Grumbling to himself, Braga hurried after her.

She led Braga through a maze of narrow alleys and cobbled streets, a mixed hand of Greys and workers and soldiers keeping step behind. They passed through several gates as they wound deeper into the heart of the Citadel, the guards stationed at each seeming furtive and uncertain. Had it been just Braga and a rabble of smiths alone, the gates would doubtless have remained locked; there might even have been bloodshed. The presence of soldiers and Greys, however, changed that. On their authority, each gate was reluctantly opened.

It was not until they were almost upon the City-Lord's towers that they met opposition. The guards there were keen and young and hungry, spread in a loose formation around the council hall. It was just where Braga had imagined the adherent would run to, and Sirle had confirmed it. He could see them now through massive glass windows, bigger than most houses: the power mongers and the power hungry, all the city's great and good. The self-titled Commissioner Dritsek Aargau and his self-serving pets, all clamouring and clinging to whomever held office.

It was Sirle who led the line. Before Braga could utter an order, she had charged the enemy formation, an axe in her hand and a cry of war upon her lips.

Cursing under his breath, Braga ran after her.

The Church is the holy protector of the Truth, rightful in its righteousness. All power and elemental forces flow from and through the Church. False and profane is anyone who contests this, proclaiming falsely to wield powers not sanctified through the Church.

—From the Tenets of Truth

CHAPTER FORTY-TWO
SOLATTA

The Citadel

Solatta's voice caught in her throat as her hair was yanked back. Fresh tears filled her eyes, though not from the pain—rather, they were born of anger and frustration at how easily this man was able to dominate her. She had the iron salt of blood in her mouth from where she had bitten his hand, yet even that belonged to the City-Lord. It tasted of satisfaction and lent her a bravery that might otherwise have been lost.

The room had fallen into the darkness of a false night. The soldiers were rounding on Dreban and the tall warrior beside him, but it was the silhouette in the dust-shrouded doorway that drew

Solatta's gaze. A woman, she thought, a warrior from some story, bloody axe in her hand.

Solatta straightened suddenly, sinking her nails into the soft and pampered flesh of the City-Lord's hand. He screeched and yanked harder, dragging her further behind the spreading ranks of grey-uniformed soldiers. She felt him half-trip on the raised dais and, in the second where his grip slackened, she threw herself away from him, wincing as her scalp burned. She scrambled towards Dreban, crawling on her hands and knees, until at last her fingers touched something soft and familiar in the murk of the hall. It was her poppet. Her Foof. She clung to it, feeling oddly thankful. Above, a statue stared down at her with cold stone eyes. He was one of the many that littered the hall: City-Lords and Council members from cycles gone, all of them lost to the annals of time. Solatta wished that she too could become lost. She could hear the City-Lord calling, searching for her, demanding her return. She crouched low behind the safety of the statue's stone plinth. *Girl* and *heathen* and *bitch* he called from the gloom, shouting and twisting and turning on the spot. She shrank back, but again it was not from fear. It was not the City-Lord she was frightened of, she realised. He was a small man, greedy and a bully at best. No, it was the priest who scared her. In him she had seen anger and hatred and lust. The voice in her head knew it too. 'Mother, no!' it wept. 'Please don't let him get the bowl.'

The adherent was crouched at the debating table, bent like an animal. His hand hovered above the bowl—her bowl. Solatta watched as the air between the two seemed to warp and bend, shimmering like heat. It seemed to shrink from his touch, or was that just her imagining? But touch it he did, his fingers latching onto it greedily like a babe on a nipple. Her Foof screamed, desperate and awful: 'No!'

The priest heard it too, his head snapping in her direction, though, thankfully, not finding her. The adherent looked back to the bowl and swiftly seemed lost in it, apparently happy with what he found there. Solatta couldn't imagine why—it was just a glass bowl. Only, at once, it wasn't. It became something else, no longer simple and beautiful, no longer hers. Instead, it was filled with light and mystery and terror. It glowed hot and bright, brimming as if with the sun made liquid. The surface seemed to ripple and shimmer at the adherent's touch, swirling around his fingers. He dipped them in, allowing the shine to spread over his hand and up his wrist. He smiled, wicked and malicious, before turning to face the melee at the hall's centre. Soulless eyes sought her out: empty glass orbs swivelling over the combatants one by one. Thin lips parted in a snarl. Suddenly, he pulled his hand free from the bowl, and with it came a shard of light, brilliant and pure. It stretched, racing across the hall like lightning. The very air seemed to shake and fizz. Solatta felt it bubbling beneath her skin. The light struck the wall behind her, punching a steaming, burning hole into the brick, the air hot and sulphurous. The priest cackled like a crone, the sound gurgling and bubbling up from somewhere deep inside of him. Solatta bit back a scream.

The fighting at the room's centre had ceased. Grey and stranger alike stood still, gaping at the adherent. Even the City-Lord looked worried and uncertain.

'It's no use hiding, you know!' the adherent cried, his voice somehow a hundred different voices, each fighting against the others. He sniffed at the air, his tongue darting out like a snake's, tasting for her. 'Tastes like fear,' he snarled.

He was right. She *was* afraid. In truth, she had never been more terrified in her life. She felt as if she had been turned to stone, just like her statue. 'You heathens are all the same, full of doubt and fear and lies! You assume to place yourself above the blessed Truth? You think yourself to be somehow outside the jurisdiction of our mother Church? I am here to disavow you of that naïve and childish notion.' The priest's fingers traced the rim of the bowl, slow and lazy, and the light within began to grow, dancing at his touch. 'You see, I understand now. I alone have answered the call of Truth, and the Goddess has gifted me this power. She has chosen me as her holy instrument. And now you too will see. All will kneel in reverence and wonder at the majesty of her blessed word, and I will burn the lies from your heart.' His hand stopped. A blast of energy spat itself free from the bowl. Solatta slammed her eyes shut just as a shockwave sent her sprawling. Where once the statue had stood in front of her, a smouldering crater of shattered stone remained.

'There you are,' Al-Eldar said, his mouth twisting into a smile. 'And not alone, I think. What fresh heresy is this?'

Solatta gasped. How could he know about the voice she carried with her? Could he somehow hear Kareti too?

'You betray yourself with your dark magic, witch. Such a silly little rabbit to think that you could hide your blasphemy when I shine the light of Truth upon you. All of your treacherous little secrets are apparent to me now, just as they must be to you. If only you could see the light of the Goddess as I do now!'

He was insane, she realised, torn apart by his own internal conflicts and desires. He had buried them deep, but still they rose to the surface. She stared at him, unblinking, and saw a thousand faces looking back at her. Some were laughing, some crying, young and old and others still, and each had the same black eyes. They locked onto hers, bored deep into her.

The City-Lord stepped between them, and Solatta breathed again, gulping in air she'd feared she'd never taste again. What was he doing? Had everyone gone mad this day? She realised that she didn't care—he was not her responsibility. For once, there was an absence of guilt, leaving only blessed relief.

'Captain-Adherent Al-Eldar!' the City-Lord shouted in his thin voice, 'clear the room of these rebels, and bring me that, that *weapon*.' His watery eyes flickered between the adherent's face and the glowing bowl, and Solatta saw the fear there.

The priest drew back a lip, bearing his teeth.

Aargau swallowed, and Solatta couldn't help but picture a lost lamb wandering into the wolf's wood. 'I am your City-Lord, Captain-Adherent, or do you forget yourself?' he asked, voice unwavering.

He is much braver than me, Solatta thought. *Or stupider.*

The priest stretched and angled his head, as if considering the lord's words. The bones of his neck cracked and popped.

'Take the bowl from the adherent,' Aargau ordered the two guards flanking him, 'and bring it to me.'

As the men approached, pale-faced, the priest growled a warning. It echoed around the hall, rising and falling in tone like a thousand voices calling out in agony. He touched his fingers to the well of light and it shimmered and rippled, a pebble dropping into a pond, then flashed red and orange, death and fury. Fire spilled from the bowl and swept towards the two men. One vapourised immediately, leaving only a fleshy mess of cloth and gore, while the other had his arm shorn away, leaving him too shocked to even scream. Yet more—Dreban's companion and a new group of fighters, an axe-wielding woman among them—were bowled over by the ferocity of the blast, cast aside like nothing more than playthings.

The priest turned his eye upon the City-Lord, his fingers twitching.

'Truth help us,' Solatta whispered.

'We need more than simple Truth,' Kareti murmured. 'Only the Three can stop him now. Mother, Sister, and Other.'

The priest's head swivelled again towards Solatta, and her plinth suddenly seemed small and flimsy. She caught a glimpse of Aargau running towards a door on the far side of the hall, and she wondered distantly whether she should follow, screaming and crying and flailing. She thought everything and nothing all at once.

Then, he was there. Dreban. He was on his feet again, his companion staring at him, his slim body glowing gold and bronze and amber in the dust-thick gloom. He was upon Al-Eldar in an instant, flicking an arm towards the priest in a short, sharp punch. And there, something else: a sliver of silver smoke arcing towards the adherent. The ghost of an arrow. It struck the adherent in the shoulder, spinning him like a top. He lost his grip on the bowl and it fell with terrible finality to the ground. The marble seared and smouldered where it fell, light spilling, turning the very stone to flame, blue and green and yellow.

'The bowl!' Kareti and Solatta screamed at once.

Dreban heard, even above the sound of cracking stone and panicking guards. He rushed forwards, reaching for the crystal bowl, its light already fading, but paused as though uncertain. Solatta remembered his reaction to her tonics. Was it the bowl he had reacted to? He was afraid, she saw. She wished she could lend him strength.

The adherent took a curt step forwards and kicked Dreban in the thigh. He cried out as he fell, knees buckling, and light flared once more, the very ground shaking. Painted tiles tore free from their moorings, thumping onto the stone floor all around. A stone column tilted, teetered, and collapsed—heading straight for Dreban. Solatta dropped to her knees. She didn't want to see, but couldn't look away. He reached out a hand, touching it to the bowl as though by instinct—and the column came crashing down. There was a dazzling flash and a great explosion of dust, and Solatta slammed her eyes shut. When she dared open them, she saw shards of stone scattered around like pebbles on a beach. The air above Dreban shimmered and hissed, blue and green and turquoise.

The adherent hissed and slunk back a step, a wolf marking its prey.

Unsteadily, Dreban rose.

Blessed is the penitent sinner who comes to the Church in search of absolution, for he shall be raised up from his lowly position by his desire for Truth. Wicked and unholy is the man who sins against the Church yet repents not, and he shall be struck down with all the force and might of the Church's holy will.

—**From the Tenets of Truth**

CHAPTER FORTY-THREE
SENTENZA

The Citadel

For cycles, Sentenza had searched. Since his run in with old Ballir, he'd remained vigilant, always watchful for any sign of the power he'd felt that day. He'd always imagined it to be a person, but now it finally dawned on him. It was a truth as brutal and confusing as the chaotic scenes unfolding before him. 'A fucking bowl,' he whispered. 'For the love of all things true and sacred, a fucking bowl!' He almost laughed. Such a simple thing. How better to keep it hidden? It was so close, almost within reach. All he had to do was race forwards and take it—Al-Eldar had dropped it and the boy was still fumbling. Surely it would be simple.

The colonel took a tentative step forwards. He had seen what had happened to Dritsek and the Greys he'd sent—the men reduced to ash, and their idiot lord sent packing, tail firmly between his legs. Through the ash, a figure came rushing towards him. Sentenza braced himself, readying both sword and Wielding, but the guard passed by, sprinting for the door. Who could blame him? Part of Sentenza wanted to join him, but he couldn't give up this one chance, no matter how slim, to claim the bowl for himself. But how? Maybe he could just wait it out, watch from the sidelines as Dreban and the adherent tore each other apart. The adherent paced, circling Dreban, looking for a chance or a weakness. He stepped too close and Dreban jerked. The bowl flared in response to his hand, liquid light spilling to the ground and searing up violently, a gleaming sheet of silver that crackled and fizzed. It almost seemed alive. The priest danced back and the barrier dissipated. The crash of falling masonry thundered through the hall.

Al-Eldar panted, his breath coming in sharp pangs, like a drunk gone too long without wine. He craved the bowl, Sentenza could tell, so much that it visibly pained him not to have it. Black raven eyes shone like grey steel in its reflection. 'I know you,' he said to Dreban. 'The Goddess has shown me everything that is in her heart, and I have seen you there. You, the priest. Ordained in the Righteous Truth, but lost. A child, wandering aimless, searching for its mother.'

Dreban watched him warily, twisting to face him as he paced, not trusting his back to the man.

'You were sold a lie,' Al-Eldar went on, 'you know that. But not by the Church. The Church has ever had your interests at heart. Search yourself—trust the things you know to be true. Those things you have seen with your own eyes and heard with your own ears.' The adherent touched fingers to his forehead, his eyes, and finally his ear.

'May you always know Truth, see Truth, and hear Truth,' Dreban intoned in answer, voice distant, almost a whisper. His eyes had grown glassy, Sentenza saw. He could almost see the memories replaying behind them.

The adherent studied his face, seeming encouraged by whatever he found there. 'Did not the Church answer your call when you knocked at our door? Did we not take you in when you thought yourself lost and adrift? Were you not nourished when you hungered for comfort, and taken into our breast when you longed to be loved and needed?'

It was expertly done, Sentenza thought. He could almost feel the tears forming in the young man's eyes. 'Don't listen to him, kid!' The words came tumbling from his mouth, surprising even himself.

The adherent crouched low, black robes splaying over his knees and onto the floor, a dog leaning back onto its haunches. His pale and pinched features relaxed and softened, making him look almost half-human. Dreban's eyes found the man, focusing on his lips.

'Ask yourself the question,' the priest murmured, 'why would the Church lie to you? What could be gained from playing you false? If you have an honest heart, your answer will be: none.'

Sentenza's skin began to itch. The man's a Cognator, he realised. It didn't quite make sense. Mind magic needed contact, the touch of flesh—how was Al-Eldar affecting the kid? Truth, even Sentenza was starting to question himself. Was it the bowl or was this something else? Some new kind of force they'd developed in the towers of the Misty City?

The priest licked his lips, pressing his advantage. 'Listen to me, listen to me. I am here for you. I can help you see clearly. You can trust me to help you find the true path to righteousness.' Al-Eldar reached out a hand, open and imploring. Sentenza watched as Dreban moved towards the man. He even felt himself edge closer.

'Yes, yes, almost there...'

A flash of something hard and cold in the adherent's other hand. The stiletto lashed out from the man's black robes and, with a sickening thud, made a sheath of Dreban's chest. Screams tore through the hall: Dreban's, the girl's, even his own voice. The adherent's free hand dropped to the bowl. He tried to wrestle it free but, somehow, Dreban's grip held true. The adherent pressed hard on the blade, forcing it deep, and Sentenza watched Dreban's face grow ashen and waxy. Sentenza knew he should do something, but to what end? The power the bowl represented had dominated his thoughts and dreams for so many cycles, and yet... the kid had come so close. He'd shown such bravery and courage where even Sentenza had faltered.

He had no time to dwell on the matter. The ground lurched beneath him and a crack tore through the roof, cracking and slapping at his ears. Great chunks of masonry fell, crashing down into the hall. The remaining Greys scattered. the girl remained, he saw, still crouched behind the plinth of the ruined statue, as did the axe-wielding woman, who was pulling her blade free from the back of a fallen Grey. More figures emerged in the doorway: rebels, he realised, and, at their head...but no, it couldn't be. The bear was dead.

Dreban and the adherent remained oblivious, as if contained in their own world. Clutched between them, the bowl shone, the air rippling around it. To Al-Eldar it would be a tool to dominate, he knew. For Dreban... well, it would likely be the lad's coffin. And indeed, Dreban's grip was slackening. His breath grew slow and calm. A look of resignation shadowed his features and, for a moment, Sentenza thought he even looked serene.

The room grew cold and still and dark.

Find community in the Truth and the Church. Look to them alone for comfort and nourishment. You are all children of the Church, and you should place it alone at the centre of your faith.

—From the Tenets of Truth

CHAPTER FORTY-FOUR
SOLATTA

The Citadel

Solatta blinked hard against the light's glare. It was morning, and the early sun was breaking over the horizon, sharing those first hopeful rays. On the ground ahead was the figure of a lone woman. She lay naked and crying, and the wind whipped her with sand and dust, covering her form with a fine layer of red and grey and brown. Beneath it, scarlet streaks spread like tendrils, criss-crossing over her back like rivers. Solatta wanted to go to her and wrap her arms around her, but something stayed her hand. She felt hidden eyes watching her from a distance. She looked around, but found no one. When she turned back, two more women had joined the first. They knelt by her side, laying hands of comfort and healing on her tired and broken flesh. Where their fingers touched, the wounds sealed together, knitting into a constellation of dark, puckered scars.

A voice cut through the silence, soft and sweet as morning song. 'Compassion for each other is one of our most amazing gifts, don't you think?'

Solatta turned to find the scarred woman stood beside her. Startled, she glanced back at where she'd seen the woman sprawled only moments before, but the sand was bare, the attendant women gone. The scarred woman smiled, and Solatta thought she seemed somehow familiar, though she was certain she had never seen her before. Her face held a fierce energy and seemed almost to glow in the morning light.

'I'm sorry, I didn't...' Solatta began, but lost the words. There was something about this woman, so serene and graceful, yet so... powerful. Yes, that was it. She seemed to hold herself with such strength and poise. Solatta found that she had quite forgotten what she had wanted to say. Odd, she thought. There was nothing outwardly remarkable about the woman—she was short and weathered, plain even, and wore a simple cotton shift—and yet Solatta found her captivating.

The woman turned to her, cheeks flushed as though she had heard Solatta's thoughts. 'Oh, I'm sure you have nothing to be sorry about, child. I think it is I who ought to apologise.'

'Do I know you?' Solatta asked. 'I'm sorry, but I don't know where I am or how I got here.'

'There you go again, apologising. Child, if we carry on like this, it's going to get mighty tiresome mighty quick.'

Now it might have been Solatta's turn to blush, but there was no malice or harshness in the woman's words; on the contrary, they made Solatta feel warmly at ease with herself.

'This here is everywhere and nowhere,' the woman said

dismissively. 'What you really should be asking is whether you even know yourself.'

It was no answer at all, Solatta thought. All her life, it felt, she had been fed half-truths and titbits in place of the full story. Because of it, she was full of holes; only part of a person. She was tired of it and she knew there was somewhere else she needed to be. Someone, somewhere was waiting for her, or was she waiting for them? She couldn't quite remember.

'Child,' the woman said, 'if you go on waiting for someone else to solve all your problems then you're going to be waiting until the day you die. You need to stand on your own two feet. Stop letting others push you around; stop dancing to their tune.'

Solatta turned from the woman sharply, holding her arms stiffly by her side. Her fingers brushed the folds of her skirt, but, instead of reaching for the hem and worrying the fabric bare, she balled her hands into fists. The action was not lost on the woman: her full berry lips pulled into a broad smile.

Solatta felt suddenly dizzy. She touched a hand to her head and closed her eyes in a bid to stop herself from swooning and, when she opened them again, the feeling was gone, and so was the woman. The landscape before her had changed too. Gone was the bare and desolate place she had occupied only moments ago. Now, she stood atop an endless path of basalt stones, each a hexagon column that seemed to have been hammered into the ground. The sea lashed to her right and left, splashing silver spray over the causeway. Slowly coming toward her was a shrouded figure. A man, Solatta saw, thin-faced and with pinched cheeks. He looked road-weary and sea-swept, but there was no mistaking him. She would know him anywhere, even if he did seem younger than when she had known him. She ran to greet her guardian on legs so light that she might have been flying. A woman appeared suddenly, her back to Solatta. She addressed Tervan quietly, and he nodded, a small smile appearing on his face. Solatta faltered, her smile freezing. It was the woman from earlier, only younger, fuller-faced and -bodied. Gone were the scars that had pockmarked her body. There was a purity about her, though she seemed almost sad, as if she carried a great burden.

Tervan too was different, she realised. He was thinner and less grizzled, even handsome. It was odd to see him that way, as an attractive man in his prime. It felt strange and uncomfortable. She smiled at him, a joyful flutter in her chest, but he did not see her. He only saw the woman. He reached out a hand to her—a slow and careful gesture that held such tenderness it made Solatta feel sad somehow. Was this some kind of memory? An echo of things past?

The woman took Tervan's hand and guided it gently to her face. He caressed her cheek and she smiled back at him. Solatta had the feeling that she was intruding upon an act of intimacy, but she could not tear her eyes away. His hand was so gentle and caring, almost touching her without touching her, and Solatta saw that the woman had started to cry. Gently and silently, her tears traced their way down the smooth features of her cheeks. They left a sorrowful track that evaporated in the morning sun, turning to tiny little sprites, brilliant and white, that spun off in all directions like lost stars returning to the heavens.

The woman moved Tervan's hand, his fingers following the lines down to her chin. When he lifted it away, Solatta could see a single teardrop glittering on his fingertip. It shone in the sun, splitting into a thousand different colours, each one more dazzling and beautiful than the last. The woman smiled warmly and looked back to Tervan. 'It's warm,' he said, looking deep into sapphire eyes that, before Solatta's eyes, turned cobalt and ruby and emerald.

'It is heavy,' the woman corrected, her voice a mournful lament that carried with it the weight of generations. Tervan looked back down to his hand. Where the tear had rested there was a shining crystal bowl. It glistened and glinted, pulling light into it, becoming brighter and brighter, until Solatta had to look away and close her eyes. When she opened them again, she was no longer on the basalt path, no longer by the lapping sea. She felt suddenly alone, and with it the pain of losing her friend anew. Somehow, she knew that it would be the last time she saw him—and, once again, she had not said goodbye.

She was in a market town, she saw, the streets bustling with people, some laughing and happy, others going about their business. She was absorbed by the smell of spices, clove and cardamom and pepper. If only she had her potions box, she thought. *No*, she realised. *That was for another time, another me.* Shouts pulled at her senses, high-pitched and dreadful. Heavy feet, marching, a steady rolling thunder that grew, drawing nearer. People starting running, calling out to their friends and loved ones. Panic spread. Solatta's heart was thumping in her chest. A bell began to toll, a song of safety, and she was drawn towards it like a moth to a flame, as were the people. They ran to it, struggling to clamber inside a large hall, though many were still waiting when the horsemen arrived. Soldiers slashed down from the saddle, swords chopping into the crowd, the street made slick with blood. An old woman slipped at the doorway, stumbling to her knees. She brought others down around her, a mass of writhing and injured blocking the entrance to their only refuge.

Solatta wanted to run to them, to help them, but her legs failed. She was a bystander, unable to move. Other soldiers moved past her on foot. They walked through her as though she was not even there. Green uniforms swarmed the townspeople. Some they dragged away, others they butchered on the spot. A big man pulled the hall door shut and barred it from inside, thinking the townspeople safe within the barricaded walls. And, for a time, they were. The soldiers stood back, watching, waiting. Solatta heard the scrape of feet behind her. A man in a black robe came to a stop beside her, and Solatta froze. The adherent. He strode on, sly and astringent lips moving in a constant mumble. He passed among the soldiers, touching each one—on the hand, on the neck, even on the cheek. It did not seem to matter. After his touch, they sprang into action. Wood and kindling were dragged labouriously through the streets and arranged in faggots at the foot of the hall. The soldiers piled the fuel thick and high, ignoring the plaintive cries from the people inside. It was the black priest himself who brought the torch. With a victorious smile, he let the flames touch the tinder. The smoke rose thick and fast, grey to begin with but swiftly growing black.

Solatta closed her eyes, not wanting to bear witness to the horror, but she could not close her ears, could not shut out or unhear the torment. It would stay etched into her memory until the day she died.

Those who did not burn, the soldiers staked. They took their time; they had no reason to rush. There was no one to stop them. The victims pleaded with their captors, offered them all kinds of treasures in return for their lives and freedom, but it was as though the men didn't even hear them. It was only the adherent they heard, him and his spiteful whispers. Heathen and heretic and unholy she heard him call them. Fornicators and idolaters. He sealed their fate with a touch and a smile, setting the soldiers into action. The screams added to the foul and putrid air already thick with fumes and agony.

Finally, the square was empty of townspeople, though it had plenty of spikes to spare. Slowly the soldiers found their places, each lining himself up next to a vacant pole. They numbered exactly. The adherent took two men as he inspected his troops before passing solemn instruction to his two honour guards. With each touch from the priest, they lifted a comrade onto his stake. The men died in silence. Not a scream or moan emerged from their lips.

When the deed was done, the adherent dispatched the final two men with a thin blade drawn from his own belt. He stood watching, enraptured, as their lifeblood spilled from them, soaking into the dust. Finally, he walked away.

Solatta felt the bile rise long before she vomited. She felt foul and soiled, as though she might never be clean again. She tried to stay strong, to carry her testimony with her, but it was too much, and she wept tears that had built up over a long, sad life. She wept for all of the people who had died, for all of the suffering at the hands of liars and false prophets. She wept for Tervan and for Dreban and for herself. She wept so much that her tears might have turned into rivers and oceans, flooding the world with their salty sorrow. When at last she had cried herself dry and sore, she opened her eyes, fearful of what she might see next, but found that she was back in the Debating Hall. Dust clawed at her throat and stung her eyes. The sudden roar of sound assaulted her ears, the brittle shattering of multi-coloured tiles ringing like explosions in her head. A slab of marble had fallen onto a statue, and its broken stone face stared up at her blankly. For a brief instant, it was her own face. She recoiled, stumbling over the debris-strewn stone.

And then she saw him: Dreban. He was grey and still, a steel blade suckling at his breast like a leech. Clutched in his hand was the glowing crystal bowl. Fresh eyes saw it anew. The light—not simple flashes, but the very essence of the Goddess. The holy instrument she'd used to defeat the beast, the sword that had punched the stars in the sky and created the world. Beside him, trying to pry the bowl away, was the priest.

Solatta almost fell by Dreban's side and the priest snarled, brandishing his blade. Solatta ignored him. She was not here for him or the bowl—she didn't need either of them. Her hand swept past the delicate crystal without even flinching, the light from it blinking out like a candle being snuffed. It wasn't a bowl, she knew—it never had been. It was the Tear of the Goddess. A piece of Truth given form. Yet she had a greater Truth; she could feel it bright and glowing inside her. Her fingers caressed Dreban's cheek just as Tervan had touched the face of the Goddess. Her lover looked to her and, for a taut second, their eyes locked. The briefest of smiles played on his ashen features, tugging on his pale lips and giving a last lustre to his eyes. As she watched, they began to close. His skin grew cold. No matter, she thought, no matter—she'd nursed him back to life once, and she could do it again.

With a final heave, the adherent ripped the bowl from Dreban's fading fingers, crowing in delight. Solatta barely looked up. The adherent thrust his hand into the bowl, a manic chuckle bubbling from his mouth, but nothing happened. There was no flash, no flare, no sudden wave of destruction. The energy had gone, dried up like a summer river. The hall echoed to the sound of his screams.

Solatta ignored him. She reached instead for the knife protruding from Dreban's chest, tugging it free. She didn't want it there, couldn't bear to see it sticking out of him. At once, Al-Eldar was upon her, his pale arms snatching the blade away from her and pushing her aside like a doll, her fingers brushing against the crystal bowl. The crystal hummed at her touch, the warmth and light suddenly returning, and Solatta jerked as if struck. Something hot and acid seemed to blossom inside of her and Solatta screamed, or at least tried to, but only light burst from her gaping mouth.

In her mind, she saw the statue with her own face, white and cold and lifeless. A corpse's face—only, it had changed. Now it was man's face. Dreban's. She thought dimly of Tervan and the Goddess and the love they had shared. 'It's heavy,' she had told him.

Behind it all, she could hear the slow growl of the adherent. There was almost nothing human about him. She saw his crooked, constantly moving lips in her mind's eye. Saw again the senseless murder of hundreds. How could she allow a man like that to live? She knew instinctively that she could end him then and there merely by ceasing to resist the power coruscating through her; if she simply opened herself, he would splutter and ignite, leaping into flames, just as the town hall had. Or perhaps he'd split apart like those staked in the square. Maybe he'd suffer one of another hundred terrible fates, over and over until there was nought left of him.

I always said that compassion in one of our best qualities. Solatta felt the voice as much as heard it. It penetrated every fibre of her being, resonating within her, full of depth and texture, buttery gold. She recognised it instantly.

'Please,' she said. 'I don't know what to do.'

Child, you do what you always have done.

What did the voice mean? She was just Solatta, an orphan of sorts—she travelled from place to place, watching from the sidelines as her guardian helped people and tended to the sick. How could any of that be of use here?

Still you do not understand. It was always you. Not Tervan. Not even the Tear. They were just the vessel—a conveyance, if you like. You were the true instrument. It was your strength and compassion. You have a deep desire to help others and ease their suffering. Tervan knew it from the very moment he sensed you being born. That was why he came to you.

'No,' Solatta protested. 'It was Tervan, it was always him. They were *his* shows, *his* performances.'

Child, you don't get to be as old as Tervan without learning a few tricks, and believe me, men are full of them. It's women who are the true power in this world. Or, at least, that was the way it was meant to be. Men are destroyers, heavy-handed protectors at best, but it's women who create. Women who birth life into the world.

Solatta was dumbstruck. It sounded inflammatory, the kind of thing a priest might label blasphemous, but then she considered it. She thought of the men in her life and others she had known. Warm and comforting memories of Tervan and Dreban, protectors both. If only all men could be like them. Her thoughts drifted to the adherent and the City-Lord, angry and greedy and selfish slaves to their own whims.

'I know what I need to do,' said Solatta quietly.

But is it what you want to do, Child?

'More than anything.'

Ask yourself: is it right? The woman's voice was not unkind; rather, there was concern there.

A warm smile spread across Solatta's face. She didn't voice her response; she didn't need to. The woman had already drifted back from whence she had come. Solatta pulled her fingers from the Tear, releasing it to the adherent. He clutched it to his chest greedily and a crooked smile sliced across his face, sly and victorious. Solatta ignored it, finding comfort in the feel of Dreban's cooling hand resting in hers. With the other hand now free, she reached forward, cupping Dreban's cheek. Slowly, she brought her face to his, and kissed him. She felt his lips part at her gentle pressure. Her mouth was full of the simple pleasure of him, the taste of him mixed with the iron salt of blood. Breath passed between them, hers to him, her love to him, her essence to him. Finally, she pulled away. She saw his warm eyes wet with tears. Felt his fingers entwine with hers. She had done what needed to be done.

She felt the relief instantly—the blessed emptiness where before there had been a tumult of energy. The Tear inside her, a violent whirlwind waiting to eat her up and devour the world. In those brief moments, it had shown her a thousand variations of what her life might have been and yet could still be. She had seen the lives she would never live and those that she might yet, but she knew that there was only one that would allow her to be happy. Her Truth.

There is no Truth but that of the Church.

—From the Tenets of Truth

CHAPTER FORTY-FIVE

BRAGA

The Citadel

The Grey lunged, striking down with his pike, the rondel snapping at Braga's axe and driving it from hands made slick with blood. The guard grinned the insolent grin of the young—all cock and no surety. These were the so-called elite, deployed only to protect the City-Lord. Braga danced back a half-step. The young Grey levelled his weapon, readying a thrust that never came. Sirle's axe bit through pad and leather, driving deep into his arm. She slipped behind in a fluid motion, finding the man's exposed neck with the short blade held in her other hand.

Braga looked to the woman he loved. There was no joy in her face, he was glad to see, none of the battle lust he had witnessed in others. There was a limit in her strength, he realised, a line that she was yet to cross. He resolved to protect her from ever needing to, if he could—if she would let him. *May this be the last time she is called upon to fight*, he thought, but he knew it was too much to hope for. If he were a man of faith, he might have offered a prayer, but he was yet to see much to convince him of any blessed Truth or righteous Goddess.

Sirle allowed the guard to drop. The fighting was growing increasingly sporadic; more Greys were trying to escape the chaos of the hall than remaining to protect it. He could hardly blame them. The air was thick with the smell of fear and dust and magic, a heady mix of sweat and plaster and something darkly sulphurous. Braga was hardly sure he wanted to be there himself, but it was where the adherent had led them. He had seen the man in glances, snatched between the cut and thrust of the faltering melee—brief visions of a twisted, black-robed ogre who seemed set on tearing the world down around him. Balls of energy had pockmarked the hall, punching holes into the brick shell, and Braga had ordered his motley hand to wait outside. At least then there'd be someone left to dig him from the rubble.

He felt Sirle at his side, her presence giving him more fight and drive than he might have imagined. The thought of ordering her outside with the rest had been a fleeting one; he knew she would ignore it. *If I'm the commander, what does that make her? Maybe she will be my colonel now that Sentenza has gone.* He smiled.

A wretched and guttural sound drew his attention. It made the big man's skin itch, and his hand searched desperately for that of the woman by his side. He found it there, soft and warm and reassuring. The black robes of the adherent shone, for a brief moment rendered bright and glowing in the glare of some spectral light. The man crouched low, his entire form trembling. Clutched to his body was a strange crystal bowl, its intricate surface glowing faintly. The gloom around the priest seemed to swell and grow in intensity until it was a thick, feculent miasma. It leeched from him, oozing over and into the young woman at his feet, who seemed to absorb it. The priest watched, manic eyes glittering, a cruel smile stretching ever upward.

At once, the woman looked up. Slowly, gently, she drew herself up, heedless of the seething miasma, her bright eyes penetrating the gloom. She looked different, Braga thought, older perhaps—no, he decided, more worldly. Wiser. Something had passed between her and the dying young man she stood over. Without a sound, she turned to the adherent and let her head fall back. He snarled in triumph, holding the bowl out before him as if it was some sacred weapon or holy relic. The girl did not flinch. Time seemed to stop, or maybe even end. The world held its breath.

Braga heard the sound of a thousand winds whistling through a thousand forests, and each one carried the dry rasping laugh of death. The great gale swept into the hall, tearing at his skin and knocking him to the floor. In the brief silence that followed, Braga thought he heard a sigh of satisfaction: the ancient voice of the mountains themselves. He found Sirle's face and pulled it close. 'Don't look,' he whispered, though he didn't know why. He closed his own eyes, screwing them tight, but even that was not enough to hold out the light. It was hotter than he thought possible, a massive blast furnace or a thousand dying sunsets—and then it was gone.

When he lifted his head, he saw men and women alike rooted and prone like bodies on a killing field. All but two. Impossibly, the adherent and the girl remained, caught in each other's stare. There was a long silence until, with a sudden chime, the bowl shattered in the priest's hands. A thousand shards burst into the air, each sparkling with colours so radiant that it made Braga want to weep. It felt like the loss of something pure; the death of Truth.

The crystal splinters fell like sand through the adherent's fingers, scattered and blown by some great invisible breath. Al-Eldar pawed at the glittering air, managing to snatch one last shard, its sharp edges slicing deep into his flesh. Blood flowed from the wounds like treacle, thick and black and putrid. With a final twisted scream, the adherent sprang forwards, almost too quick for Braga to see. When he withdrew, his hand was empty, and a silver spear was embedded in the girl's heart. It glowed there for a moment, too beautiful to behold, and then it vanished.

The adherent staggered back, peering down at the ashen boy below. His eyes glowed black and red like burning coals. Braga was already on his feet, moving incredibly fast. He raised his arm, finding the weight of his immense battle axe reassuring. He did not remember picking it up. He swung, the axe describing a perfect arc of light, slicing through the ash and dust and dark, and facing satisfying resistance, the metal struck home, its beard slicing through flesh and neck and bone and gristle. There was no blood this time. No scream, no tears, just the pale face of the adherent, empty and lost, dead eyes seeking the girl even as they fell. The head landed with a wet thud, coming to rest beside the adherent's body and the silent form of the boy. The girl was nowhere to be seen.

Tiredness hit Braga like a hammer blow. He slumped into himself, dropping his axe. It clattered to the ground like the tolling of a bell announcing the death of a king. Emotion washed over him, and again he found himself close to tears. He did not hear the approach of City-Lord Dritsek Aargau until the man was on top of him, stolen sword in hand. He heard Sirle's shout, felt the anguish in her voice, saw her trying to reach him. It was no use; she was too far away. He regretted the time he hadn't spent with her, the cycles he'd wasted searching for a family when she'd been there already, waiting for him. He felt the breath of death as the sword sliced through the air, saw the smoke-grey wisp as it struck out like a whip. Heard Dritsek cry out, the sword go skittering across the stone.

It was the colonel's face that appeared at the City-Lord's shoulder, though it was not his blade that stroked the flesh of Dritsek's neck. It was something less substantial, though just as deadly. Air, Braga realised, stretched thin and sharp as a razor.

EPILOGUE

The last of the summer heat had long since passed. The months had gone from monkey to fox to wolf, bringing rains and a cold that cut deep into the bones. These were not nights for being out on the road, he knew, but the inns and taverns held their own dangers. Not that thieves and cutpurses held much of a threat for him these days. It was eyes and ears and questions he shied away from now.

The roads had become busy with traffic and trade of all kinds. Refugees and migrants moved in both directions, some fleeing the city, fearful of change, while others hurried in the opposite direction, eager to find prosperity in the new order. There were others, too, who hid among the faces. Bandits, footpads, and Truthless Churchmen, all of whom he'd rather avoid. Blessedly, he had not happened upon any since leaving the Citadel.

The huge pioneer sergeant, Braga, had tried to convince him to stay and help rebuild, but he found the walls held too many memories for him, even if they had been forever changed. The breaking of the Debating Hall had decimated whole sections of the old town, the quaking ground causing more than one tower to fall in on itself, though it was not only the buildings that had been left in ruins. The Other had stalked the Citadel that day. Ancient dynasties and peasantry alike had fallen foul to her icy grip, and panic had spread. Without direction, the people fought against one another for food, shelter, and control. Rioting and looting became commonplace. The old signs and symbols were torn down and desecrated, little more than weeds being cleared from a garden bed. Statues toppled, and even the old house markers and family crests were ripped from their fixings and thrown upon the amassed rubble like the towers that had once been great symbols of power. It was clear that this would be a city marked with the stylings of heraldry and privilege no longer.

Those House-Lords that survived were powerless to defend themselves and, fearing for their survival, they took the only option left open to them: they turned to Braga and those forces that remained loyal to the big man. He became their reluctant colonel, though not without price. In place of the old Council of Nine, he proposed an elected council of representatives, to be picked from the old House-Lords and the peasantry alike. He demanded the collectivisation and redistribution of wealth across the citizenry, where everyone would benefit from the plentiful resources of goods and services produced within the region. He insisted on fair and apportioned taxation that would be met by all and, most dangerously of all, he petitioned for the expulsion of the Church. Unsurprisingly, the demands were refused and the House-Lords clung to power, hoping beyond hope that the king might send forces to stabilise the region. But no one came and, after a grim period of unsteady quiet, the lords had no choice but to capitulate and accede.

When the time came for the clergy to be removed from their churches, they were found to have already vacated, and not a single black-robed capercaillie was found within the city walls. Even the great mansion of the Premiero had been left abandoned and stripped of its finery and riches, although whether that had taken place on the orders of Premiero Irmao himself or at the hands of the quick-fingered crowds, no one could be certain.

And so the young man had politely declined the offer to stay, knowing that however much he threw himself into the work of rebuilding, his mind would forever be dragged back to that day. Even now, his dreams were beset by glimpses of those events: half-lost memories that haunted his sleep and plagued his waking moments in almost equal measure. Hardly an hour passed without his thoughts wandering, and he would find himself subconsciously twitching at some phantasm of the past. This was the real reason he had developed a dislike of towns and cities. It wasn't out of fear of being stopped and challenged by some official, for Braga had arranged his travel papers easily enough using the chits and permits left behind by the priests. Rather, it was the wearisome conversations and lies that he found himself constantly repeating in order to steer conversation away from the recent past.

He followed the lower branch of the Waipera to the old island fortress where she had first found him, crossing it at a ford before continuing northward. He had to push his horse hard to make it so far in such a short time, but he did not want to stop, least of all there. The crossing at the Tyne was simpler—from there, the First Great Canal struck deep into the interior, where it branched off into the many lesser waterways that made up the complex branches of the king's grand network. The further north he pushed, the fewer people he came across. He had scant idea of where he was heading. He followed only a faint tug felt somewhere within him; a feeling that he would find answers when he got there, wherever that was. Not for himself, mind. He knew there were few places he would be able to find those. The answers he sought were for someone else. Someone more important.

A noise in the darkness caused him to hold his breath. The sharp snap of a twig, disturbing the still night air like a beacon fire warning of danger. He listened intently as he slowly and silently slipped himself from under his deer hide. His grip tightened around the hilt of the short sword—a gift from the pioneer sergeant. He'd developed the habit of sleeping with it since leaving the Citadel. More noise: a clumsy rock fall, as though someone had stumbled in the dark. With cat-like stealth, he drew the sword from its sheath, gritting his teeth against the slight rasping sound. His skin tingled and itched as if he was being swarmed by hundreds of biting insects. A heavy weight pressed on his shoulder. He spun in the darkness, sword cutting through the air, ready to bite into the fool that tried to assail him. There was no one there.

'Fuck's sake,' came a familiar voice, 'you could take your eye out with that thing.'

Stone scratched against metal and a flame flared into life, illuminating the creased and weathered face of the colonel, whose cold eyes fixed upon Dreban. The young man let out a slow breath. 'What are you doing here?' he asked.

'Good to see you too, kid,' Sentenza answered.

'Yeah, well, I've been going out of my way to not see anyone,' Dreban replied, almost petulantly.

Sentenza nodded slowly as if mulling over Dreban's words. 'Listen,' he said at last, 'I know you're hurting still, but running away won't make things better. You can't outrun yourself.' He stepped from the shadows, carrying a small bundle of twigs. He set it down and began building a small fire.

'Well, shows what you know then, doesn't it?' Dreban said glumly, sitting back down upon his blanket with a thud.

'I'll tell you what I do know,' Sentenza said, meeting Dreban's eyes and holding the stare. 'I know what you're looking for.'

'How could you know what I'm looking for?' Dreban asked sharply; he didn't even know that himself.

'I've been there.'

The look in Dreban's eyes changed; a tiny flicker of hope.

'And what's more, I can help you find it.'

* * *

Even when he had known it, the path had not been an easy one, twisting as it did through the tangled depths of the Marandum Forest. Now, though, more than ten cycles on, the trees and creepers had grown so dense as to virtually cut out all sunlight at ground level, leaving only the hardiest of bracken and clasping bushes. It was only the old stones—straight-edged black rocks jutting out of the soil every five to six hundred paces—that enabled him to find his way at all. He remembered how smooth they felt, how strangely warm to the touch they were, and took care to keep his hands to himself.

At length, he approached a clearing, the terminal point in his journey. Somehow, the atmosphere was thicker here and it was harder to breathe, as if the air held less of whatever life-giving ingredient it was meant to hold, or was for some reason reluctant to share it with him.

A gnarled old ash tree stood at the centre of the clearing, bent crooked like an age-befuddled old man. It appeared half-dead and presented only a smattering of leaves, none of which seemed to hold any colour. Slowly, the man stepped to the tree, appearing almost hesitant in his approach. Despite having practised this same art elsewhere, here it felt different—primal, almost, and less controlled. He took a stone from his pocket, one that almost exactly matched the marking stones he had passed, and clutched it firmly in his left hand before grasping a hard and shrivelled branch with his right. Both the tree and the earth below reacted immediately to his touch, emanating a green and swirling mist that thickened and collected in front of him. Slowly, the mist coalesced, growing in stature from the ground up until it appeared to resolve into the approximation of a man, tall and heavily robed. He wore a cowl that obscured his face, but there was no disguising him.

The man made a clumsy attempt at bowing in the presence of the swirling image before him, though it was made awkward by the necessity to remain in contact with the tree, and inwardly he cursed himself for taking hold of a branch and not just touching the trunk.

'Be still, you oaf,' came a distant yet authoritative voice that somehow seemed to echo, even out here in the forest clearing.

'I apologise, my lord,' the man responded, head bowed. 'If my position allowed, I would prostrate myself at your feet and await upon your will until the blessed Goddess wrought her justice upon the world.'

'You were meant to bring that justice into being at the Citadel, though with your bungling you have created nought but chaos. Instead of a puppet government, we have anarchy and mob rule. Even the holy institutes of the Church stand empty and forlorn thanks to your incompetence, *Premiero*.' The speaker spat the moniker, lacing it with so much venom that Irmao felt it almost as a slap.

'But my lord,' Irmao began, though his voice was faltering and his words sounded pitiful even to him, 'if I might be afforded just one more chance—'

'Enough,' came the silencing response. 'We have wasted

enough time and energy already on your exploits and schemes. You will return to us in the sacred city of Togat By before the closing of Lobo Satti. There is time yet to rescue the situation.'

Irmao brightened at the comment. 'There is, my lord?'

'There is ever time for the Goddess to empower her Church in the name of Truth. Though the king is away working on his projects, we cannot keep news of this magnitude from him for long. Luckily for you, it may yet work in our favour. The Crown will have no option but to enact his royal prerogative in this time of civil emergency. He will announce the month of ghosts and the advantage will be with us once again.'

For a brief moment, Irmao thought he detected the sound of a smile in the spectre's voice, but as quickly as the idea faded, so too did the swirling image before him. The luminescent green mists dissipated like they had never even existed, leaving the former Premiero with the familiar feeling that he was perhaps really insane.

'Sombra Satti,' Irmao wondered aloud, 'month of ghosts.' It had been many cycles since the last, and each one before it had brought change and upheaval. He wondered how long this one would last for—only the king could decide. These were strange and dangerous times indeed.

The thought made Irmao shiver, and an icy feeling crept over him that left him slightly nauseated. Warmth in his fingers reminded him that he was still holding the stone, and, with distaste, he slipped the impossibly smooth black pebble back into his pocket.

'Well,' he announced to the forest, 'it is a long walk from here to the Misty City. If I am to make it before the month of wolf is out, I should really get moving.'

Distantly, a wolf howled as if in response and, for a fleeting moment, Irmao felt an unnerving sensation engulf him, as if he had been suddenly plunged into icy water. This time, he chose to ignore it, and began to look for the path back the way he'd come.

ACKNOWLEDGEMENTS

First things first, thank the Goddess that we made it this far. I had no idea how difficult writing a book could be. In truth, I couldn't have done it without the wonderful people that have helped me along the way. There are so many that have directly or indirectly supported me through their friendship, work, influence, kind words or just blind belief. I don't have enough space to list them all here, so I will name check some and trust those that know me well enough not to take offence if they aren't mentioned.

To You. Thanks for the trust, belief and encouragement that you have provided throughout. I would have given up cycles ago without your inspiration. Mum and Dad, thanks for being gangstas. See, Dad, people like us can write. Sue Bateson, thanks for being the wonderful person you are and all the dinner parties. Nick Kell, Maureen Wafer and John McCumiskey; my alpha readers that kept me going with support and criticism in enough measure to keep me grounded and believing. David Livesey, had you not been a writer neither would I. Chris, I await Memoirs of a Gay Sir with hot, bated breath. Tony Burns, Dame Dr Harvey, the Oddingtons, Ruth, James, Alex and Fin—our adoptive family—Sara and Bella, Michelle, Anna and Amaya, Harriet and Frank, Paul, Jen and Pumpkin, Matt, James—I'm still working on the fantasy version of our Euros trip—Matty and Claire at the Liverpool Editing Company, Chris, Helen, Dr Frank, Trev, Ben, Harriet, Fred and all in Heroic Books that work so diligently behind the scenes to make this all real. Finally, to my family for being fantastic—Aunty Kay, I knew you'd read until the very last word...

Thank you to everyone for reading this book. I hope you enjoyed it and those yet to come. Welcome to Alytheia.

In Truth,

Quillem

ABOUT THE AUTHOR

Quillem McBreen wrote the The Tenets of Truth in his hometown of Liverpool where he lives with his partner and best friend. Despite having a wide-ranging background, which has seen him try his hand at everything from a fire dancer to the watcher in sky, even the keeper of the keys, and many things in between, this is his first time working as a writer; though his experience of security and politics certainly helped to create the shadier elements that form the world at the centre of the Alytheian Cycle series.

Quillem's love of literature no doubt began with the read along 'Story Teller' magazine and cassettes of the 1980s. He would spend hours in the back of his parent's caravan as they toured with the travelling menagerie listening to stories like Anansi the Spiderman and Gobolino the Witches Cat. No wonder he became a daydreamer with a vivid imagination and eventually wound up as a fantasy author!

To this day, Quillem has an appetite for audiobooks, and when he's not reading, he's probably listening to a book, although his parents have since sold the caravan—to a well-dressed gentleman and a young girl, he seems to recall...